KINGDOM

A YA / FANTASY NOVEL

By
RACHEL E. WOLLASTON

Published by Rachel E. Wollaston
www.rachelewollaston.com

Cover design by Rachel E. Wollaston
Cover Image Copyright © Unholy Vault
Designs/Shutterstock.com

ISBN: 1533300410
ISBN-13: 978-1533300416

Dedicated to my amazing grandad, 11th May 2016.
You inspired me. You will be greatly missed.

CONTENTS

Acknowledgments	vii
1. Bad Impressions	1
2. Strange Happenings	9
3. Unfortunate Circumstances	25
4. Curious Developments	39
5. Incredible Sights	51
6. Unexpected Invitations	65
7. Crazy Fantasies	75
8. Revealing Truths	85
9. Mystical Beginnings	95
10. New Adventures	113
11. Bold Admissions	127
12. Unlikely Friendships	137
13. Old Acquaintances	151
14. Friendly Faces	163
15. Rational Fears	183
16. Perilous Choices	199
17. Dangerous Quests	211
18. Growing Suspicions	219
19. Deadly Foes	233
20. Evil Twists	247
21. Wicked Plans	263

22. Inspiring Words	273
23. Small Fortunes	279
24. Turning Tables	291
25. Untimely Encounters	303
26. Glad Returns	311
27. Cunning Devices	321
28. Further Complications	339
29. Ordinary Heroes	349
30. Rising Questions	357
31. Happy Reunions	369
32. Strengthening Bonds	381
33. Painful Discoveries	393
34. Vile Betrayers	401
35. Hopeless Situations	415
36. Shocking Revelations	423
37. Powerful Enemies	435
38. Magical Friends	447
39. Brave Sacrifices	461
40. Final Disclosures	473
41. Lasting Legacies	479
Epilogue	487
About the Author	495

Acknowledgments

I would like to give special thanks to Kate McGinn, Katy Rees, and my dad for helping me get to this final draft.

Also thanks to family, friends, and teachers who always supported me.

KINGDOM

A YA / FANTASY NOVEL

1

BAD IMPRESSIONS

'*Long live King Calpacious!*' *the troll bellowed as he aimed. His club clouted Alzabar's shield, dented from the many mêlées it had endured over the decades. Sweat slithered down Alzabar's forehead in rivulets and he could taste the familiar tang of blood on his tongue. Maybe he punctured it with his own teeth.*

The war waged for a mile round. The combatting bodies of men and beasts alike peppered the rocky terrain. The fallen lay like dead leaves, trampled beneath the boots of soldiers from both sides. It was a scene of devastation, yet the battle had barely begun.

The troll's treasonous words drove Alzabar's sword forward. 'Calpacious is no more a king than yourself!' he spat, his bull-like eyes seeing red. He took a swing at the troll's protruding belly. 'Would you defy your true leader so?'

'True leader? Ho!' the creature guffawed, sidestepping the slicing blade. 'Where have you been for the last five years? A king's first duty is to his subjects. You're not a king at all!' The troll narrowed his eyes. 'I could kill you right now. I could kill you, and this whole feud would be over. We don't need you anymore!' His face grew tighter. He roared as he turned to the offence, charging straight towards Alzabar, when suddenly-

'MISS FAIRFIELD!'

I gasped and jolted to my feet, dropping the book to the floor. An older woman scowled down at me. She looked official in her mauve business suit, but I doubted she was much older than forty. Her slim glasses enhanced her steely eyes and the condescending look she gave me.

I gulped, feeling like she'd caught me committing some heinous crime.

I looked down to see the book lying face-down on the stone floor, the embossed lettering adorning its tattered cover: *The Kingdom*.

2

'I—I'm sorry,' I bumbled, stooping to retrieve the timeworn book. 'I didn't mean . . . I didn't realise . . . I—I wasn't snooping!'

The mysterious woman said nothing. I locked my eyes on her lilac shoes, clutched the book close to my chest, and rose. I wanted to return her scowl, but at the same time did not want her to see my blush of embarrassment. I tried to hide my face behind a curtain of hair. I felt pathetic, like a cornered mouse.

Come on, I mentally urged the woman, *say something!* But she remained silent. The awkwardness in the air became almost palpable.

I pulled together my dignity and cleared my throat, willing myself to speak first.

'I'm here to see Mr. Calthorpe,' I announced. I tried not to grimace at the strangled sound that escaped my throat.

'I know why you're here,' she snapped back. Her gaze skimmed the length of my body, taking an uncomfortably long time. Her expression stayed stoic. I shivered at her blatant appraisal. I guess I did not meet her expectations. Or maybe it was the fact I'd let myself into the house without awaiting an invitation that narked her.

I knew what she saw: a meek young girl who looked like she belonged anywhere but there. I would sneer at me, too.

3

I felt fine on the train here, imagining how I could impress my new boss. But this snooty lady had now ruined that vision, turning me into a snivelling wimp. So much for acting sophisticated and professional.

'I'm afraid Mr. Calthorpe has taken the children out for today,' the woman said. 'You will just have to wait until he is ready to see you. That is, *if* he wants to see you. In the meantime, as his housekeeper, I will be—' She cleared her throat. '—happy to show you to your room. Follow me.' She flicked her perfect blonde ponytail and marched off.

I grunted to myself before following, more angry with myself than anything else. I wasn't used to being outside of my comfort zone, but here I most certainly was.

The pictures of this place on the internet hadn't done it any justice. The house was magnificent to the very definition of the word! Mr. Calthorpe clearly had a lot of money. Why did he hire me, an unqualified eighteen year-old, to be a live-in nanny for his two children?

Were they even his? I vaguely remembered the website mentioning what relation they were to the owner, but I'd long forgotten now.

I squeezed my bottom lip between my front teeth as the woman led me through the various rooms. Each was identical to the last, both in size and decoration, bedecked in gleaming burgundies and browns. I knew I was going to get lost here.

'If you intend to keep your job, then you must abide by a firm set of rules,' the woman said as her heels clacked against the floor.

The words fell from her mouth like they would from an automated machine. She must have gone through this routine many times. 'No shouting, no running, no inviting friends, and no disturbing the Master.' She stopped and span round. She pierced me with an icy glare and added, 'And NO touching the antiques!'

Staring at her out-held hand, I was puzzled for a moment. Then I realised, mortified, that I was still clutching the book from the foyer. She snatched it from my hands.

'Thank you.'

My heart sank. That book—*The Kingdom*—had been one of my favourites during my childhood. I'd lost it one day at school. I couldn't have been older than ten. I never found another copy since. I was so delighted to see it on the manor's bookshelf, I couldn't help myself—I had to delve right back into that fantasy world which had always been so close to my heart.

I stared at the book in the cranky woman's firm grip. Now it was untouchable again.

'Now I trust you'll have no problem following those instructions, will you, Miss Fairfield?' She drew her left eyebrow upwards in a look which stank of cruel authority, as if her words hadn't already done the trick.

I gave her the sweetest smile I could muster. 'Please,' I said 'I'd much rather you called me Pepper.'

But my attempt at being civil smashed like a kicked-in window. She gave me a peculiar look, as though I'd suggested she paint her face green and do the moonwalk on the ceiling. She leaned forward and spoke with bitter emphasis, '*Miss* Fairfield.' I staggered backwards. 'And you will call me Miss Sharpe.'

How fitting, I thought to myself. The name suited her perfectly.

It took her a full moment before she gave me room to breathe, and led me in silence down one of the corridors. After a short while, she opened one of the giant creaking doors and led me inside.

'This is where you will stay.'

At first, the only thing I registered was the bed and the urge to jump straight into it. My legs were killing me from the long journey on the trains. I was just about ready to collapse, and the mattress was calling my name.

6

The bed was not the only thing I noticed, though. Solid oak furniture skirted the rest of the room, matching the grand four-poster bed in the centre of the room. This was far fancier than anything I had ever been accustomed to.

'That is all, Miss Fairfield,' Miss Sharpe said with a weary voice. 'May I be of any other service?' I nearly found myself laughing at how plastic and scripted the request sounded. The temptation rose to come up with some absurd demand just to infuriate her, but I refrained. I couldn't imagine having Miss Sharpe as an enemy would result in any positive outcomes for me.

'No, thank you,' I said instead. 'I'm fine.'

Miss Sharpe's expression did not waver, but I did see her stance relax a little. She turned and left me alone in my room without even a goodbye. Beneath the light of the chandelier, I shuffled over to the inviting mattress and flopped down. The poufy bedding swallowed me whole.

That was better. I could have gone to sleep right there and then if . . .

Damn it!

I left my luggage in the foyer.

2

STRANGE HAPPENINGS

*M*y mother wasn't too keen on me taking a year off before going to university. Though perhaps it was what I was planning to do with my year that concerned her.

'You want to do *what*?' she'd exclaimed when I showed her the online advertisement two weeks ago.

'Well, look here,' I'd said, and pointed to the screen. 'They're offering every Thursday off, plus holidays. And look how much they're offering to pay per week!'

Mum leaned in, squinting to see the illuminated words on the laptop. She saw what I was pointing to and raised her eyebrows. I think that was what made her finally come round.

'Well, if it's what you want to do,' she'd eventually said with a complacent shrug.

I didn't have the heart to tell her it wasn't. I mean, I liked children, sure! I was pretty good with them, too—I had often thought about going into childcare someday. But I had bigger motivation behind my actions.

I loved to write.

From the day I learnt to hold a pen, sentences flowed from me. Writing had been my only true passion, though I still wasn't sure I was ready to tell my mum. I wasn't sure how she'd take it.

What really caught my attention about this job was the location. I mean, what other chance would I ever have to live in a Gothic mansion for a whole year? I could think of no better place for finding inspiration.

I never expected to get the job. From what I saw, a whole bunch of people already had their eyes on it. I could hardly believe my luck when the acceptance letter came through. Though it baffled me as to why they'd choose me, a young woman with little childcare experience, I eagerly snapped it up. This year could be exactly what I needed to get my life underway, without having to scavenge money off my parents.

10

I had a lot of expectations about Calthorpe Manor. One which had already come true was how difficult it would be to find my way around.

I found my way back downstairs while only getting lost twice, but getting back up to my room was going to be a different matter entirely.

My cases were right where I left them, with the blue one lying on its front, teetering forward with its top-heaviness. The smaller, handheld bag was propped up against the bookshelf. My eyes trained along that bookshelf, scanning the rows and rows of labelled spines right down to the floor. I couldn't help but imagine, as I had done countless times before elsewhere, my own print book perched upon that wooden shelf. Yes, it would look good there. You know . . . when I actually got round to writing it.

I couldn't help but notice the book I'd been reading earlier. *The Kingdom.* Miss Sharpe must have put it back here after taking it off me, meaning she must have seen my bags lying here. I had to chuckle. If she hadn't already made it clear she didn't like me, then she was doing a pretty good job of it now. Why else wouldn't she have brought them up to me?

After checking to make sure Miss Sharpe wasn't within sight, I reached out to take the book. But the moment my fingers grazed the spine, a strange noise filled my ears. With a frown, I turned round,

11

completely forgetting about the book. There it was again! It sounded like laughter . . . like a little, childlike giggle. But it was higher pitched. The sound carried what I could almost describe as a metallic reverberation. I froze for a few moments, my wary eyes scanning every inch of the space around me, waiting for the noise to come again. Silence was all that ensued.

I shook my head, telling myself it was nothing, and picked up both of my cases, heading back towards the staircase. But I stopped dead in my tracks when I heard the laugh again. Okay, this was odd. Miss Sharpe told me that Mr. Calthorpe and the children all were out for the day, so what was going on?

I heard it again, only now I could identify that the noise was coming from my left. Discarding my bags once again, I turned down an unfamiliar corridor and followed its direction. The further I ventured, the clearer the laughter became. I walked past door after door, the sound becoming louder, and more pronounced, until it stopped. I found myself next to a door, standing ever so slightly ajar.

There was a light on inside, though I couldn't see much else. The sound had definitely stopped here. I didn't even think about what I was doing as I pushed the door open to see inside. I was in an office, where there were desks of paperwork stacked so high, it looked like one gust of wind would cause a paper blizzard. I peered around, but could not find the source of the laughter. There was only a man sitting at his desk, laboriously scribbling down notes on the sheets in front of him. There was no way the sound could have come from him. I nearly giggled to myself at the thought.

He hadn't spotted me, so I turned round to creep out before he noticed my intrusion. But I collided with something in the doorway. It grabbed me by the shoulders and began to shout.

'What on earth are you doing in here, child?' yelled the angry voice of the sharp-tongued housekeeper. 'I told you not to come down this way and you deliberately disobeyed me! Why, I have a mind to . . .' She trailed off, and I watched as Miss Sharpe's attention shifted from me to something behind me. Still gripping my shoulders, she span me around to face the inside of the room and pulled me back against her front. The man at the desk ceased what he had been doing earlier and looked bemusedly in our direction.

'Oh, I'm so sorry, Mr. Calthorpe. I didn't realise. But, you see, this girl, she—' Miss Sharpe stuttered, but was cut off by Mr. Calthorpe, as I now knew him to be. The master of the house. Miss Sharpe must have lied to me when she said he was out. Hmm.

13

Perhaps I'd confront her about that later. If I could work up the courage.

I squinted in suspicion as I studied him. Mr. Calthorpe looked to be no older than twenty—surely far too young to own an estate like this, but perhaps I was being judgemental. His hair, dark and straight, had been parted perfectly down the centre, and he sported his business clothes casually, with his shirt sleeves rolled up to the elbow and his top button unfastened, framing his collarbone.

'It's okay, Prudence, I understand,' the young man assured Miss Sharpe.

'But you don't see, Sir. I told her that—'

'It's perfectly all right. Now, let the poor girl go.'

Miss Sharpe lessened her grip, but she did not let go. 'Right, Sir,' she agreed. 'I'll take her to her room and—'

'*Now*, Prudence!' I felt her flinch. 'Am I going to have to report you?'

Finally, she began to back away. As soon as I was free, I shuffled away. Miss Sharpe was holding both her hands out in front of her as she backed out of the room.

'Oh, no, Sir,' she pleaded. 'No, I didn't mean to offend, Sir. I'm sorry to have taken your time.' And with that, she turned into the corridor and fled, but not before directing a glare at me. I was going to have to

14

deal with her wrath later. I wondered just who Mr. Calthorpe had threatened to report her to. Whoever it was had Miss Sharpe quaking in fear.

'I'm sorry about Prudence,' said Mr. Calthorpe after she had left. I was suddenly aware I had been left alone with the master of the house—my employer. I tried to swallow down my nervousness, but it bobbed back up. 'She can be a bit . . . over-zealous at times. She's a pain in the butt, but we just can't seem to get rid of her!' He chuckled, blue eyes shining. I smiled and breathed out a little, glad to relieve some of the tension from my body. 'Come and have a seat,' he offered, gesturing towards a comfy-looking armchair in the corner of the room. I did so with haste, still tired having not yet had a chance to rest.

'So, you must be Pepper Fairfield,' he said with an easy smile as he reclined back in his black, leather chair. 'I wish I'd known you were here. I would have shown you round!'

'Thanks.' I smiled back. 'But I'm afraid you've been beaten to it.'

'So Prudence found you first, did she?' he shook his head in a tut-tutting manner as he rolled his pen between his fingers. 'Oh man, what a first impression! I hope she didn't put you off the job.'

I shook my head, twitching my own fingers in my lap. It seemed not all my nervousness had dissipated.

'Not at all,' I assured him. 'As a matter of fact, I'm looking forward to working here!'

'Good, I'm glad to hear it.' He stood up from behind his desk and strolled around it before stopping in front of it. Then, he must have changed his mind, because he started walking the short distance over to where I sat and extended a hand. 'Sorry, I should introduce myself. I'm Max. Maxwell Calthorpe.'

I took his hand and returned the handshake. 'It's nice to meet you, Mr. Calthorpe.'

'Whoa, hey.' He took back his hand and held it up in front of him. 'Only Pru calls me that. The name's Max.'

'Okay, sorry,' I said, dropping my gaze, though I'm not quite sure why I felt the need to apologise. For some reason, the man was making me feel uneasy. I looked back up at him, deciding to voice what had been playing on my mind. 'I thought Miss Sharpe said you were taking the children out someplace this evening.'

He looked at me strangely. 'Oh, really?' he asked with a bemused expression. 'Now I wonder why . . . oh, oh right! Yes, well, I think she meant to say Peter and Lilly are out with a relative today. I have been home all day, so she must have been mistaken.'

I frowned in thought. 'Oh, I see. It's just,' I began, now feeling foolish, 'I think, well, I thought I heard children laughing when I came down here earlier.' This time, when I looked at Max, his eyebrows were drawn low across his forehead. He didn't say anything. 'I guess . . .' I carried on, 'I guess I must have imagined it.'

'I guess you must have,' Max spoke solemnly. I almost shrank back from the shadow that seemed to cross over his features. But then, as quickly as it appeared, the shadow vanished, and he was smiling at me once again. Perhaps it had never been there at all.

'Would you like me to go and get you anything, Pepper? A cup of tea?'

I shook my head, but smiled with gratitude. 'I'm good, thank you. It's getting late. I should probably go and unpack before meeting the children tomorrow.'

'That sounds like a good idea,' Max agreed with another smile. My breath caught in my throat as I suddenly realised he actually had a pretty nice smile. I felt an inexplicable warmth heat my cheeks at the thought.

'The children,' I began as another thought struck me, unsure how to state my question. 'Are they . . .'

Max caught my meaning. His smile widened to an almost mischievous grin as he shook his head. 'They're not mine,' he said. When I gave a questioning look, he added, 'They're my cousins.'

I nodded in understanding, and I knew my face was

17

now flushing all shades of red.

'I . . . I need to go and grab my bags.'

'Can you find your way back to your room all right?'

I told him that I could, and turned to leave his office, making sure my gaze remained lowered.

'Pepper?' I stopped when he called my name. I looked up long enough to see him say, 'Sleep well,' and I could have sworn he threw a wink at me before I exited along the corridor.

It took me a moment to gather my bearings and remember what I was doing.

Bags. Foyer. Right.

I headed back towards the entrance to retrieve my things. When I did, I found myself stealing another look at the book from before.

Whether it was out of spite or interest, or maybe both, I do not know. But I reached forward and grabbed the book from its perch and shoved it into my bag. I scampered quietly away before Miss Sharpe could catch me—I didn't want another reason to be in her bad books!

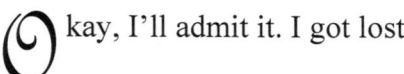 kay, I'll admit it. I got lost.

18

Which wasn't difficult when each corridor looked just like the next. The never-ending walls were making me dizzy as I desperately tried to find a familiar-looking door.

Sighing in frustration, I leaned my back against the brown wallpaper, taking a moment to gather my bearings. I felt something rocking precariously behind me—I hadn't looked where I was leaning. Releasing my bags, I lurched forward and span round, thrusting out my arms just in time to catch a heavy painting as it slipped from its position on the wall. I tried to calm my heartrate as I cradled the large frame just feet from the floor. I surveyed the area around me to make sure no one had noticed my near catastrophe.

I glanced down at the picture I had pinned between myself and the solid wall. A beautiful oil painting depicted a magical forest path, meandering its way between illuminated tree trunks. I brushed a gentle finger across the textured surface. The picture felt smooth, with slight bevels where the paint was thicker, making my finger run across it in waves. Tiny orbs of light were speckled artistically across the piece. They reminded me of fairies dancing through an enchanted woodland. A perfect backdrop for a fantasy tale.

With a smile, I lifted the frame back up onto its hook, where it hung central on the otherwise bare wall. I wondered how I could have missed it before.

The tinkling laughter sounded again, and with it came a worried feeling in my stomach which hadn't been there before. Both Max and Miss Sharpe had now stated that the children weren't in, so something wasn't right. Would I say I was scared? Probably, yeah. But, once again, my curiosity got the better of me.

The sound was a lot clearer than it had been before, and I could say with certainty it came from my right, further down the corridor.

Darkness crept up on me, and the smell of dust assaulted my nose. It was clear this area of the building was rarely used. Hence Miss Sharpe's omission of it earlier, I assumed.

The end of the corridor was scarcely lit—only enough for me to read the sign on the door at the end; the only door along this stretch of space. 'PRIVATE: NO ENTRY' it stated in red capitals, and it was looked as though no one had done so. At least, not in a long time. This forgotten region of the house hadn't even been dusted for . . . well . . . I dreaded to think. I shivered at the sheer number of cobwebs dangling from the ceiling. I didn't particularly want to imagine the kind of spiders capable of that craftsmanship. Did Miss Sharpe know about this area? If so, then why didn't she tell someone to clean it once in a while? Or

20

turn the lights on? It looked and smelt like someone had died here.

I was about to turn and walk away when I heard the giggle again. I inched with caution closer to the door. There was no doubt that the sound had come from behind it.

The moment my skin touched the cold metal of the doorknob, an electric sensation came over my body. Discordant voices filled my head with a loud, unbearable screaming, at the same time as my insides felt like they were being slowly filled with water. My vision blurred, and before my eyes shone a rainbow of glittering, bright lights. It felt like I was falling, and for a moment, I lost all sense of self. I snatched my hand from the handle, and just like that, the feeling vanished. What the hell?

Gasping for breath, I stared at my palm. That couldn't have been real. My mind must have been playing tricks on me. Everything was becoming too much for me today, and it was having an effect. I needed to lie down, and somehow get rid of the sugary-sweet taste suddenly filling my mouth.

My room was only a few doors down from where I had been. Relieved to have finally found my way back, I collapsed straight onto the bed, belly down, my luggage already discarded at its base. Yes, that was much better.

21

I lay there, listening to the sound of my own breathing for a while. So, this was going to be my room for the next year then, eh? Well, I guessed I could get used to it. Provided I could figure my way around the house without getting lost. Miss Sharpe was only a minor nuisance, but I could not shake that cryptic door from my mind. There was no way I could have imagined that laughter. And the eeriness of that corridor . . . I shuddered. My head swam with all kinds of far-fetched possibilities. Was Mr. Calthorpe hiding something?

I decided to forget about it for now. I'd worry about all this later. I convinced myself I was going to enjoy this job, and if not that, then just the experience of living here. Perhaps I was just blowing things out of proportion, and maybe there was a plausible explanation behind it all.

Rolling round onto my back, I surveyed my room from this new perspective. To the right were two doors which led to both an en-suite bathroom and a small kitchenette. It looked like I was expected to cook and care for myself. Not that I minded much. I was kind of prepared for it.

I was quick to get into my nightclothes, but as desperate as I was to get a good sleep before my first day of work, I couldn't resist reading a quick chapter of *The Kingdom* beforehand.

After all, I did just steal the book from my boss.

KINGDOM

3

UNFORTUNATE CIRCUMSTANCES

searing pain to the brow was among the first things to light the king's consciousness as slumber passed over him. He released a moan and caressed a calloused hand 'cross his face.

'I see you wake, good king,' an unseen voice spoke in tender manners. Alzabar could not mistake the kind words of the friar, a loyal friend from times he could not think back far enough to remember.

With lids still drawn, Alzabar tasted the words on his own tongue. 'Good king,' he echoed. 'Such title has not graced my being for many a year. Spiteful;

negligent; cowardly: those are all tags I have been dealt. I desert my people to crusade, only to return with coats stained more by my home blood than that of my enemies. And yet I am told I am good. Tell me, my friend, how am I so?'

Peeling open his eyes from where he lay on the cold church floor, Alzabar's gaze fell upon his dear friend, his face fraught with worry.

'Dark times have descended upon us all, Your Majesty,' he spoke gravely. 'In your stead, your kinsman has pilfered the throne and now reigns over us with a tyrant's intent.'

Alzabar's arms, strong, yet weak from tireless years of crusading, levered him up from the stone. 'I am aware of my brother's disloyalty,' he glowered.

'Do not blind yourself with daisy'd falsities. Look deeper. The kingdom is split. Where the sylphs have remained loyal, the unicorns have sided with Calpacious. The goblins and centaurs are not to be trusted and the banshees are causing havoc. One by one, the creatures are turning faithful to the unworthy leader. You must see that we are in great trouble.'

'Of course I see that,' the king answered in retort. 'They are all after my blood.'

But the friar shook his fraying head. 'Your kingdom was rife with deadly blades since long before your return. The blame lies not with your good self. I admit some inhabitants may want your head, but not all are as cold at heart. Many of us welcome your appearance. You are precisely what we need in this dark age. Alzabar, your majesty,' spoke the friar, 'please be our salvation. We need your help.'

' S he's dead!' a boy screamed, his hands thrown high above his head. The seven-year-old was dressed in *Batman* pyjamas and his dark ginger hair stuck up in tufts where it had yet to be combed. 'She's dead! She's dead!' he kept screeching as he rocketed round the room with no apparent concern for what he might be running into in the process.

It was still early in the morning, and I was groggy. With the aftertaste of coffee lingering on my tongue, it was a matter of time before the caffeine started to kick in. The Calthorpe children, Lilly and Peter, however, looked like they could both run two full marathons, back to back, without even breaking a sweat.

'I'm not dead!' Lilly complained in protest. 'You need to touch my head to make me dead! You only hit my shoulder. I don't like this game, anyway.'

Peter climbed up onto one of the old armchairs,

27

standing on the cushion to make himself even taller than his younger sister. He poked his tongue out at her and resumed his little victory dance.

'Peter, could you get down off the chair, please?' I requested. I hadn't specifically been told the children weren't allowed to play on the furniture, but I got the impression a young child's feet jumping on the manor's decades-old upholstery was not a good thing.

Peter made sure to perform a few extra high jumps before finally springing off and landing on the rug with a loud thud. I gasped and ran over to him, but he just looked at me, an impish grin on his face, and skipped off, giggling. He began to chant.

'Ding dong bell,

Pepper's aunty smells,

She has weird hair,

And she dresses like a bear.'

Lilly clutched her belly, giggling hard, clearly amused at her brother's poetry. 'My turn, my turn!' she proclaimed. She looked around the room for inspiration, sucking in her pink lips as she thought.

'Roses are red,

Violets are blue,

Pepper likes garlic bread and eats cabbage for breakfast.'

Smiling at the two siblings' antics, I figured they were safe by themselves for now (i.e. they weren't throwing themselves off antique armchairs) and turned into the adjoining kitchen while Peter chastised his sister, telling her how poems worked and that the words had to rhyme.

Now, what was it Miss Sharpe had told me they liked for breakfast? Was it porridge for Peter and Frosties for Lilly? Yes, I was pretty sure that was it.

I left the door wide open to ensure I could hear everything the children were doing. With my ears straining to hear into the next room, I got to work preparing our breakfasts.

This morning, I'd had some time to think about the strange occurrences which took place the day before. At first, I had considered simply asking Max what was behind the signposted door, and whether it had anything to do with the strange laughter I heard, but, upon further judgement I'd figured it rude to ask my employer such a question. Perhaps the room was kept private for a reason.

Maybe I would do a bit of investigating myself. Later that night, after the children had gone to bed, I would sneak upstairs and discover what, if anything—though I was pretty sure there was something—was hidden behind the door.

'Be sure to put some cold milk in Peter's porridge.'

I jumped in alarm at the voice. I hadn't even noticed Max entering the kitchen, let alone standing directly behind me.

'Jeez, you frightened me half to death!' I gasped, slamming a hand against my pounding chest.

Max chuckled. 'I tend to have that effect on women,' he said as I opened the door to the bleeping microwave. 'I see you've met the children, then.'

'Yeah, well.' I set the bowl down on the side and, as per Max's instruction, added a dollop of cold milk to the gloopy mixture. 'It was kind of hard not to when they came bounding into my room at half five in the morning, pretending to be cowboys.' I checked to make sure I could still hear them in the lounge. From the sounds of it, Peter was still explaining to Lilly what rhyming was.

Max laughed again. 'Don't be put off by them. They're doing it on purpose. Probably to wind you up.' Today, he wore more casual attire. A pair of navy blue jeans went with a washed-out green shirt, and his hair had been brushed sleepily across his forehead.

'I'm used to it.' I shrugged. 'Have you ever lived with cats? Mine make a habit of walking over my face half an hour before my alarm goes off.' I poured some Frosties into Lilly's bowl then half-filled it with milk. I managed to find two colourful plastic cups in the cupboard above my head and set them on the side, shooting an inquiring look towards Max.

'Orange juice,' he informed me. 'Fridge. Top

shelf.' I located the carton and promptly filled the two cups. 'Yeah, well, this house really isn't best suited for pets,' he said in response to my earlier comment. 'I've always wanted a dog, but could you imagine the mess?'

I giggled at his grimace. 'Oh, yes,' I said. 'Scratches on the tapestries!'

'Fur in the fireplace.'

'Paw prints on the armour!'

We both chuckled. 'Nah,' said Max, 'we have enough problems with these kids. Though they're nothing you can't handle, I'm sure.' He grinned. 'They can be a little trying at times, but you'll get to love them. I have a feeling you're exactly what they both need right now.' He looked at me for a long while, and I suddenly felt myself becoming rather uncomfortable under his intense gaze. Squirming, I decided to change the subject.

'So, uh,' I faltered, 'you must be rather busy here, what with running the place and having to look after the children and all.'

'Oh. Well, uh, yes, I guess I am.' Max reached back with his arm and scratched the back of his head. 'Yes, keeping this place up and running does take a lot of effort!' he said. 'You know, the life of a busy businessman, right?'

I opened my mouth, about to ask him exactly what

kind of business he ran, when a noise from beyond the kitchen made me stop.

'I said it would catch fire! I told you to move the furniture before you lit the match!' came Peter's irritated voice. Max and I exchanged horrified glances before scrambling into the lounge.

Lilly and Peter stood side by side, no match at hand and with all the furniture perfectly intact. They were both grinning from ear to ear, and when they saw our expressions, they burst out into fits of hysterical giggles.

As my heart rate regained its natural rhythm for the second time that morning, I found myself chuckling along.

'Okay, you two,' I said, 'I think it's time for some breakfast.'

Both little faces lit up and they raced each other into the dining room. I turned to Max, and he turned to me. Goodness, what energy! Were they always like this? I got the feeling that I was going to need to stock up on coffee if I was to have any hope of keeping up with them.

'I'll leave you to it,' Max said, amused. 'I just came by to check how you're coping. I'd take them out somewhere later to let them burn off some of their energy if I were you, or you'll never get any sleep tonight!'

I nodded. That sounded like a good idea.

'Just call Miss Sharpe or me if you need any help with anything,' he offered, then paused before adding, 'though I'd rather you called me.' With that, he turned and left the room. I watched him retreat. I hadn't quite made my mind up about Max. Sure, he seemed nice. Maybe he was a little too sure of himself. I guessed I would soon get to know him better.

Without wasting any more time, I grabbed the bowls from the kitchen and sat down with the children, my own plate of jammy toast in front of me. My stomach growled. I tucked in.

'Why is your name Pepper?' Peter asked around the spoonful of gloopy porridge he was shovelling into his mouth.

Five-year-old Lilly glared at her older brother. 'You shouldn't ask that!' she scolded him. 'It's not nice!'

'I was only asking.' Peter shrugged. 'It's a funny name.'

'Well I think it's a lovely name,' countered his ever-argumentative younger sister.

I smiled at her. 'Thank you, Lilly,' I said, and then turned to answer Peter's question. 'My name is Pepper because that was what my grandma was called.'

Peter kept his eyes lowered over his bowl, a scowl

33

across his features. 'I think it sounds like something you put on a salad.'

'Peter, don't be mean!'

Peter shrugged. 'I'm only telling the truth, Lilly,' he said, cramming another large spoonful into his mouth.

Lilly decided to divert the conversation. 'Is your grandma a nice person?' she asked me.

Smiling down at her, I nodded. 'She used to be a very nice person, yes.'

'What happened to her? Did she leave?' Peter caught on to my use of the past tense.

'In a sense, yes.'

Neither of them said anything for a while as the three of us continued to nibble at—or in Peter's case, gulp down—our breakfasts. After a few seconds, Lilly leaned in close to me and whispered, 'She died, didn't she?'

Swallowing down my mouthful, I told her, 'Yes. Yes she did.'

Then she did something I was not expecting. She lifted her small hand and gently placed it on top of my own. I looked down at her, and she looked up at me with wide eyes of the palest blue. What the young child said next made my heart ache.

'My mummy and daddy died,' she said plainly, without taking her intense eyes away from mine.

'They died in a car crash a few weeks ago.'

'Lilly,' came Peter's voice from the other side of the table. His words were strained as he spoke them through gritted teeth. 'We're not supposed to talk about that.' His knuckles turned white where he was gripping his spoon.

'But Pepper can know,' she insisted. 'She's almost like our mummy now.' Peter said nothing, just continued to stir what was left of his porridge with his spoon. We ate in silence for a while. It was obvious we'd hit a bad topic. I needed to change the subject, and fast.

'Max suggested we go out someplace later today,' I began. 'Is there a park or anything nearby you like to go to?'

Lilly sucked in both her lips as her young face made slight, thoughtful furrows. It didn't take her long to think. 'Ooh!' she exclaimed. 'Eaststreet Park! We like that one, don't we, Peter?' Peter grunted in affirmation. 'We've been there hundreds of times already with Miss Sharpe!'

Oh no. The poor kids hadn't had to put up with her, had they?

'Don't exaggerate,' said Peter curtly, now a much different person than he had been before the mention of their unfortunate parents. 'We've been twice.'

'Lilly it sounds like a great idea.' I grinned. 'Is that

35

okay with you, Peter?' I tried to be sensitive with my words. Peter was in a bad mood, and I didn't want to make him any worse.

But it looked as though I had done so anyway. He frowned and sighed, dropping his spoon dramatically on the oak table. He looked up and shot me the dirtiest of glares.

'I don't like that park!' he spat, taking me aback somewhat. 'It's old and it's creaky and it only has two swings. I don't like this place either, because it's full of weird stuff and it smells funny. But most of all, I don't like having a nanny, and I'll never want one.' With a scowl, he pushed up from his chair and stormed out of the room, leaving his empty bowl and spoon on the table.

'He does that,' whispered a little voice by my ear. I looked down to see Lilly still leaning towards me. 'He's upset because he misses Mummy and Daddy. He thinks you're trying to be like them.' She pointed to the door her brother had just fled through. 'He gets like that sometimes, but then he gets better. Soon he will be a happy Peter and not a grumpy Peter.'

With understanding, I reached an arm out and squeezed her shoulders lightly. 'Don't worry, sweetie,' I told her, 'I've been through it all. I miss my nanny, too.' I glanced down at the sweet, little redhead under my arm. Lilly's skin was pale, like her brother's, but her hair was lighter than his. Ginger curls sprouted from her little head and tumbled down around her face where some of the wispy tendrils had escaped from their bunches. Her cheeks were rosy beneath a slight smattering of freckles and her blue eyes were as soft as the summer sky. She smiled at me. She didn't look like a child who had lost both her parents recently.

'What about you?' I asked her quietly. 'Do you miss your parents?'

She cocked her head to one side. 'I do,' she spoke softly, 'but I'm not upset. Mummy and Daddy are happy where they are. They are with people who love them. If I cry, I will not bring them back, so I need to save all my crying until I really need it.'

I was momentarily stunned by the wisdom behind Lilly's words. How different she was from her brother.

What was I supposed to do about Peter? Should I go and see if he was all right? Or leave him to calm down of his own accord? My reasoning told me the latter would probably be the better idea, or I feared I would only make things worse again. Lilly had said he would come round eventually, and if anyone knew him better than everyone else, it would be his own sister.

'I like you.' She nestled into my arm. She smelled

powdery, with the clean, childish smell I was so used to smelling on my own sister.

'Do you want to know a secret?' I said with a little smile, looking down at her

She nodded eagerly. I leaned in closer and whispered in her ear, 'I like you too.'

Lilly grinned back at me and giggled girlishly. Her laugh was contagious. I ruffled her hair before grabbing the dirty dishes and carrying them out into the kitchen. I hadn't realised Lilly had followed me until I was halfway through loading the dishwasher. She handed me one of the dirty bowls with a shy smile.

'Pepper?' she said quietly. Still in her pink nightdress, she held her hands clasped behind her back and rocked back and forth on the balls of her feet. She looked like a child who was about to ask her parents for more pocket money.

'What is it?' I asked as I rinsed the remaining Frosties down the sink.

'I have a secret to tell you, too.'

4

CURIOUS DEVELOPMENTS

*R*ather puzzled at the little girl's behaviour, I humoured her, and followed as she led me along the halls and up the stairs, round corners and through doors. She seemed to know exactly where she was going despite having only lived here for a couple of weeks. The five-year-old seemed to have better navigational skills than I did.

Lilly led me all the way to her bedroom. Though it was still in the process of being decorated, Lilly's bedroom certainly had the feel of a little girl's room. The walls were light pink and gentle beige in colour, and on the one wall, a large, detailed fairy castle mural was mid-way through being painted. Most of her belongings were held in cardboard boxes which were scattered chaotically across the purple floor, but a number of stuffed toys sat atop decoratively placed shelves. On the whole, the room was large—which was not surprising given the scale of the house—and would look stunning when it was finished, in a whimsical, fairy-tale sort of way.

'What's the matter, Lilly?' I probed when she offered me no further clues as to whatever was on her mind.

Lilly kicked one of the boxes out of the way, spilling its contents onto the floor in the process. She beckoned for me to follow her. I did so, pulling the door closed after me until it was slightly ajar.

Her eyes were alight and dancing as she stood close to me and looked me in the eye.

'I think I found out something secret about this house,' she said, her words hushed. 'Nobody knows apart from me. Not even Peter!'

My mind instantly flashed to yesterday and the mysterious door I had come across. She hadn't . . . had she? 'I hope you haven't been poking around anywhere you shouldn't have been, Lilly,' I warned her, but she shook her head.

'It's not like that!' she insisted. She slumped down onto her unmade Disney Princess duvet cover, and I

40

followed suit. 'Can you keep a secret?' she asked. I wasn't sure how to answer. What if she told me something I would have to report back to Mr. Calthorpe?

'You *have* to keep this a secret, okay?'

The look she gave me was so intense, I found myself relenting.

'Okay.'

My assurance gave her back her smile. I watched her with interest as she peered around the room, seemingly looking for something.

'Fifi?' she called out quietly. 'It's okay, you can come out.'

My eyes widened as, from behind her cluttered wardrobe emerged a small, white bunny. I gasped as it hopped towards us and jumped onto Lilly's lap.

'Should you be allowed an animal in the house?' I asked in shock as the creature began to nuzzle Lilly's hand. Its fur was the most brilliant white I had ever seen. It almost glistened in the sunlight from the window.

'Pepper, meet Fifi. Fifi, this is my new nanny, Pepper.' The bunny turned its head towards me, and if I didn't know any better, I'd have said it was giving me a look of appraisal. I stared curiously at its eyes— a bright, sparkling violet colour. Rabbits didn't have purple eyes, did they?

Lilly carried on with her introduction. 'Fifi is a magical bunny,' she explained as she stroked its fur. 'I found her in my room the day we moved in. She's really kind and lovely.'

I panicked. I had no mental scenario for five-year-old-child-has-a-wild-rabbit-in-her-bedroom. What the hell was I going to do about this? 'I think you should tell someone about your rabbit,' I told her. 'I don't think it belongs to this house and it needs to be outside where it belongs.'

Lilly pouted. 'She's not an "it"!' she protested. She shielded the little rabbit with her arms, cuddling it closely when I moved to take it away from her. 'No!' she shouted. 'You promised! I told you, Fifi is a magical bunny! She belongs in this house and she belongs to me!'

'No, Lilly.' I shook my head. 'I'm really sorry. This is a wild bunny which belongs in the forest. Maybe if you ask Mr. Calthorpe nicely, he'll let you have a rabbit as a pet. But this one needs to go back to her family.' I leaned forward to take the animal away from Lilly, but just as I was about to touch it, it vanished.

'What the . . .' I stammered. 'Where did she go?'

Lilly giggled at my stupefied expression. 'I told you, she's magical! She turned herself invisible because she wants to stay here with me!'

My heart began to race. The bunny was nowhere to be seen. What was going on? There was something strange about this house. It was a glaring fact I could ignore no longer.

'Lilly, this is serious,' I announced, jumping up off the bed. 'Tell me, exactly where did Fifi come from?'

She pinched in her lips. 'Well, I don't know *exactly*,' she started, 'but I do know where her family lives.'

'And where's that?' I asked her, although I already had a worrying suspicion.

'Down the hallway,' she pointed beyond her room. 'Behind a door with the big words on it.'

I dropped my head into my hands and rubbed my face with my fingers, stretching the skin as I ran this all through in my head.

'Have you been inside that room?' was my next question.

'No.' She shook her head. 'Fifi wouldn't let me.'

I looked around, but the invisible bunny had yet to re-materialise. 'Does Fifi talk?'

'Oh no, she can't talk. But she listens to everything I say.' Right at that moment, the rabbit in question appeared on the windowsill to my left. I stared at her. She stared right back at me. Her fur began to shimmer, and right before my eyes, her sparkling white coat began to change and she turned bright

43

blue!

'You've hurt her feelings!' said Lilly, laughing at the bunny's reaction. I began to edge my way across the disorderly floor towards the mystical creature. My hand reached out to her, but this time, Fifi just twitched her whiskers and remained perfectly visible as I ran my fingers across her silky, azure fur. I could have been imagining it, but it looked like she was smiling. My fear told me to turn and run in the opposite direction, but my curiosity was a force to be reckoned with.

'Hello, Fifi,' I greeted her uncertainly. It felt odd, talking to a bunny. Especially one with . . . magical powers, if that was what they were. She made a funny little chirping sound in response, one I had never heard from a bunny before.

Lilly was delighted. 'I knew you would be able to see her!' she said. I asked her what she meant. 'I tried to introduce her to Peter, but he couldn't see her. He told me I was teasing him. He can't see any of them!'

'Wait, what do you mean, any of them?'

Lilly grinned from ear to ear. 'Didn't I tell you?' Her big, blue eyes swam with delight once more. She pointed at Fifi. 'There are more like her!'

Okay, now I was officially weirded out. I needed some fresh air.

'Come on, Lilly,' I said, ushering her out of her

room. 'I'm sure Miss Sharpe is wondering where we are!'

To be honest, I just needed the moment to clear my head. What I just saw couldn't be real. Could it?

After I left Lilly's room, it came to mind I had yet to see Peter since he stormed out of the dining room. I should probably go and check on him. I asked Lilly to show me to his room and, sure enough, when I got there, there he was.

Peter lay in his bed, the green sheets pulled right up over his head. He made no movement to show he was aware of my presence.

Unlike Lilly's room, Peter's was very minimal, with green and white horizontally striped walls and black furniture. All was coordinated. However, like his sister's room, cardboard boxes of unpacked belongings made it difficult to see the carpet.

I continued to stand in the doorway.

'Peter?'

He made no response. Only the slow rise and fall from beneath the blanket kept me from fretting.

'Peter, would you like to talk to me?'

'Go away,' he grumbled. But I defied his request. I'd been through this scenario before with my sister, so I began what I had done countless times before, and tiptoed over to where he had cocooned himself in his bed and crouched before him. With his head

45

buried beneath the sheets, I couldn't even tell which way he faced.

'Peter, have you ever met a troll?'

There was movement beneath the duvet as Peter rolled round. With two, small hands, he peeled the covers from his eyes. 'Trolls don't exist.' His face disappeared once more.

'Oh, well, you've never met my friend, Archie, then.' I said, and waited. Out came one hand. Then the other. Soon his eyes were back on mine, only this time they were drawn beneath lowered eyebrows.

'That's right,' I said, 'I once knew a troll. And he was a very nice one, too.'

'But aren't trolls supposed to be horrible creatures?' Half of Peter's face was still concealed behind the blanket, absorbing the sound of his voice.

I gasped and put my hand against my chest. 'Why, whoever told you that?' I said with exaggeration. 'Trolls are the nicest, gentlest creatures you will ever meet.' I smiled as he lowered the duvet a little more. I levered myself up from the floor and perched myself at the foot of Peter's bed. The action caused him to wriggle even further up his end. 'You know,' I continued, 'you kind of remind me of Archie.'

'Yeah?' replied Peter. His eyebrows inched back up his face. 'What's he like?'

'Well,' I began, making myself more comfortable.

'He is brave, intelligent, and his heart is one of the strongest I have ever come across.' In the low lighting, a mouth became visible. Then a chin. 'And—' I leaned forward a little. 'The amount of love he had for his family was second to none.'

At the word 'family', Peter's head retracted again, back into its duvet-shell. I sighed.

'Archie had his fair amount of difficulties, too.' I went on with my story. 'He was brave, indeed, but his bravery did not come without cost. The village Archie lived in had been under threat from an angry phoenix for as long as the trolls could remember. This phoenix terrorised the villagers by endangering their lives and destroying their crops. It came by every week. The villagers were too scared to face it. One day, when it returned, it was Archie and his brother, Frederick, who made the decision to defeat the beast once and for all.

'The hunt did not go as planned. Unfortunately, the two strong brothers were no match for the bird of fire, and it found them first.' I reached forward and lay a soft hand on where I supposed Peter's shoulder to be in the hope it would coax him back out of his nest.

'What happened?' Peter mumbled, still submerged.

'Archie lost his brother that day,' I told him. 'He returned home to his mother, but he did not speak to her. Instead, he went straight to his favourite rock, where he lay down and cried. For days, nobody could speak to him, not even his own mum. He blamed himself for what happened to Frederick. He thought if he had seen the phoenix first, if he had been brave enough to kill it before it found his brother, Frederick would have survived.

'Archie's mum didn't feel as though she had lost one son. She felt like she had lost Archie, too. She barely saw him, and she wished she could do something to bring him back to the cheerful troll he had once been.'

Peter folded back the duvet and sat upright in his bed, interest now lighting his eyes. 'But that's so sad!' he said. 'It wasn't his fault!'

I smiled sadly. 'Yes, I know. But Archie wouldn't believe it. One day, when he felt as though he could not live with himself any longer, his mum came up to him. She had bad news. The phoenix had returned to the village.'

'No!'

'Archie's mum didn't quite know what to expect from him. Would he cower even more? Would he storm outside in a rage and attack the bird on the spot?'

'I would have.'

'Well, what Archie did next surprised everyone in the village. Unarmed, he ventured out into the path of the phoenix, where no troll would ever consider himself stupid enough to go. He stood before the phoenix as it lit its trail of flames in the blazing sky. The firebird shrieked and flapped at the young troll, expecting him to retreat in fear. But Archie stood there, unflinching. The phoenix was stunned at the absence of fear in Archie's eyes. The fire in its tail died down, and the bird landed in front of him.

'For a while, the two creatures did nothing but look into each other's eyes. Archie stared at the beast and saw the eyes of his brother's murderer, but anger was not an emotion which crossed his mind. In that moment, a glimmer of understanding passed between the two enemies and they both saw each other, not for what they were, but for what they could make each other. Archie reached out and stroked a hand along one of the bird's glistening wings. While fearful trolls shuddered from behind their windows, a bond was struck between two life-long foes.'

Peter's head cocked to the side as he looked at me with curiosity. 'But why?' he asked. 'If the phoenix had killed his brother, then why wasn't Archie angry?'

'Frederick may have died,' I replied, 'but no matter how much Archie missed him, he knew he could never bring him back. Instead of seeking revenge on the bird, who was just as scared of them as they were

49

of him, Archie made the decision to turn Frederick's passing into something positive for the village. He made a friend of the phoenix that day. Archie became the greatest hero the trolls had ever known, and the village was finally free from the bird's attacks. The phoenix became a part of the village, helping the trolls to grow their crops, and they in turn gave it all the supplies it needed, and a loving home for the rest of its life.'

I waited a moment to gauge Peter's reaction, and was pleased to see a grin spread across his face.

'That's a happy story,' he beamed. 'I think I like Archie. Maybe one day I'll be like him!'

'Perhaps you will,' I said, smiling back.

5

INCREDIBLE SIGHTS

I really hoped this wasn't one of those 'three strikes and you're out' kinds of contracts, for if it was, I would already be out now, on just my second day. One strike for snooping around the house in places I wasn't allowed to go, another for stealing the house's property (*The Kingdom* still lay open on my unmade bed where I'd left it that morning) and one more just now for neglecting the children's scheduled bedtime and sending them to bed an hour early.

Okay, I couldn't really justify the first two. It was my fault for venturing too far in the manor, and I'd only taken the book to spite Miss Sharpe.

After the whole ordeal with the disappearing bunny earlier that morning, I found myself counting down the hours until I would be able to fully investigate the house that evening. The whole afternoon while I'd been at the park with the children, I couldn't seem to get my mind off the strange happenings.

The outing had worn out Lilly and Peter, who'd now calmed to a happier mood, thank goodness—I wasn't sure I could handle a stroppy Peter for a whole day—and both were willing to go straight to bed after supper. So now, as I tucked the covers around Lilly, who was already fast asleep, I whispered for the magical bunny.

'Fifi, are you there?' I called. 'I need you.' I didn't need to wait long, for no sooner had I spoken those words, the white rabbit materialised at my feet. I jumped, even though I had been half expecting her. She began rubbing herself against my ankle in a happy greeting.

'Hello to you, too,' I chuckled, scratching her head between her ears as she chirruped. 'Now listen to me.' I crouched down in front of her, hesitating—would she really understand me? Despite my doubts, Fifi's ears pricked up in anticipation. 'I like this house,' I told her. 'I like you, and I like the children. I want to stay here.' The muscles in Fifi's face moved in a way that looked almost like she was smiling. I relaxed a little, feeling a little less stupid. 'I need to know what's up with this house,' I continued, holding the bunny's violet gaze, which stared unblinkingly back at me. 'Lilly told me there are more of you. Can you show me where they are?'

The rabbit just cocked her head, her expression unchanging. She remained this way for a few seconds, showing no sign of responding to my request. Feeling dejected and foolish, I slumped.

'You can't understand me, can you?'

Again, Fifi gave no indication she heard me, just gave her left ear a thorough scratching with her foot.

'Fine,' I sighed. 'I guess I'm just going to have to find out for myself.' I stepped over Fifi and went to exit Lilly's room, being as quiet as I could in closing the door behind me. After a brief circumnavigation, I ventured off to find the mysterious corridor and forbidden door.

Now, I was sure I hadn't taken a wrong turn. I'd walked right past my own room, and was certain the corridor hadn't been far from there. And yet I found myself trailing in circles, unable to find the cordoned off area of the house I had stumbled upon so easily before. I was going crazy, I had to be! There was no sign of a hidden, darkened corridor. All the corridors were fully lit, and not one of the ones I searched contained a signposted door. And the picture, the striking oil painting, was nowhere to be seen. How odd. Had I imagined it?

I rounded the same corner for the umpteenth time, my frustration now starting to get the better of me.

After twenty minutes of walking in circles, I finally resigned to my room.

Peeved after my fruitless search, it took some strength to close the door without slamming it like a stropping toddler. I didn't have time to consider my painful failure at locating the door, though, because something else seized my attention.

Butterflies. My room teemed with them. Hundreds upon hundreds of the insects, all different colours and sizes, fluttered in a myriad of wings around the space. I stood, my mouth agape, and with my back flush against the door as I absorbed the spectacle before me. The sight was breath-taking. Some of the butterflies had landed on the posts of the bed, flaunting the shimmering hues of their expansive wings which glinted in the fading light of the sunset. It was truly magical.

But how did they get in here? To my knowledge, the bay window had been closed all day. There was no way they could have got in. Unless someone did this on purpose. But who would do such a thing?

Being careful not to crush any of the fragile

creatures, I crept over to the window, which took up most of the wall opposite my bed, and pushed it open on both sides.

'Go on,' I whispered, 'get out!' I made scooping motions with my hands to push them out but, no matter what I did, none of the butterflies would venture anywhere near the open window. This was ridiculous. They couldn't stay here. I looked over to the door. Would Max be mad if I let them out into the rest of the house?

'What's she doing?' came a whispered voice from behind me. I snapped my head around, in search of the source. There was no one there. 'Is she trying to get them out of the house?'

'I told you she was nutty,' said another voice. Whereas the first one had been unquestionably male, this voice was a lot higher in pitch. 'Did I tell you I saw her talking to a rabbit earlier?'

I scoured the room, but I could not work out who was speaking. Were they talking about me? All I could see were the butterflies, and they couldn't talk. Could they?

'Who's there?' I called out, my voice shaking, to the invisible voices, suddenly feeling as though I needed to arm myself with something. All I had around me was a desk, a chair and a pile of unfolded clothes.

'Wait, can she hear us?' whispered the female voice to her male friend.

'I don't know, try asking her.'

There was a clearing of a throat. 'Hey! Girl!' shouted the female, as though we weren't in the same room. 'Can. You. Hear. Me?'

'Who—' I swallowed. 'Who's saying that?' I batted at some of the butterflies collecting around my face.

'Up here,' said the male. I looked up. 'To your left!' I looked left. 'No, our left!'

And there, right on top of the bedpost, sat . . . well . . . I wasn't quite sure from down where I was standing. But they certainly weren't butterflies.

The two voice sources fluttered down from their perch, and for a moment, I thought my eyes were having me on.

Two tiny human figures landed side by side atop the old chest at the foot of my bed. That wasn't what startled me, though. No, what had me backing up to the wall were the glittering wings which sprouted from each of their backs, not too dissimilar to those of the butterflies. My brain struggled to comprehend what my eyes told it.

'You-you're,' my tongue stumbled over the words in my disbelief, 'you're fairies!'

The girl peered at me. 'Fairies?' she repeated, and

then began to giggle, her pretty features crinkling with humour. Her laughter turned raucous. Even her companion stifled a chuckle, though more at his friend's antics, it seemed, than at what I said.

'What? Aren't you?' I asked in confusion. The girl now laughed so hard that she lay on her back, crumpling the red-brown, leaf-like dress she wore. The air around her shimmered with an orange glow.

'Scarlett, get up,' urged the boy. Chocolate brown hair stood spiked on the top of his head, giving him a boyish, playful look. His garments had a similar, rustic appearance, but were moss green in colour and had the texture of, well, I could only liken it to a sort of soft tree bark. Like the girl, he wore pointed brown shoes on his feet. 'The poor girl's probably never seen a sylph before!'

'But it's just—so—funny!' she rasped between laughs. Childish; tinkling. The same sound I chased around the manor the day before.

The boy sighed. 'She's like this sometimes,' he said to me with an apologetic smile. 'I'm Cade.' He pointed to the giggling fairy—no, sylph—at his feet. 'That's Scarlett.'

'Um . . .' I had yet to move away from the wall, and the butterflies still flitted above my head, occasionally colliding with my face. 'Nice to meet you.' I said it almost as a question.

Pepper, what are you doing? Spoke a voice in my head. Your room is full of butterflies and you are talking to fairies. You've either lost your mind or you're in big trouble. Get out of here!

'Ahem!' Cade cleared his throat with implication. Scarlett stopped her laughing and snapped up into a sitting position, legs apart, and her huge bush of white-blonde hair flopping over her tiny face as she did so. With both hands, she drew apart the tight waves like a pair of curtains and peered at Cade, her cheeks glowing.

'What?' She grinned. The boy fairy made a pointed gesture towards me with his eyes.

'Oh!' She levered herself up and brushed herself down. 'Yes, hi, I'm sorry about that.' Her orange tinted wings fidgeted behind her—huge in proportion to the rest of her body. 'I'm Scarlett.'

'I just told her that,' said Cade with a smirk.

I cleared my throat. 'My name's Pepper.'

Scarlett offered me a quizzical look, tilting her head to the side, her pink lips pursed. 'Are you good or evil?' she asked with suspicion.

'Am I what?'

'Scarlett, you can't just ask that!'

'Why not?' She scowled at Cade with her hands on her petite hips. 'Wouldn't you want to know?'

'Of course I would, but—' Scarlett wouldn't hear

him out. She fluttered away from him and flew right up into my face, her features drawn tight in scrutiny. She peered into my eyes, and what she saw there must have shocked her as she pulled back, a startled expression on her face.

'She's human!' she exclaimed.

'What?' Cade matched her expression. 'That's impossible. How can she see us?'

Scarlett shrugged. 'I don't know,' she said. Then she turned back to me. 'How *can* you see us?'

The look I gave back was dumbfounded. 'I'm not sure,' I said, a warble in my voice. 'Until a few minutes ago, I had no idea fairies—I mean, sylphs—even existed.'

Cade and Scarlett exchanged funny glances, like they were communicating with each other telepathically. I used the time to rub my eyes, take deep breaths, pinch myself—anything which might tell me I was in some strange kind of dream, and not conversing with fictitious beings. After closing and re-opening my eyes numerous times—each time to a room still filled with butterflies and fairies—I inched my way along the length of the wall, feeling for the door handle. I had to get out of there and get some fresh air.

'Human girl?'

I jumped. Cade and Scarlett were both looking at

me. I gulped.

'We need to speak with you,' said Cade, his small form hovering in front of me alongside Scarlett.

There came a knock at the door. I went white.

'Pepper? Are you in there?' My eyes danced around, panicked.

'Um, yes,' I called back. The problem was, so was a swarm of butterflies and a couple of fairies! 'Er, one second!' I turned to Scarlett and Cade with wide eyes. Both their expressions turned vigilant.

'Who is it?' Cade asked.

'My boss.' I made shooing motions towards the open window again. 'How do I get rid of these butterflies?'

'Is he good or evil?'

I ignored her, keeping to the main issue at hand: the butterflies. 'What do I do?' I asked.

Cade's eyes peered into mine. 'He can't see us!' he stressed.

None of the stubborn butterflies would budge, continuing to flit around my room as though they owned the place. Why wouldn't they leave?

'That won't work.' I turned to the sylph who spoke up. 'They can't leave the house,' Cade explained.

I gave him a stupefied expression. 'What?'

Three more knocks.

'Pepper? Are you okay?'

I grabbed a T-shirt from the floor and commenced flapping it, attempting to usher the critters out that way.

'I'm fine! Just a sec!' I continued to flap. 'Why aren't they going?'

'We told you!' Scarlett said. 'They cannot leave this house!'

'Why not?'

'What are you doing in there?' Max's muffled words, now laced with a hint of concern, only heightened my sense of urgency.

'Nothing!' I glowered over my back at the two sylphs who were still watching my hysterics. They showed no sign of leaving, either. 'I'll be right there!' I swatted my way through the forest of insects towards the door, opening it a fraction—only enough to allow my head to poke through.

'Hi!' I greeted Max, trying my best to not to look suspicious. I probably looked crazy. Max peered at me, which only succeeded in making me more antsy.

'Were you talking to someone in there?' he asked.

'What? Me?' I laughed. 'No, there's no one in here.' However, my reply did not appease Max. He just smirked, and then craned his neck in order to see past me and into the room. I blocked his gaze by raising my head and inching the door just that extra bit closed. He raised his eyebrows.

61

'Sorry.' I grimaced. 'It's a bit of a mess in here. I haven't finished unpacking yet!' I rolled my eyes in a silly-me kind of way. I knew I was over-playing it. Drama was never my forte. Max kept his squinting gaze on me a while longer. I squirmed. He knew I was bluffing. He held his stare for a few more seconds, and then smiled, his features and stance relaxing.

'Did you have a good day with the children?' he asked.

'A great day,' I said. This time I really did smile, and it wasn't forced. 'They had a lot of fun at the park.'

Max smiled and leaned against the doorframe. 'Good,' he said, 'I'm glad you're getting along.' I looked at him as he looked at me. It was the same casual, lopsided expression he'd offered me on both of our previous encounters, but his sudden nearness had me edging back a little. I fumbled to keep my gaze from catching his, which eyed me like I was the most interesting animal at the zoo.

'Sorry, did you want something?' I asked as politely as I could, hoping to put an end to his staring, which, as flattering as it was, made me a tad uncomfortable. With his hand, Max smoothed down the back of his russet hair.

'It's not much,' he began. 'Only . . . you were told about the party tomorrow night, weren't you?'

I stretched my memory back to the day before. Miss Sharpe was decidedly vague with the information she gave me yesterday, and I didn't recollect anything about a party.

'It's for a few business friends of our family's. It's a real bore, but it's become quite a tradition,' Max explained.

'I'll be sure to stay out of your way,' I said, and made to close the door, but it stopped at the impact of Max's hand before it could shut. With his strength, he pushed it open, so this time all of me was visible. With nothing to hide behind, I felt exposed.

'That's not what I meant,' he said, his smile suggestive. His forwardness made me feel quite uncomfortable. I blushed and took a step back into my room. His eyes trailed after my retreating form, then came to rest on something beyond me. I watched as his expression altered from seductive to confused. 'What's that?' he asked, pointing at something that caught his eye. My heartrate peaked.

'Nothing!' I ducked in front of Max in an attempt to mask his view, but I was much shorter than he was . . . and weaker. In one movement, Max was able to move me out of the way and open the door wide enough to walk right past me, into the enchanted room.

.

6

UNEXPECTED INVITATIONS

*T*he room was empty. I peered around, befuddled, as there was not a butterfly in sight, much less a duo of chatty fairies. What on earth happened? Had they really gone out through the window? Or had they simply vanished into thin air? Well, I'd seen a bunny do it, so why not a flock of winged insects?

'I've read this one!' I glanced over at Max. He'd noticed the stolen book lying open on the bed. He picked it up and flicked through the pages. 'How much have you read?'

'I've read the whole thing a few times before,' I

answered, 'but not in a while. Last night, I reached the part where the King went into hiding.'

Max's eyes showed recognition. 'I remember that bit! Doesn't he get offered to stay at the old witch's house?'

I nodded as he continued to leaf through the pages, enwrapped as he relived the story.

'You like to read then?' I asked.

'It's all right,' he said with a small shrug, though his eyes never left the browning pages. 'When I get bored, I read some of the books we have here. This is one I actually enjoyed.' He closed the cover and flipped the aging book over in his hands, peering up at me with raised eyebrows. 'Did you steal this?' he queried with a smirk.

Warm blood flooded my face. 'No! I-I didn't! I just borrowed it.'

'Without permission?'

I clenched my lower lip between my teeth and remained silent.

'Isn't that stealing?' He snickered and tossed the antique in question back onto the bed.

'I'm sorry.'

He sauntered a little closer, hands buried in the pockets of his grey suit trousers. 'It's a good thing I like you,' he said with a hint of teasing in his voice, 'or there might have been consequences.' I hid my deepening blush behind a curtain of blonde hair. 'Keep the book,' he said. 'You've obviously taken a liking to it.'

'Oh,' came the surprised sound from my mouth at his kindly gesture. 'Thank you.'

Max perched himself on top of the chest at the bottom of the bed. Right where the two sylphs had been not too long ago. A jitter started to form within the depths of my stomach. As decent, if somewhat forward, a man as Max seemed, something about having him in my room—even though it had barely been my room for a day—left me feeing uneasy.

I leaned against the corner post of the bed in an effort to act casual as he surveyed the room, which was still a total mess from where I had yet to sort out my things.

'I see you're a fan of books, too,' Max stated. I looked to see where his eyes had landed. On the cushiony floor beside him lay my open suitcase. A stack of books, read and unread, as well as a handful of note-bearing writing books, sat uncomfortably inside, having fallen from the impeccable formation I piled them into before I left home.

Max reached forward and grabbed the top book from the pile, regarding me as he lifted it up. I raised an accusatory eyebrow.

'What are you doing?'

67

'Borrowing one of your books.'

'Without permission?'

His eyes gleamed. 'Apparently so.'

'Isn't that stealing?' I smirked, quoting his own line. He shrugged.

'An eye for an eye?' he offered with a smile, peeling open the hard cover. He peered at the first page, his face intrigued at first, before contorting into an expression resembling bafflement. 'What's this?' He turned the double page, clustered with hastily written scribbles, round to face me.

'Oh, *that*.' Trust him to pick that one up. 'They're my notes.'

Max scrutinised the words I'd jotted onto the lined paper during one of my bursts of inspiration.

'They make no sense,' he said. 'What do they mean?'

I took the notebook off him and squinted at my own writing. The words were an absolute jumble, but to me, at least, they were just about decipherable. 'This page has notes on character,' I translated for him, 'ideas for personality and appearance, as well as information sheets on my existing characters.'

'You're a writer?' He raised his eyebrows with interest.

'Well . . .' I folded the book and dumped it back in the case. 'Aspiring.' I pulled out the wheeled office chair from beneath the wooden desk and plonked myself down on it. Embarrassed, I fiddled with the ends of my hair.

Max folded his legs beneath him and continued to look at me with unwavering intrigue. I didn't mind this Max—the one who had a deep passion and who clung to every word I said with interest. Perhaps I had him all wrong. This Max wasn't half bad.

'What do you write?' he asked with the same glint in his eyes.

'I like all genres.' I grinned, my own enthusiasm for the subject coming through in my voice. 'I've tried my hand at most, to a certain extent, but I always find myself going back to fantasy.'

'Fantasy, eh?' he mused. 'You mean, like *The Kingdom*?' He pointed to the book on the bed.

'Yes, something like that,' I said. 'I like the idea of inventing a brand new land. A whole world where nothing is as it should be. Where trees have feelings, and houses can fly, and there is no limit to what can happen!'

Max looked amused by my outburst. 'So you're *that* kind of writer then, are you? The wacky sort?' I chuckled. 'Well, if you ever need someone to help you out, I'm your man.'

My smile turned grateful, but I made sure to tell him, 'I haven't actually started anything yet. I'm still waiting for the right idea to hit me.'

'I'm sure it will,' he assured me. 'It sounds like you know what you're doing.'

I sighed. Sounding like I knew what I was doing and actually knowing so were two entirely different things, and quite probably the difference between whether or not I got the career I so desperately desired.

'So . . . the party.' Max jumped back to the topic we had all but deserted. 'Would you like to come? There'll be a live band and an open buffet. We even have some spare dresses in the manor. You can borrow one if you like.'

I dropped my eyes to my hands on my lap. 'I don't know,' I said. 'I don't know any of your friends. I'll just get in the way.'

But Max insisted. 'Come on, Pepper,' he said, 'it'll be a great chance for you to get to know some people.'

I frowned. I didn't particularly want to get to know anyone new. It was enough for me at the moment just getting to know the few inhabitants of the manor. I always struggled when it came to friends. I'd failed to keep in touch with any of my friends from school, and doubted I'd ever resume contact. I'd never really been extremely close to anyone, anyway.

'The parties are something you're going to have to

get used to,' he continued. 'We host sometimes up to four in a month. If you come along to one it might make it easier for you.'

I wasn't quite convinced with his reasoning, but he seemed so insistent, I found myself saying, 'I'll think about it.'

He continued to look at me with that intense way of his. I fidgeted a little in my seat. 'I don't just invite anyone to these parties, Pepper,' he said. 'You should feel privileged.' With that, he released his legs from beneath him and stood from his perch and made for the door. 'I'll see you tomorrow,' he said with his hand on the handle. 'Sweet dreams.'

'You too,' I called after him above the sound of the latch catching.

'Ooh, who was that,' chirped a tinkling voice from behind me. I jumped when I turned round to see Scarlett and Cade hovering in the exact same position they were in when I last saw them. My brow furrowed with confusion.

'Where did you go?' I demanded. 'You weren't leaving! I was worried he was going to spot you!'

'We told you he can't see us,' spoke Cade.

'Yes, so why weren't you hiding? He could've . . .' I trailed off as the switch finally clicked. 'You mean he literally cannot see you?' Cade nodded. 'Oh!' It made sense now. Kind of. That explained why I couldn't see them either while Max was in here, I guess. I peered around again. 'Where did the butterflies go?'

Cade just shrugged. 'Who knows with butterflies?' he said. 'They do whatever they please.'

'You still haven't answered my question!' interrupted Scarlett. 'Who was that?'

'I told you. He's my boss.'

Scarlett giggled as she flew round in a full backflip. 'I think someone has a bit of a crush on you!' she sang.

'What?!' I said, aghast. 'Why would you say that?'

'It's obvious!' said the playful sylph, still grinning. 'Do you like him, too? I wouldn't blame you if you did.' She mimed fanning herself with her hand. Cade nudged her with an irritated elbow, but she just grinned back at him.

'No!' I was quick to say. 'I mean, not that he's not a nice person, but I don't feel, you know, like that.'

Scarlett sank down in the air, clearly disheartened by my proclamation. But the sadness was short-lived. Her wings pricked up again behind her as she said, 'Still, you're going to his ball!'

'It's a party, but—'

'Oh, I can't wait to help you pick out an outfit! You're going to look amazing! Oh, I'm just so excited!'

'Scarlett, please!'

She trailed off at my plea.

'I'm sorry.' I sighed. 'I have a lot of questions right now. Can you please just tell me . . . why couldn't Max see either of you?'

It was Scarlett who came forward and offered the information. 'He's not one of us,' she explained.

'A sylph?' I questioned. Scarlett shook her head.

'A magick.'

KINGDOM

7

CRAZY FANTASIES

I twitched at the sensation on my ear, giggling at the tinkle on my skin. I used my awakening fingers to bat at the afflicted area. My eyes were still closed as I rolled myself under the bedsheets from my side onto my back, but still the source of the tickling persisted. I felt it move further up the side of my face until it was my cheek being brushed.

'Stop it,' I murmured, transitioning back into consciousness. With my hands behind me, I used them to lever myself up, but my face collided with something prickly in front of me. I jerked back, swatting away whatever just attacked me, spitting it away from my face. 'What the . . .?' My eyelids blinked open.

I was in my bedroom at the manor. Or, at least, I thought I was. The entirety of the space was painted in pink, and not in the literal sense. The colour came from the hundreds upon hundreds of soft, blushing roses that had taken over the room. They entwined the bedposts, swathed the furniture, dangled from the ceiling—it looked like some kind of floral explosion had taken place overnight, dousing everything with silky pink petals and thorny vines.

There was a nudging at my side, tearing my focus away from the spectacle before me. Fifi, her white whiskers fidgeting, watched me as I took in the new décor. It must have been her who woke me. I smiled as I ruffled the top of her head and she made a happy, purring noise. An odd sound for a bunny, but then she was an odd bunny.

'How did you get in here?' I asked. Her luxurious fur disappeared under my hand and I was left stroking the air. Fifi re-materialised in the centre of the floor in a nest of flowers, where she squatted and commenced washing herself. Oh, right, I forgot: magic bunny.

With as slow a transition as possible, I manoeuvred myself out of the bedclothes and tried my best to clamber down from the bed without crushing any of the delicate flora. I only managed to get so far before I found myself stuck, one leg on the bed and the other not quite touching the floor, with me hovering precariously above a swirling vine of nasty thorns. The sleeve of my flannel pyjama top was caught, snagging on one of the branches on the bed. I couldn't move, not without causing myself an injury. I tried to tug free, but these weren't ordinary thorns. One of them had hooked right through the material. I was caught fast.

But it wasn't for long. Fifi appeared on the bed beside me and, clenching the fabric between her teeth, unhooked me so I slipped down without catching myself further. The rabbit appeared at my feet.

'Thank you.' I smiled at her. She bobbed her little head in a small bow. I peered at her. 'Can you . . .' I began. 'Can you actually understand me?'

She sneezed.

I sighed. 'I guess not.'

My eyes scanned the enchanted room around me. I felt like I was lost inside a fairy tale book, and at any given moment, a Big Bad Wolf would leap out from behind the bed and gobble me up, or a fairy godmother would swoop in and grant me three wishes. Just like with the butterflies the day before, my brain could find no logical explanation for this craziness.

'Scarlett?' I called out. 'Cade? What's going on?'

I waited, but neither of the sylphs came to answer me.

'Hello?'

Again, nothing. They'd left the night before without much of an explanation, just Scarlett complaining she was tired and bored. I'd had no idea where they went, and they were still nowhere to be seen.

I had to get out of here. Someone had to know what was going on.

I hopscotched over the vines, leaves, and flowers to the door. I had to pull it with some force in order to move it through the crazed vegetation. A cascade of petals and various other plant debris fell into my face and hair as it opened, and I shook it away as I walked out of my bedecked room and into the hallway.

The plant life continued out there. Along the wall opposite me trailed a vine of ivy, the leaves all pointing one way. Against my better judgement, I followed its path.

I stood still, my breath catching in the back of my throat, for the sight before me . . . well . . . there were simply no words to describe it. All thoughts that my room had been beautiful beyond compare seemed almost laughable as my eyes struggled to take in everything before them. I had to be dreaming.

Nothing this marvellous, or this beautiful, could exist in real life.

But no. This was better than a dream. No dreams I'd ever known could imagine anything this vivid, this glorious or this . . . unutterably fantastical.

From my position on the upper floor, I could see all the way across to the balconies on the other side and over the railing which separated me and the drop down to the grand foyer. A flourish of flowers clung to every available surface. There were pale pink rosettes like the ones in my room. But there were also roses of other hues, as well as a myriad of other flowers spiralling, tumbling, and poking out from every crevice. Leaves of green and silver fluttered in an impossible wind which carried through the hall like the ghost of the building's hidden secrets. The house was alive, its regal and ancient designs concealed behind the thriving nature that sprang from all corners, and there were the butterflies again! The majestic insects flitted among the shrubbery, and even a few birds glided overhead.

I wasn't scared. Why should I be? How could anyone even think of fear in the presence of such majesty? I breathed in, the sweet smell filling my lungs with air so light that I thought I might drift from the ground. The aroma remained in my mouth, playing with the senses on my tongue. And the sounds

. . . the gentle lyrics of the birds carrying through the building; the leaves and petals chiming in the wind. The flowers themselves burst so full of life, I could almost hear the energy they exuded.

And then there was the sound of gushing water. I edged closer to the railing, and leaned over to see the most glorious sight I had ever witnessed.

Down the Gothic staircase of the manor cascaded a silvery waterfall, flowing into a shimmering, turquoise pool that was the grand foyer. Like an old, abandoned house which nature had reclaimed, the manor sang with its newfound beauty. It was as though I had awoken from a long sleep, only to find everything I had once known and recognised had been long lost to the abyss of time.

A lone bluebird fluttered over to me, chirping its sweet melody. I felt the urges of a grin tug at my lips as it soared in circles above my head, trying to get my attention. Then it dove, and grabbing a section of my hair in its beak, it tugged.

'Ow, ow!' I cried out, but the bluebird did not stop. It pulled me towards another corridor. I had to watch my step as it led me along the thriving passageway, afraid to trip on the winding vines. It took me left, then right, and then left again. Finally, the bluebird came to a stop outside a closed door, flying in a frenzy around its metal handle.

The corridor was lit, and there was no sign in sight, but I knew this was the same door. My stomach tightened in a knot of trepidation as I reached forward.

The familiar surge of power flooded my body, but this time I kept my hand on the doorknob and, taking a deep breath, I let myself through.

Into a closet. And even by closet standards, this room was tiny. Aside from that, there was nothing much about this place that was particularly different from any other part of the house—still decked from top to bottom with bursting plant life.

'Why did you bring me here?' I asked the little bird. I felt silly talking to it, but I did so only to hide the nervousness building up in my stomach. Thoughts such as, 'Where is everyone?', 'Are they seeing this, too?' and 'Am I ever going to get out of here?' slithered through my mind. I didn't want to get stuck here alone. As beautiful as this was, I was now getting a little scared.

The bird followed me into the cupboard where it perched on top of a swirling, moss-covered tree root emerging from one of the corners, only to disappear again somewhere nearer the ceiling. The bird watched me with its beady eyes, its head at a tilt.

'What is it?' I asked. It hopped, flapping its impatient wings.

I was about to walk back out of the cramped room

81

when a glinting caught my eye. My gaze flicked to the opposite wall, where the bird still watched me, and there I saw it—a flash of silver concealed behind a tangle of vines and branches. I closed in towards it and, with hesitation, pried the foliage away in order to gain a better look.

Beneath the twisting vines and plush petals hung a mirror, positioned right in the centre of the wall, perfectly unharmed by the activity around it. The mirror was ovate in shape and surrounded by a heavy, decorative border. Carved from wood, the frame showed signs of superb craftsmanship. Within the intricate twists and swirls of the wooden structure showed hidden shapes that resembled animal forms. Some of them I recognised, such as a galloping stag and the face of a cat, but others looked more fictitious. One such creature bore the head of a horse, but an ape's face and a fish's body.

At the very head of the frame, the face of a roaring bear had been carved. The image invoked both fear and wonder within me. The level of detail within the carving was remarkable, and I found myself wondering how long such a masterpiece took someone to create.

The mirror began to shudder, rocking against the wall to create a dull, thudding sound that picked up in speed. I stepped back, unable to peel my eyes away from the glass as it started to glow. That was all the warning it gave before a large, twisting vine of purple wisteria burst out, pushing past me and out of the closet. It travelled along the corridor and round the corner, out of sight, along with two robins and a baby raccoon, which jumped down from the mirror and chased down the hall after the ludicrously proportioned plant.

The vine stilled with a final rustle of leaves, and the light from the mirror died down. I almost found myself stooping down to the floor in search of my jaw, which had surely dropped from my face after that spectacle. I inched towards the mirror instead.

'So, this is where it all comes from,' I marvelled. It was probably a bad idea, but I felt my hand lifting up to the reflective surface of the magic mirror. Furrows lined my brow when the surface regained its white glow, growing brighter and brighter the nearer my hand came. The surface of the mirror changed, turning from the solid glass it had once been to a rippling, watery texture. What would it be like to feel? To touch? My fingertips were almost upon it.

'Pepper Fairfield?'

I started, and snapped my head around to see the face of an unfamiliar man. I no longer stood in the cupboard, but instead found myself in the middle of the hallway. All traces of the beautiful land the manor

83

once was were gone. A heavy feeling of loss embedded itself in my stomach at the sight of the russet wallpaper and auburn carpet.

'I didn't expect to find you here,' said the older man. 'I would have introduced myself earlier, but I had other matters to attend to. So, how are you enjoying it here at Calthorpe Manor?'

Dumbfounded, I just stared at the man. Dressed in a crisp, blue shirt and suit trousers, he didn't look like a member of staff.

'Um, yes,' I said. 'I'm sorry, but do I know you?'

The man laughed, the deep sound coming from within his belly. 'Of course!' he said, 'How silly of me!' He smiled and extended a hand in friendly greeting. 'I'm your boss, Adrian Calthorpe. It's a pleasure to finally meet you, Pepper.'

8

REVEALING TRUTHS

Scarlett was only too eager to help me prepare for the evening. For the sake of the party, the children were sent to bed early, and Adrian kindly picked out a few dresses for me to choose from.

Max's father insisted I address him by his first name, consigning formalities to things of the past.

After the initial surprise of learning Max wasn't actually my boss, as I was led to believe, the real Mr. Calthorpe and I took some time to get properly acquainted. Adrian was a good-humoured man. Unlike his egotistical son, he appeared to be a genuinely lovely person.

A selection of five dresses lay on top of my bed, and Scarlett took joy in pointing out the flaws of each one.

'I can't believe this is all they have!' she pouted. 'They're so outdated, they're basically fossils! I don't understand why you didn't bring any dresses of your own.'

I sighed as I fingered the curls Scarlett helped my style my hair into. 'I didn't think part of my job would entail attending my boss's own party.'

It wasn't that I didn't want to go. On any other occasion, I would lap up the opportunity to go to a fancy ball in a flouncy dress. It was more the fact that I would have to look Max in the eyes again which made my stomach queasy.

'Out of all of them,' Scarlett spoke up, still adjudicating the dresses, 'I think the beige one is the least vile.'

I turned my attention to the one she—finally— pointed out. The dress had an A-line skirt and was made of pure chiffon which ruched at the bodice. The top of the dress started at a pure, clear white, and graduated to a soft cream as it went down. Tiny, beige rosettes adorned the neckline. The style was simple, but effective.

Still, I liked it a lot more than Scarlett did. She

turned her nose up as I held it in front of me and looked at myself in the mirror.

In this house, and with this dress, it was easy to imagine I was a princess from a fairy tale. In fact, it was the same fairy-tale vibe I had from this place ever since I arrived.

'What's going on?' I asked Scarlett, out of the blue. 'There's something odd about this house. Ever since I stepped foot in here, strange things keep happening. What do you know about it?'

From the expression Scarlett gave, I knew it was a heavy question to ask. She landed on the bed and I sank down next to her. Having left the bed this morning in such a hurry, I realised the covers were still a mess. I made a mental note to sort them out later.

'This house has a story,' I continued. 'It's so strong, I swear I can feel it in the air sometimes. This place—I feel like it's trying to tell me something, but I just don't understand.'

Scarlett turned serious. For the first time since I'd met her, her face showed no sign of joking or bursting into hysterics. For a moment, she no longer looked like a child.

'You know,' she began, speaking at a slower pace. 'Cade and I were talking about this last night.' She dropped her head down, so all I could see was her

87

incredible mass of hair, masking her face. 'We're not sure why you can see these things. It's not normal for a human.' She breathed in, as though she was about to add something else, but thought better of it.

'This morning,' I told her, 'the whole house transformed. It was beautiful at first, but then I was scared. Everyone had disappeared.' I took a deep breath. 'I-I came across a room with a mirror . . .'

'You saw the mirror?' Scarlett's head snapped up with a swish of her crazy hair.

'Well, yes. I was led to it.' Scarlett did not reply, but a slight frown began to cross her even features. 'That's where you come from, isn't it?' I asked, even though I was pretty sure this was the case by now. 'Behind that mirror. Is there another land?'

The young sylph looked conflicted. 'I don't know how much I should say,' she said. 'Some humans have seen us before—those with strong imaginations. But no one has ever found the mirror. It might be dangerous for me to tell you.'

'Scarlett,' said another voice, and I glanced up to see Cade flying over towards us. 'It's fine. I think it's best she knows.'

'Best I know what?' I felt my pulse quicken.

Both sylphs stared at me with a look of, what? Fear? Intrigue? Whatever it was, it was nothing short of intense.

'The mirror is a portal to another land,' explained Scarlett. 'You were right about that. It's where us—the magicks—live. We always have done, ever since Marcius Calthorpe banished us there one hundred years ago.'

Cade glanced at Scarlett in surprise. 'Wow, someone's been doing their research!' he commended.

Scarlett beamed, flicking her hair from her face with pride. 'I know.'

'So . . .' I rubbed my forehead, trying to absorb what she said. 'Who are these magicks? What are you?'

Cade shrugged. 'Oh, anything. A magick could be a tree, a fox, an elf, a sprite—but what links us all together is that we all come from the same land.'

'The one through the mirror?'

'Correct.'

I was beginning to understand. 'I see. So, how come it's in this house? Why here?'

Cade grinned. 'Excellent question. Scarlett, would you care to explain?'

'What? Oh, uh, sure! See, one hundred years ago, Marcius Calthorpe banished us to another land.'

'You mentioned that,' I said.

'Right, yes well, you see, he sent us there because he, er, didn't like our singing? Um . . .'

Cade sighed. 'You didn't learn it, did you?'

'I learnt some of it!' Scarlett folded her arms in front of her chest, pouting. Cade just rolled his eyes and chuckled.

'For a long time,' he said, taking over, 'this house was well-known for its books. As one of the biggest collection of vintage books, people would come from across the globe to get their hands on some of the most obscure stories. Books were read here, written here—many were stolen—but for the most part, this was a place where literature was celebrated.

'Popularity grew, with books being read so much, the air remembered the stories. Images of the characters began to be sighted, like ghosts. It wasn't long before the stories leaked from the pages of the books. The characters became real. At first, it wasn't a problem. It wasn't until the visitors started to find themselves caught up in battles between ogres and minotaurs in the lounge!'

'Whoa, whoa, whoa.' I held out my hands in front of me to stave off his onslaught of information. 'Do you mean to tell me the characters—from storybooks—turned into real people?' Cade and Scarlett nodded. 'Because their stories were being read so much?'

'That's the long and short of it,' answered Cade.

'And that's what you are?'

They nodded. Okay, I think I was getting it now.

'So what happened next?'

The door creaked open, stealing my attention. A sleepy-eyed Lilly walked into the room, the white skirt of her nightdress swinging at her ankles.

'I can't sleep,' she said, rubbing her eyes. 'Uncle Adrian's making a lot of noise and Peter keeps complaining that . . .' she trailed off, and blinked a few times, before her eyes turned to round spheres and her jaw dropped open. 'Fairies!'

Scarlett clasped her hand over her mouth as she tried to contain a giggle. Cade elbowed her in the side. 'Sorry,' she said.

Lilly's intrusion reminded me I only had a matter of minutes to get ready for the party. I wasn't even dressed yet!

Suddenly wide awake, Lilly galloped over to the two little creatures and crouched in front of them.

'Wait,' said Scarlett, scrunching up her face. 'She can see us too?' I shrugged. Apparently so.

Scarlett squeaked and jumped back along the bedsheets at Lilly's approaching finger. The little girl giggled at her reaction, and reached forward again.

'Lilly, no touching the sylphs,' I ordered her.

'Aw!' she complained, her bottom lip drooping. 'But they're so pretty! Can I play with them? Please?'

I sighed, still aware of the time. 'Okay,' I said. 'But only for a few minutes. Then you have to go back to bed.' Or Miss Sharpe would have my head mounted on the wall, I reckoned.

Leaving a delighted Lilly, a perplexed Scarlett, and a disgruntled Cade, I scooped up the dress and headed for the bathroom.

Approximately 90 seconds later, I came back to find the three of them giggling, my room alight with colour.

'Do it again, do it again!' Lilly sang, and I watched as the room flooded with light and a burst of colour erupted in the centre of the room. Tiny butterflies of light fluttered out, dissolving into the air and generating a cascade of red rose petals that rained down onto the carpet below. The remaining sparks clustered together, swirling into a formation resembling a dragon's head. I stood in stunned silence as the dragon swooped down towards Lilly. It closed its eyes and nuzzled her hand as she reached out and stroked the bridge of its nose. The dragon then burst into one final surge of light and fizzled out into the air. Lilly gasped in pure wonderment. Some of the retreating sparks landed in her ginger curls, transforming her hair into a glowing beacon.

'Time to go, Lilly,' I said, breaking the spell. She slumped.

'I don't want to go to bed,' she said. 'Can me and Peter come to the party with you?'

'I wish you could, sweetie,' I said, 'but if you don't go to sleep now, the fairies won't come again.'

She let out a little huff. 'Oh, okay then,' she said. 'Can the fairies tell me a bedtime story?'

I looked over my shoulder at Scarlett and Cade, and they agreed to the idea. They went to lead Lilly out of the room, but not before Scarlett turned to me and said, 'Don't forget to smile when you make your entrance.'

KINGDOM

9

MYSTICAL BEGINNINGS

*C*linging to the handrail, I teetered down the staircase, trying my utmost not to let my posture drop. My upper back already ached from this posture.

I pinched a section of the champagne chiffon and inched it up a little. There. Now I could walk without tripping up!

Crikey, how many steps were there? It never felt like this many before.

Finally, I reached the foyer, and released my skirt so it floated back to its perfect A-shape. That was the first ordeal over with. Now to actually talk to people!

'Pepper! So glad the dress fits you.'

'Adrian.' I beamed.

'Thanks for letting me borrow it. It's beautiful!' I said as I fingered the white lace bodice.

'My pleasure, dear. Come, there's someone I'd like you to meet.' His hand on my shoulder, I followed the greying head of my boss through the throng of attendees. Upon inspection, these guests—about eighty of them—looked to be of mature years. Business people, I assumed. With everyone dressed to the nines, and a string quartet playing on the rostrum, it felt like I'd gone back in time. It was clear these parties derived from tradition. I relished the moment, adding it to my mental list of scenes I could include in my writing. I barely registered when Adrian forced me to a stop.

'Ah, Pepper, this is my son. Maxwell, this is Lilly and Peter's new nanny.'

A gaze of azure blue met mine.

'Actually,' I turned to Adrian, ready to let him know Max and I had already met the other day, but I was interrupted.

'A pleasure to meet you, Miss Pepper,' Max said with a bow. 'I do hope you enjoy your stay here.'

I gave him a look which I hoped said, 'what the hell?' but played along anyway.

With my eyes slit like those of a snake, I grasped

his outstretched hand, being sure to convey my message through clenched fingers.

'The pleasure's all mine,' I said, un-gritting my teeth long enough to let the words out. Max closed forward. 'Would you give me the great honour of leading you through this first dance?'

I forced a back a smile. 'I would be delighted.' Ugh, it felt like I was reading from a script.

'Go and enjoy yourselves you two.' Adrian chuckled. 'I'll be around if you need me.'

Max moved to hold me in a typical dance position and I felt my nerves piling up. I was relying solely on him—while I had a fair idea how it worked, I never had the chance to give this type of dancing a go.

'What do you make of the party?' asked Max over the music as he twirled me in a full circle.

'S'all right.'

We weaved between other couples on the dance floor. I was surprised we didn't collide with any of them. It was clear Max had done this many times before and was quite the pro.

'This ensemble is phenomenal,' he said as he led. 'You see the one in the middle? That's my father's cousin; my godfather. He plays with his orchestra every time Father hosts one of his parties. They're very popular among our circle.'

I couldn't see much of the musicians through the

flowing sea of dancers.

'Oh.'

Max continued to stare at me as our feet span across the dance floor. I tried my best to keep my gaze away from his—over his shoulders, at my feet.

'Pepper, come on, speak to me. I can tell you're upset.' I brought my face up from the floor, the muscles tense.

'Upset?' I echoed. 'You lied to me!' His expression did not waver, so I continued. 'You told me you owned the house.'

Our spinning slowed as the musical number faded to its conclusion. I followed the crowd's suit as they turned to applaud.

'I never told you I owned the house.' I turned back, taking in his solemn expression. Well, until it broke into a sly grin. 'You just assumed I did,' he said.

I felt the blood in my face sizzle. 'You could have at least told me the truth.'

Max said nothing. The next piece of music started up, and he resumed his hold. This only succeeded in irking me further.

'Okay, so what was all that about just now with your father? "A pleasure to meet you, Miss Pepper."' I attempted an impression of Max, which I hoped was offensive. 'Do you have any idea how stupid I felt?'

He sighed and dropped his head, showing off his

perfectly parted hair. Then he looked back at me, the cocky smirk back in place. 'Listen, I can't help that you thought I was your boss. When I first realised, I couldn't resist playing along for a bit. I guess I was just trying to impress you. You've gotta admit, Pepper, you are quite the catch. As for my father— would you really deny an older man the simple privilege of introducing the two of us for the first time?'

I got the impression he was trying to infuriate me on purpose.

I watched my feet as I focused on stepping in time to the music. Front. Side. Together. Back. Side. Together.

'All right, I'm sorry. Is that what you want? I'm sorry for letting you think I was Mr. Calthorpe. Now is that better?'

What was he doing? He was trying to make me feel like I was overreacting. I opened my mouth to answer back when a hand on Max's shoulder pulled him out of the hold.

'Excuse me,' interrupted a portly gentleman in a waistcoat. 'May I cut in?'

'Absolutely not,' Max snapped, replacing his hand on the small of my back. 'Find your own dance partner.'

This time, the man wrested Max's arm away from

me, holding it in his podgy fist. 'You've had your turn, Max. You know how it goes.'

A dark expression clouded Max's features and I could almost feel the air heating up around him.

'It's all right, Max.' I removed his other hand, which gripped my elbow like a vice. 'You go and have a drink. I'll come and find you in a minute or two.'

Max turned to me briefly, eyebrows drawn low, and spoke nothing as he stalked away towards the punch bowl.

The older man turned and smiled at me before grabbing my shoulder with one hand and my hand with his other. His palm felt warm and clammy in my own, and as he leaned forward. I tried not to cough. He smelled like the kind of cream my mum made me use when I had tight muscles.

'You're the Calthorpes' new nanny, aren't you?' he said as we began spinning. His steps were smaller than Max's. It took me a couple of rotations to learn his pace before I could step without standing on his toes. 'Adrian is a good man. Secretive though. Much like his house.'

'Secretive? What do you— ?'

'How long have you been working here, Pepper? A couple of days?' He didn't even give me a chance to question how he knew my name. 'You've probably had more than enough time to explore the splendour of the manor.'

'Well, yes, I've seen a fair bit,' I answered. I wished the music would end so I had an excuse to leave.

The gentleman held my gaze for a while, his face stoic, yet pointed. I felt my spine shudder.

'I'm sorry, sir, I really have no idea what you're getting at.'

'Cedrick.'

'Huh?'

'My name's Cedrick.' He leaned forward so his lips were beside my ear. The stench of muscle cream became overwhelming. 'And I think you know exactly what I'm getting at.' I stiffened. Fifi . . . the sylphs . . . he knew about the house.

Over Cedrick's broad shoulder, I spied Max still over by the punch bowl. He was leaning his weight against a pillar, his legs apparently failing to support him on their own.

'Look,' I said, 'I've got to go and see Max. It looks like he could do with a hand.' But as I turned to leave, a moist hand grabbed my wrist.

'Not so fast.' The once smiling face transformed into a mask of contempt. 'You've seen it, haven't you?' Cedrick growled. 'Tell me, where is it?'

I swallowed, feeling pools of sweat manifesting in

my own palms. 'Where is what?' My voice shook. 'I have no idea what you're—'

He yanked me harder. 'Don't lie to me!' He glanced around to make sure no one was watching our debacle. Keeping his voice low, he said, 'Adrian's been keeping this a secret from me for too long. He trusts me, you know. If I was to tell him you've been harassing me, he'd believe me. You could say goodbye to this precious job of yours. We wouldn't want that, would we?'

Dread rose in my throat, making my voice creak. 'What do you want to know?'

Cedrick dragged me off to the side of the room, away from the twirling dancers. He spoke to me menacingly, emphasising each word: 'Where is the mirror?'

'I don't know.' My mouth was dry.

'You're lying!' he boomed, without realising he had raised his voice. A couple of heads turned our way, but none of them were really bothered. Cedrick straightened himself out, putting on an air of decorum, and cleared his throat. 'You are not ordinary, Pepper,' he said, though he spoke what should have been a compliment with dark tones. 'Adrian hired you for a special reason. Surely you must know that.'

I took a step back. 'Well, I'm flattered, but I'm—'

'Miss Pepper, is this man harassing you?'

I wasn't sure whether to be grateful or furious to see Max intervening. Slightly ruffled, he glared at Cedrick with eyes which appeared a little, well, glassy. 'Back off, mate. Or I'll get my dad to kick you out.'

Cedrick shot a glance over at Adrian. I read the turmoil in his face. No matter how much Mr. Calthorpe trusted Cedrick, his word was nothing against his own son's, and he knew it.

'Of course.' Cedrick smiled. 'I didn't mean to keep your lady for so long. Lovely to meet you, Miss Pepper. Maybe I'll see you again, soon.' But the endearment came off more as a threat.

I only just managed to catch hold of Max's fist as it swung back, ready to take a hit at the man who had to be at least twice his size.

'Max?' I said as he stared daggers at Cedrick's retreating form. 'How much have you had to drink?'

'Drink?' He turned to me, though his eyes failed to lock onto mine. 'Not much. Why?'

I took the glass of clear liquid from his hand and gave it a whiff.

'That's not punch!' I said, horrified, and banished the offending glass to the table behind me. As my back was turned, I felt Max's hands come down onto my shoulders, then slide slowly over my biceps.

'How's about another dance?' he said into my ear.

'Um, no, I don't think so.' I tried to wriggle free of his grasp.

'Aw, come on! Just one more.' He dragged me over to the dance floor where couples now trotted at a much livelier gait. I could not see this ending well.

'Max, wait!' I had to shout over the loud music and my heaving breath. 'I don't want to dance. Stop!' But he wasn't listening. Using my peripheral vision, I guided us, still galloping, out to the side towards the staircase. Max didn't even notice we had moved until his back collided with the base of the handrail.

'I'm sorry, Max,' I said when he was still enough to listen. 'I'm not in the mood for dancing right now.'

'What's up?'

Placing a finger on my lips to silence him, I scanned the floor to see where Cedrick had gone. I wanted to get as far away from that creep as I possibly could.

'It's me. You're still angry at me, aren't you?'

'Shh!' I didn't take my eyes off the main hall. 'I . . .' I breathed. 'I think I need some air.'

Without listening to another word he might have to say, I span around and ascended the stairs. I had to force myself not to run. That would draw attention.

I became aware of another set of footsteps beside my own. I picked up my pace. As soon as I stepped foot on the landing, I bolted down the corridor, tracing the way back to my room. The steps behind me also quickened, their beat heavy.

When I got to the door, I flung it open and sealed myself inside. I didn't turn the light on—that would give me away.

'Pepper?' came Cedrick's enraged voice from the other side of the door. 'Show yourself!' I steadied my frantic breathing as he stomped dangerously close to my hiding spot.

In the near darkness, I fumbled around for the light switch, but it was not where I thought it would be. Baffled, I leaned further along the wall, but I tripped over something which felt like a bucket on the floor. I covered my ears as I crouched and an avalanche of mops and brooms landed on top of me. Okay, so this wasn't my room. I needed to reconfigure my mental map.

'Open up!' The oak door shuddered under the fistfalls of the burly man, as he had clearly heard the crash. I scrambled away from the door, only to collide with the solid wall behind me. It was too late. I couldn't get out of this one.

As the door handle turned, my hand came into contact with something cold. It was hard at first, but then my fingers sank as the object softened.

The door cracked open, but that was all I saw before a white light consumed my vision, and I fell.

*I*t was the strangest feeling. I could only liken it to being sucked into a vacuum. But the air felt dense, like water, almost.

The sensation lasted only a couple of seconds, and then I landed. At least, I assumed I did—I didn't feel any impact.

I did feel my neck, though. My head snapped back, thudding against a moist surface. The drop hadn't hurt my head, but I could tell without moving my neck that I had whiplash.

The floor beneath me was uneven, and the woodsy smell told me I had somehow found myself outdoors.

I rubbed my eyes, the bright light singeing them. I grunted at the pain in my neck as I heaved myself from the ground. I must have blacked out. What happened? And how did I get out here?

Peering around, I saw no sign of the manor, or even if it was close by. Had Cedrick found me? Knocked me out and left me for dead in the forest?

But this was unlike any forest I'd ever encountered before. The colours were bright; more vivid than I could have ever imagined. Each tree spiralled high up into the sky, looking more like artistic sculptures than the trees I was used to. Even the sky was different, swirling with sparkling shades of turquoise.

It wasn't until a butterfly the size of my palm came to perch on my shoulder that I remembered.

The portal. In my haste, I must have shut myself in that room—the one I could for some reason never find when I consciously looked for it. The one with the sign warning people to keep out. Because it held the portal to another land.

The mirror had sucked me through.

Stay calm, I told myself. It's okay. I found my way in, so I'll find my way back.

Woozy, I dragged myself through thick foliage. My shoes sank into the damp moss beneath me, and I realised I still wore the cream ball gown. The water had seeped in, dampening the base of the skirt, and I didn't want to know how filthy my back was. I silently thanked Mr. Calthorpe for picking me out some flat shoes, for heels would have left me completely grounded in this soggy terrain.

I was in such a daze as I gazed up at the twisted tree branches and crystalline sky, that I only managed to catch myself three feet from falling off the edge of a cliff. I used a hand to steady my heart, which was now in my mouth. That was too close.

Something beyond the cliff caught my attention— something golden glinting off in the distance. I inched ever so slowly closer to the edge to get a better look, but the ledge didn't look all that secure.

Below me stood a castle. No, a fortress! The structure was made from stone, but gleamed golden in the light of the sun. It stood proud above a glistening waterfall which cascaded from the magnificent rocks that were its foundation. The water collected in a huge lake, spreading far out below me. It streamed off in several directions, but I couldn't see any more from where I stood due to the dense trees surrounding me and the moat beneath.

The vision was mesmerising, and I found myself staring in awe at the sight before me.

If I hadn't already worked out I was in some fairy-tale land, I sure would have by now.

An arm grabbed me from behind, a hand silencing my mouth before my brain could send the message to scream. It happened quicker than I could think. I was too shocked to fight back as the person wrestled me to the ground behind a fallen tree.

'Stay quiet,' a voice urged in a whisper. I heard it then—marching, slow and rhythmic, accompanied by the clattering of metal armour. From our low position, I saw nothing, but felt the ground vibrating as the procession passed. How many? Ten? Twenty? It felt like more. I kept silent, though my body was twisted uncomfortably and my neck was burning. When the noise passed, I wrenched the stranger's hand from my mouth.

'What the hell do you think you're doing?' I struggled free, surprised my captor didn't put up any resistance.

'Seriously? You're asking me this? Don't you know this part of the woods is monitored by the King's guards?'

The man who rose from the floor to stand beside me looked no older than I, with chocolate brown hair that hung haphazardly down into his eyes. And his clothes, they were tattered—possibly made by hand. He walked barefoot on the hazardous ground, though he didn't look like it bothered him. But it was his eyes that got me. They were as green as a summer meadow, but laced within them was something darker—he had the eyes of someone who had seen a lot of hardship in his time.

Something about him shocked me into silence. Was it the way he looked like he had just come off the streets? Or was it because he just saved me from being spotted by the king's guards? Either way, I found myself unable to respond.

'I'm sorry, ma'am,' the young man said, catching himself, and bobbed his head. 'I should have thought better than to insult a person of high standing.'

'High standing?' I questioned, then realised. I

109

looked down at my dress. 'Oh no, no. There's been a mistake. I'm not high on any social ladder! Heck, I think I'd even struggle on the bottom rung!' I managed a strangled laugh.

'But, your clothes . . .'

I grimaced. 'Yeah, see, I was at a party before . . . oh. It's a long story.'

Now it was the stranger's turn to fall silent. For a while, he simply watched me, quite intensely. Unlike Max's scrutinising stare though, this man's gaze didn't make me feel uncomfortable. Within his eyes wasn't that look of hunger which usually left me feeling queasy. Instead, he eyed me with an expression of curiosity, and maybe a hint of trepidation, as though he expected me to lash out at any given moment.

'You're new here, aren't you?' His words were slow and tested. He inched forward a little.

'What makes you say that?'

'I just got that impression.'

'Oh.' So I stuck out like a sore thumb, huh? 'I'm sorry,' I said, as though being an outsider was an unforgivable sin.

He peered at me a little closer. 'What's your name?'

'Pepper.' I managed a small smile.

He returned the smile. 'Pepper,' he repeated. 'I'm

Therron. Welcome to Tantary.'

10

NEW ADVENTURES

Max

*O*nce, there lived a simple man. He never wanted for much. He respected nature as nature respected him—with true appreciation of its hidden value. In a land ravaged by war, the young man stood firmly above it.

Anyone would take him for a normal man, but his talents defied impression. He bore power that far surpassed the other inhabitants of the land; he was truly a rarity.

Cheery and with a gentle persona, he was born

with the courage and ability to overcome any evil. He had the potential to become a great hero. With magical powers of the likes no others had seen before, the hero who was destined to bring redemption to the kingdom was the young man named Therron.

'That's it?'

Father shrugged.

'And this took you, what, two years?'

'Well, I haven't touched it for quite some months.' He twizzled his pen between his fingers as he sat, tense, in his chair. The worry lines on his face pronounced themselves.

'Surely it should have worked by now.' I re-read the notes Father had given me, but nothing seemed out of line.

'I don't know, son. I included everything. Something must have gone wrong, I just wish I knew what.' He used his thumb and his forefinger to pinch his forehead, something he often did when he was stressed. Though it seemed to me he was always stressed.

I slumped on the chair across from Father and rested my feet on his desk, gnawing at the stumps I called nails. I wanted to get back to the party. This was so lame. I really didn't like the idea of being cooped up in here, trying to help Father find a solution to our haunted house problem, or whatever the hell it was, while I could be out there trying to woo Pepper.

Except she had to go and ditch me, didn't she? After all I did for her, she just upped and left. And now here I was with my father, rabbiting about fairies and what else not.

'What if it did work?' I spoke to my fingers. 'Would we even know?'

Father shook his head, reaching round my feet to retrieve his piece of writing. 'Alzabar is many times stronger than Calpacious,' he said. 'If he had been found by now, he would have taken back the throne. With Calpacious no longer in power, the portal would be restored and we would not still be tormented by evil magicks.'

I was growing tired of this, and my head was really giving me a hard time. I needed to get back to the party. Maybe a few more drinks would numb the pain.

'Isn't the solution obvious? Just write "Therron freed Alzabar. Alzabar defeated Calpacious. The end." Then we can all go back to living normal lives, like normal people.'

'You know it doesn't work like that.' I didn't reply. I just continued to chew my nails. 'Max, what's the problem? Why can't you help me with this? This is your home as well, you know.'

I mumbled an incoherent response, but Father made me repeat it.

'I said, maybe I don't want this to be my home!' I shouted. Then I sighed. Damn. Now he was going to get angry. 'Father, I'm getting tired of this. Everything's "Tantary this, Tantary that, pixies, rainbows and unicorns". Who cares if the spell is weakening? No one can see the story creatures anyhow. The last I checked, they were unable to leave the house. So how about we just pack up and move somewhere else? Is it that difficult?' To emphasise my frustration, I lifted my crossed legs from the desk and slammed them back down again the other way round.

'Why do you think no one can see them? Just because you can't?'

'Okay, so the only people who can see them are people with strong imaginations,' I said. 'Of all the people you've invited to your parties, nobody has shown any signs of seeing anything. To find someone like that, you'd need an artist-type person, or a writer, or . . .'

It finally hit me.

'Pepper,' I said, my feet falling from the desk, scattering piles of paper in the process. 'That was why you hired her, wasn't it? All this time, I told you we didn't need a nanny. It was all part of your plan!'

Father sighed at the mess I made, but didn't comment.

'You're right,' he said instead. 'Pepper is one-of-a-kind. Though I hadn't intended for it to happen this way. I advertised for a nanny because I thought we needed one. It wasn't until I read Pepper's immaculate application form that I knew there was something special about her. She has the kind of imagination I've been looking to find for years. If she is able to communicate with the magicks, then there is a chance she can find out what's going on in Tantary and why Calpacious is still on the throne. Max, you need to talk to her! Get her to speak to the magicks.'

'Yeah,' I said with a grimace, 'there could be a slight problem with that.'

'What's that?'

'Well, it's complicated,' I told him. 'Let's just say she probably doesn't want to talk to me at the moment.' And that's just normal talk, I thought, let alone talk about mythical creatures.

'What have you done to her?'

'Oh, it's nothing.' I shrugged. 'She's just overreacting.'

My eyes snagged on the open notebook Father had written Therron's description in, and my face contorted in alarm.

'Father,' I said, picking it up with hesitation. 'You

may want to have a look at this.'

'I want to thank you for earlier,' I said. 'For saving me. From the guards.'

Therron glanced at me briefly over his shoulder before continuing to plough through the dense shrubbery. 'Um, thanks,' he said. 'You know, for thanking me.'

My skirt kept getting caught on the thorns jutting out of the bushes. What had once been a beautifully pale fabric was now stained with various shades of brown and green, and ridden with tears. I had no idea what these plants were, but I certainly hadn't come across any before.

I had to marvel at the way Therron navigated through this forest like it was second nature to him. To me, each direction looked identical to the next. I was afraid—I couldn't help it. Therron seemed like a genuine person who was willing to help me out, but what if I was wrong about him?

But then again, what if he knew how to get back to the manor?

'Excuse me,' I called from behind him. On our journey to escape from the King's forest, Therron hadn't spoken to me all that much. It was clear he was a man of few words. A slight turn of his head was all that told me I had got his attention. 'Have you heard of Calthorpe Manor?'

'Sure.' He pushed a low-hanging tree branch aside. 'The house all our stories are kept in. Why?'

I hadn't had much time to ponder what the sylphs told me that morning, but parts of the conversation came back into my head. If all the story characters had really been banished to this other land, then everyone here was part of a story. So Scarlett, Cade, Therron . . . they were characters! They were all creations of someone else's imagination, and they lived here, in flesh and blood! Had I not been scared out of my wits, I would have been enthralled.

'Do you know how I can get there?' I asked Therron.

'I don't.' He shook his head in apology. 'But I know someone who does.' I saw his face again. His features were hard and tight, as though his skin had been carved from wood. I suddenly wanted to touch him, to smooth out those lines and tell him it was all right. I wondered what could have happened to give him such a haunted expression.

Something cracked behind us. With a sharp breath, I whipped round to see a dark silhouette moving in the shaded greenery.

'We need to get out of here,' whispered Therron.

The shadow loomed closer. A guard must have spotted us.

'Run!' Therron bent down to retrieve a brown satchel then grabbed my wrist and we hurtled through the trees and bushes. I barely had time to hoist my dress up to avoid getting caught by the branches again. We were still too slow though, and the guard was catching up to us with increasing speed, bellowing for us to halt. Soon, he was no more than a few feet behind us.

'Go,' Therron yelled, and I felt his hold loosening.

'What?' I said through gasps off air.

'Just go! I'll hold him back. Go straight through those trees and you'll be out in the open. You'll be safe there.'

He stopped running and my wrist fell from his hand. 'Hey, wait!' I watched the guard approach him, but could not watch for long as I had to look where I was running. I did as he told me, tearing straight in the direction he pointed me in. I hurdled over logs and avoided tree stumps, until the trees grew sparse, and sunlight surrounded me. I slowed my pace to a jog, my hand over my thrumming heart. I took a moment for the burning in my chest to subside. I really needed to get into shape.

Turning back to the forest, I saw no sign of

Therron, or whether he got away. What was he doing? Turning himself in to the king to let me escape? No, he wouldn't. We'd barely met.

Once the rushing of blood died from my ears, I became aware of the sound of trickling water. I looked up, only now taking notice of my new surroundings. Vibrant grasses tickled my ankles, swaying in the mellow breeze as flower heads bobbed to a silent tune. I recognised the rich flora from the manor, from when the plant life took over the building. It was far more beautiful out here, in its natural habitat.

Close by flowed a gentle stream. The transparent waters drew me closer. The melodious babbling made me realise just how dry my mouth was from all that running. I crouched down on the rocky bank. The water sparkled where the sunlight kissed it, giving it a shimmering, almost iridescent quality.

My fingers swam through the shallow stream in a figure of eight, the frigid current soothing against my skin. Lethargically, I used my cupped hands to scoop up some of the luscious water and held it to my lips. It tingled as it trickled down my throat. I couldn't help myself. I took another handful and poured it over my face, allowing the liquid to drip down my hair, styled into ringlets for the ball earlier. I drew in a deep breath of the freshest and cleanest air I ever tasted.

I stood from my perch, but my skirt weighed me down. The end of it had fallen in the stream, clogging the fabric and making it rather heavy. I couldn't carry on like this. I scanned the stream for a sharp stone, and sure enough, a small-ish and sharp rock came into view. I used the sharpened edge to slash through the soggy layers of chiffon. It took some work, and a lot of arm ache, but eventually I had the dress trimmed so it sat comfortably above my knees. There. No more snagging or waterlogging. Proud of my handiwork, I performed a little twirl, giggling at the way the skirt flared when I span. Something Lilly would have loved.

I came to a stop when I spotted the figure watching from within the trees.

'How long have you been there?' I called out.

Therron stepped out of the shadows, running a hand through his tousled hair while he cast his gaze downwards. 'Not very,' was all he said.

I walked towards him. 'What happened to the guard?'

'Don't worry, he's fine.' His mouth turned up in a small smile. 'He may find he has a long walk back to the castle, though.'

I gave him a questioning look. 'Why? What did you do to him?'

'Nothing bad.' He wandered over to the stream

where he dropped his satchel to the ground and crouched down by the water's edge. He took a long sip. I joined him, gulping down more of the fresh water until I quenched my thirst.

Out of the shadows of the trees, I could see Therron a lot clearer. Though he couldn't have been much older than me, he looked like he could pass for older, especially with the swirling ripples of the stream casting twinkling reflections across his features. He had thick eyebrows that matched the chestnut hue of his hair, which hung unevenly across his forehead. His movements were small and guarded, like he was unsure of himself.

Therron peeked up from his hands, spying me watching him. Embarrassed, I turned away. I went to remove my shoes so I could slip my warm feet into the soothing stream. I relaxed the second the cooling water hit my skin.

'So, who is this person who knows how to get to the manor?' I asked Therron once he finished drinking.

'Her name is Penelope,' he told me, following my lead, sinking his own bare feet into the water. 'She goes back and forth from the human world regularly, though I have never been there myself. She'll know where and when to catch the portals.'

It was really beginning to sink in now that I was

nowhere near home. Heck, I wasn't even in the same realm as home! I was in some distant fantasy land I never even knew existed until that very morning. I tried my best to keep my emotions at bay. There was a way back—Therron had told me. I needn't get upset. And, hey, maybe this whole adventure could result in an idea for a story.

'How long have you been in Tantary?' I didn't realise Therron was watching me. I met his gaze, astonished once again by the depth of colour hidden in his eyes, now even more visible in the daylight.

'I arrived only moments before you found me.'

Therron smiled a little, and though it was only small, it completely altered his appearance. 'I know it's tough when you arrive here for the first time,' he spoke with a reassuring tone. 'Even after being here for two years, I still find it difficult.' He paused. 'Do you know anything about your story?'

'My story?' I repeated, confused. 'I don't know what you mean.'

'Hey, it's fine,' he said, smiling again. 'Some of us don't know much about the books that brought us here. I assume that's why you want to go to the manor? To find your story?'

Oh. He thought I was a book character.

'Um, well, yes. I suppose it is.'

Okay, I was lying. So what? With any luck I'd be

out of here soon anyway, so what would it matter?

'What about you?' I probed, ignoring the guilt punching my stomach. 'Do you know anything about your story?'

Therron poked at the pebbles beneath his feet with his toes. 'I'm not sure I'd want to know,' he answered. Before I could ask anything else, he stood from the bank and shook his feet dry.

'Okay,' he said, 'we'd better get going now. If we head this way, we should make it before sundown.'

I followed suit, slipping my shoes back on. They felt tough and constricting after the cleanse. I looked up into the sky. The sun appeared to be at its peak, telling me sundown was quite some time from now. My legs felt weak beneath me and my eyelids were heavy. Back at the manor, it must have been close to midnight.

'Therron, wait,' I called as he started walking away from the forest. 'I'm really tired. Is there a place we can rest first?'

Therron paused and looked thoughtful. If he was wondering why I could be so tired in the middle of the day, he didn't ask.

'Sure,' he just said, and smiled. 'Follow me. There's a little place down at the foot of the hill where we can rest awhile.' He waited for me to catch up before we waded the rest of the way through the long grasses. Sure, I was stuck in a magical foreign land with a total stranger, but if one thing was for certain, it was that I absolutely could not wait to lay down my head and close my eyes.

11

BOLD ADMISSIONS

I curled my toes by the fire, allowing the heat to ease the shivers racking my body—while it was beautifully warm outside, this cave was dark and carried a chill from the damp rocks.

'We should be safe in here for a while,' Therron said as he added more wood to the blaze. 'This is something of a safe haven round here—away from the guards, the ogres . . . no one ever comes to these parts.'

'I take it you do.' Weary, I sank down to my front. The flames from the fire made me even drowsier than I was on the journey here.

He didn't look at me as he prodded at the fire with a long stick. 'I like to come down here when I'm out on my own.'

I listened to the fire as it crackled and spat, mesmerised by the patterns it cast on the cave's walls. Just a hollow forged into the base of a hill, the cave was easily the size of an average lounge, with room enough for a small family.

Yes. Family. I smiled a little to myself. I already missed my parents and sister. I'd never spent much time away from home in the past—something which did give me cause for concern when I applied for a year's job as a live-in nanny. At least back at the manor I could be certain I was going to see them again. But now . . . a sickly feeling rose in my throat and I pushed the thought aside before it could materialise.

'What were you doing in the King's forest?' Therron's words stopped my mind from producing any more depressing thoughts. I paused, unsure how to respond. 'I-I'm sorry,' he said, misinterpreting my silence. 'I didn't mean to pry.'

'No, no, it's fine,' I told him. 'Honestly, I don't really know how it happened. I just opened my eyes and . . . I was there.'

Therron looked across to where I lay on the opposite side of the fire. It wasn't the most comfortable floor, but it was something.

'So, you really are new here.'

I shrugged. Technically, shrugging wasn't lying. For a moment, I contemplated what would happen if I told him I was human. Perhaps I ought to. Lying to him wasn't fair, and what was really the worst that could happen? Maybe he had some kind of grudge against humans.

'What about you?' I said to him instead, probably out of cowardice. 'If the woods are so dangerous, why were you there?'

Therron snapped the stick in two and threw both halves into the fire, where the flames promptly devoured them. 'That forest is used as a private hunting ground for the King and his guards. Being so close to the castle, it makes the perfect place for their training. From the edge of the trees, on the clifftop, you get the most spectacular view of the castle. It's nice to sit up there some days and just admire the scenery.'

'The clifftop. That's where we met!' I realised. 'Aren't you scared you might get caught?'

He shook his head. 'Sometimes I am, but from my spot, I know no one can see me.' He allowed the silence to linger a while longer before speaking again. 'May I ask you another question?' His words were low in the quietness of the cave. I found myself

129

strangely at ease with Therron, concealed in this protective enclave. Nothing about Therron felt in the slightest bit threatening. I felt oddly . . . secure. 'Why are you so eager to find the manor? It can't be just about your story. No magick I ever heard of has seen their story before.'

I hooked a strand of hair behind my ear, searching for the right thing to say. 'I guess all I can say is that I don't belong here,' I told him. 'This place isn't for me.'

'What makes you think the manor will be any different? What if you don't fit in there, either?' I sensed something deeper laced within his words. I wished I could see his eyes in the dim light.

'I . . . don't know. I guess we all have to fit in somewhere. Don't we?'

Therron cast his gaze back down. 'Maybe.' His voice was so quiet, it was practically a whisper.

'What is it?' I sat back up from where I had been lying on my stomach in order to see him properly above the fire. He sighed.

'It's such a cruel fate,' he said, 'to be granted life. I was not supposed to live. I am a character in a book, created with the intention to entertain people.' He looked up and blinked when he saw me, like he forgot I was there. 'I—I'm sorry,' he said. 'I didn't mean it like that.' His face drew into a frown. 'I just get upset sometimes. I shouldn't have said anything.'

I mustered a smile. 'Hey. It's all right, I get it. You're angry at the person who created you this way, aren't you?'

He shook his head. 'No. Whoever it was, they knew what they were doing. The fault lies with me. I couldn't be who they wanted me to be. I was born with these powers . . . but I didn't know what to do with them.'

'Powers?' I repeated. 'What do you mean?'

His fingers toyed with the hair at the base of his head as he let out a sigh. 'There I go, speaking before I think again. Yes, I was created with these strange abilities. Somehow, I am able to control things— water, plants, air—it's weird.' He frowned. 'Why am I telling you this? I promised myself I would never let anyone else know.'

'Anyone else?' I shuffled round the fire to sit a bit nearer to him. 'Therron, what happened?'

'It's not important. It's over now anyway.' He turned to me, and his previously taut face relaxed into a smile. 'You look tired. You should get some rest.'

I knew he was trying to change the subject, but I really was tired. Dropping the questioning—for now—I swivelled round to get comfy. In the process, I knocked over the satchel Therron had placed near the fire. Something black dropped out onto the

131

ground.

'I'm sorry,' I said, and reached over to pick it up, but before I touched it, I recognised what the object was. 'Wait, is that . . .?'

'Pepper, please.' He grabbed the bag and stuffed the item back inside.

I peered towards him. 'What were you really doing on that clifftop?'

'It doesn't matter. Go to sleep.'

'You weren't taking in the scenery, were you?'

Therron ignored me as he pretended to make himself comfortable, moving the satchel aside. And the binoculars inside it.

'Were you spying on the castle?' Again, nothing. 'Hey. I'm not going to get mad. I just want to know the truth.'

He had his back to me. 'Okay, yes. I was spying on the castle. On the King, to be exact.' He took a deep breath before turning back around to face me. 'I didn't mean to lie. It's just . . . the truth is too long.'

'Don't worry about it.' I smiled in what I hoped was a reassuring way. He'd told me the truth. It was only fair that I did the same. 'You know what, we may as well get off on the right foot,' I said. 'I haven't been entirely truthful with you, either.' Turning back, he peered at me quizzically. 'I'm not from a story.' I paused, gauging his response. 'I came here from the human world. That's why I'm trying to get back.'

'Oh.' A mixture of conflicting emotions passed across Therron's face. It was not a reaction I was expecting. Dropping his head down, he stared at the fire between us. I was tense. What was he going to do? Would he refuse to help me? Was he going to abandon me in the night?

Then he surprised me. He smiled a little, his expression sincere, and said, 'I will do everything I can to get you back home.' He didn't look angry. He didn't look scared, either. I could have been looking too deeply into it, but I thought I detected a hint of sadness.

I relaxed, touched by his kindness. Maybe I was going to get home. Maybe this was going to be okay after all.

'*A brother; a brother.*'
    Whene'er Calpacious' tongue stroked the word, down drew his brow a little more. 'Not once a brother to me. This throne was never his to keep.' His fingers enwrapped the wooden arms in possessiveness. 'This chair has borne my name since my birth!' he bellowed into the air. Had only he not

fled to fight a year afore his crowning. Mayhap his parents would not have disgraced him, bestowing the kingly title upon their youngest son—Calpacious' timid brother—Alzabar.

After reigning for no longer than a year, Alzabar was summoned to the crusades. In his five years of absence, Calpacious stole back the kingdom with ease, using propaganda to turn the population against their legal ruler. The ogres had been easy to persuade, though there were a few, harder-headed creatures who stood firmly by the side of their deserter.

There was a knock on the door to the throne room. 'My lord,' greeted the High Constable upon his entry. 'I have news. King Alzabar has been sighted on the battlefield.'

'KING?' Calpacious rumbled, his fist almost splintering the wood of his throne. 'How dare you name him a king in my presence!' He levered himself from his chair, his cape swishing like a shadow at his back. 'I am your leader now. Not that treasonous villain.'

'Your Majesty, you fail to see the facts,' protested the tired official with a sigh. 'Half the inhabitants of this town still side with your brother. Remember, while he lives, you are still just the regent.'

Calpacious' face heated at that word. Regent—

Bah! He was the firstborn. He should have been the one to whom the people bowed. But no matter how hard he tried, there was always that one person obscuring his path.

'Then there is but one thing for it.' Calpacious stood with his toes touching those of the High Constable. As one who respected himself for his fearless heart, the official felt his body recoil in the regent king's foreboding presence. 'Alzabar must die.'

12

UNLIKELY FRIENDSHIPS

*S*lept right through the afternoon and the following night. Apparently, crossing worlds really took it out of you. I already apologised several times to Therron for oversleeping.

'Seriously, you should have woken me,' I insisted as we tread the dirt track. 'You shouldn't have stayed up that long.'

'It wasn't a problem,' he answered. 'You must have been pretty tired.'

Though the journey to Penelope's house was short, I was glad we took the time to rest earlier, as I'm pretty sure I would've been asleep on my feet by now.

My eyes kept getting distracted by the giant mushrooms and odd-shaped boulders lining our path on either side. This world was so different from my own, yet in ways that were strangely similar. The road, for example. It looked just like any dirt path back home, except for the odd chip of soft crystal here and there, making it sparkle.

My stomach let out a long grumble. I'd been so absorbed in the scenery, I barely acknowledged the fact that I was starving. The last time I'd eaten anything had been before the party. Oh gosh, the party! It had still been going on when I left. Had anyone noticed my absence yet? Or maybe time worked differently here, I considered, remembering the *Narnia* books I loved to read in my childhood. Perhaps I'd go back and it would be the same time as when I'd left.

My tummy rumbled again, this time louder. Therron heard.

'When we get to my house I'll prepare us a meal,' he said. 'We could be waiting a while until the next portal opens.'

'Wait, your house?' I looked at him in confusion. 'I thought we were going to see Penelope.'

'We are.'

It took me a while to realise what he meant. 'Penelope is *at* your house?' He nodded. I should

138

have left it at that, but my curiosity kept me speaking. 'And Penelope is . . .'

He turned and smiled. 'My pet.'

'Oh.' I felt foolish for assuming anything otherwise. And for having had the urge to ask.

I didn't notice when we arrived. I initially wondered why Therron stopped in the middle of the track, as I could see nothing resembling a house, only trees.

'We're here,' Therron announced. We'd stopped beside a particularly thick-trunked tree, which Therron proceeded to walk around. I assumed he meant for me to follow.

That was when I saw it. Built up against the tree was a structure of wood and stone, its roof carpeted with luscious green moss. Small, the house was barely the size of a single room—I failed to see how it could function as a home. I ran my palm along the rustic surface of one of the stone walls.

'It's perfectly safe, if that's what you're wondering,' said Therron as he hung his satchel on a wooden post beside the front door.

The hut looked just like something out of a storybook. I laughed at that thought—it most probably was! 'It's beautiful! How did you find it?'

'I built it.'

My jaw fell loose. Seriously? He made this all by

himself? I eyed the immaculate structure, from the jutting chimney to the circular windows and the glorious window boxes, bright with vivid flowers, hanging below.

'I know. It's not the best job in the world. It could've been a lot better.'

'Are you kidding? This is incredible!' I wished I could live here myself. Quiet; secluded—this place was everything I could've dreamed of!

'Thank you.' He smiled. 'I'm glad you like it. I don't think anyone's ever been down here to see it before.' I was about to ask why, but he continued to talk. 'I'm, uh, going to light the fire. Are you okay with roasted sadgia?'

'Um, sure,' I said, not telling him I had no idea what a 'sadgia' was.

The inside of Therron's house was very cosy indeed, with soft, quilted fabrics covering just about every surface. Therron battled with two pieces of flint by the hearth as he tried to get the fire going. I took a seat on what I supposed to be a solid rock covered by a quilt, but was actually soft and squishy, like a sofa. It was actually pretty comfortable. The chair stretched the length of the room, and at the one end was positioned a pillow. I assumed this must double up as Therron's bed.

A corner of the room was cut off by a partition,

with a door at the one end. That must have led to the bathroom. The hut may have been compact, but it appeared to have all the necessities for living. I loved Calthorpe Manor and all its Gothic splendour, but there was something equally enthralling about this little cabin, in a cosy, charming kind of way.

'When do I meet Penelope?' I asked, more in a way to make conversation than out of impatience.

Therron stepped back from the stove as the tiny spark he had generated from the rocks began to ignite the pile of wood. 'I'm not sure,' he said without taking his eyes off the flame. 'She's probably at the manor, but I don't know what time she left. She rarely stays for longer than a few hours, so I wouldn't imagine she'd be too long. Don't worry.'

The odd thing was, I wasn't worried anymore. Should I have been? Probably, yes. But Therron had been nothing but kind to me, and the only threat I came across in Tantary so far was the King's army. But if Therron was correct, we were safe from them here. I trusted Therron. Having never been much of a people person, I rarely found myself gravitating towards anyone. But there was something different about Therron. Perhaps it was that, beneath his apparent aptitude for survival, I saw a struggling young man.

It wasn't long before the meal was ready. Sadgia,

though I had initially imagined it to be some kind of animal, was actually an orange-coloured vegetable. Therron served it on a wooden plate alongside a couple of other foods I had never seen before. I pushed aside my trepidation and took the first mouthful, and was surprised to find it tasted much like potato, only much richer and with an earthy twang. The rest was equally delicious. I scarfed it down, my stomach thoroughly grateful.

'Do you live here all by yourself?' I asked Therron between mouthfuls.

Therron seated himself on a low stool beside the fire, which still crackled away. 'I have Penelope here for company,' he said, 'but aside from her, yes. I live alone.'

A hundred more questions bubbled up inside me, but I didn't wish to voice them for fear I would offend him by asking too much. Instead, I tried to find something else to talk about.

'I don't suppose you could tell me a bit more about this place, could you?' I probed. 'I mean, I know that everyone here comes from a storybook, but how did it happen? How did you all get here?'

Therron actually looked pleased I had touched upon this topic. He sat a little more upright as he continued to munch at his food.

'Are you familiar with the story of Marcius

Calthorpe?' he asked me.

'Vaguely,' I replied. 'The original owner of Calthorpe Manor?'

Therron nodded in affirmation. 'That's right. When the popularity of the manor began to decline, Marcius sought out the help of a powerful wizard to banish the characters to a new realm. The wizard used this spell to create an enchanted mirror. The mirror, I assume, you used to get here.' I confirmed this. 'But the mirror's strength was limited. It wasn't able to keep out all the creatures; only half. This wizard was clever, and he specially calibrated the spell to secure the evil characters, and allow only those with good intentions to pass through. There is one catch, though.'

'What's that?'

'Should the mirror ever be broken,' he said with a grim expression, 'so shall the spell. The bridge between realms would close and we would be stuck here forever. There are a few people who fear us who have tried to locate and destroy the mirror, but it has been an oath for the Calthorpe family to ensure that we are kept safe.'

I did not know what to say or think to that onslaught of information. I had really underestimated how complicated this matter really was.

'You really know a lot about this,' I said, at a loss

for any other words.

Therron shrugged. 'Yeah, well. Reading the history books helps to pass the time of day.' He inhaled as though about to say more, but the intention drained from his face, and he finished off his plate before setting down his fork, which was fashioned from a tree branch. 'You finished with that?' he asked, extending out his arm for my empty plate. I nodded and handed it to him. 'Follow me.' He stood from his seat and exited the hut, a plate in either hand, with me not far behind.

Outside, I followed Therron down an uneven slope, wondering where he could possibly be taking a couple of empty dishes. The trees grew tighter together, making everything darker and more enclosed the further down we went. Therron stopped at a curtain of vines and turned to me, a beaming smile on his face.

'Go in,' he urged, gestured towards the hanging plants. Obediently, and with just a hint of excitement brought on by his eager grin, I drew back the vines, and gasped at what lay beyond.

Hidden away in the depths of the forest sat a lake of sparkling turquoise, displaying its crystalline colouring where the sunlight pushed through the overhead trees. For such a concealed part of a secluded forest, the place burst with life. Insects such as dragonflies and fireflies skimmed across the lake's surface, as well as a few tiny sylphs with glowing wings. They danced around the vibrant water lilies and bobbing fruit that fell from the surrounding plants. The vegetation that perched along the bank seemed to prosper from the water's proximity, the leaves and petals shiny and radiant. One flower in particular had long, glowing stamen that reflected on the lake's surface.

A trickling stream flowed into the lake at one end, before spilling out in a glittering waterfall at the opposite. It was barely audible above the rustling of the leaves and vines hanging from every draping branch.

'What do you think?' asked Therron, entering the secret grotto from behind me. I did not answer, simply gawked at the scene. 'This is my favourite place to come,' he continued. 'It was one of the reasons I chose to build my house in this spot.' He crouched down by the outgoing waterfall and began to scrub one of the dishes in its flow with a sprig of fresh moss from the bank. I grabbed the other plate and mimicked his actions.

'Thank you for this,' I said as I scrubbed.

'It's no problem. I always have enough food in the house.'

I decided to move my legs from underneath me and let my feet dip in the flowing water. The bottoms of my feet rested comfortably on the river bed. There was something about the water in this land—it just felt so good. 'I don't mean just that,' I said. 'I mean for everything. For helping me get home. And for being so kind.'

Though he kept his gaze downcast, I noticed Therron's cheeks redden at my words. 'It's the least I can do for a stranger to the land,' he said. His plate was now clean, but he stayed sitting. I finished with mine shortly after, setting it on top of his.

'This place is beautiful,' I breathed in admiration. 'Every time I think I could never see anything more stunning, I do!'

'I guess it can seem like that when you're new here,' said Therron with a smile. 'I doubt you'll see anything more amazing than this, though.' He nodded towards the lake. 'The waters here descended from the mountains, from the North Spring.' He pointed upstream. 'By the time it gets here, it's still fresh. The best thing about the stream is that it is so hidden, hardly anybody knows it exists.' He chuckled. 'I almost feel like I own it!'

I laughed too, and Therron swung his feet down into the water next to mine where he promptly crossed one leg over the other, splashing my skirt in the process.

'Oh gosh,' he said. 'I'm so sorry. I didn't mean to .

. . hey!' He looked down at his trousers, damp from where I splashed him back. His look of total surprise was too much. I held a hand up to my mouth, but it didn't suppress the escaping giggle. The corners of Therron's mouth twitched up in a mischievous grin, and I could do nothing to hide as he scooped his hands into the water and flung it in my direction, soaking me from the waist down. Before long, we both stood in the stream, the water at our ankles, kicking and throwing it at each other.

Caught up in our little scuffle, I almost missed the strange squeal that came from beside us on the bank.

'Penelope, you're back!' Therron exclaimed.

Standing beside us, her fur completely drenched, was a fluffy, white rabbit. At first, I didn't think much of it, but then she looked at me, and I saw her bright, violet eyes.

'Fifi?'

The bunny hung her head, ears sagging to the ground.

'Fifi?' Therron echoed, confused.

I stepped out of the stream, shaking my feet out, though the rest of me remained totally soaked. 'I've met her before,' I explained while slipping my shoes back on. 'In the manor. Only . . .' I shot her an accusatory look. 'I thought she couldn't understand me.'

'Penelope,' spoke Therron with a stern tone. 'What have I told you about lying to people?' Fifi—or, Penelope, I should say—dropped her head even lower. Therron turned to me apologetically and explained. 'She does that sometimes to people she's unsure of.' I gave him a questioning look. 'I—I don't think she meant it personally. She does it a lot, you see. Quite the cantankerous little bunny.'

Penelope let out a little grumble to show she did not appreciate being spoken about in such a way. Whipping round to give us a good view of her rear, she hopped off towards the hut.

'I'm sorry,' Therron said. 'She's not usually like this. Well, sometimes. I can try and calm her down, but it may take a while.'

'It's fine,' I told him. 'I think I know why she doesn't like me.'

'Oh yeah?' he said, intrigued. 'Why's that?'

Therron scooped up the plates and the two of us sauntered back up the hill. 'Back at the manor, I asked if she could show me the way to your land. She didn't respond to me. I don't think she wants me here.'

'So you were looking for Tantary?' he asked. 'If you were trying to find it, then why do you want to go back so soon?'

'I wanted to find out about it, yes.' I squeezed out my hair, watching the drips fall to the soft soil. The dampness was now starting to make me feel a little chilly. 'But that was before I knew about the history, and the spell. I never had any intention of actually coming here.'

'Are you glad you did?'

His question caught me by surprise. 'Um,' I began, 'I suppose so, yes. Yes, I am.'

And the more I thought about it, the more I knew it was the truth. The whole thing had been an enlightening experience, and it was a pleasure to have met someone like Therron. I started to get excited about telling Lilly and Peter all about Tantary when I returned. No doubt they would both love to hear!

Back in the hut, the fire had long gone out, but Penelope lay by the hearth, enjoying the heat that continued to ooze from the embers.

'Penelope, we need your help,' Therron told her, but she didn't move, only twitched her front paw as though in slumber. 'Don't pull that one on me,' he told her, though through his warning, I still heard a hint of affection. It was easy to tell these two were old friends.

Penelope yawned and rolled onto her front before glaring at her master. I could not get over how un-bunny-like so many of her movements were. It was quite comical.

'Pepper needs to get back to Calthorpe Manor,'

Therron continued to explain. 'Could you please tell us when and where the next portal is?'

Penelope made a series of twitching and blinking movements while Therron watched, apparently understanding what she was trying to communicate.

'Are you sure?' he asked with a frown. 'And you're not lying to me this time, are you?' He sighed, and I felt dread at the displeased look on his face. 'We have a day's wait,' he told me. I nodded. Okay. That wasn't too bad, was it?

I smiled and nodded. 'That's not a problem.'

'We've also got a day's journey.'

Ah.

I made a face. I was never a massive fan of journeys.

'Okay then,' I sighed. 'We'd better get started now. Where's your car?'

The look he gave me was one of complete bafflement. 'What's a car?' He asked.

'Oh, you know.' I made a gesture with my hands. 'A big machine with wheels. It gets you places.' He still looked blank. 'Are we going by boat then?' Again, nothing. 'By horse?' He shook his head.

'You seem to be mistaken,' he said with a hint of a smile. 'We're going to be walking.'

13

OLD ACQUAINTANCES

Max

'You're insane.'

'It's the only way.'

'Not a chance. There is no way I'm going—'

'MAX!'

I fell silent, startled by my father's sudden rise in tone. It was just as I feared—things were getting even more complicated. Just as I began to believe I would be off the hook regarding this whole Tantary nonsense, what with Pepper's apparent involvement, Father had to go and throw this in my face.

'Why me?' I asked, this time choosing a more

indirect method of protesting. 'You said anyone can enter Tantary now that Pepper has, so why me? Why not you? Or one of the kids?'

Father leaned over his desk, his elbows sitting on the worktop and his chin resting on his clasped hands. He regarded me with a solemn expression. 'I called you here, Max, because I trust you,' he said. Oh, great, I thought. Not this again. 'When you take over as master of the house, you will be responsible for the portal. It is not a job to be taken lightly—it is a serious business.'

Yeah, yeah. 'They're fictional characters.' I knew as soon as the words left my mouth I had said the wrong thing. Father glared at me.

'You know they're a lot more than that,' he said. I sighed, defeated. I may have prided myself for being stubborn, but there really was no one worthier of that title than my father. To argue with him was futile, as I knew from many previous experiences.

'Every character written into one of these books is now a conscious being with thoughts, feelings and ambitions. They have control over their actions, which is why we can only write characters into existence, not circumstances. They are real people. We must treat them as such.'

Whatever. I'd heard it all before. That, and the reason why we couldn't simply write in a body-building warrior with skills in karate. Father was afraid a killing machine with no compassion would just destroy everything in, and out of, its path. And, of course, we couldn't have that. It wouldn't be 'humane'. Like it doesn't matter there are already fictional psychopaths and cunning criminals wreaking havoc over there, thanks to some of the gorier books in this house.

'So when are you banishing me to this forsaken land?' I asked. There was no point trying to hide how disgruntled I was about his stupid arrangement.

'Now,' father replied.

'What, as in right *now*, now?'

He nodded. 'Pack your things and go straight to Pepper. Use the book to help you find her.'

alking. Again. For someone who was not a great fan of any kind of exercise, I was certainly getting my fair share of it these last few days. At least, I thought, it might do something to get rid of some of the excess flab on my thighs. The portal was to open on the other side of the city the next morning. According to Therron, there was a shortcut that would have us got there a lot quicker, but unless I wanted to be gobbled for lunch by a chimera, this was the safest route.

Penelope—I was going to have to get used to calling her that—made it clear she still didn't trust me. Back on the dirt track, she kept an unreasonable distance in front of us at all times. At moments, I thought she was going to hop off on her own and we would lose her, but Therron wasn't worried. He assured me she was a smart bunny; she could take care of herself.

Therron and I walked side by side. At one point, I turned to look at him, and saw him smiling to himself.

'What are you smiling at?' I asked. He nodded towards the hopping bunny in front of us.

'I've never seen her like this before,' he said with a low chuckle. 'She must really hold a grudge against you!' He raised an insinuating eyebrow.

'Yes, well,' I said with a grimace. 'I wasn't exactly kind to her the first time we met.' We rounded a corner, and I mentally groaned when I saw the steepness of the path ahead. What I wouldn't have given to have my car right then!

'Speaking of grudges,' I continued, 'are you going to tell me why you were spying on the King yesterday?' It was a subject I wanted to approach all day, but failed to find the courage. I watched his expression change, hoping I hadn't overstepped the boundaries. Therron exhaled before speaking.

'There are some . . . difficulties in this kingdom,' he explained with some reservation. 'The King is mainly responsible. Because of this, the kingdom has been split in two: those who are with him, and those who want to see him gone.'

His description of a split kingdom reminded me of the book I read at the manor.

'Which side are you on?'

'I don't know.' I remained silent, allowing him to continue. He sighed again, rubbing the hair at the base of his neck. 'I mean . . . I'm not entirely sure myself what's going on. I think the King's up to something; something the other townsfolk don't know about. I haven't gleaned much, but it's definitely bad. From what I've seen and heard, I believe it has to do with the manor and the spell the wizard cast years ago. I . . . I think he's trying to break it.'

'And you figured all this out just from spying on his castle?' I asked, scarcely believing it. Just as I suspected, Therron shook his head.

'Do you remember what I told you yesterday?' he asked, staring along the road ahead. 'In the cave. About having been born with strange powers?'

'I think so.'

'I don't like using them. When I do, bad things tend to follow. But, once or twice, I've used them to

155

enhance my hearing. From the clifftop in the forest, I picked up on some of the conversations from within the castle. Only a few words, but enough to give me cause for concern.'

I wanted to ask some more about this controversial king, and was also intrigued by Therron's talk of his powers, but an air-splitting shriek resounded from the path beyond. Startled, I turned to my knowledgeable travelling companion.

'Hide,' he commanded with panic-stricken eyes, seeking out the source of the noise.

'What is it?' I asked as he steered me off the track and into the brush.

'I don't know.' He tugged on my arm so that we crouched down behind a tangle of blue leaves. 'But I don't want to find out.'

The next cry was accompanied by a loud *thwump* that sounded like the beating of wings. A whole four seconds later, we were hit by the gust it had generated. Well, whatever it was, it certainly wasn't small.

Through the matted branches, I made out a speck of white chasing up the track, heading towards the deafening noise.

'Penelope!' I exclaimed, shooting up from my hiding spot.

'What are you doing?' Therron barely raised his

voice above a whisper. 'You'll draw attention!'

Disregarding his warning, I darted out from the bushes and chased up the path after Penelope. I almost reached her when another gust came at me from the side, making me lose my footing. Pushing against the blow, I threw myself on top of the bunny, shielding her as the force grew stronger.

My face down, I watched as a black shadow spread over the dirt track. I could hear the mighty creature descending over us. With a thumping chest, I squeezed myself into a tighter ball and winced as the flapping continued. My thoughts blurred in such a way, I couldn't even register my own fear.

There was a whooshing sound, and a cry from above. The air grew lighter as the shadow passed over, and I inched my head up to see a gloved, and rather large, hand reaching forward to assist me. I didn't take it. Instead, I raised my gaze to find the face the kindly gesture belonged to.

My eyes travelled further than I anticipated, as the frame of my rescuer stood several feet above me in my crouched form. I took in the large, peaked ears, rounded nose and grey skin of the man in front of me. The odd shaping of his face was the kind that might have given me nightmares as a child, but his smile was warm and genuine.

'It's all right, Miss Pepper,' he said, his voice deep.

'The dragon has fled.'

'H-how . . .' I could not find the voice to complete my sentence through my quaking. The greyish man smiled in understanding.

'I don't suppose you remember me, do you?' he said as he hefted me up from the path. Penelope scampered away, grunting in dissent.

What did he mean? Had we met? You'd think I would remember meeting someone like him. Now that I stood, I could see he had to be at least eight feet tall and his bulky frame only added to the impact. Across his back was slung a bow and quiver and his attire was an unusual hybrid of armour and mufti. He was certainly not a man I would forget in a hurry.

Running footsteps on the trail behind alerted me to Therron's arrival.

'What's going on? Pepper, are you all right?' He stopped a short distance away from us, noticing the stranger. 'Who are you?' he asked the towering figure in the middle of the pathway.

'My name's Archie. I've been trying to hunt down that moody dragon all day. Thanks for catching his attention.' I knew he meant it ironically, as that attention could likely have cost me an appendage or two!

'Wait,' I said, holding up both my hands as my brain tried to comprehend what it just heard. 'Archie?'

The kind-natured troll smiled. 'Ah, so you remember me now?'

'Hold on,' Therron intervened, 'you know him?'

'Yes, but . . .' I peered closely at Archie's face. 'I-I don't understand.' I turned back to Therron. His confused expression was similar to my own. 'This . . . he . . . I created him. In a story. One I told to Peter to try and cheer him up.'

'Looks like the boy enjoyed your story so much, he decided to write it down.' He held out his hand to Archie. 'I'm Therron, by the way. Thanks for helping us out.' The troll took Therron's hand and told him not to worry about it. 'So, where's the dragon now?' Therron asked as he searched the skies, as though he feared it hid in one of the treetops.

'He's been deterred,' Archie answered. 'I sent off a few arrows to turn him the other way. The way he's headed, he should make it to the mountains where he won't disturb anyone until his mood has settled.'

I still stared in awe at a character my imagination had created just the other day. It was strange. I'd often wondered what it would be like to meet one of my characters in person, and now here he was.

I guess it made sense—all the characters from the manor's stories became real. Why hadn't it occurred to me before that Archie could actually exist?

'Archie.' I beckoned his attention. 'How did you

recognise me? Did you know I was the one who created your story? Does it even work that way?' I gave voice to just a few of the questions queued on the edge of my tongue.

Archie shook his head. 'In my story,' he explained, 'you and I knew each other. We were close friends.'

Had I said that? It made me smile to think Peter might have remembered that little detail, if it was indeed him who wrote the story down. It was also nice to know there was someone here in Tantary I knew. Well, in a sense.

'It's really nice to see you . . . Archie,' I said, trying to get used to the whole concept. 'Thank you for helping me out.' Archie just nodded in gratitude, in much the manner I imagined for his character.

'Where are you both headed?' He took a swig from a flask which he unfastened from his belt.

'The city,' said Therron. 'We need to get to the other side in time for the next portal opening.'

'And you're walking?' he asked with an incredulous look. We both nodded. 'Follow me,' he offered. 'I have a much quicker way.'

My legs sighed in relief. I did wonder how exactly he knew so much about Tantary, considering he couldn't have been here much longer than a day. I asked my question to Therron as we, along with Penelope—who was still in a huff with me—followed

Archie.

'I don't really know how to explain it,' he replied. 'It doesn't feel like you've just arrived. You have a whole existence behind you. Memories; experiences. It's like having lived here your whole life.'

'So surely you knew then.'

He cocked his head to the side. 'Knew what?'

'That I wasn't from this land,' I said. 'I had no idea about this place, I even said as much. So why didn't you say anything?'

He looked down sheepishly at his moving feet. 'I figured you would tell me in your own time,' he said. 'I didn't want to push you. You were clearly shaken by the transportation.'

I had more questions, mostly about his own past, but I decided to let them slide for now.

I continued to study Therron from the side. I had really taken to him over the last day. It was so refreshing to come across someone as pure and unselfish as him. I had to admit, it made a welcome change from having been around Max lately. He and I were going to have a real heart-to-heart once I got back to the manor. I wasn't sure I forgave him yet for his lies.

'Why did you do that?' Therron spoke up after a while. 'You purposely put yourself in harm's way to protect Penelope. Why?'

161

I thought about this awhile. 'It was a natural reaction, I guess. I wouldn't have willingly let her walk into danger. Wouldn't you have done the same?'

'I'd like to think I would,' he answered, though he seemed unsure of himself. 'Thank you for spotting her. If you hadn't gone after her like you did, I hate to think what would have happened. You're a brave person.'

I was going to reply, to tell him it wasn't bravery, but compassion, when Archie drew us to a stop. At the side of the track, he stood in the entrance of a small cave in the face of a cliff. He gave a shrill whistle. There was a noise from within, and the hole began to glow, getting brighter and brighter. Then, right before us, stood a blazing bird of fire.

14

FRIENDLY FACES

'This is Belinda—or Bel, as she prefers to be called.'

The phoenix bowed her head in our presence. Upon instinct, I flinched away from the dancing, orange flames that leapt from her skin in place of feathers. The magnificent bird stood almost as tall as Archie, and that was without the added height of her fiery wings. Unlike me, Archie was unafraid of the spitting flames, and used his hand to reach out and stroke the phoenix's hawk-like beak.

'Is that . . .' I gawped.

Archie nodded. 'This is the phoenix that killed my

brother,' he stated while peering into the bird's beady eyes. It was astonishing. It was just as I'd imagined it: these two lifelong foes could communicate everything in as much as a simple gaze. Then Archie did something that totally amazed me. He moved his hand from the bird's beak and up to her face, then ran his fingers down the flames on her neck—flames which surely should have burnt him.

Archie turned to look at me. He could tell what I was thinking.

'It's perfectly all right,' he said in response to my alarmed expression. 'She won't hurt you.'

I turned to Therron for assurance. He nodded. 'It's phoenix fire,' he told me. 'It only burns when the bird is scared or trying to defend itself.'

Archie motioned for me to come over, to pet the phoenix myself. Defying all my natural instincts, I closed up to the fire bird. Being nowhere near as tall as Archie, I couldn't quite reach her neck, where the bulk of the flames resided, so instead I ran my hand along her flank. The flames that swallowed my fingers were warm, but no more so than a hot water bottle, or a mug of warm cocoa you'd have to comfort you on a snowy, winter's day. They were also soft, like real feathers, and the intriguing thing was that they all clustered around my hand, like through some magnetic force.

'She seems to like you,' Archie said with a pleased smile. 'It's just as well, because she's going to be flying us to the city.'

My eyes bugged. Flying? He couldn't be serious! Archie looked a little smug at my response.

'Um, may we have a minute?' Therron excused us from Archie's presence before escorting me behind a tree at the side of the track.

'Pepper,' he said, 'it's your choice. I can see you're scared. Don't think that because you created this guy you're obliged to do what he says.'

I had to smile at Therron's consideration for me. 'I won't deny it,' I told him, 'I am scared. Most things about this world scare me.' I looked down at my feet at the admission. 'The way I see it, there is a big difference between fear and danger. I don't know. Maybe it would be a good idea to follow Archie's advice. He seems to know what he's doing.'

Therron nodded. 'Look,' he said, 'I understand if maybe you don't want my company anymore. If you want to travel the rest of the way with Archie, then I'll be happy just to have got you this far.'

'No!' Somehow, the idea of carrying on without Therron gave me a great sense of loss. He'd been by my side since my arrival in Tantary. I was not about to let him go now. 'Please, I would much rather you came with me.'

The gleam in Therron's eyes shone brighter than the demure smile he offered me.

*I*t was decided: I hated flying.

I was never keen on it in the first place—the few times I'd been in a plane with my family, I always found myself counting down the minutes until we landed. It wasn't that I was afraid of heights—I wasn't— it was more the thought of being suspended in mid-air. It was unnatural. I was beginning to wish I'd taken Penelope's initiative and decided to stay on the ground.

Maybe now, though, I wouldn't be quite as reluctant to go on a plane as I used to be, for it was certainly preferable to riding on the bare back of a phoenix! I clung tightly around Archie's wide waist as we swooped over various terrains—forests, moors, mountains, villages—until I thought I was going to be sick. Behind me, Therron sat with a similar grip around my middle. The pressure of his arms around my midriff, I found, was actually quite pleasant, so I tried to focus on his touch to try and take my mind off the nausea.

We flew for quite some time, and for most of the

journey, I had my eyes sealed closed. It wasn't like I could have seen anything around Archie's body if I did have my eyes open, though. I had to admire Archie's phoenix—Bel—as she continued to maintain a reasonable speed despite her large number of passengers.

Once we levelled out and were no longer being tipped from side to side, I dared a peek around Archie's broad form. Bel soared in a clear, level path in perfect alignment with the clouds. But then, in the haze beyond, I spied a new shape rising from below. We were heading straight for what looked like a solid wall! I expected Bel to slow as we approached, but instead she accelerated towards the wide blockade.

'Um, Archie?' I stammered as we drew nearer. I looked up into his face and saw a determined expression as he stared at the fast approaching wall. It wasn't until we were almost upon it that I could see the texture of the partition. What I'd initially believed to be a brick wall was actually a well-tamed row of impossibly tall trees.

But we were still getting nearer. I closed my eyes and prepared myself for the impact we would experience when we crashed into it. But, at the very last moment, I felt a rush of air as Archie steered Bel up and over the treetops. I felt my stomach lurch as we careened upwards and I grabbed tighter on to

Archie. Fearing for my life, I stayed that way for a while, my head buried into his back.

I flinched at a gentle tap on my shoulder. 'Pepper,' Therron spoke into my ear above the rushing of the wind and the whooshing of Bel's monstrous wings. 'Open your eyes!'

His soft hold on my shoulders coaxed the tension out of my body and allowed me to lift my head a little. When I peeled open my eyelids, I understood Therron's enthusiasm.

We soared high above a city of towering, metallic buildings that glinted in the sun like a thousand shards of a broken mirror. From our height, it looked like we were flying above a mosaic of silver. Constructed in peculiar, angular shapes, some buildings were incredibly high, while others lay flat, but covered a lot of low-level space.

But it wasn't what was down below that was the most intriguing; it was in the sky. Nobody would have to worry about looking conspicuous riding above the Tropolis on top of a flaming phoenix, as it looked like such creatures were the standard form of transportation. The sky around us was alive with people travelling on the backs of dragons, griffins, phoenixes, and a number of other fantasy-type creatures I failed to identify. The sound of the bustling traffic made the air around us hum with its energy.

Animals screeched out to one another, and people laughed and yelled as they darted through the sky.

In one smooth move, we dove down, swooping closer to the city. Once level with the buildings, we wove in and out of the silvery architecture, flying over—and even under—the elaborate designs. It was then I heard the music. Pipes, drums, and strings sang in a merry tune, filling the air everywhere we went. It sounded like it was coming from everywhere, as though the entire city was joining in to create this joyful melody.

'We're just in time,' Archie shouted back to us over the clamour. 'Festivities begin today for Bawntide. You should have some time before the next portal opens, so if you get the chance, I thoroughly recommend you go and take a look around. Nobody celebrates quite like we do here in the Tropolis! Or, so I've heard. I've never been to one myself!' I asked Archie what Bawntide was all about. 'It's our annual celebration for the creation of Tantary,' he explained. 'Traditionally, it is the time to give thanks to the people who helped create us—the authors, the publishers, and the original Marcius Calthorpe and the wizard who created this land. The celebrations last for a week, then on the last day, we give special thanks to our king. On this day, each subject is to present the King with one of their most cherished possessions.

The donations are collected in a wagon and then taken to the castle.'

The grim tone the troll's voice took on informed me he wasn't too happy about this particular tradition.

Archie landed Bel on a flat area of land, a little like a field, with occasional tufts of yellowy grass poking up through the trodden-down mud. A number of other creatures landed here too, and a few others were preparing for take-off. Off to the left was a large paddock, where it seemed all the animals were housed and fed. After dismounting, Archie offered Bel a large fish for her labour. She snatched it off him greedily and swallowed the whole thing with only a couple of chews. I grimaced. He led her off towards the paddock.

'Is that true?' I asked Therron while Archie was busy making Bel at home. 'Does everyone really donate their worthiest possessions to the King every year?'

Therron's face was set firm as he adjusted his satchel on his shoulder. 'It's our way of thanking him for all he has done for us,' he confirmed. 'I think you'll find quite a lot of the population disagrees with his rules, not just me.' He made a sound between a sigh and a grunt as we walked off the landing pad. 'It didn't always used to be like this. I've heard stories of a time when we were once ruled by a fair king. But that's all it is now: a story.' He peered around himself to make sure no one was listening in before leaning in closer to me and speaking in a hushed voice. 'Many of our people would swear blind Calpacious is the best king this land has ever had, but I stand by my belief. That man should never be trusted.'

'Wait.' My heart shuddered in recognition. 'What did you say the King's name is?'

'Calpacious.' Therron spoke the word like he was having trouble getting it to pass his lips.

My memory jolted. Calpacious. The tyrant king from the book!

'Therron,' I spoke, now feeling my fear towards the situation at hand. 'What if I told you your doubts about the King are justified?'

The look he gave me was questioning.

'I've read the book Calpacious is from,' I explained, and Therron egged me to elaborate. 'I used to read it when I was younger, but I found a copy of it at the manor. In the story, he steals the throne out of greed when his brother, Alzabar, leaves for the crusades. He divides that kingdom in half, too. Half of them want Alzabar to return, and the rest of them believe Calpacious is the greater ruler.'

Therron's eyes widened at the parallels between the two stories. 'So what happened?' We had now travelled to the side of the bustling landing pad where

171

we waited beside the paddock for Archie to join us.

'When Alzabar returns,' I continued, 'war ensues. Calpacious hears his brother has come back and becomes intent on killing him so he can retain the throne. Alzabar goes into hiding, and Calpacious' thirst for his blood splits the kingdom even more. A lot of stuff happens, but by the end of the book, Alzabar vanquishes Calpacious and the land becomes peaceful once again.'

Therron looked wistful. 'It would be nice to think this land could be restored to the way it was in the stories I've heard.' The weight of his worries drew visible lines in his sun-bronzed brow. In that moment, I felt all his pain of knowing something was wrong, yet having to act like everything was fine. He looked distraught. I didn't like it. I wanted to see the Therron he had been down by the lake again.

'Why don't you speak up?' He turned to me at my question. 'You've seen and heard probably more than anyone else has regarding the King's intentions. Why don't you say something? If the land is divided like you say, there should be many people who are willing to stand by you.'

Before even taking a moment to consider my words, Therron shook his head. 'It's not my place,' he said. 'I agree some things need to happen, but it's not going to start with me.'

I was about to rebut, but just then, Archie re-joined us. He offered to accompany us around town for a while before sundown. As soon as night set in, Therron and I would have to find a place to sleep before everywhere became full with people staying for the Bawntide celebrations.

Out on the streets, there was barely any room to walk as parades wove between the buildings. We had to tuck right into the sides of the roads to squeeze past the crowds, watching the patrolling guardsmen as they marched to the beat of the music. Through the peering heads, I caught glimpses of the procession. It was an odd combination of soldiers, acrobats, and horses. No, wait, unicorns! A band of drummers rode astride a line of crystal-white unicorns! As much as I wanted to, I didn't get to watch for long, as my vision was soon obstructed again by the ever-flowing crowd.

The shops were an entity all of their own. Despite their steely tops, their front faces were highly decorative, with stained glass windows embedded into their stone walls. Each was beautiful in its own right. Just like back home, each shop specialised in a different craft. Today, every company had adorned their products with the emblem of Bawntide—a black pentagon inside a larger, silver circle. All five corners touched the infinite wall of the ring.

'It's the symbol of Tantary's creation,' Therron

explained when I asked him what the symbol meant. 'The points of the pentagon represent our five forms of life—humans, humanoids, beasts, plants and, the top corner, royalty—all coming together here in this united circle of equality.' I raised my eyebrows. Equality? The fact that the monarchy had, not only its own category, but sat at the top of the pentagon, already spoke otherwise.

I noticed Therron took in the city sights with nearly as much wonderment as me.

'Have you been to the Tropolis before?' I asked out of curiosity.

'Once,' he told me. 'But it was a long time ago.' The taut expression on his face told me there was more to it he wasn't telling me. 'This is my first time here for Bawntide, though.'

The music was just as audible inside the shops as it was outside. The sound made my bones warble with the vibrations, making me feel an energy of the likes I had never before experienced. But for all that the music was powerful, it wasn't that loud—I could speak to both Therron and Archie without having to raise my voice to a shout.

One of the shops we came across was a dressmaker's. I insisted on popping into this one, because I was getting rather uncomfortable in this shortened version of the ball-gown Adrian had lent me for the party. Apart from anything else, it was becoming quite filthy, with mud and dirt stains tinting the formerly beige colour a horrible, murky brown. I didn't suppose I would be returning this one to Adrian. Maybe I could make up some excuse about an accident with the punch bowl.

Therron graciously gave me a couple of silvers to get me outfitted, and left me to do my girly grooming in peace, going off to explore the rest of the market with Archie. We agreed to meet back outside the store in half an hour's time.

The shop was a small one, tucked away in a dim alleyway. If we hadn't ducked in there to avoid getting crushed by the crowds, we would never have come across it.

My arrival was announced by the clacking of a wooden wind chime above the door. The ornament set the tone for the rest of the shop, which was bedecked with wooden antiquities. The soft, cream colour of the unfamiliar timber worked as the perfect background colour to show off the voluptuous dresses on display on three of the four walls.

'Oh my, my, my. Visitors. And look at this place! I haven't even swept!'

A podgy little woman with tan skin, darker than the blonde ringlets draped over her shoulders, shuffled out from between a cluster of boxes behind the

175

counter at the far side of the shop. The middle-aged woman clearly had difficulty clambering over the mess.

When she finally got to me, she took one look at my grubby get-up and gave a huge grin that looked quite comical on her small, rounded face.

'Welcome!' she sang with jubilation. 'I'm Tharva.'

I smiled back and offered my hand. 'Pepper.'

Tharva's hand met mine in a strong and enthusiastic handshake.

'Been getting into the festive spirit a little early, have we?' She pointed her look at my torn and stained dress and laughed. It was a deep cackle that sounded directly from her belly, and it was extremely contagious. 'Don't worry,' she said between chuckles. 'I'll soon get you all cleaned up! I'll go and find something especially pretty for you.' I thanked her as she directed me to the changing cubicle, where I promptly drew closed the curtain and relieved myself of the now offending garment.

'I'd like to congratulate you on finding me,' Tharva called over the sound of her rummaging. 'Not many folks know I'm here. I've been thinking about moving to a more central part of town, but I ain't got enough dimes to my name! Such a shame. Such a waste of stock.' Tharva's arm emerged into my cubicle bearing three different garments, all of them long, flowing dresses. I guessed jeans and T-shirts were alien to this civilisation. A house full of old stories clearly meant old-fashioned characters with old-fashioned customs. For as long as I was to be among them, I would be expected to dress like them.

'Here, try these on,' she said as I took the dresses from her outstretched hand. 'I made them with my own two hands! Pass me the one you're wearing and I'll give it a good cleaning. I'm never one to waste good material!'

I took the immaculate dresses off her and hung them all up on the curtain railing before handing over the filthy one from before. I doubted even she could salvage that one.

The first dress I tried on was a dusty blue colour and had a full skirt, with hooks all down the back of the bodice. It was tricky, and quite a reach for my un-flexible arms, but I was adamant that I was going to fasten the dress myself.

'Say, you're not from around these parts, are you?' Tharva commented, presumably noticing the material of the dress I had just given her. 'Where're you from?' she asked, intrigued. 'Go on, I won't tell!'

I did toy with the idea of telling her, as Tharva came across to me as such a genuine, kind-hearted woman, but in the end I decided to play it safe.

'I'm from somewhere far away from here,' I said

vaguely. 'I got lost, and now I need to get back.'

'Oh, you poor dear!' Tharva said with sympathy, but thankfully did not pry any further.

I exited the changing area to give her a view of the dress on my figure.

Her hand flew to her chest. 'Oh!' she exclaimed. 'It looks perfect on you! Just the way I hoped it would!' I blushed at her words.

'It's only because you made it so well,' I said, throwing the compliment back at her. 'This dress is gorgeous. You have such a talent. You really should advertise more!'

Tharva smiled sweetly. 'Oh, Pepper,' she said with a sigh. 'You're like the daughter I never had!' Did I see tears welling up in her eyes? 'You be careful on the road, now, won't you child? I know you're unfamiliar with our land, and there are many tales of evil lurking here.'

'Thank you for the caution,' I said with a light smile, 'but I'm sure it'll be fine. I won't be staying here much longer; I should be safe.'

Tharva's mouth drew into a flat, grim line and her eyes narrowed as she peered at me. I found myself leaning backwards a little at her scrutiny.

'I have a feeling your journey has only just begun,' she told me cryptically. I was startled for a few moments, unsure how to respond, but then she relaxed, her expression morphing back to the way it was. It was as though she hadn't said anything.

'Would you like a cup of tea?' she asked with a warm smile. The previous discomfort gone, my British tongue started craving the taste of a hot brew. I accepted her offer and went to try on the remaining two dresses while she went to make the drink.

I was fitted in a billowing, burgundy frock by the time Tharva returned with the steaming cup. In between the blue and red dresses, I had tried on a beautiful number with a firm corset and halter-neck strap, but the milky colour of the material had completely washed me out, what with me being so pale and blonde.

I took the drink from Tharva and, upon her insistence, took a seat next to her on the comfy sofa in the middle of the room.

'So when do you plan on returning to Calthorpe Manor?' she asked me before blowing into her own cup.

I stared at her, dumbfounded. 'Wha-how did you . . .'

Her eyes twinkled. 'There's more to this here face than meets the eye!' She chuckled. 'From looking at you now, I am able to tell you more about yourself than you would ever wish to hear.' The look on her face showed mischief. So was that why she'd been looking at me funny? 'So when do you leave?'

'Tomorrow morning,' I said. 'I'm catching the next portal.'

She nodded, but did that strange peering thing again, which I'd now learnt was her seeing deeper into . . . what was she looking at? My soul? My destiny?

'How much do I owe you?' I asked her. 'For the dresses?'

'For a young girl in dire circumstances?' She looked shocked. 'No charge.'

'Really?' I was taken aback by her generosity. 'No wonder you're going out of business if you give all your stock way for nothing!'

But Tharva chuckled and patted my leg. 'Not to everyone, my dear,' she said. 'Just to those in unique situations.'

The sound of wind chimes filled the room. Tharva and I both looked up in surprise as someone entered. I recognised Therron immediately, though he had a strange look on his face. It hadn't been half an hour already, had it?

'Pepper,' he said. His voice had an apprehensive tone to it. Something was troubling him. I set my tea aside and went over to him to check he was okay, but his words preceded mine. 'Do you know this man?' He asked. He stepped aside to reveal someone else standing behind him in the doorway, and I gasped.

How could I mistake the formal attire and smug expression of Maxwell Calthorpe?

KINGDOM

15

RATIONAL FEARS

'*Y*OU.' Tharva screamed, shooting up from the chair. Some of her tea spilt on her skirt as she rose. 'I know who you are!' She ran round to the back of the chair, away from Max and Therron.

I looked between them. She knew Max? How?

Max stepped forward out of the doorway, closely followed by Therron.

'Stay away from me!' Tharva ordered as she flinched. 'You . . . you heathen!' She grabbed one of the cardboard boxes from the floor and shielded herself behind it, as though it would protect her.

183

The man making her shake stepped forward again, and Tharva recoiled in fear. She had no more room to go back. But it wasn't Max she was cowering from.

It was Therron.

'Stay back!' Tharva ordered, her voice trembling. 'Get out of here or . . . or I'll sound the alarm!'

'Wait!' I moved so I stood between both of them, facing Tharva. 'Therron won't hurt you! He wouldn't hurt anyone.' I glanced at him over my shoulder for backup, but he avoided my gaze, staring instead at the wooden floorboards. He didn't say anything. 'Would you?'

'I don't know what kind of lies that monster has been feeding you,' Tharva said, now a completely changed woman from the one who'd given me dresses and made me tea. 'But don't listen to him, Pepper. You remember the evil I was telling you about? That's him.'

Therron still did not look up. He neither confirmed nor denied Tharva's allegations.

No. She had to be wrong. Therron was a kind person. The kindest I'd ever met! Perhaps she mistook him for someone else.

'Therron?' I asked him. 'What's going on?'

He looked up a little, but only enough to look me in the eyes. His gaze passed from me to Tharva. The strange thing was, he looked almost as scared as she did.

'Therron,' spoke Max, 'maybe you should go and wait outside.' Therron turned his wary expression to Max before turning and exiting the shop. Okay, something was definitely up. I would have gone after Therron, but now I was faced with a new dilemma: Max.

'What are you doing here?' There was an accusing bite in my tongue.

Max smirked. 'Is that the greeting I get after following you all the way here? Somehow I thought you'd be happier to see me.'

'Who are you?' Tharva inched forward. Therron may have left, but she still held her cardboard barricade firmly to her chest. 'And why are you working with that monster?'

'Okay, slow down there.' Max held his hands out in front of him. 'I admit the guy may not be on my best friends list, but he's not a monster. Not technically.' He walked away from the door and slumped down on top of the sofa like he owned the place. He reached his arm down beside him to grab my mug of tea and took a huge glug before releasing a satisfied sigh.

I shot him a dirty look. He caught my eye, and just winked as he took another gulp, taking huge pleasure from infuriating me. I deepened my scowl. I didn't want him to know, but underneath it all, there was actually a hint of joy at seeing a familiar face in this foreign land.

'Why are you here?' I tried asking him again. I folded my arms across my chest, unsure of what else to do with myself since Max lay horizontally across the only sitting space. Tharva wasn't so tactful, though. She flapped her arms at Max, shooing him off the chair, grumbling something about feet on the upholstery. She grabbed the mug from him.

'I was following you, naturally,' he said once he stood, giving Tharva the stink eye. 'I'm not the kind to sit idly by when a damsel's in distress.'

'I am not in distress!' I argued. 'I was on my way home. I was in good company!'

Max gave me a curious look. 'With Story-Boy?' He laughed and jerked his thumb in the direction of the door. 'Are you telling me you'd rather have help from a fictional character than a real human being?'

'You're from the manor, too?'

Until Tharva spoke up, I'd almost forgotten she was still there.

Max turned an accusing expression my way. 'You told her you're human?'

'What would it matter?' I said with a shrug. 'You just basically told her, anyway.'

He frowned. 'That was a simple slip of the tongue.

Who else knows you're human? If this gets out, we could be in serious trouble!'

'Then why did you come here?'

'To fix this mess you created!' He raked his fingers through his hair and grunted. 'After you managed to wiggle your way in through the magic security system, the only way to get hold of you was to follow you. That makes this whole damn thing your fault! My father sent me to try and fix things. He seems to think you have some sort of connection to this land through your imagination, because you write stories and stuff.'

Max began to pace the room, pulling out random garments from their hangers, only to sneer and cover them back up. His passiveness was really infuriating me. I was about to demand more answers, when my eyes fell to a spiral-bound notebook that had fallen out of his jeans pocket onto the sofa. I went over and picked it up, but Max was quick. Before I could even open the front page he snatched it off me, ordering that I be more careful with such things.

'What is it?'

'This,' he said, waving the book in my face, 'is the exact mess that I was referring to. It's Therron's story.'

'Therron's . . . wait, give me that!' I reached for the notebook, but I was far shorter than he was. He simply raised the book into the air, causing me to collide into his chest as I tried to grab it. He tilted his head down over my face and smirked. That was when I realised what an awkward position we were in.

'If that was what you wanted, all you had to do was ask,' he said, his voice dangerously husky.

I grunted and pushed him back, turning away to hide the embarrassed colour of my cheeks.

'Why do you have that?' I asked without looking him in the face.

'Because, Oh Naive One, the outcome of Therron's story might just save the whole of Tantary's existence.'

That caught my attention. I looked him in the eyes to find a rare serious expression gracing his features.

'That freak?' Tharva clamoured. 'I refuse to believe it! I've heard some of the things he can do with his magic. It's not natural!'

Oh, I thought. So that was why Tharva was so terrified of him.

Max looked up to the ceiling, his face an image of exasperation. 'I do hate being the voice of reason,' he said to himself as he shook his head. 'Go and fetch us some more tea,' he told Tharva. 'I have a feeling this is going to be a long discussion.'

Tharva was reluctant, but she did as she was told. I went and made myself comfortable back on the sofa and Max came and sat beside me. I scooted further up the other end. He noticed.

'You're still mad about the whole Mr. Calthorpe thing, aren't you?'

I ignored him, suddenly finding my chipped nail varnish extremely interesting.

'You know why I did it though, right?' I still refused to answer. He sighed again, and then tried a different approach. 'I've thought about what you said at the party—and—I understand why you're upset. It was wrong of me to lie. So I'm sorry.' Catching the sincerity in his voice, I chanced a look up, and gave him a soft smile of gratitude.

'But you did overreact, you must admit,' he added. The look I gave him must have scared him, as he held his hands up in front of him and swiftly added, 'Hey, hey, I was just saying!'

A few minutes later, I heard Tharva's muttered cusses as she scrambled through the mess of the stock room with the hot cups of tea. Running to her aid, I took two of the drinks from her to save her from scalding herself. With her free hand, she dragged the chair out from behind her desk and placed it beside the sofa. She and I turned to look at Max expectantly.

I watched him struggle for words for a few moment, not knowing where to begin. Failing to find the right words, he changed his mind and instead reached down for his rucksack he discarded on the floor earlier. I hadn't even noticed him bring it in.

He fished out a large book and flung it onto my lap. 'Recognise that?' he asked.

In front of me was the novel that I had been reading in the manor: *The Kingdom*. I understood what he meant, remembering my earlier conversation with Therron.

'I already know,' I said, doing nothing to help the smug smile that surfaced. 'Calpacious is the King of Tantary.'

Tharva's eyes widened in wonder at the book on my lap; the King's story.

Max tilted his head in challenge. 'Well then,' he said, 'you must already know Tantary is under huge threat. Calpacious is no less power-hungry here than he is in the book. If you've been paying any kind of attention, then you should know only the well-intentioned characters can cross into our world.'

'Yes.' I was unsure as to what he was getting at. 'So . . .'

'Well it's not that way anymore. That spell is weakening. It has become old and fragile. There have been reported sightings of other magicks—darker ones—who have made it through the portal. And now, thanks to you and your escapology act, it's getting even weaker. The only reason I was able to follow you in was because you've loosened the barrier between the two worlds.'

I dropped my gaze back down to the book.

'How did you get through, anyway?' Max probed.

'I was hiding.' I grimaced at the memory of running from the party, and that awful man, Cedrick. 'I found a cupboard. Or, what I thought was a cupboard. I don't really know how it happened. It was so fast. I just remember waking up in a forest.'

'That was the mirror.' Max nodded. 'You used up too much of its energy. It couldn't cloak itself after you left, so I was able to find it.'

'I'm sorry. I didn't mean to.' A child-like echo rang inside my head, screaming how much I wanted to go home.

'So what's this all mean?' Tharva interjected. 'Anybody can just pop in and out of Tantary as they please?'

Max looked relatively relaxed about all this, considering. 'Maybe not yet,' he said as he reclined against the back of the sofa, 'but in time, yes. It's all part of Calpacious' plan to destroy Tantary and live in the real world like in the old days.' His expression remained unconcerned as he added, 'It is rumoured he plans on using our world as his new home. He has enough story characters now to build an entire army, and with the spell breaking, they will be able to take over much more than just the manor.'

Tharva remained silent, clinging to Max's every word. I could see the confusion creasing her brow. I don't think the idea of leaving her shop for a full-fledged war had her all that excited.

'That's really his plan?' I asked Max.

'That's what my father said. I don't tend to argue with him when it comes to Tantary stuff. It's not really my domain.'

'But surely Calpacious couldn't have planned on me coming here.'

'No,' he said, 'but you've certainly sped up the process.'

I sipped my tea as my brain tried to take in all of this. So, somehow, the combination of writing stories and being chased from a party by a madman had led to a threat for the destruction of the world. Apparently.

'How do you plan on stopping this?' Tharva asked when nothing else was said.

'We have that under control,' answered Max. 'Or at least, we thought we did. This is why Therron is so important.' He handed Therron's story to me. 'Here, read this,' he said.

I only peered at him for a few moments before opening the cover of the tiny notebook. Tharva peered over the book from beside me, trying to read it too.

The jerky handwriting read:

Once, there lived a simple man. He never wanted for much. He respected nature as nature respected him—with true appreciation of its hidden value. In a land ravaged by war, this young man stood firmly above it.

'Did you write this?' I asked incredulously as I read.

'Not me. My father.'

With magical powers of the likes no others had seen before, the hero who was destined to one day rescue the land's rightful king, Alzabar, was the young man named Therron.

The handwriting suddenly changed. The words became more flowing, looking nothing like any handwriting I'd ever seen. Upon Max's prompting, I read on.

Therron stood atop the cliff, concealed by the trees in his advantageous viewpoint. Through his spyglasses, he saw the castle in all its foreboding glory. The King was up to something. He felt it.

But he felt something else, too—another's presence. Instantly alert, Therron grew still as footsteps drew nearer, presuming it to be one of the King's guards. But his stance only grew tighter when he realised the footfalls were too soft, too delicate, to be those of a soldier. His body was as rigid as the tree he stood behind. Who else knew of his hiding spot?

The steps came to a stop, not far from where he stood. Breath held, Therron chanced a glance around the trunk of the tree, and swallowed a gasp when he saw the person standing there.

He had never seen her before, that was for sure. For if he had, he would have certainly recognised her. Blonde hair blew in billows behind her back and a serene smile kissed her flushed cheeks with dimples. Her elegant attire suggested nobility. Who was she?

Therron kept back in the shadows, for fear of disturbing her. He was about to turn away and leave when his enhanced hearing picked up on the sound of soldiers patrolling the perimeter. Usually, he would make as little noise as possible, staying hidden in this blind spot on the cliff's ledge. But what about the girl? If they found her trespassing in these woods, they would take her to the King, and who knew what would happen then?

Therron tried to tell himself it wasn't his place to get involved, and he should let the girl succumb to whatever fate awaited her. But there was this other, unfamiliar part of him that felt he needed to help. The guards were almost upon them when, in an act of either bravery or stupidity—he wasn't quite sure— Therron charged towards the girl and clamped his hand around her mouth before pulling her down to the floor behind a fallen tree.

'I'm not sure I want to read any more,' I told Max, my hands shaking a little as I closed the book and began to hand it back to him. I knew without reading any further that the girl in this story was me. Reading our first meeting from Therron's perspective felt like a breach of privacy on my part. I couldn't do it.

Max took the book.

'How does it do that?' I asked. 'How am I in Therron's story?'

'Because you messed things up,' Max reiterated. 'Thanks to your meddling, we can't complete Therron's story. We can't make him into the hero he needs to be to free Alzabar. We're going to have to undo everything you've done here.'

'And how are you going to do that?' asked Tharva. Having read the first few pages of his story, she didn't seem to have quite the prejudice against him she'd had before.

'By deleting Therron and starting over again with a new hero. You're a writer—you should be able to help us create one who won't fail this time.'

My eyes widened. 'Deleting?' I echoed. 'You mean . . .' Max nodded. 'No!' I snatched the book back from him. 'I can't let you kill him! You've met Therron—he's a real person with a life and a past! You can't take that away from him. I won't help you.

Not if it comes at the cost of Therron's life.'

I knew I'd angered him when Max's face started to burn red. 'Are you really trying to defend him?' he fumed. 'Pepper, he's not real! You can't let compassion get in the way of what has to be done.'

'I don't care,' I refuted. 'There is no way you can get me to agree to this. Even if you were planning to spare Therron, I wouldn't help you with whatever plan you're trying to conceive. For whatever reason, my presence is changing Therron's story. If I stay here, I can help him write his own destiny. I've seen his potential. He can become a great hero! Just you wait and see.'

'Fine!' Max bellowed. An angry vein on his forehead popped forward as he spat his words at me. I tried my best to stand firm and not let myself shrink back. 'If you think Therron is so great, you go and teach him. It won't work. He's an incomplete character; he'll never be able to rescue Alzabar. It's a good thing I never cared about Tantary, because it will soon be dead!' Grabbing his empty rucksack, he didn't even bother retrieving *The Kingdom* from where I left it on the sofa before he stormed out of Tharva's shop, slamming the door behind him.

I only had one choice now. I had to turn Therron into a hero. If I couldn't, then the spell would break, and all hell would be let loose.

16

PERILOUS CHOICES

Tharva offered for Therron and me to stay the night at her place. I was extremely grateful, knowing she was still wary of Therron and his powers.

After Max's dramatic exit, Tharva and I agreed not to tell Therron about the book just yet. In the morning, things would be different. But right now, it was getting dark, and both of us were weary from the long journey.

Getting to Tharva's place was like walking through a maze in the angular, reflective architecture of the Tropolis. Tharva lived high up in the city. Her apartment—which is what I guessed it was called—was perched on top of two other buildings, joining them kind of like a bridge. I enjoyed another sample of Tantary's weird yet wonderful food, as prepared by Tharva, before we settled down to rest for the night.

Tharva's compact, sparsely decorated home had only been built to accommodate one. Two at most. Tharva kept in her room, leaving Therron and me to choose between the sofa and the floor.

While I was more than happy to bunk on the floor, Therron insisted I take the sofa. After a lot of persistence, I finally gave in. I took the sofa, and Therron camped on the patchwork blanket—the only thing protecting him from the cold metal floor below.

From where I lay, I had a full view of the entire room around me in the dim light of the gas lamp on the table top. If you were to strip back all the furnishings and the decorative upholstery, that were clearly the work of Tharva's talented hand, you would be left with a bare, tin-can kind of structure. The walls, floors and ceilings were pure metal, which would account for the mirror effect when you were up in the sky. You could see that Tharva had done her best to add as much of her personality to the house as she could, but the genericity of the building still crept through. I decided I much preferred Therron's handmade cabin in the woods.

'What did you say to Tharva?' Therron asked me out of the blue as I was about to drift off to sleep. 'While I was out of the shop, what did you say to her? She seems to have forgiven me for being . . . me.'

I twisted myself under the thin blanket to look at where he lay across the room from me. In the darkened room, I could barely discern his silhouette on the floor, staring up at the ceiling in thought. My hand instinctively went to the notebook I had wedged against my skin under the bodice of Tharva's dress. Gifted seamstress though she was, she had no suitable night clothes to lend us.

Therron's question was a weighted one, and I had no inclination to tell him the whole truth. Not yet, anyway. For now, I decided to take a side-on approach.

'Tharva has an ability of her own,' I told him. 'She can see glimpses of people's destiny—their intentions, and a few other factors beyond our control. Her power is weak, but Max and I convinced her to open herself up to your fate.'

Therron quieted. Whether he was annoyed about having his intentions read or not, I couldn't tell. I was nearly asleep when he spoke up again.

'Who is this Max guy?' he asked me. 'How do you know him?'

'Lives in the Manor,' I mumbled in my semiconscious state. 'One of the people I'm working for. Must've followed me when the portal sucked me in.'

'After Archie left, said Therron, 'Max approached me outside one of the shops. When he said he knew me, I thought he was going to tell me what an unnatural abomination I am, like Tharva did. But then he told me he was looking for you. I don't know how he knew you were in the Tropolis. Did you know he was here?'

I told him I didn't.

It was the book. I knew that, though I couldn't tell Therron as much. It was the book that led Max to me. The book that transcribed everything Therron did and felt as it happened. The book that I could so easily reach out from under my clothing and show him. I couldn't deny the temptation that kept prodding me to sneak a peek, but my conscience kept the urge at bay. Despite what Max said, Therron was a real person, with a real person's right for privacy. It angered me that Max could think anything otherwise.

'I'm not interested in anything Max does. He infuriates me too much,' I said. I smiled to myself, imagining his hurt little face if ever he heard me saying that.

I heard Therron let out a sigh of relief. 'Oh, that's good,' he said.

'What?'

'I don't feel so bad for disliking him myself, now.'

I chuckled. By this point, in my mental scenario, Max would be storming right out of the room, making a big show of slamming the door behind him, much like he had done in Tharva's shop.

I wondered where he was now. I assumed he went straight home, but considering the portal didn't open until the morning, that couldn't be. I hoped he found a place to stay the night. As much as I despised him at the moment, I didn't want him sleeping out on the streets. With the Bawntide celebrations, we were extremely lucky to come across Tharva, even if she was a little hostile towards Therron at first. I thought about the confrontation more and, tired though I was, the cogs finally began to click themselves into place.

'You mentioned you've been to the Tropolis once before,' I said, testing my words. Therron's ensuing silence egged me on. 'Tharva's not the only one here who fears you, is she?' I heard a subtle change in Therron's breathing as it became heavier. I could tell I'd hit a raw spot, and I probably shouldn't have kept on, but the curiosity was too much. 'Therron, what happened?'

I expected him to remain silent at my probing, but to my surprise, he began to explain.

'It was two years ago,' he said. The depth and weight of his reflective voice told me to be prepared for a long story. 'When I first arrived in Tantary, like all new characters, I appeared in the Square—the centre of the Tropolis. Each new arrival is reported to the King, and he is the one who decides what happens to you, where you're to live, et cetera.

'But it wasn't long after my appearance that I started exhibiting these weird, unnatural abilities. I was thirsty; I got water to float in the air in front of me. I was tired; I softened the road below so I could sleep. I had no control over what I did—it just happened. A group of ten guards came to escort me to the King's castle, a little over a day's journey away. We barely got half way before I was on my own again. Whatever I thought, it would just happen. My mind barely had to graze the idea, and that was it.'

I propped myself up on the sofa, intrigued by his story.

'I tried my best, I really did, but one stray fear led an eagle to swoop down and carry one of the men off. A wish for better weather made two more pass out from the heat. And a pang of hunger turned another into a full roast sadgia dinner.'

I bit down on my lip to prevent a giggle escaping at that one. Turning into a fictional vegetable was no laughing matter.

'It would have been fine, had a chimera not intercepted our path, initiating what should have been an easy battle for the trained guards. But my disobedient powers interfered. In a torrent of raging emotions, the rest of the guards, and the beast, were left incinerated, asphyxiated, or running for the hills. I didn't know what to do, so I fled. People were going to find me. They would kill me for what I did. I built myself the discreet cabin beside the lake and worked on controlling my powers.'

Throughout his whole retelling, there was not a single break in his voice—no sign he was about to lose hold of his emotions. And I admired him for that.

'But you've got control over them now,' I commented, in reference to his abilities. 'At least, if the fact that I haven't been burnt to a crisp is anything to go by.' He did chuckle a little at that. 'So why haven't you come back?' Still looking at where he lay, I saw that his posture had not changed in the slightest. The only movement I could make out was the regulated rise and fall of his chest as he breathed.

'For a few reasons,' he answered. 'Penelope and I have worked out a thriving, self-sufficient life alone in the woods. I'm happy there. I wouldn't want to leave.'

'And?' I probed, noting he'd only given me one reason.

'And . . . I guess there was always the fear they wouldn't accept me here,' he admitted. 'A lot happened back then. Many people got hurt because of me. I wouldn't blame them if they never want to see my face again.'

So Therron had lived alone the entire time he had existed here. He cast himself out through his own fear of hurting others. He may have been keeping a tight lid on his emotions, but I couldn't control mine so well. My eyes stung as my tear ducts swelled.

'And yet you're back now,' I observed. 'You're back . . . because of me.'

This time he did move. I heard the swoosh of fabric as he rolled himself around, though I couldn't tell if he was facing me or the back of the sofa.

'You're the first person to ever accept me for who I truly am, Pepper,' he said. 'That, I will never forget.'

I wanted to say more, expected him to say more, but neither of us did. In the silence of the silvery room, I fell asleep thinking about the secret I was keeping from him.

'*P*epper . . . Pepper, wake up! PEPPER!'
I jolted awake. My hip hurt from where it was pressed against the hard sofa, and I could feel my neck had cricked, too. I expected it to be light when I opened my eyes, but when I did, there was

only the sheath of darkness lingering outside the window. I couldn't have been asleep for more than a few hours. It was Tharva who shook me from my slumber.

'It wasn't me,' she insisted, her face fraught with fear. 'I swear, I didn't tell a soul!'

I rose, rubbing my eyes, and asked her what she was talking about. It was then I heard the sound of a blaring siren.

'It's the alarm,' Therron said. He was already up and fumbling for his satchel. 'It means everyone needs to evacuate. It's only sounded when the Tropolis is under threat.'

'I overheard a conversation down on the street through my open window,' Tharva went on to explain. 'One of the guards was alerted there are humans free in this land. Bawntide celebrations have been cancelled and everyone is to flee the Tropolis and report to the castle immediately where a census will be reviewed.'

Panic-stricken, I jumped off the sofa and started looking for my things, before realising I didn't have any. 'What do we do?' I asked Tharva.

'You run,' she said.

Tharva raced around the apartment, grabbing various items and sticking them in a blue shoulder bag. Food, flasks, flannels, and clothes, as well as

Calpacious' book, were squashed into the sack before she shoved it into my hands. She saw us down the outside stairs and into the bustling street. 'You need to find Alzabar,' she said. 'Calpacious knows you're here—he will stop at nothing until you and Max are both dead. Me too, probably! This is it. The war is nearly upon us. This madness has to end. Find the brother!'

That was all she said, no goodbyes or anything, before she pushed us away and we scrambled through the frenzied crowds in an attempt to escape the Tropolis. I wondered briefly where Archie had got to now, and whether he was caught up in this chaos, too. Above me, I could see all the phoenixes, dragons, griffins, and their respective riders all travelling in the same direction—towards the castle. The troll was probably up there with Bel.

I relied on Therron to lead us out of the Tropolis, for I had no idea where I was going. Each road looked just the same as the next, especially in the dark and among a frantic throng of people. For the most part, we followed the grain of the horde, veering away when the on-looking guards turned the other way.

There was only one exit from the town: through a large opening in the surrounding circle of trees. Once we got through there, there would be no hiding from the King's guardsmen. It had been Therron's move to pull both of us round the back of a small shack, where we crouched awhile to wait out the crowd and recapture our breath. The gap was large enough to fit the two of us, but small enough that people weren't using this as a path to get to the exit. We remained veiled until the worst of the crowd died down. It felt like longer than it was. In this compact alleyway, we had to press together quite tightly so as not to be seen. I surprised myself how aware I was of Therron's bicep pressed against mine, rising and falling with his breath.

'Pepper,' Therron said once his breathing had evened out. 'I'm not sure we should be doing this.'

'What?'

'Finding the King's brother. It-it's not a good idea. It's really not our place to intervene. Maybe we should leave it to someone like Archie to deal with.'

I slumped my shoulders. This was not the way it should be going. I considered right there and then to tell Therron all about the book, but something inside me urged me not to. What if he resented it and ran away?

'Listen to me, Therron.' I looked him right in the eyes. 'There is very likely a bounty on my head at this moment, and I can't even imagine the price they must have set for yours by now. The King is obviously up to no good—by the looks of things, he's planning for an all-out war. If we've got the chance to try and hinder his plans, then why turn the other way? The question you should be asking yourself is, why *not* you? Why shouldn't you be the one to bring an end to all this? I believe in you, Therron. I know you can do this. And I am going to be right here, by your side.'

From the side, I saw the muscles in his jaw twitch as he deliberated. 'But what about you?' he said. 'You're supposed to catch the portal in a couple of hours. I can't ask you to give up going home in aid of saving a land that isn't even your own.'

I calmed a little. That was a reason I could deal with. I turned and smiled at him, which caught him a little off-guard. 'That's a pathetic excuse,' I teased. Now that the roaring of the mob had died down, the atmosphere around us was a lot more tranquil. I kept my voice down, anyway, just in case there were any lingering guards. 'I'm not giving up anything. I want to see this land free of the tyrant king as much as you do. As far as I'm concerned, this *is* my land. I have friends here. You, Tharva, Archie—you're all a part of my life now. The truth is, home isn't what you pay the rent for. It's where your heart truly lies.' And I didn't feel bad for saying that, because I knew, book or no book, it was true.

17

DANGEROUS QUESTS

*I*t was a while before we felt secure enough to walk at a leisurely pace. Once the crowds dissipated, we'd squeezed out through the trees and sprinted far away from the Tropolis. By now, the whole kingdom would be alerted there was a human on the run, so we tried to keep as low a profile as possible, taking all the mountainous routes and hidden valley paths, and avoiding any built-up areas.

We crested a hill where we stopped to rest our feet. The balls of my feet were still bruised from all the walking we did the day before, and they were throbbing now in protest, sensing another long journey ahead of them.

Therron retrieved his spyglasses from his satchel

and surveyed our surroundings while I delved into the bag of goodies Tharva gave us. I dug around inside to find two loaves of rich, fruity bread. My tummy gurgled in anticipation.

The view was, once again, spectacular. I silently wondered if there was anything in this land that would fail to take my breath away. Since we deliberately took the hilly route, every direction we turned in we were greeted by the land swelling up and plunging down, with little views of anything man-made. The sun was now waking from its slumber, squinting through the bevels of the horizon as it prepared to climb the rest of the way. The landscape flooded with a warm, orange glow. I was grateful for the heat. Though I was fairly warm from climbing the hill, I was fast becoming chilly as my heart rate slowed back to resting.

It was Therron's idea to climb the peak. He decided it would be good to gain a full vision of where we were and which direction we were heading in.

'Do you have any idea where this other king might be?' I asked him when he was done with the surveillance check and came to join me for some breakfast. He shook his head as he took a bite of the moist bread.

'For all that I've been eavesdropping on the castle,'

he said when he finished his mouthful, 'I have never heard the name Alzabar. Above that, I didn't even know Calpacious had a brother. I hope your friend's right, and he really is here in our land.'

I fished *The Kingdom* out of the Tharva's shoulder bag and laid it in front of me. 'Maybe there are some clues in here as to where he might be,' I pondered. I opened up the pages, but when I slid it over to Therron for a closer look, he flinched away, eyeing the book like it was about to bite him.

'Is there something wrong?' I asked.

'No.' Therron blinked, shaking his head as though trying to wake himself from a daze. 'It's just . . . it's well known that magicks can never see the books from the manor. When they visit the real world in person, they remain invisible to our sight. Just the way we do to humans.'

Well, I guess that explained Tharva's astonishment at this book the day before. 'Maybe things work differently here,' I suggested, but his words created a knot in my stomach. I hoped nothing bad would come of having books in this land. I was breaking the rules faster than I could understand them.

I was on edge. I knew that. Especially since our abrupt flee from the Tropolis. That whole debacle had brought to light just what a risky business this all was.

That wasn't the only thing scaring me, though. I

213

didn't like the idea of being in control of Therron's fate. I was letting what Max said get to me, and found myself looking out for every possibility where things could go horribly wrong. It's fine, I tried to tell myself. Nothing bad is going to happen. Max wouldn't have brought *The Kingdom* and Therron's book here if they were going to endanger the magicks . . . would he? Well, I assumed that, if somehow having the book here would send Tantary spiralling into a black hole or something, it would have happened before when Max brought them here.

Therron startled me when he went to pick up the book and commenced flicking through the pages. I gasped and waited, but Therron didn't disintegrate, the book didn't explode, and no black holes appeared. I breathed out with relief, feeling foolish.

'How much have you read?' Therron asked me, realising that simply leafing through the pages wasn't going to give him any answers.

'I read the whole thing back when I was younger. I'm afraid I don't remember a lot of it, though.' I'd wanted to read more at the manor, but the whole incident with getting spontaneously sucked into a magical portal hindered me from doing so.

'Do you remember any significant details that might help us find him?'

I stretched my mind back. 'For five years, before

he came back to the kingdom, Alzabar was out on crusades,' I said, unable to think of anything else that could be marginally helpful.

'For a whole five years?' Therron questioned. 'He must have rested at some point. Did he set up a camp? Or was there somewhere he visited a lot?'

Something in his words triggered a vague memory. 'Hang on a second,' I told him and took back the book. I flicked through the pages before coming to a stop. I found it!

'"A week's rest he'd have, though far from often,"' I read aloud, '"wherehence he'd shelter down past the battlefields of old 'til war called upon him once again."'

He peered over my shoulder and re-read the words himself. 'I don't understand.'

'The battlefields of old—fields which had been destroyed by the battles and then discarded,' I explained.

Therron's eyes widened, understanding what I was saying. 'It's genius!' he said. 'No one would have expected him to set up camp there!'

I was only temporarily delighted. 'But that's only in the book,' I stated. 'There aren't any old battlefields around here, are there?'

'Not as such, no.' Therron's optimism did not dampen. 'But there is talk of a city—an ancient city—

that got destroyed when Calpacious took the throne. The place is real, but the story is just a legend; no one remembers far back enough to know the truth. Though I'll bet you anything it's where the real Alzabar is hiding.'

'Perfect!' I said, happy we were actually getting somewhere. Maybe everything was going to be okay after all. 'How do we get there?'

Therron pulled me up by my arm to standing, then, with his hand on the small of my back, span me around and held the spyglasses up to my eyes. 'You see that patch of green over there? The one that's a slightly different shade to the rest.'

'Yes. I see it.'

'That's the Old City. A place steeped in more mystery and legend than the rest of Tantary put together.' He lowered the binoculars and I looked up to meet his eyes.

'Tell me.'

At first, I thought he wouldn't, as he continued to stand there, with one palm against my back, gazing down at me. I nearly lost my breath at the depth of his eyes, sparkling emerald in the light of the rising sun. It couldn't have been more than a few seconds before he remembered himself and stepped away.

'There is a legend,' he said, staring out at the little patch of brown-green off in the far distance, 'of a beast who fought in the Initial Battles—the revolt that occurred soon after all the magicks found themselves banished here. This monster, an ogre, was driven crazy by the endless years of conflict, and eventually became unable to distinguish which side he was on, attacking anyone who came near him. And, as an ogre, with his formidable size and strength, he always won. Legend has it, he still lives there, alone in the Old City, battling the ghosts of the war victims. It's said he believes the wars have been carrying on for the last hundred years.'

'What a sad story,' I remarked, gazing off into the city where the ill-fated beast allegedly roamed. 'Is it true?'

Therron shook his head. 'No one has ever gone back to find out. But if it's true, and he's as dangerous as rumours say, then we'd do best to keep our profiles low—remain on the outskirts and stay hidden.' At his warning, my confidence went, and I was left once again with a heavy weight of trepidation.

'It'll be fine though, right?' I asked, hoping for assurance. 'I mean, if we do happen to run into the monster, you can deal with it, can't you? Just like you did with the guardsman in the forest the day I arrived.'

'Yeah,' Therron said, though his resigned tone and the way he dropped his head to the grassy hilltop

217

countered his words. 'Sure. Just like that.' I was going to ask what the problem was, but he quickly regained his natural posture. 'I guess we'd best get going then,' he said, 'if we want to make it by nightfall.'

'Nightfall?!' I repeated, my eyes bulging. It was barely dawn! 'Wait, don't tell me,' I said to Therron's bemused expression. 'We're walking again, aren't we?'

18

GROWING SUSPICIONS

*T*herron had exaggerated about the time it would take to get to the Old City. He did it just to wind me up, which I was annoyed about, but not overly. Frankly, my feet were thankful for the short—ish—journey.

We approached the outskirts of the city shortly after noon. The restricted view from the hilltop earlier hadn't given the slightest hint about what was really down here. I had to swallow down my heart as I took in the huge, dilapidated stone archway that was the once ornate gateway to the city. Reclaimed by nature, the extinct town was being slowly strangled by vines, weeds, and various species of fungus. It was clear this place had been neglected for many, many years.

The crumbling arch was a frame for the two-tiered flight of stone steps that ascended on a steep incline. From what I could see from down here, it looked like something out of a horror movie. Everything about it gave me excited shivers. Perhaps the most haunting detail of all, though, was the plethora of metal armour pieces that had sunken into the earth around us, becoming features of the mossy ground.

All was deathly silent.

'How can anyone live here?' I whispered, as though speaking any louder would shatter what was left of the place.

'You'll be surprised what a man can scavenge when he's desperate for survival.' Therron hauled his satchel higher up on his shoulder.

Without waiting for him to say so, I started heading for the stone steps.

'Where are you going?' called Therron from behind me.

I paused and turned back to face him. 'Um . . . to find Alzabar?'

'Not that way,' he said, 'it's too dangerous. We need to stick to the outskirts.'

'How do you propose we do that when Alzabar's in there?' I argued, pointing back up the stairs.

I half expected Therron to get mad and raise his voice, but he remained surprisingly calm and collected. 'We don't know that yet,' he said quietly. 'It's not worth risking our necks if he's not in there. We should search around for clues first.'

He was right. Barrelling straight in there probably wasn't the wisest idea, as much as the thought excited me. I turned to continue walking around the edge of the city, when I noticed Therron had stilled, staring at something beyond the rocks.

'What is it?' I asked, feeling my body go cold.

Without moving his gaze, Therron put his finger to his lips and beckoned me over towards him. When I approached, he pointed towards what caught his eye, just the other side of a shattered boulder. As soon as it came into sight, my jaw fell slack.

'Is that—' I rasped. Therron nodded.

'A wild pegasus.'

I watched in awe as the crystalline-white horse took a drink from the stream that trickled out from the ruins. Its mane and tail were pale brown, and shimmered with iridescence in the reflections from the water. The ends of its flowing mane floated on the surface of the water she drank from.

'They're extremely rare, you know,' Therron informed me as she drank. I assumed it was female. 'One of the rarest species in Tantary. But one of the

221

most beautiful, too.' He wasn't wrong there. The creature had such elegance, the likes of which I had never seen before. 'I had no idea they lived around these parts.'

I kept my breathing steady as I studied the winged horse, afraid any sudden sound or movement might startle her. As though sensing our presence, the pegasus lifted her head from the water, her tresses dripping with the sparkling fluid. Slowly, she turned her head to face us. Her eyes were a striking azure blue. They immediately spoke of magic and wisdom. She couldn't have been more than twelve feet away. I could easily walk up and stroke her.

But I didn't have to. After blinking at us once, she stretched her enormous, feathery wings out behind her and came sauntering, ever so slowly, towards us. My heart fluttered inside my chest.

About five paces in front of us, she stopped. Her ears twitched, like she heard something we hadn't. Still entranced by her majesty, I watched her flip her head to the side, narrowing her eyes at whatever seemed to have caught her attention. She began to stroll away from us, her gait speeding up to a trot. Soon, she was inside the city, and we lost sight of her. I wanted to go after her, but Therron held me back.

'This is her territory,' he said. 'We should leave her in peace.'

We only moved a couple of steps away when a loud whinnying sounded from within the city. Therron and I looked at each other. The noise came again, only this time it was more urgent. It sounded like the pegasus was in pain.

'Stay here,' Therron said, and moved to take off after the sound, but this time it was my turn to pull him back.

'You can't leave me here,' I told him. 'And I'm not leaving you to go in there by yourself.'

He pulled away. 'No,' he resolved, 'it's too dangerous in there.'

'Which is exactly why I won't let you go alone.' I left no room for him to argue. I took off in the direction the pegasus had gone with Therron trailing closely behind me. We hurried up a slope, not quite as steep as the one the steps were built on, but steep enough to give us—or at least me—difficulty keeping a fast pace. We followed it up a ways, but the pegasus was nowhere to be seen. Out of breath, I leaned over so my hands were on my knees and I tried to take big gulps of air. Man, I really needed to get fit.

'Pepper,' Therron said. Something about the way he said my name made me look up. I saw exactly what he did.

The place was eerie. Stone houses lined up in perfectly straight lines across several streets, hauntingly symmetrical. All of them were covered in ivy and crumbling to the ground. Again, more armour was strewn across the landscape. Only this time, some of the formations resembled the figures of the people who died wearing them. The bones probably still lay inside the metal casing.

There was still no sign of the pegasus.

We strode down one of the streets, cautious not to make too much sound. Our silence was probably futile, considering how we stormed in here just moments ago. The primitive stonework of this city was a far cry from the chrome labyrinth that was the Tropolis. The magicks had certainly evolved a lot over the last hundred years. I scoured the streets and what looked like shop fronts for any clues as to where Alzabar might be, but considering I didn't really know what I was looking for, it didn't do much good.

Tree roots had prised the cobbles up from underneath the road, and earth and rocks created hazards everywhere I stepped. I still wore the flat, beige shoes from Adrian's party, except they definitely weren't beige anymore. They were soggy and grimy, and starting to fall apart. I was beginning to wish I'd asked Tharva for some new ones. It occurred to me then how, this whole time I had known Therron, he'd never worn anything on his feet. I wondered how much they were hurting him right about now.

'Have you found anything?' I asked after skipping over several mounds of shattered rock to catch up to him.

He nodded. 'Yes.'

'Where?' I asked, wondering why he hadn't pointed anything out before.

'All around you.'

I looked around, but failed to catch his drift.

'You see the emblem on that wall over there?' he asked, gesturing to a symbol etched into one of the stones. The mark was an outline of an eagle standing tall in the centre of a six-pointed star. 'That's the Royal Crest. Or similar to it, at least.'

I cocked my head to the side as I peered at the engraving. 'I've seen that mark before,' I said, and traced my steps back a few paces. 'Right . . . here.' I pointed down at one of the cobbles on the road. It had been dislodged from its original position and lay on its side, but the mark was as clear as day.

'It's like I said.' Therron pointed along the whole road. 'It's all around you. Just like the mark of Bawntide at the Tropolis.'

My eyes widened as I suddenly began to notice the exact same design repeated several times in the stonework around me. But I was still confused.

'What does it mean?' I asked him.

'This isn't the mark of King Calpacious,' he answered. 'It's very similar, but it's not the same. It means this city, when it was inhabited, was reigned over by a different king.'

'Alzabar!' A touch of glee brightened me for all of two seconds before curiosity hit me once again.

'Weren't some of the magicks in Tantary here from the time the land was created?' I asked. 'Shouldn't they remember?'

Therron walked further down the street, avoiding the piles of rubble as he did. I followed.

'You would have thought so. So much of this doesn't add up. There are a few survivors old enough to remember the Old City, yet no one can recall being governed by anyone other than King Calpacious. I have a feeling we are dealing with a lot more here than we could have ever imagined.' He looked contemplative. 'We need to get a hand on this town's records,' he stated. 'As far as I know, no one's seen them since the Initial Battles. Perhaps they can give us some idea as to what we are dealing with. The only explanation I can find at the moment is that those who do remember a hundred years back do not remember as clearly as the think they do.'

I thought about his words. I guess it kind of made sense; I was only eighteen, and even I struggled to remember further than a few years back. For someone who'd been alive for a hundred years, it was understandable for some of their memories to be a little dubious.

'So, this other king,' I said as I contemplated, 'do you really think it was Alzabar?'

'I guess we can only find out.'

Coming off the road, we merged onto some crossroads, with what must have once been a spectacular fountain standing in the middle. Now it was just a moss-clad ruin.

'Therron, look!'

I needn't have said anything though, as Therron spotted what I had at exactly the same time: A castle.

The structure stood upon a hill, not far away from where we stood. From its position, it would have had the perfect view of the entire city.

It may have looked close, but it took us a fair while to reach it. Up close, the castle was even more breathtaking. I couldn't imagine what it looked like back when it was still intact, but the ruins themselves were a sight to behold.

The door groaned in protest as Therron heaved it open. Debris and dust rained down as it squeaked on its blackened hinges. Inside, every sound echoed off the stone walls, and the whole place looked and smelt dingy. From the outlook, it certainly didn't seem as though anyone could survive here: dust and rubble lay on the floor inches thick, and the non-existent roof made it very hard to imagine living here.

The two of us looked all over, searching for any sign Alzabar still lived here—a half-eaten loaf of bread, or a clean bedsheet, or something like that. But there was nothing.

'Looks like we've found a dead end,' Therron said as he walked back over to me.

'Stop!' I said, holding my hands out in front of me. He gave me a funny look. 'Go back a few steps.' He was hesitant, but did as he was told.

No, my ears were not deceiving me—there was a very audible creaking sound every time Therron stepped on one particular area of the floor. Considering the floor was made of stone, this was very odd indeed.

'Help me move some of this.'

Therron joined me as I began digging at the mud and wreckage. I continued to scrape away until my nails scraped against something solid and flat. It only took a little more clearing to reveal the rest of the wooden hatch in the middle of the floor. Therron and I exchanged glances.

A tiny hole, just big enough to fit my finger through, served as a handle. To my surprise, when I lifted it, the trapdoor came easily open. I inched towards the ladder that plummeted into the darkness below.

'Are you sure about this?' Therron questioned when he saw the intention in my eyes. 'From the looks of that dirt we just removed, no one's been down there in years.'

'There might be some clues,' I reminded him. 'Plus I've always wanted to investigate a haunted castle cellar! You got a light?'

Therron shook his head.

'What about your magic? Can you light a candle? There's bound to be one around here somewhere.'

'I'd rather not—'

'Never mind. I think I might have some matches in here.' I reached into the bag Tharva had packed for us, and sure enough, out came an unopened box of matches. I knew I'd seen one in there earlier!

I took a deep breath, looking down into the black abyss before me. 'Are you coming?' I asked Therron. He shrugged in response.

'Apparently so.'

I lit a match and descended the steep ladder, which moaned in warning with every step I took. Therron wisely decided to wait until I got to the bottom before beginning his descent. Once down, I handed the matchbox to Therron so he could light one himself. It wasn't much of a difference, but at least now we could see one another.

My bravado was false. I think it was pure adrenaline which kept me going. I landed on the floor of the cellar, my heart thumping an unnatural rhythm as we surveyed what looked to be some kind of armoury. Swords and spears poised along the one wall in perfect alignment, and I couldn't help but run my hand over the hilt of one of the silvery weapons. It was cold and smooth, and hummed at the prospect of going back into battle.

Along the far wall was an entire collection of armour pieces: breastplates, helms, and gauntlets, as well as many other parts I didn't know the names of, were stacked high against the wall, all in pristine condition.

I walked around the crypt, looking everywhere to try and find some sort of clue. Something personal of Alzabar's, perhaps.

'This place is incredible,' Therron remarked. His words bounced off the stone walls, reverberating around the room. I held up the match in front of me, intrigued by the sight before me. Like the rest of the castle, the place looked barren and felt isolated. No signs of life anywhere. It looked like we had reached yet another dead end.

'Maybe we should go,' Therron suggested. 'I don't think we're going to find Alzabar here.'

Therron moved back towards the ladder, and I

moved to follow him, but something caught my eye.

'Hold on,' I told him.

Tucked away in one of the corners sat a wooden writing desk. The top was coated in dust, and the chair had tipped onto its side. The top of the desk was empty, save for a single piece of paper. In my curiosity, I picked it up and read the hastily scribbled note. My breath caught in my throat. I thought I was going to be sick.

'What is it?' Therron asked in concern when he saw my expression. He joined me over by the desk, where I handed him the piece of paper, my hand shaking.

'STOP HIM' it read.

But it wasn't the words that made me shudder. It was the splatters of dried blood surrounding them.

Therron's expression matched my own.

'Who is this referring to?' he asked me, but we both knew the answer: Calpacious. Whoever inhabited this castle wrote this as a warning, in the hopes someone would find and read it.

Just then, the room began to shake. The first time, Therron and I just exchanged horrified glances. It wasn't until the second rumble that the two of us darted back up the ladder, but not before I snagged a sword from one of the holdings on the wall. Better to be safe than sorry.

We made a run for the exit, but stopped dead at the sight greeting us just beyond the threshold.

It was the pegasus. She lay directly opposite the castle entrance, crying in agony, her wings twisted and bent in horrible, unnatural ways. Fresh blood marred her otherwise perfect complexion.

'It's a trap,' Therron conceded, looking around himself warily for the danger. I moved past him and out the door, but he grabbed my upper arm. 'Pepper, what are you doing?'

'I can't just leave her there like that!' I protested, pointing at her broken wings. 'At least let's get her inside!'

'You can't keep putting yourself in danger like this. If you ever got hurt, I'd—'

But I never got to hear the rest of the sentence, as a dark shadow loomed towards us. 'Look out!' I cried and pulled Therron out of the castle and down onto the ground. The doorway we'd been standing in crumbled to the floor with another earth-shattering crash. Once the bricks and dust stopped flying, I dared myself to peek up from where my head lay against the ground. Rising up from the wreckage that had once been a castle was a huge, snarling ogre.

19

DEADLY FOES

S tanding at six feet tall, the portly ogre eyed us both with murderous intent. His weight alone had destroyed the centuries-old castle doorframe—what was he going to do to us?

I searched the ground around me for the sword I grabbed from the armoury, but I couldn't find it.

'There's no time for that,' said Therron, ushering me to my feet. 'Come on!' He was ready to sprint away.

I felt a sting in my index finger, and looked down to see blood oozing from a long gash. My hand had brushed against the blade of the sword in my frenzy. I grabbed the hilt and bolted up from the ground, but refused to catch up to Therron. When he noticed I wasn't there, he slowed, and turned back round. He saw what I was doing.

'Pepper, what are you doing with that?' he shouted. 'Put it down!'

The ogre growled, taking a defensive stance as he circled me and the sword I pointed at his chest. The weapon felt foreign to my hands. Far heavier than I anticipated, it weighed down my arms. I tried to keep them outstretched to give as much distance between me and the beast as possible, but it was too heavy.

'Go get the pegasus,' I said to him without taking my eyes from the monster. 'We can't leave her here like this.' As afraid as he was, I knew Therron didn't want to leave the injured pegasus any more than I did. Keeping a wide berth, he inched his way around us, towards the hurt creature.

The ogre took a swing with his fist, and I thrust the sword out to catch his blow head-on. The vibration of the impact trembled through the metal all the way down my arm, and I nearly dropped it. I gripped tighter.

With the blade angled in front of my chest, I stumbled backwards as the ogre closed in towards me. His eyes were wild with swirling shades of white and grey. His stout figure, clad in frayed rags, moved clumsily, and the sounds coming from his rotting mouth were unlike any I ever heard before. This was the monster—the one from the legend Therron warned me about. The crazed look in the monster's eyes told me as much. This ogre had become victim to one of the cruellest things imaginable: his own mind. Just as I wondered whether an ounce of the man he used to be remained inside of him, he launched at me with another attack.

With a roaring lunge, the ogre grabbed my sword-bearing hand and twisted the other behind my back. A gurgled yelp made it past my lips.

'Pepper!'

'N-no!' I spoke to Therron through grinding teeth. 'Just save the pegasus!'

The stench emanating from the beast strangled me. I felt the ground sloping beneath my feet where the steep hill descended to the village. If I lost my footing, even for a second, I would tumble, and that would be it.

I pushed forward against the ogre's giant form, but he must have been at least three times the size of me. He twirled me around so he held both of my arms behind my back. I wiggled my wrist blindly in the hopes of slashing him with the blade, but the effort was futile. Within mere seconds, the ogre had me face-down on the rocky ground, my sword arm splayed out to the side. The sword dropped to the floor too, the hilt mere inches from my fingertips. The ogre had a podgy hand pressed up against my back, rendering me unable to get back up. I grunted as I stretched my arm to its limit to try and retrieve my weapon, but it was no use. My middle fingertip merely grazed the edge of the silver. The ogre noticed my attempts and I had no time to react before his foot came slamming down on top of my forearm.

I couldn't scream. The pain was too much. Only a strangled gurgle made it from my throat when the cracking sound of the impact reached my ears. The ogre hefted me up from the floor and slung me over his shoulder, and then started to run. From where I hung upside-down, I could not see where he was taking me, but I knew it was in the direction of the castle ruins. With a rusty voice, I called out Therron's name, knowing what was about to happen.

The ogre had just hooked his hands around my waist, ready to fling me against the protruding remains of Alzabar's castle, when a voice shouted, 'Stop!'

I was jostled as the monster came to an abrupt halt, my damaged arm rebounding painfully against his back.

'Put her down!' Therron's voice commanded. The monster rumbled. He did as he was told, but he did it with such a force that I landed flat on my back. The throbbing in my arm made the world around me spin, but I could just about see Therron standing in front of the crumbled wall the beast was about to bash me against. He held the same sword I was using earlier. The ogre grunted, now even more enraged than before. I watched as fear drained the courage from Therron's face as the ogre strode towards him with a look of death. He fumbled with the sword, exchanging it from his right hand to his left, and then back again.

'Fight him!' I whimpered from the ground below, so quietly that I doubted he heard me. 'I know you can do it.'

The sword trembled in his hand. He had himself cornered, and the ogre was getting ever closer. I couldn't move. I willed him on silently as my vision started to blur.

I heard the clatter of the sword falling to the ground and feared the worst. By now, my eyes were closed, and I could see nothing but a swirling vortex or colour flashing through the darkness of my mind. I was, however, aware of my body lifting from the ground once again and being carried down the hill. The angered roar of the monster from behind told me that it wasn't the ogre coming to finish what he had left off, but Therron coming to my rescue.

A few seconds later, I was led down on a bumpy

floor. I groaned as I tried to battle off the sleepy haze trying to consume me.

'It's all right,' Therron said as he brushed my hair away from my face. 'Just stay with me.'

With effort, I was able to peel open my eyelids to see Therron leaning down over me in one of the ruined streets.

I slapped him.

'What are you doing?' I asked as he cradled his reddening cheek, a look of shock behind the mark my hand left. 'Why didn't you fight him? You just endangered us even more!'

But he didn't listen to me.

'Pepper, you're hurt. This was a bad idea. We need to leave, now.' There was a loud thundering from the direction we'd come from. Because of the ogre's size, he was a slow runner, but it wouldn't be long before he found us again.

'Why didn't you fight the ogre?' I asked him again. 'You had a sword! Magical powers! Why didn't you use them? You fought of the guard in the forest. What's so different now?'

Furrows of distress lined his forehead. 'I'm sorry,' he said, 'I didn't want to tell you. I can't use my magic. I've never combatted before in my life!'

I blinked and stared at him, though the world was still spinning. 'You told me you got control over your powers.'

Therron sighed. 'I did. I learnt to suppress them. I haven't used them in so long, I don't even know how to reach them anymore.'

Deafening crashes came from not too far away. The ogre was almost upon us, crushing the already damaged buildings as he searched between the roads.

'How did you escape from the guard that day in the forest then?' I asked him, anxieties weaving their way into my stomach, making me feel queasy.

'I outran him,' he admitted. 'Look, Pepper, I don't want you to see me as some kind of hero, because I'm not. This is who I am: an outcast. A nobody. I was never supposed to amount to anything, and I never will! I wanted you to see me differently. I really did. I tried so hard to be different for you, but I'm just too much of a coward. I'm sorry!'

If only he knew, I thought. If only he knew he was destined for so much greatness.

'Therron,' I said, 'there's something I should tell you.'

But I never got the chance, as right then, the building in front of us shook, and through the brickwork barged the ogre, looking more murderous than ever. I couldn't move—I was too woozy, and my one good arm wasn't enough to heft me up from the street floor.

239

'Run,' I urged Therron. 'Get out of here!'

But he refused. 'There's no way I'm leaving you,' he said. He tried to pick me up once more, but stumbled on the uneven cobbles and fell flat against the road.

This was it. With a solid brick wall behind us, there was nowhere for us to move to. The monster had us trapped, and he knew it.

He also had the sword.

The ogre lifted the blade high above his mighty head, poised to deal a double death blow with a single fatal slash. I was unable to detach my eyes from the blade as it swooped down towards us.

But it never made contact.

A glistening ball of flame appeared from nowhere, colliding into the vengeful beast. The impact sent it flying down the road and crashing into a brick tower several feet away with an almighty thwack. Both the beast and the blazing object crumpled onto the cobbles below.

Therron found his footing, and carefully helped me up, being mindful of my arm which now throbbed intensely. When we saw the beast was no longer moving, we ventured over to where he crashed and now lay, unmoving, on the street floor.

The supposed ball of flame was there too, beside him. I recognised the form of the beautiful phoenix,

Bel, before I was even close enough to stroke her dwindling flames.

'No!' I cried when I saw her lifeless, beady eyes staring up at the heavens. 'No, Bel, please!' I collapsed down to my knees, watching helplessly as the last of Bel's flames died down to a simmering flicker. 'Come on, Bel!' I pleaded as a tear brimmed on the edge of my eyelid. 'Don't do this!'

Therron laid a gentle hand on my shoulder. 'I'm sorry, Pepper,' he said.

'No! She's a phoenix! Aren't phoenixes supposed to regenerate from their ashes?'

'I'm not sure what kind of phoenixes you've read about,' he said, 'but here, I'm afraid there's no such thing.'

I stroked the magnificent bird's wing, now clad in dull, brown feathers in place of the flaming inferno that were once there. The tears fell loose. 'But . . . what am I going to tell Archie?'

'That she saved both our lives,' he said with a rueful smile. 'But, unfortunately, it came at the cost of her own.'

I stroked the bird's silky feathers once more as I grieved. I was the one who granted her life. That day I told Archie's story to Peter in an attempt to cheer him up, I brought Bel into existence. And now it had been brutally taken away from her, because she tried to save me. It wasn't fair.

But what about the ogre?

'Where's the ogre?' I asked. He was not where he was before. We looked around for him, but could not see where he went. Had he run off? Or was he waiting in the shadows for a moment to strike out?

Something grabbed my better arm, and I yelped as I was tugged down to the ground. The ogre was behind me, blood pooling in the corner of his mouth as he lay, barely breathing, on the grimy street. He'd tried to get away, but had now given up. He kept his grip on my arm as he looked me in the eyes. My heart pounded in my ears.

'Thank you,' he whispered in one, final, dying breath, and closed his eyes. His hand became slack, and I writhed free, shuddering back to standing.

'What was that?' Therron asked as I struggled to compose myself.

'I-' I began. 'I think we saved him.'

'From what?'

I looked back to the lifeless form below me. From here, he looked like much less of a monster, and more like an actual person. One with a past; a story. Maybe even a family.

'Himself,' I said.

Therron's satchel and Tharva's shoulder bag were exactly where we'd left them when it had all started—outside the castle on the top of the hill. When we got there, the pegasus was gone. I assumed it meant she was still alive and had gone back home to her family.

'I'll carry that for you.' Therron took the blue bag from me before I could hoist it onto my shoulder.

'Are you sure?'

'Of course. You're hurt.'

I looked down at my arm which I supported in front of my chest with my other hand. Every time I let go of it, it would instantly hurt again.

'Let me have a look at that,' he offered, holding out his hand. I recoiled, which only elicited a laugh from him.

'I'm not going to bite!' he joked. I slowly extended my injured arm, allowing my wrist to rest in Therron's hand. 'Now try and wiggle your fingers,' he said. I tried, but could barely manage a twitch before I was wincing in pain again. 'Looks like a fracture,' he conceded.

'How do you know?'

He quirked an eyebrow. 'You really think I can

hunt for my own food every day without sustaining a few injuries?' he said. 'Here, I'm sure Tharva packed something we could use.' He gave me back my arm and dove into the bag, fumbling around for a few moments before pulling out a length of stretchy, black material. 'Here,' he said. 'I'm not sure what it is, but it should do the trick.'

I looked at what Therron had found, and I couldn't help myself. I giggled.

'What?' he asked, baffled at my reaction. 'What is it?'

I pointed at the fabric he held in his hands. 'That,' I told him, 'is a pair of women's tights.'

Therron's cheeks turned bright red. 'Oh . . . um . . . I didn't realise . . .'

'It's fine,' I assured him, trying to control my laughter. 'Don't worry, it'll work.'

Tenderly, Therron threaded the nylon around my arm and behind my neck, creating a perfect sling. I had to admire his handiwork: it didn't hurt in the slightest. When the job was done, the two of us headed back down the hill to make our way out of the city, ready to resume our quest for the King's brother. Now that the whole ordeal with the ogre was over, we both felt a little more relaxed about continuing with our journey.

Little did we know, though, our troubles were only

just beginning.

20

EVIL TWISTS

I exhaled and reclined against the dry moss, soaking up the warmth of the glittering sun. I felt gross. The sweat from the previous exertions had dried to a sticky sheen down my back and across my face and my hair was suffering the effects of not being washed in a few days. My new dress was ruined. Much like the old ball gown, it was muddy, bloody, and torn. To top it all off, my right arm still ached considerably, despite its new support.

But I felt at ease. Or at least, I tried to feel that way. This would likely be the only respite we would get for a while, so I tried to make the most of it.

247

Large birds in the trees cawed, hoping to scavenge some of the leftovers from our hastily thrown together meal. Tired of the bread Tharva had given us—as tasty as it was—Therron speared and fried two fish from the stream beside by the city ruins. It was a satisfying dinner, yet my tummy gurgled for more . . . or for something else. I found myself salivating when the thought of a sticky toffee pudding came to mind. It was too long since I last tasted human food.

'So,' said Therron, interrupting my daydream. 'What do we do now?' He, too, lay on the mossy earth, enjoying the refreshing rays of golden sun. Lying a few feet from me, he had his arms folded up behind his head while he watched the clouds pass. The place we rested in was a beautiful, open spot beside the stream—a perfect location to refresh and rejuvenate.

I wiggled my bare toes in the cold leaves beneath me. We still had a long quest ahead of us, but right now, I savoured the peace and quiet. And the lack of walking.

'I don't know,' I said with a reluctant sigh. I didn't really want to talk about missing kings and evil plots. 'We still need to find Alzabar, but how? The book led us to the Old City, and the only thing we came across there was near-death.'

'Maybe we haven't been looking hard enough,'

Therron suggested. I rolled my head to the side to look at him. 'Perhaps the clues were right there in front of us,' he continued, 'and we just weren't looking in the right places.'

'You think we should go back in there?' I asked, referring to the crumbling city.

Still gazing into the sky, Therron shook his head sleepily. 'Not right now,' he said. 'I think we deserve some rest first.'

Now, that was something I could agree with. My eyelids were becoming harder and harder to keep open. After a disrupted night's sleep in the Tropolis, my body was basically running on reserves, and now any energy I had left was working to digest the food in my stomach. It may have been mid-afternoon, but I was ready to fall asleep right there and then.

'Bel didn't have to save us,' I said as I felt my eyelids drooping.

'But she did. Phoenixes are incredibly loyal creatures—they never forget a friend. For her to consider us as such was a great privilege.'

Therron's words did little to console me. 'Archie's going to be so upset,' I said.

Though my eyes were closed, I felt a warm set of fingers lace themselves through my own at my side. 'I don't know Archie that well,' said Therron. His voice sounded a lot closer than it had moments ago. 'But if I were him, I would be proud of Bel.' He gave my hand a gentle squeeze that filled me with hope and reassurance, and another feeling I couldn't identify. 'Bel's sacrifice shall not be in vain. She gave up her life to save ours, and with that gift, we will save the kingdom.'

No other words he could've said right then would have been more encouraging to hear. He may not have been able to see it himself yet, but Therron was a hero. He was going to rescue Alzabar and I would return home, safe in the knowledge that both Tantary and the real world were safe.

But something was wrong. No matter how hard I tried, I could not shake the feeling something wasn't right. I didn't understand. This was what I wanted, wasn't it? For Therron to save the day and the land to be free. Then why did the thought of succeeding make me feel so empty inside?

With a deciding yawn, I attributed the emotion to tiredness, and fell asleep.

My sleep was a perturbed one. Dreams were plagued with strange sensations: the sound of syncopated footfalls against a muddy terrain. The smell of fresh upholstery—crisp and clean. The feeling of rocking forward and back, and side to side. A strange taste of citron. And at one point, I thought I caught a glimpse of the hooded face of a man.

The first thing I was aware of when I woke up was that it was cold. Very cold. I opened my eyes. It was also dark.

'Therron?' I called, my voice lowered to a whisper. The sound reverberated with a chilling echo all around me, but there was no response. I tried to lever myself up, forgetting my right arm was broken. Still strapped to my chest with a pair of tights, the appendage refused to move. Using my good arm, I rolled myself onto my side instead.

The surface was rough against my palm, and undoubtedly the reason I was so cold. I rubbed my eyes and peeled them open a little wider. I was in a small, stone room that was completely empty, all except from the raised platform I slept on.

How could this be? The last thing I remembered was falling asleep beside Therron. Where was he?

It wasn't until I tried to stand up from the platform that I felt and heard the metal clink of chains. They were attached to my ankles, tethering me to the stone below. The sick feeling in my stomach was only made worse when I saw the wall of bars behind me, confirming my nightmare.

I was in a prison cell.

I tried to move towards the iron bars, but the shackles kept me from advancing the last few feet. Keeping my feet still, I leaned my body weight forward and grabbed the cold metal with my hand.

'Hello?' I called out. 'Is there anyone there? I think there's been some mistake!' Once again, a hollow echo was my only answer. I peered left and right. Nothing but a stone corridor containing similar, though hauntingly empty, cells met my gaze. There was no one there.

Sconces lined the walls, but none were lit. It was more like a medieval dungeon than a prison. Only a single skylight at the end of the corridor made it possible for me to see anything. Dust and cobwebs told me this place had not been used in a long time, and only added to the chills slowly turning my bones to ice. I tried to tell myself not to panic. That I would get out of here. Therron would come and rescue me. Or Archie.

I tried shouting a couple more times, but was answered only by my own echoes bouncing off the stone walls. How did I even get down here?

I went quiet for a while, and tried to listen for any sounds—any signs to tell me I wasn't the only living person here in this . . . wherever the hell I was.

At first, I could hear nothing above the drumming of my heartbeat and my heavy breathing. But then I heard it: scuffling. Something moving further along the passageway. I leaned forward as far as I could with the bars and the shackles to see down to where the sound was coming from. But in the limited light, I couldn't see anything. The noise wasn't coming from down the corridor anymore. It was coming from beneath me.

I screamed and leaped back up onto the platform— which I now realised was supposed to be a bed—as a little pink tail disappeared out through the bars. My stomach churned again.

My next instinct was to check the bars, hoping one of them may be loose. No such luck. The lock wouldn't budge, either. Great. What was I supposed to do now? Stay here until I rotted?

Out of options, I sank back down onto the 'bed' and wondered which I would die from first— dehydration, starvation or madness?

I was only about two hours into my depressing reverie, with a grand total of twenty-seven possible ways I could die in here, when I heard another noise. I thought it might be another rat, but I then heard a door open and close. No rats I knew of could open doors.

More light came in through the skylight now, so I assumed it must be some time in the morning. That knowledge gave me little solace.

I leaped to my feet at the sound of footsteps drawing near. Three woman wearing conservative, black dresses shuffled up to my cell. I nearly cried with joy when one of them pulled out a key and proceeded to open the cage. All three of them had their heads downcast and showed no intention of telling me what was going on.

'Thank you so much,' I said when the same woman unfastened the shackles. 'Could you please tell me where I am? I have no idea what's going on.'

But the three women said nothing. They just ignored me, like they didn't even hear me. Wordlessly, they escorted me through the dungeon and out the door they had come in through. I asked where they were taking me, but again, to my increasing irritation, they did not answer.

A spiral set of stairs took us out of the dungeon and into another dingy corridor. This one, at least, looked a little more inhabited. Sconces on the walls were lit with healthy flames, and a throng of similarly clad people—all mute—darted back and forth carrying baskets of clothes, food and what-else-not. It appeared I was in a servants' quarter, but of where? I surveyed the internal architecture once more, and a lead weight formed in my tummy.

A castle. I was in Calpacious' castle. He found me.

What was he going to do? Execute me? I tried to writhe free of the servants' grip, but there were three of them, and only one of me.

Several doors later, we entered the main part of the castle. Now, this was much more like what I imagined Calpacious' castle to look like. I had to tilt my head back in order to get a full view of the maze of staircases that zigzagged in and out of one another, climbing all the way up the huge, vaulted ceiling. Dazzling marble and gold surfaces gleamed in the light of the chandeliers. This was one king who had plenty of money.

They towed me up two more flights of stairs. Our footsteps echoed the whole way, even with my flat pumps. I kept searching for possible escape routes, such as leaping over the banister, or bolting across the landing. But the maids seemed to anticipate my moves before I made them. Still, none of them spoke for the entire journey.

After yet more walking, they ushered me into a highly decorated bedroom. Unlike my one in Calthorpe Manor, this room shone in glossy hues of white and gold. Both the four-poster bed and the bathtub on the other side of the room were bedecked in vibrant jewels. The stones reflected a rainbow of colour around the entire room.

The tallest of the three maids, the same woman

who freed me of my shackles, span me around so my back was to her. It took me a while to realise she was trying to remove my dress.

'Hey!' I protested and sprang away from her cold hands. 'What do you think you're doing?' I tugged the skirt back down to cover my modesty.

'I'm not supposed to talk, miss, but you really are trying my patience,' she spoke. Like the other two, she had her hair tied into a solid knot at the back of her head. She was clearly the oldest of the bunch. At least, if the number of wrinkles marring her face was anything to go by. 'You need to get washed and cleaned up before your audience with the King.'

The King. So I was right.

But I refused to cave.

'Or else what?' I challenged, but by the way her face paled and her eyes glassed over, I figured it was best I didn't find out.

'Fine,' I stated. 'I'll get cleaned up. But I'll have you know I can undress myself, thank you very much.'

I was more anxious than I let on, but I hoped they couldn't tell that. My courageous words were just a façade to disguise the trembling butterflies in my tummy. I disappeared behind the screen in the corner of the room, and unveiled the real reason I wouldn't let those controlling women undress me.

Therron's book. It was still tucked away, secured within the bodice of my dress. Since I had yet to find my bag anywhere, I assumed Therron was still in possession of *The Kingdom*, but this one was with me. And I was determined to do whatever it took to keep both it and Therron safe.

After shedding my garments, I folded the spiral-bound notebook within the dress, which I made a big show of placing neatly on the bed. 'I would appreciate it if my clothes weren't touched, if you please,' I commanded the women. 'That was a dress that belonged to my mother, and I would not wish for anything to happen to it.'

The maids eyed the mud-splattered and shredded fabric I pointed to and, after a few quizzical looks, conceded.

The bath had already been run, so I slipped myself in and begrudgingly allowed the maids to do their work, washing my hair, scrubbing my skin, and soaking the grime off my face. I actually found myself being grateful to be cleaned and pampered after my long trek through the woods.

What I didn't enjoy as much, however, was when they then proceeded to dress me up like a mannequin. Now, I always liked wearing dresses, but there was a point where I did draw the line. Poufy, meringue-style dresses did not fit into that comfort zone.

I had no choice but to stand there as they forced me into a vanilla-coloured wad of tulle that was about three times my body mass.

'Excuse me,' I wheezed, struggling to breathe in the tight corset, 'but do you happen to have anything a little less . . . flamboyant?'

But the maids had reverted to being their mute selves. I sighed. Or, at least, I tried to, but the bodice of the dress didn't allow for that kind of movement.

As well as getting outfitted with a new wardrobe, I was also given a fancy hairstyle to match. It took thirty minutes, three maids, and quite a few screams on my part, but the knots were finally teased out, and my hair was styled into a neat blonde braid that wound right down to the middle of my back.

We exited the room, and began travelling once more. Of course, I had to walk a little slower this time, for the simple fact that even placing one foot in front of the other caused me pain. It wasn't until one of the maids knocked upon a set of giant, double doors that my nerves kicked in again. This was it, wasn't it? I wondered for a brief second, if I were to die here, would I die in the real world, too?

The doors opened almost immediately to a grand throne room that did not disappoint the rest of the castle's lavish architecture. I saw Calpacious before anything else. His presence was so dominant, it was impossible not to notice him.

He wore a coat of crimson velvet which wrapped around his neck and cascaded to the floor below. Accents of black within the fabric made him look even more foreboding. Dirty blond hair spewed from his scalp and billowed in waves around his sturdy shoulders, complemented by a thin line of hair running the length of his jawbone.

A pair of steely, grey eyes was the centrepiece of his angular face. Those, paired with the structure of his abnormally pale skin, gave the King the effect that his entire being had been carved from stone. He was perched upon a golden throne, hands resting upon the snarling bear heads on either armrest. Both hands hid inside a thick pair of black gloves.

'Pepper Fairfield.'

Those two words were all it took for what was left of my heart to shrivel up into a frozen cube of ice.

I narrowed my eyes. 'How did you find me?'

'I have my resources. Your name is only one of the many things I know about you. Come. I believe we have some talking to do.' He signalled for the robot-like maids to leave the room, and the two guards standing over the King soon followed suit.

I swallowed a lump in my throat, but the tightness of the dress only pushed it back up again.

'I believe you know why you were summoned

here, correct?' he questioned as soon as we were alone in the throne room.

'I—um . . .' I cleared my throat. It took me a while to find my voice again. 'I'm afraid I don't,' I said. Calpacious peered at me through those disturbing, grey eyes of his.

'You must have some idea,' he said, his mouth cracking into a smile, and it wasn't a very pleasant smile, at that. 'Go on. Take a guess.'

I didn't want to. My stubborn nature urged me not to play along. To give him a run for his money and not give in. But something about the way he looked at me told me I was not dealing with a sane man here.

'This is to do with where I come from, isn't it?' I answered, vaguely. I didn't want to outright say I was human in case he, by the off chance, wasn't already aware. But I was in no such luck.

'You're close,' he said, 'but not quite close enough. You see, little Earth-dweller, you possess something exceedingly rare and valuable in these parts. Yes, you have infiltrated our system and endangered the lives of us all, but right now, what you have might just be the thing that saves your life in this case.'

In this circumstance, only one point he was making stuck out to me. 'Wait,' I said, 'so you're *not* going to kill me?'

'Kill you?' He guffawed. 'Not just yet. Though time might lead to that.' He grinned. This was all a game to him.

I failed to see the hilarity. 'What is this thing that is so important to you? What have I got that could possibly be of any use to you?'

He angled his head and leaned forward, the fabrics of his clothes chafing as he moved. He was building this up on purpose. I forced myself not to recoil. 'Your words,' he said.

I stared at him blankly, totally blank.

'Pepper,' he said, 'I want a story.'

21

WICKED PLANS

*C*hildish enthusiasm glinted in his grey eyes, which flitted all around my face. He never once made direct eye contact.

I raised my eyebrows and peered at the King. 'A story?' I repeated. 'Is that all you want from me?'

Calpacious' lips curled open in a widespread smile. The breadth to which it spread reminded me of how a shark would open its mouth before devouring its prey.

'Were it only that simple, dear girl,' he said. I shivered at the low growl which accompanied his words. 'No, I desire a specific story. One that has yet to be written.'

He rose from the throne, managing it with grace despite his hefty robes. For some reason, his height shocked me. I expected him to be taller.

'I want us to be friends, Pepper. I believe we can become great allies.' He kept his distance, pacing left and right in front of his throne on the raised platform. 'Do you like the castle?'

I resented the change in subject, but decided for the time being to keep him happy. As much as I wanted to get back to this 'story' business, and whatever the hell he was talking about, I figured it was best to play safe for now.

'It's lovely,' I said in an attempt to appease him. 'Grand. Very homey.'

Calpacious grinned again, bearing his stumpy teeth. They were short, like they had ben ground down over the years.

I had come to understand quite a bit about the rules of Tantary and how things worked here: no one changed in physical appearance. They couldn't age or reproduce, but they could still be killed.

I'd asked Therron about this phenomenon on our way back from the Old City.

'It wasn't always this way,' he explained. 'When the magicks first began to take corporeal form, they were immortal. As long as their books were in the manor, so were they. It was when the wizard cast the spell that we lost that trait. Perhaps it was intentional. Guess he didn't care about us much.'

Calpacious still smirked down at me. I hated the way his eyes kept skipping around my face, never keeping contact with my own. It made him look crazed.

'Good,' he said, 'because this is going to be your home for the next few days.'

I didn't even hear the door opening behind me before I felt someone grab my shoulders. It was the same three women from before.

'Wait! No!' I shouted. 'You can't keep me here! This isn't right. I refuse to go back to the dungeon!' I kicked and wriggled, but there was no escaping the maids' strong grip. Crikey, what did these women eat for breakfast?

'Dungeon?' Calpacious scoffed. 'Why would I send you to the dungeon? You're my guest! You'll be staying in the room you were taken to earlier.'

'And let me guess.' I grunted, still trying to get loose. Every movement sent shooting pains down my injured arm. 'I'm going to be locked up in that room until I complete whatever task it is you want me to do?'

He grimaced. 'Locked up is such a strong phrase. Why don't we try, restrained?'

I scowled, unable to conceal my irritation any longer. 'You can call it picking flaming daffodils if you want, but it's still imprisonment.'

'Now, now.' Calpacious held out a finger. 'Let's not get off on the wrong foot here. I'm sure you'll be very compliant and keen to work with me during your stay, but we must start now as we mean to go on. Being friends will come later, so how about we stick with being civil for now?'

I quit my struggling and focussed all my energy on giving Calpacious the dirtiest look I could muster. 'What on earth makes you think I will even help you, let alone be civil to you?' I spat. 'You kidnapped me, *and* had me locked me up. I've heard more than a fair share of stories regarding your dirty deeds, and half the kingdom wants you dead. So why, *why*, would you possibly think I would want to work with you?'

The look he gave me was pitiful.

'Oh, Pepper,' he said. The maids towed me, much to my protest, over towards where he stood. He must have been about the same height as me, but from his position on the rostrum, I had to angle my scowl upwards for it to reach him. 'You see, I'm not the kind of man who does things impulsively. I always have a plan. And it just so happens this one comes with a certain leverage that just might sway your decision.'

I leaned forward, getting as close to him as I could against the grip of my captors. 'I don't care what you say. You have chosen the wrong person. Not only can I not help you, but you cannot make me.' It was all I could do not to spit on his leather boots.

Calpacious countered my scowl with another. He spoke in a tone just above a whisper, 'Oh, I know I've chosen the right person for the job. I don't think you realise what a power you have, Pepper. You have an imagination that is unrivalled; your words have more influence than you ever would have thought. Think about it. You told a story to a little boy, and those characters became real without even committing them to paper. That has never happened before. Your actions in this world are manipulating the story of a character already living here. Again, there is no record of that ever happening before. So what do you say to that?'

I blanched. 'How-how do you know . . .' I trailed off. Knowing who I was was one thing, but this . . .

Calpacious grinned again, the corners of his mouth stretching up so far this time that all his flattened teeth were on show. For the first time, his eyes latched directly onto my own. Something cold, cruel and terrifyingly sane swirled inside his irises, forcing me to draw back. Earlier, I mistook him for a madman, but this was far, far worse.

'That, young girl,' he said, grey eyes gleaming, 'is the leverage I spoke of. You want to know who told me about you? You're a smart girl—have a think. Because that is the very person whose life you will endanger should you refuse to comply.'

I already knew who he was referring to, but he clearly still felt the need to demonstrate. With three claps of his gloved hands, one of the side doors opened, and in marched two guards, dragging with them a bound and gagged Max.

I rolled my eyes. Figured it would be him.

'My guards found this young fugitive on the outskirts of the Tropolis, trying to escape during the evacuation. I have to give him credit, he was a tough nut to crack, but after a thorough beating, a day of starvation, and a number of other, unmentionable horrors, he finally caved. He told me a lot about you, you know. With a little persuasion, of course.'

Max's arms were tied behind him and being held by the two guardsmen who had escorted him in, and he stared down at the floor. He looked awful. He couldn't have been here for longer than a day, and yet he looked like he'd experienced a month's worth of torture, with dried blood caking his clothes, and fresh gashes streaking his face. For all that I wanted to slap him for the spectacle he'd thrown back in Tharva's shop, this was not fair.

'What have you done to him?' I yelled. The maids tightened their grip, and one of them pulled my good arm behind my back. 'Let him go! You're a monster!'

I heard a scream, and looked over to see Max wincing in agony. One of the guards held something against his upper arm.

'Now, Pepper,' said Calpacious with a condescending tone. 'I thought you would be smarter than to do something like that. You see,' he pointed over to Max and the metal band the guard had just strapped to his arm. 'That device is a beautiful little thing that one of our wizards came up with. Every time you step out of line, an impulse is sent into the band, and it generates a wave of shocks that sends Max's body into excruciating spasms. Would you like to see another example?'

'No!'

But despite my protest, another cry escaped Max.

Calpacious grinned, revelling in my distress. 'I was hoping you'd say that,' he said. 'I'm afraid defiance constitutes stepping out of line. See, one of the personality traits I hate the most is stubbornness, and you have it in bucket loads. I hope this little device your friend is wearing will help eliminate that pesky little quirk of yours.'

I glanced over at Max, who was panting from the pain he just endured. He looked weaker than ever.

'Oh, yes,' Calpacious said. I waited for his icy breath to pass me before I turned to face him. 'There is probably one more thing I should mention. With each spasm he endures, the weaker he becomes. It probably won't take many before he dies altogether!' He chuckled as though it was the most amusing thing he'd heard all day. 'And the best part is, I'm not even the one inflicting the pain: you are.'

I looked up at him, then at Max, then back at Calpacious again. Max may have been a jerk to me, and Calpacious' reasoning was far from acceptable, but I had my morals.

'What do you want me to do?' I asked, and tried not to scowl too much when Calpacious' mouth widened to another toothy grin.

'I'm glad you asked that,' he said. 'This is what I've been looking forward to explaining. Not here, though. Allow us to escort you to your room, first.'

Of course, I could do nothing to protest as Calpacious took the lead and the three maids, still holding me tight, led me back up to the room I would stay in. It was just as it had been left—the clothes untouched. I only felt a small drop of relief.

Max hadn't been brought up with me, so I figured the guards took him back to wherever they held him captive. Clearly not in the dungeon, as it looked to me like I was the first person to be held down there in a

270

long time.

Unless Calpacious had more dungeons, I suddenly thought. Or torture chambers. I wouldn't put past him.

The maids were excused, and Calpacious and I stood face to face in the middle of the room. The door was unguarded, but he knew I wouldn't risk Max's life by making a dash for it. The fact that escape was within my reach made the whole situation even worse.

'It's like I said, Pepper,' Calpacious explained. Now he was off his podium, we stood eye-to-eye, but it didn't make him any less imposing. If anything, it made him seem scarier. 'I need a story from you. Whoever wrote my story didn't know what they were doing. They made me a villain, and a powerless one at that. I need to get through the portal and into the manor, but, as you probably know by now, villains can't cross through the portal.'

I stared at him, quizzically. 'You want me to make you a good guy?' I asked.

'No.' He frowned. 'It's too late for that, now. No, what I want is power. I want to have enough magic so I can push through the curse that's keeping me here. I want magic of the likes no one has ever seen before!'

'Well, there might be a slight problem there,' I said, and glanced down at my arm. My writing arm. 'Afraid I got caught up in a bit of a scuffle with an ogre earlier.'

He just stared at me. 'And how is that a problem?'

I raised my eyebrows. 'I'm right handed. I kind of need that arm to write with.'

Calpacious shook his head. 'Do you not pay any attention to yourself?' he asked. 'You don't need your arm! How do you think you managed to bring a troll and a phoenix to life?'

'I didn't!' I shouted. 'That was Peter!'

Now he was glaring at me. 'Do you want Max to live or not?' he asked, his face reddening. His beard seemed to bristle, and even a vein bulged on his forehead. 'Now either you write this story, or he dies. I may even find some more of your friends out there to help convince you. That little dressmaker, perhaps. I'm done explaining to you. You figure it out yourself!'

With a swish of his cloak, he strode out of the room, with an angry elegance only an arrogant king could achieve.

22

INSPIRING WORDS

Therron

I returned to the place where it all happened. It was the first place I could think to look.

Maybe it was because I was in such a state of panic. When I woke up and saw Pepper wasn't there, my mind assumed the worst. That perhaps . . . no, I couldn't think like that. She had to be around, somewhere.

It was a good thing I chose to search the scene of the ogre's death, for had I not, I wouldn't have stumbled upon Archie.

'You're here.' It was all I could think to say under the surprise of seeing him here in the Old City. He was bent down over the form of his lifeless friend. 'How did you know?'

The troll had his back turned to me, making no movement to show he acknowledged my presence. His hand ran up and down Bel's extinguished feathers.

'I asked her to follow you,' he said. His hand stilled, and the rest of his body remained motionless, as though he were a statue. 'I needed to make sure the two of you were safe. I couldn't come myself, for I got caught up in the evacuation, so I asked Bel to go.' He twisted his head round to look at me. 'It's strange,' he said with a wan smile, 'because she and I have only really existed for a couple of days, and yet I feel I have known her for lifetimes. When she died, I just knew. I felt it. Deep inside.'

I clambered over the rubble towards him and sat down. 'How do you mean?'

'Where I come from, it is a well-known fact that the bond struck between two souls is the strongest bond of all.' He appeared thoughtful for a moment. 'That's what I remember, anyway. I don't suppose the land from my story really exists, does it?' I could only shrug. At least he had a past.

And there it was—another secret I was too scared

to share. All the other magicks here seemed to have a recollection of their past—of some of the events that happened in their own stories.

I had nothing. And it made me wonder why. I wanted to know the truth about my story, about who had made me this way, with no memories, and a strange set of powers that condemned me to a life on the run.

I didn't spend long in my reverie before I snapped back to the present, the matter at hand weighing on my mind. 'Listen, Archie,' I said, 'Pepper's missing.' He narrowed his eyes. 'I can't find her anywhere. I-I'm afraid something might have happened to her. You don't think Calpacious might have . . .' I couldn't bring myself to complete that sentence.

Archie's mouth drew into a firm line. 'We mustn't rule out the possibility,' he said with a solemn expression. I raked my fingers through my hair, turning my helpless gaze to the sky above.

'Therron, I know you have feelings for Pepper.'

I dropped my head back down and fumbled with my fingers.

'How can you tell?'

'I'm a good judge of these things,' he said, 'knowing how people are feeling; observing their personalities. The only reason I approached Bel the first time was because I saw the fear in her eyes.

Somehow, I just knew she wasn't going to hurt me.' He smiled, and at the mention of his beloved phoenix, he stroked her cold form.

'Bel was an amazing bird,' I said, looking down to where she lay on the stones in front of me. She looked so peaceful. 'I may not have known her well, but she had the spirit of a real hero.'

Archie nodded. 'That she did.'

'I'm really sorry about what happened.'

Archie did not respond. After a few moments, he stood, and dusted himself down. I did the same.

'I need to stay here for a while. Say my last goodbyes. You go and save your young Pepper. You can take the griffin I flew here—he's waiting just beyond the city.'

'What?' I nearly choked. 'Me? No, no, I can't go on my own.'

He gave a reassuring smile. 'Don't worry, this one is a very experienced flyer. He knows the way back to the Tropolis.'

'It's not that.' I stared at my feet. I'd felt pathetic enough before, just standing in front of the giant of a troll, but now I felt worthless. 'I can't do it,' I said. 'It's not my place. I'm not a hero like you and Bel.'

He pulled his cloak up around his shoulders and folded his arms. 'You think this is about heroism? You know, there was a time, when I was as young as you, when I didn't believe I was capable of anything, either. The day Frederick and I went to save the village from Bel, we thought we were being strong, doing what no one else was willing to do. As it turned out, it wasn't an act of bravery; it was an act of fear. Going out to kill the so-called beast that threatened us was weak—a last hope. It was foolish. I didn't know it then, but my only true act of bravery would be when I finally befriended Bel.'

'But that was you!' I pointed out. 'This is me and . . . I'm just not cut out for these kinds of things. It's not my—'

'Place,' Archie finished. 'Yes, I know. But how do you know that? Because you are not brave? The thing I am trying to tell you, Therron, is it doesn't matter how much courage or strength you have. True heroism doesn't come from bravery. It comes from the heart.'

23

SMALL FORTUNES

othing.

I groaned and slumped my head on the desk. I don't know what I expected, but this was ridiculous.

What did Calpacious think I was capable of? I had no idea how I was supposed to change his character. Before, when I created Archie, it was an accident. I didn't know what I was doing then, and I very much doubted I could do it again.

Unable to use my writing hand, I opted to use my voice, speaking out loud the story I'd conjured in my head, the same way I did with Archie's story. I directed the words onto the sheet of paper, hoping they'd magically appear. They didn't.

A fully-functioning writing desk, with stacks of blank paper and a collection of pencils, pens, and quills, was set up for me on the one side of the room. I sat at that desk now, rocking my forehead against it while wondering what the hell I was going to do now.

I lifted my head, and stared at the empty page in front of me. I had no idea how long I had been in here, but by the rumblings in my stomach, it must have been at least a few hours. I wondered where and how Max was. Was he suffering from my lack of productivity? Was that considered 'stepping out of line'? Knowing Calpacious—probably.

I mean, I was trying. I really was. But it seemed the harder I concentrated, the more difficult the task became

I decided to take a risk. I held out the sheet of paper in front of me for the umpteenth time and concentrated hard. This time, however, the words I spoke were different:

'King Calpacious was a kindly man,' I began. 'He cared for his subjects, and ruled over them with benevolence. He would never—'

'That's not going to work.'

I jumped. I thought I was alone. I turned to see the three maids from before were back in my room. I groaned. Why couldn't they just leave me alone?

'Don't talk to her, Louisa,' said the matriarch of the group. That was when I noticed there were four women in the room this time, not three; the one addressed to as Louisa, I had not seen before. She was dressed much like the other three, but the ginger hue of her hair made her distinguishable.

Louisa dropped her head and continued with her tasks.

The four of them flitted around the room. At first, I didn't know what they were doing, but then I noticed the way they opened and closed the drawers, lifted up the bedding, and checked behind the changing screen. They were looking for something. A weapon, perhaps.

'What are you doing?' I demanded. 'Do you think I'm plotting to kill the King? Because, trust me, if I had a dagger, I would have used it already.' They continued to rummage around the room, my frustration growing with every silent second. Why did they have to be so mute?

The redheaded maid walked over towards the bed and the pile of my clothes on top. My mind instantly went to Therron's book, tucked away inside the dress.

'Hey, wait!' I called out. 'Please, don't touch those!' But she didn't listen to me. Instead of rifling through them, though, she picked up the pile and carried it out of the room, following her colleagues.

She was the last to leave. I glared at her just as she was about to close the door. She caught my gaze, and smiled.

I was alone. I sighed and rubbed my hand over my face. The maids had left a plate of fresh bread on the bed, and though the smell was enticing, I wasn't hungry. I was more concerned about the fact that they still had Therron's book.

Speaking out loud to the piece of paper didn't work, so I tried a bunch of other techniques, including writing with my left hand, and even taking my right arm out of its sling and writing through the pain. But for some reason, the words were only committed to the paper for a few seconds before they faded away as if they had never existed at all. In the end, I tried to picture in my head exactly what I was trying to write down, and project my thoughts onto the sheet. That didn't work, either.

This was getting stupid. And I was bored. More time went by, and I remained alone. I got up from the desk and stretched my legs for a few moments, taking a stroll around the room to get familiar with my new surroundings. After all, it looked possible that I could be here for quite some time.

Though the furnishings in this room were lavish, possessions were few. Inside the wardrobe was a small collection of clothes. The garments consisted of both men and women's wear, but with such variations in size and style that made it clear they were meant for emergencies. Such as my stay. I'd already changed out of the flouncy dress the maids forced me into and now sported a much comfier outfit. The piece wasn't as comfortable as Tharva's creations, but it would do.

The drawers and dressers were empty. It was more like a showroom than a lived-in space. I ran my hand along the dust-free surfaces, walking with an absent mind around the room's perimeter. My fingers traced over the swirling curves of the intricate mirror frame, then fell to the wall, where they continued to brush along the shiny, golden surface, leaving finger marks as they went.

The texture changed from cold metal to solid wood, and I lifted my hand just as it was about to touch the rounded doorknob.

It was there. Escape was literally within my reach. Damn Calpacious and his stupid mind games! If it wasn't for Max, I would have slipped out right there and then.

I turned my back to the door. It was tormenting me, and I needed to take my mind off it. I walked over to the bed, considering jumping straight in and taking a nap. But no. There was no chance I would be able to sleep. Not under these circumstances. I inspected the sheets that covered it. The silk, embroidered with tiny, hand-stitched rosebuds, shone in the light of the chandelier. I lifted up the blanket and stroked the fabric beneath. I felt the plush, softness of the mattress through it. What luxury for a little guestroom.

Something caught my attention as I ran my hand over the sheets. A dark colour showed through the pale material, but only when I pressed down on it. Confused, I picked up the edge of the sheet and lifted it to reveal the mattress beneath. I gasped, feeling sick to the stomach.

Patches of dark brown stained the otherwise white pad. Blood. Some of it older than others. The stains were everywhere, marking the entire length of the bed. That was when I realised. This wasn't a guest room.

I dropped my eyes to the stone floor, where the stains repeated. Many were hidden beneath a red rug, but they were still there if you knew to look for them.

Something glinting under the bed caught my attention. I bent down to take a look, and felt my skin go cold.

Chains.

Now it made sense why the dungeon was so empty—Calpacious kept and tortured his prisoners in the main rooms of the house. Somehow, I found that fact even more sick and twisted than if it were the other way round.

There was a knock at the door, and I jumped up. Was this Calpacious? What kind of awful torture did he have in mind for me?

It opened, and one of the maids poked her head around it. It was the redhead from earlier, the one who took Therron's book. My heart settled, but not by much.

'Oh, thank goodness!' she said after seeing me, and let herself into the room, closing the door behind her. 'By the stars above, that was way more difficult than it should have been! Do you know what it's like having those three breathing down your neck all the time?' She let out a weighty breath and brushed her hands over the front of her skirt before giving me a beaming smile. 'Are you ready?' she asked.

I stared at her, baffled. 'Um . . . ready for what?'

'To escape, of course!'

My blank expression didn't change. After a few seconds, the maid pulled a face and slapped her forehead with her palm. '*Durh*, of course, how dumb of me! I forgot about this stupid glamour! It's me!'

I watched as her appearance shimmered and, through the maid's rounded face and coppery hair, another face showed through. This one had sharper features and a rather distinct mass of white-blonde hair. The biggest giveaway, though, was the glittering of orange behind her back in the shape of a butterfly's wings.

'Scarlett!' I exclaimed, and ran to give her a big hug. 'What's going on? How did you find me here?'

Scarlett, now back in maid form, put a finger against her lips. 'Shush,' she said, 'I've already raised their suspicions here enough without your help as well!'

I raised my eyebrows. 'Oh no, what have you done?'

'Not much.' She rubbed a hand up and down her arm. 'Well . . . I might have accidentally used magic once or twice to help clean up the kitchen.'

'You what?!'

'And I dropped a basket of laundry. And I think I may have given one of the guards the wrong cup of tea—'

'Scarlett!'

'It's fine, though!' She clasped her hands in front of her. 'I don't think anyone noticed. At least, not many.'

I shook my head, and a little chuckle escaped. I couldn't disguise how happy I was to see a friend like her. 'All right,' I said, 'I think you'd better get out of here before you do something stupid and they catch on!'

'Okay.' She turned to exit, then looked back at me.

'Wait, what do you mean, me? Are you not coming? This is supposed to be a rescue mission. I can't rescue you if you don't come with me!'

I dropped my head. 'If it wasn't for Max, I would. As it is, Calpacious has made it so I cannot leave this place without endangering his life.'

She shook her head. 'Don't worry about Max,' she said. 'He's fine, trust me.'

'Fine? But I—'

'What's going on in here, Louisa?' The door opened, revealing the face of Miss Sourpuss herself— the surly, old maid who appeared to be the one in charge. Funny. She reminded me a lot of Miss Sharpe.

'Oh, nothing, ma'am!' Scarlett straightened herself out. 'I just . . . I came to collect Pepper's dishes!' She headed over to the bed and picked up the plate of untouched bread.

The older woman glared at Scarlett for a few more seconds. 'Just make sure you are out of here soon.' She turned her attention to me. 'The King has requested an audience with her.' With that, she walked out, shutting the door behind her. I pulled a face at the closed door. I hated the way she spoke about me as if I wasn't even in the room.

Scarlett grabbed my hand. 'Okay, let's go!' she whispered.

'Wait!' I pulled away. 'What do you mean about

Max? How do you know he's okay?'

'Pepper, now's probably not the best time to discuss this. How about we wait until we get outside the castle? There's a portal about to open on the other side of the forest. If we hurry, we might be able to catch it.' She exited through the door and I followed close behind. She paused.

'Okay,' I whispered, 'so what's the plan?'

She looked at me. 'The plan?' she repeated. 'Oh! The plan. Darn it, I *knew* I forgot something!'

'So . . . you don't have a plan?'

'Well, no. Not exactly. I was just going to make it to your room and then—'

This time it was me who grabbed her hand. 'Okay, follow me.' I ran down the hallway with her in tow. I counted three doors down, and pulled her to a stop when we got to the door to the servants' quarters. I remembered the door from earlier when the maids came to prep me. 'That glamour thing that you've done,' I said, pointing to her gingery hair. 'Can you do a similar thing on me?'

She shook her head. 'I'm sorry. It doesn't work like that.'

'Okay, well,' I said and pushed her in front of me, 'then you pretend you're taking me to Calpacious.'

She looked baffled, but nodded. We turned back towards the door. I felt the adrenaline kicking back in.

Scarlett had only just put her hand against the door when a loud cough made us stop.

'And where do you think you're going?' spoke a gruff voice.

I span round, coming face-to-face with none other than Calpacious himself.

KINGDOM

24

TURNING TABLES

Calpacious started to grin, and then laugh. Slowly, his appearance shimmered away. I watched in confusion as, before us, stood a chuckling Cade.

'What are you doing?' Scarlett scolded her friend, giving him a slap on his arm. 'You just about gave me a heart attack! I thought I told you to wait outside!'

Calpacious—well, Cade—gave a throaty laugh. 'Yes,' he said, 'but that was before I came up with the fantastic idea to disguise myself as the King to get you both out of here. What do you think? I got you pretty good, didn't I?'

Scarlett punched her friend on the shoulder. 'You,' she scolded him, 'are an irritating genius. Come on, we need to get going!'

Cade ignored her. Instead of following her command, he turned to me and asked, 'What happened to your arm?'

I ran a protective arm over the sling. 'It's quite a long story,' I said. 'I'll tell you when we get out of this damn place.'

We assumed a convincing position, in which Cade took the head, and Scarlett gripped onto my arm as she dragged me after him. We took the servants' route, hoping there'd be a lesser chance of us running into the real Calpacious there.

The other servants pressed themselves up against the walls as we passed, dropping their heads in respect as Cade strode past them. I made a show of putting up a fight against Scarlett, squirming and shouting the entire way. I was rather impressed with Scarlett's performance, too, as she remained silent and expressionless; as robotic as the real maids. Some of them gave us funny looks, perhaps wondering why the King was in the servants' part of the castle, but none of them spoke up.

We made it down to the ground floor, and exited into the main part of the building. Cade came to a stop, and, since there was no one else around, I asked him what was wrong.

'I don't know how to get out,' he stated.

'Well, it's easy,' Scarlett said. 'You follow that corridor along, then you turn right and . . . actually, wait. Where are we? Cade? What's going on? Cade, we're lost!' She started hyperventilating. 'What are we going to do? We're going to be stuck here forever!'

'Scarlett, shush!' Cade said, turning around. 'You're overreacting again. We need to keep our voices down. It's fine, we'll find a way out. Just follow me.'

Despite the busyness of the servants' quarters, the rest of the castle was surprisingly quiet. We only passed another staff member every couple of rooms or so, but that didn't stop us from dropping our formation. I quit my protesting, though. I didn't want to give Calpacious any reason to come and investigate.

Several rooms later, we still weren't getting anywhere. I was getting a little worried, as we had now traversed most of the lower floor and still had no clue where the real Calpacious was. The surly maid had told Scarlett that Calpacious was about to come and see me. He would realise I wasn't in my room and send out a search!

We rounded a corner, and there it was! A set of

double doors looked out to an expansive and decorative garden. This was our escape route!

Before we could venture any further, a sound caught my attention.

'Wait!' I whispered. Scarlett and Cade both stopped.

Another door that led into a room not far away from us was propped slightly ajar, and the sound of voices could be heard from within. Trying not to make a noise, I beckoned for the two sylphs to come closer before I tiptoed across the room and held my ear up against the tarnished wood.

'For the last time, I know you think this is a bad idea, but this girl is going to help us.'

It was Calpacious voice, and he didn't sound happy with whoever he was talking to.

'You know what, I don't really care what you think anymore,' he continued in a rage. 'You've been doing things your own way for too long now. Can you not see that your plans don't work? Trust me. This is exactly the step we need to take if we ever hope to gain access.'

'But—' another voice—a female voice—interrupted.

'I know, I know. My subjects may suspect something is up. But you never know. If it's true, and this girl really can change my story, then she can make the people trust me. I need you to find out more about her. She trusts you. Discover her weaknesses.'

Footsteps started moving towards the door, and I felt myself being pushed away.

'Move!' I heard Cade whisper. Without making too much of a noise, I slipped away, making a beeline for the exit, the two sylphs at my heels. My heart hammered, but not from the running, or from nearly getting caught.

That person who Calpacious was talking to in there . . . he'd told her I trusted her. That meant it was someone I knew. And not only that, but someone who I thought was on our side.

But I had no time to ponder over that now. We had to run.

We fled through the doors and into the garden. In our hurry to get away from Calpacious, it completely escaped our minds to be on the lookout for staff. Gardeners and guardsmen turned to us in confusion as we bolted out of the castle, making us come to a dead stop. Damn. What now?

Cade cleared his throat. 'Um,' he began in his deep Calpacious voice. 'Don't mind us. Er, back to work, my good people.'

Their suspicious gazes followed us as we inched towards the row of trees that was the entrance to the forest—the same forest where I first met Therron. In

295

fact, if I squinted, I could just about make out the ledge where he hid me from the patrolling guardsmen. I smiled to myself at the memory.

Once we were concealed by the foliage, Scarlett gave Cade a hefty thump.

'Hey!' he protested as he shrank back to sylph-size. His glamour was now gone. 'What was that for?'

Scarlett fluttered beside him and flicked her long curls, happy to be back in her normal form.

'Did you really think they were going to fall for that?' she asked. 'I mean, really, could you have *been* anymore un-Calpacious-like?'

'Well, I don't know!' Cade replied. 'I've never met the man. What do you think then? Should I have been more menacing? More controlling, perhaps?'

'Ooh, I think maybe you could have dropped your tone a little bit more. Maybe made eye contact with them to enhance your physicality—'

'Look, guys!' I interrupted. 'Can we save the drama class for later? Calpacious is going to be looking for us and we've left a pretty obvious trail. I suggest we get out of this place as fast as we can!'

Cade and Scarlett agreed, and we commenced racing through the trees. I had no idea where I was going, and just hoped to come across an exit if we continued to travel in a straight line.

'This is all your fault!' I heard Scarlett accuse

Cade as we travelled.

'My fault?' he rebutted, 'I think you'll find it's your fault. You're the one who came up with the idea of rescuing her!'

'Well, I wouldn't have known she needed rescuing if you hadn't been spying on the castle!'

'What, so you'd rather we hadn't found out, and we'd just left her there instead?'

'Hey!' I shouted between pants. 'I'm right here!' But the two of them carried on like they hadn't heard me.

'I never said that!' said Scarlett in defence. 'Anyway, I told you to wait outside!'

'And what would you have done then?'

'. . . I'd have thought of something.'

'Hey, shush!' I shouted at the two of them. They stopped their quarrelling and turned to look at me. I slowed to a stop. 'You two arguing isn't helping. It's only going to get us found quicker. We need to find this portal. Do you know where it is?'

Cade gave Scarlett one more dirty look before answering me. 'Absolutely,' he said. 'It's just off the northern border of the King's forest. If we head . . .' He paused, looked around himself, and pointed left. '. . . this way, it should be a twenty-minute journey.'

'Twenty-one and a half, actually,' added Scarlett, her arms crossed in front of her. Cade hit her shoulder,

Twenty-one and a half minutes later, the trees began to spread out. Scarlett had been giving Cade some more pointers for his acting methods, but, under my insistence, had been a lot quieter about it.

'Look, there it is!' she exclaimed, forgetting about the volume of her words. 'Sorry,' she said when she realised.

I wouldn't have noticed it if it wasn't for the small cluster of magicks all waiting in line, ready to cross into the manor. It was funny—it almost reminded me of seeing people waiting for a bus back home.

The portal itself was almost invisible. All I saw was a patch of air where the shapes and colours were distorted, kind of like a heat haze. Circular in shape, the portal had a diameter of roughly twice my own height.

I watched as a frog spontaneously appeared out of the centre of the portal and plopped down to the ground. He was soon followed by a short, chubby gnome-like creature, who sauntered away, a grouchy look on his face.

Similarly, already on the ground, a group of five different magicks all disappeared one at a time through the magical portal. Amongst them, an elegant looking elf in a white dress, and a beefy giant, who had to get down on his hands and knees in order to get through.

'I never got the chance to ask,' I spoke to the two sylphs as we waited. 'Why is the portal scheduled like this? And why only on this side?'

'It all has to do with the spell the wizard created,' Cade explained. 'He wanted to limit the traffic as much as he could. It was only under Marcius' command that he allowed us into the human world at all.'

Soon, we were at the front of the queue, and I hesitated.

'Are you sure this is going to work?' I asked, feeling nervous. 'I go through here now, and when I go back in through the mirror, it will land me somewhere different?'

Neither of them could give me a straight answer.

'It's impossible to say,' admitted Scarlett. 'When the portal is open our end, wherever it is is where you will end up. But if there is no portal here when you enter from the manor, you could end up anywhere.'

'I suppose it's worth the risk.' I fiddled with the fabric of my sling. 'Listen, I don't suppose you—'

I was cut off by the sound of movement coming from behind me. I span round. There was no one there, but we were definitely being watched.

'Cade,' I whispered. 'Change. Now!'

My back was to him, but I heard the impact of

Cade's feet hitting the leafy floor as he transitioned back into the form of Calpacious.

There was silence for a few seconds. Not even the wind through the branches could be heard. We turned round, and were just about to walk away when a rough hand grabbed at my wrist. I looked up to see the hooded face of one of the King's guards—I could tell from the regulation red and gold armour that they all wore variations of.

'Let her go,' Cade said from behind me.

'But . . . your majesty—' replied the guard.

'NOW!'

My arm fell back to my side and I stepped away, trying to avoid the guard's menacing glare.

'Get back to your post,' Cade continued. 'I can handle it from here.'

The guard nodded and turned away, trudging back to where he came from.

'All right!' cheered Scarlett, performing a loop-the-loop. 'That was so much better! You could've had me fooled, then!'

'Um, Scarlett?'

Scarlett and I turned our heads at the sound of a new voice. When I saw who it was who had spoken, I gulped.

There were two Calpaciouses.

RACHEL E. WOLLASTON

25

UNTIMELY ENCOUNTERS

'What's going on?' Scarlett grasped her head in both hands.

It was clear what was going on: we were caught. Calpacious saw Cade for the first time, and did a double-take. Well, so would I if I saw myself standing in front of me.

'Who are you?' asked the real Calpacious to his lookalike.

A mischievous smile spread across Cade's face.

'I am King Calpacious,' he said.

Calpacious glared at him. 'I will have the guards execute you for your impersonation,' he threatened.

Cade just smiled back. This was a game for him.

'Not if I get them to execute you, first!'

Calpacious frowned. 'And what gives you the authority to demand that?'

'I am the King.'

'Preposterous!'

'No, Calpacious!'

'What?'

'I said I'm King Calpacious. Not King Preposterous. Maybe you're King Preposterous. But not me.'

Calpacious' face reddened. 'This is treason!' he bellowed. 'I will not let you get away with this!'

'Psst, Pepper!' whispered a still tiny Scarlett into my ear. 'This is your chance! Go! Now!'

I slipped away from the exchange between Cade and Calpacious towards the shimmering portal. Maybe I could slip through without him noticing.

As I inched closer, I started to feel the pull of the portal's strength. I was nearly there. I could have escaped right then without being noticed, but I hesitated. Did I really want to leave Scarlett and Cade here to suffer Calpacious' wrath?

The hesitation cost me, as soon after, I felt the hands of one of Calpacious' guards grabbing my shoulders. At the same time, I watched as another pair of hands flew forward and trapped Scarlett inside a glass jar.

Calpacious caught my eye and gave me a triumphant grin. Of course he wouldn't come here without backup. He hadn't been distracted by Cade at all—it was all a show. The impish joy slipped from Cade's face as he, too, realised this.

'I originally came here just for Pepper,' he sneered, 'but now it looks like I've caught myself a couple of fairies, too.'

'We're sylphs,' said Cade through gritted teeth.

Anger bubbled up inside me, and with it came a burst of adrenaline even I hadn't seen coming. With a surge of energy, I slammed my heel down onto the foot of my captor and dug my elbow into his stomach. With a groan, he loosened his grip, and I was able to spin around and land a punch straight to his mouth.

Cade followed my lead, and one smooth kick brought the other guard to drop the glass jar onto the floor where it promptly smashed, and out fluttered a slightly woozy-looking Scarlett. After only a moment's hesitation, she grew to human size, her hand pressed up against her forehead.

'Stars above!' she said. 'Be more careful next time, will you, Cade? You almost knocked my wings off!'

Both the guards went to grab us again, but now they were outnumbered. Well, outnumbered, maybe, but out-skilled? Between the three of us, and with my injury, we were only able to hinder some of the attacks.

I didn't get much of a chance to look around, as I was too busy defending myself, but I was aware that Calpacious was gone. Or maybe not gone, so much as hiding.

A fist flew towards me, and I barely had time to dodge the blow. But as I bent down, another hand grabbed my elbow—the bad one. It started to slip from its sling. The guard tugged, and a jolt of pain racked through my forearm.

'Let go of me!' I said as I tried to squirm away, but the harder I resisted, the more my arm hurt. I repeated the moves I performed earlier, but none of them worked. This was a different guard, and he was a lot more resilient.

'Scarlett!' I heard Cade shout. 'Now!'

It took a while, but I managed to squirm myself round to face him. I aimed my fist at his face. I launched my punch, but when it struck, it collided with something solid. Where there should have been soft skin was a rock hard surface.

I didn't realise until then, but my eyes had been closed. At the unexpected impact, I opened them again, and was baffled by the sight.

The man was frozen. With one hand still wrapped around my waist and his eyelids half shut, he was completely still.

'Run!' Cade yelled. I turned my head and saw Cade's arms stretching out towards the guard who held me captive, an intense look of concentration on his face. Scarlett was doing the same, her arms pointing out to the other one. 'We can't hold them for long!'

The guard's stance unyielding, I sucked in my breath and squeezed out under his arm. I took off towards the portal, but stopped when Scarlett called out.

'Wait!' she said. 'I nearly forgot something. Come over here!'

'Scarlett, be quick!' said Cade.

I did as Scarlett told me.

Carefully, she drew back one of her arms and reached her hand into a hidden pocket in her leafy dress. All the while, she did not take her gaze from the guard.

'Here,' she said, removing whatever it was from her pocket. 'It's Therron's book. I hid it from the other maids. Take it back; keep it safe.' She placed the little notebook in my hands just as a sound escaped from one of the guards. 'Now run!'

Without any more prompting, I sprinted away, but by now, the guards were beginning to move again. Cade was right—they really couldn't hold them for long.

But I had a head-start. I hooked the notebook inside my sling and ploughed towards the portal. It was only a few feet away; I would make it with one leap.

I closed my eyes as I felt the cold pull on my face. I was about to jump, but a leathery grip caught my hand, keeping me grounded. I opened my eyes to see the familiar, un-focusing eyes of Calpacious.

It was too late, and he knew it. Already half inside the portal, I continued to be sucked towards it. My legs drifted out from beneath me, and soon I was hovering horizontally, Calpacious' grip the only thing tethering me to Tantary.

His eyes latched onto mine. I hated when he did that—it made him look only half-mad. I found it easier when I believed he was insane.

'This isn't over,' he warned. The whooshing of the air past my ears did its best to block out other sounds, but I heard him clearly. 'And to prove it, here is my parting gift.'

His other hand reached over and clamped something around my arm. He then removed his gloved fingers, revealing a golden bangle that looked much like the one I saw around Max's wrist back at the castle.

'You still have a job to do,' he said. 'Your friend

may not be in danger, but I have other ways of making you comply.'

My friend . . . Max? What was he saying?

But I didn't have much time to speculate. Calpacious loosened his grip and I shrieked as the portal sucked me in further. He caught me just before I disappeared, pulling at the ends of my fingers.

'By the way,' he said, 'did you really think you could go gallivanting through my lands without me knowing what you were doing? You are never going to find my brother. You want to know why?' He lowered his bushy blond eyebrows and leaned his face in towards me. 'Because I killed him.'

And with that, he let go, sending me screaming into the dark abyss.

26

GLAD RETURNS

I barely had a chance to think before my body slammed against a wall and I crumpled down to the floor.

My bad arm was saved from the hit, but my head was not. I winced and cradled the side of my head in the palm of my hand, willing the pain to stop.

It took a while for the headache to ebb enough for me to open my eyes. I was in the cupboard back at the manor. The mirror I fell out of glowed and swirled in a frenzied way which I could tell wasn't just from my entry.

Max was right—the portal had been weakened. It

was not meant to support humans travelling through it. I wondered how long it would be until even Calpacious could breach it.

Not that he would even have to wait long, if I did what I was told. But then, what power did he have over me here? I was back in my own land, now. I need never see him again.

Then I remembered the band he slapped onto my wrist during my departure. I looked at it again now. What the hell was it for? While it looked like he had wrapped it around my arm via a hinge, there was no sign of any opening, and it refused to slide up or down my arm. Maybe I could cut it off?

I tried to tell myself it was nothing. Maybe now that I was back here, it didn't even have any power. I pushed back the knowledge that Calpacious never did anything without a thorough plan. Today's fight proved that to me.

No, I had bigger problems to deal with now. Such as telling Adrian his son had been kidnapped by an evil fictional king.

My mind replayed the last thing Calpacious told me before he sent me falling through the portal. He killed Alzabar. His own brother. No, not just his brother—the rightful ruler of Tantary.

I felt sick to my stomach. All this time, we were hunting for a dead man. I had to let Therron know. I had to . . .

Oh God. Therron! What happened to him? The last I knew, he had been abandoned outside the Old City when Calpacious' guards kidnapped me. Would he think I left him on purpose? Oh, what had I done? Anything could have happened to him!

I still hadn't moved from the enclosed cupboard, having squeezed myself into one of the corners where I shook with heavy breath. I barely noticed when the door opened and I was taken by the hand and led downstairs. Soon, I found myself on a plush armchair with a plaid blanket covering my legs. I raised my head to see Adrian entering the room and placing a steaming mug of cocoa in my hands. From looking up, I recognised where I was—in Adrian's office; the room I met Max in for the first time.

Thinking about Max caused my breathing to hitch again. How was I going to explain to Adrian what happened?

'How are you doing?' Adrian asked as he took a seat on a chair next to mine.

'Um,' I said, testing my voice. 'Okay. I think. What happened?'

'You had a panic attack.'

I said nothing for a while as I stared at my cup, waiting for my breathing to slow.

'I suppose all the secrets are out now, then,' Adrian

spoke after a few moments passed. 'So, what do you think of Tantary?'

'Is this why you brought me here?' I looked up, watching his face through the billowing steam of the hot chocolate. 'Calpacious told me about my imagination. Was that why you employed me? To send me off into that fantasy world and do your dirty work for you?'

Adrian rubbed at his forehead, stretching and pinching the wrinkles embedded there. 'I didn't have much of a choice,' he said. 'I had no intention to send you there, mostly because I didn't know it was even possible. Of course, I wouldn't have made you do anything without your full understanding and consent. But, as you know, situations robbed us of the opportune moment to work it all out.'

I could see he wanted to say more. Probably to ask questions, like what happened to my arm. But he decided to keep quiet. I took a few sips of the cocoa, hoping to ease the jitters a little more. It was a weird feeling. I'd never had a panic attack before, not even through my school years, but I knew I never wanted one again.

'I'm sorry,' I said. 'It's all my fault. I knew what you wanted me to do—to find Alzabar and stop Calpacious coming through the portal. But I couldn't even do that. If anything, I've just made things worse.'

'So, Max found you, did he?' Adrian asked, 'I take it he explained everything.'

I took a deep breath. He would have to know sooner or later, anyway.

'Listen, Adrian,' I began. 'About Max. He's—'

'Right here.'

Adrian and I span round at the same time to see Max standing in the doorway, alive and uncaptured. I nearly spilled my cocoa.

'Max!' I shouted. 'How did you . . . what are you doing here?'

'Why?' he asked, defiance in his tone. 'Do you not want me to be here? Would you rather I went back to Calpacious' castle?'

That caught his father's attention.

'You were in his castle?' he asked as Max strutted into the room and launched himself up to sit on the top of the desk. 'What in heaven's name were you doing in there?'

Max raised both his hands in the air. 'Don't look at me,' he said. 'It wasn't any of my doing. That dumb king kidnapped me because he thought it would give him leverage over her.' He pointed an accusatory finger my way. I glared back.

'Don't you think he wouldn't have found you if you hadn't left Tharva's house in a strop?' I said.

'You could have escaped the Tropolis with Therron and me and helped us find Alzabar.'

'And look where that got you!' he shot back. 'The only thing you returned with was a broken arm. I'm lucky I got out of there when I did.'

I peered at him. 'How *did* you escape?' I asked. 'The last time I saw you, you were restrained by Calpacious' guardsmen, looking like death itself. And now you come waltzing back in here with barely a scratch on you. There had better be a wild story behind all this.'

'Oh, trust me,' he said, 'there is. But right now, the point is, your quest was futile. I know Alzabar is dead. I found out long before you did.'

'Whoa, hold on there.' Adrian interrupted. 'Slow down. Alzabar is dead? What . . .'

'So, it turned out you and Story-Boy went on a life-threatening mission for nothing!' Max snickered.

'Don't call him that!'

'What, that's what he is!' He smirked. 'He is a made-up figment of my father's imagination, with no soul. He shouldn't even exist.'

My blood boiled and I squinted my eyes so narrow that I felt the pressure against my eyeballs. 'You're lucky my arm is in a sling,' I said, 'otherwise I would come over there beat out whatever sense you have left. Therron has more soul and personality than you ever will!'

'Please!' Adrian stood up and stretched his arms out, one flexed palm facing each of us, as though scared one of us really was about to charge at the other. And trust me, I was tempted.

'We have a big dilemma on our hands. I'm still not sure what's going on, but we need to work things out, and you two bickering isn't going to solve anything.'

'She started it,' Max mumbled.

'Enough! Am I going to have to ground you for the next month? Maybe you would like to work with Miss Sharpe for a while.'

Max opened and closed his mouth like a goldfish. 'You can't do that!' he protested. 'I'm twenty-one. I nearly own this house! You wouldn't!'

'Adrian?' I piped up. 'How much do you know about Tantary?' He turned to look in my direction, anger still evident in his features. 'I mean, do you know much about their magic? Or, more specifically, about Calpacious' magic?'

'I know some,' he said. 'Most of what I know I've gleaned from studying all the books we keep here and the notes of my ancestors. Everything you see in here is work I've done based on that.' He gestured around at the masses of paperwork. 'Why do you ask?'

'I have something to show you.' I lifted my left arm from where I had been resting it at my side,

317

showing him the golden band Calpacious fitted me with. Adrian peered at the contraption. 'I saw Max wearing a similar one earlier, but this one seems different. Do you know what it is?' I asked him.

To my dismay, Adrian shook his head. 'I'm afraid I have never seen the likes before,' he said. 'That land has evolved much since the time of Marcius Calthorpe. No one else of our heritage has had the ability to speak to the magicks since. What do you think of this, Max?' He lifted my arm, indicating to the wristband. Max shrugged.

Adrian's revelation made me think about Lilly; his niece. She could see, not only Penelope—or, Fifi, as she lovingly dubbed her—but Scarlett and Cade, too. She could see them. And Adrian didn't know this. Well, it looked like that was a conversation to have later down the lines.

'What did Calpacious say to you?' Adrian asked, interrupting my thoughts. 'Maybe we can work out what this thing is together.'

I sighed and leaned back into the chair.

'Calpacious said many things,' I said. 'But I don't feel like talking about it now.' Without really meaning to, I closed my eyes. The cocoa was making me drowsy. Or perhaps it was the after-effects of the panic attack.

'Understood.' I heard Adrian grunt as he stood up

from the chair. 'Come on, Max,' he said. 'I think we could all do with getting an early night tonight.'

I picked up what was left of my drink and got ready to follow Adrian out of the door. Max mumbled something about girls being weak before he shoved past me and into the quiet, darkened hallway. It must have been some time in the middle of the night here, or at least late in the evening. It was odd adjusting to the time change, kind of like coming home after a long flight. But after today's exertions, I was more than ready for a full night's sleep.

The three of us walked in silence up the dimly-lit staircase, trying not to wake the sleeping children. I was about to turn down into the corridor that led to my bedroom when a thought occurred to me.

'Adrian?' I whispered. He paused. 'What day is it?'

He smiled. 'It's July 27th. When you wake up, it'll be Thursday.'

'Thank you.'

I walked back to my room with a comforted smile on my face. It may have seemed trivial, but just knowing what day it was brought back a vague sense of normality.

That night, I went to bed with a contradictory sense of achievement. My sleep was fitful, but my dreams were pleasant.

27

CUNNING DEVICES

woke up the next morning feeling, for the first time since I had landed in Tantary, that things were going to be okay.

Waking up in my room at the manor felt so comfortably familiar. The first thing I did after getting out of bed was take a lovely, warm shower, washing out all the grime and terror that had accompanied the last few days. I savoured the feeling of the water running down my face, invigorating me with their cleansing sense of natural energy.

Rescuing Alzabar may be a task now in the past, but I still had one person worth saving: Therron.

While falling asleep the night before, I was

thinking. Knowing both Max and I managed to escape from Calpacious' castle gave me hope. Perhaps he wasn't as undefeatable as we all assumed. Maybe there was a chance that, if we all worked together, we could thwart the King's plans.

Yeah. Work together. Now, there was an unlikely possibility. I rolled my eyes in remembrance of Max's antics last night. He really had it out for Therron, and probably most of Tantary. I doubted he would be willing to help.

I got myself dressed, and turned my nose up in disgust when I saw most of the food in my private kitchenette was now horribly out of date. But having been away for almost two Earth-weeks, that wasn't much of a surprise.

I headed downstairs. It was a Thursday—my day off. I had to go and see my family. There was a bus nearby I could take to the train station, and I intended to have a hearty breakfast before the journey. And when I said hearty breakfast, I meant hearty breakfast!

I raided the kitchen and piled my plate up with a full fry-up . . . with extra everything. I just sat down at the kitchen table to dig in, when I heard voices coming from the room beyond.

I stepped through into the lounge and saw Max and Adrian sitting on opposite chairs, having what looked like a heated discussion.

'I don't care what she said to you,' Adrian said. 'You've got to bury whatever this grudge is you have against her. Whether you like it or not, you are a part of this. Now act it.'

From where I stood, the back of Adrian's head was all I saw of him, but the whole of Max's face was visible. He hadn't noticed me lurking in the doorway.

'Father, I cannot work with that girl! She is rude and stubborn and . . . I just dislike her.'

It didn't take a genius to work out which 'her' they were talking about. I leaned against the doorframe, folding my arms over my chest and crossing one leg in front of the other. Man, it felt good to wear jeans again.

'Because she doesn't fancy you?' Adrian asked. Max said nothing, and I felt heat rising into my cheeks. Should I really be listening into this conversation? As guilty as I felt, though, I was intrigued.

Adrian sighed in frustration. 'When are you going to recognise what is happening to this house is more important than your social life?'

'She chose that story kid over me.' Max sounded like a toddler who didn't get what he wanted for Christmas. 'Who would do that?'

'Hey!' I called out from my corner of the room. 'I'm right here, you know.'

Max didn't even look like he heard me.

'Look, I'll help you, all right?' he said. 'Just don't expect me to be too enthusiastic about it.'

'Excuse me?' I said. 'I can hear you!' With my arms still folded in a defiant position, I marched over to where the two of them sat. 'Listen, Max, I do not appreciate you talking about me behind my back. If you have a problem with me, I would much rather you said it to my face.'

Max stood up and, without even looking in my direction, said, 'I'm going to make some toast,' and headed into the kitchen.

'What,' I called after him, 'now you're just going to ignore me?'

I turned to Adrian for backup, but he was leafing through a stapled document in his hands, paying me no attention.

'God, anyone would have thought I didn't exist!'

Adrian put the paper down on the coffee table and walked towards me. I blocked his passage, hoping to get some words out of him. But then the strangest thing happened.

He passed straight through me.

I felt my face go cold as a chilling shiver drained the blood away. Okay, what the hell was that? They couldn't hear me, they couldn't see me, and now, it seemed, they could walk right through me. What was

RACHEL E. WOLLASTON

going on? Was I dead? I certainly couldn't remember dying, and I didn't feel like that was something you would forget in a hurry.

I inspected my hands, but they weren't transparent, the way you'd expect a ghost's to be.

The bracelet was still on my wrist. I forgot it was there. This had to be why they couldn't see me.

My heart started racing again. Why would Calpacious make me invisible? What could he possibly gain from this?

Another shuddering thought occurred to me. I had been so looking forward to seeing my family today. But how could I possibly do that when no one could see me?

Nothing made any sense. I needed to get out of the house, to get some fresh air and to clear my head. All the 'what ifs' and 'maybes'—I had to get them out of my mind before I drove myself crazy.

My breath heavy, I hurried through the rooms into the foyer, making a beeline for the front door. I threw it open and took a step forward, but I was hurled back, as though by a magical force-field.

I stared at the open doorway, at the leafy trees that were part of the manor's grounds. I inched forward and reached out my hand. As soon as my fingers came level with the door frame, they struck something solid. Yet I saw nothing keeping me from leaving. It was like an energy; a magnetic field.

'Pepper!'

I turned round to see Lilly beaming her sweet little face up at me.

Wait, she could see me? Knowing that calmed me down a little. Maybe the invisibility was just a temporary thing.

'You're back! You were gone for ages and ages and I thought I would never see you again!'

Lilly launched herself at me, trapping my legs in a tight embrace.

'I'm so happy to see you!' she said. I told her I was happy to see her, too. 'And Peter missed you!' she continued, her voice slightly muffled where she held her mouth up against my thigh. 'Uncle Adrian told us you went on a special adventure. Is that true?'

As pleased as I was to see her, I had to peel Lilly away from me slightly. Her grip was beginning to hurt. I crouched down so I could look her in the eyes, lit with an excited twinkle.

'You would have loved it,' I told her, trying to equal her enthusiasm. 'I saw everything! Fairies, trolls, phoenixes . . . and I saw where Fifi lives!'

'You saw Fifi's home?' Lilly exclaimed, eyes wide. 'The one behind the scary door?'

I nodded. 'The very same.'

I heard the footsteps of someone approaching, and

looked to my right to see Adrian heading towards us. He smiled when he saw Lilly, as I imagine anyone would, seeing her beaming face.

'Morning, Lilly,' he said. 'Have you seen Pepper this morning?'

Lilly giggled. 'Silly!' she said and pointed at me. 'She's right here!'

Adrian rubbed the skin around his eyes, and I noticed the dark circles framing them. It looked like I wasn't the only one having trouble sleeping.

'No games now, Lilly, please. This is important.'

But Lilly insisted. 'I'm not playing games! See? She's right here!'

'I'm really not in the mood for this, Lilly,' Adrian said with a sigh.

Lilly's head cocked to the side in confusion, but then realisation dawned on her face as it clicked. She looked back at me with an amused expression.

'Pepper!' she said. 'He can't see you, but I can. Just like the fairies!'

It took me a while, but eventually I caught on to what she was trying to say. I was just like one of the magicks—invisible to all those without the ability to see the characters, and unable to leave the confining walls of the house. My eyes found the gold band on my arm. So, this was Calpacious' game?

'What do you mean?' Adrian asked Lilly. 'What

327

fairies?'

Biting her lip, she turned to look back at me. 'I wasn't supposed to say that. Was I?'

'It's fine.' I gave her a reassuring smile. 'Go on. Tell your uncle about what you can see.'

She looked worried for a moment, then, with some uncertainty, began to explain to Adrian, 'There are fairies. Two of them. I saw them in this house. I think they live in one of the rooms here—a room I'm not allowed to go into. And . . . and there's a magical bunny, too! I called her Fifi. And there's—'

'Lilly.'

Lilly shrank a little at Adrian's interruption. 'Am I in trouble?'

'No! No, of course not. But I . . . I think you and I need to talk.'

I could tell Adrian was struggling to digest this new can of worms. I felt guilty for making Lilly launch her ability on him right now, what with everything else going on, but she was my only hope of communicating with him while this stupid band was still on.

A little shell-shocked, Adrian appeared indecisive as he beckoned Lilly to follow him towards his office.

'What about Pepper?' she asked him. Adrian glanced to the empty space where I stood.

'You say you can see her?' he asked, and Lilly

nodded. 'Then I guess you should—both—come with me.'

With a befuddled look, Adrian turned and walked down the corridor. Lilly turned to me, and I gestured for her to follow.

It was weird, being seen by one, but not the other. Adrian asked me questions, but my answers had to be transmitted through Lilly.

Lilly took the whole situation in her stride. I was rather impressed at the way she handled being told she lived in an enchanted manor. I suppose, when you've been seeing disappearing bunnies and chatty sylphs for the last few weeks, something like that wouldn't come as much of a surprise.

It was Adrian who struggled to take it all in. I explained as well as I could, through Lilly, about everything I knew regarding the bracelet. It wasn't much. I mentioned the similar one I saw on Max back at the castle.

'Max is at his mother's house this morning,' said Adrian with a pensive expression. 'He must have got his band off somehow. I doubt he's got his phone on him—he never has—so when he returns, we'll have to ask him how he removed it.'

I examined the band more closely. Completely smooth all round, there was no visible way of getting it on or off. I wondered how Calpacious even got it on me in the first place. There had to be some kind of magic around it.

I remembered Calpacious saying something about wizards. So, was that who he hired to do his dirty work?

Lilly looked bored. She rested her cheek against her palm, staring down at her bare toes as they scuffed back and forth on the grey carpet.

'I want to go,' she said, 'I think Fifi might be back.'

Adrian stood from where he sat behind his desk, his thoughtful expression turning into an affectionate one as he looked at his young niece.

'Of course,' he said with a smile. 'I've kept you here long enough. You can go now. And, um, tell Pepper I say thank you for coming and speaking with me.'

Lilly giggled. 'She can hear you!' She stood up from the armchair and took my hand. 'And she says you're welcome.'

Adrian watched as we left the room, a bemused expression on his face. I knew he was uncomfortable about this whole situation, and I couldn't blame him.

I followed Lilly back to her bedroom. I surprised myself by how much I missed her while I was in Tantary. I took this job to mind the young niece and nephew of Mr. Calthorpe, but for my first two weeks of the job. I had spent more time away in a fictional fantasy world. In many ways, I found myself glad to be back.

'Fifi!' Lilly called out, crouching down to get a view of beneath her bed. 'Fifi, where are you?'

We both waited for a few seconds, but there was no glimpse of a feisty white rabbit. Lilly's smile turned down.

'I thought she would be here by now,' she said, looking dejected. 'I haven't seen her for days and days! She never goes away for this long.'

I placed a comforting hand against her back. 'I wouldn't worry,' I told her. 'Fifi is a very busy bunny. She probably has a lot of work to do back home.'

Lilly sniffled, but managed to compose herself in record-breaking time. Funny how her attention could be diverted.

'I forgot to ask you!' she said, and pointed at my broken arm. 'What did you do to it?'

I sat down on her pink duvet, and beckoned for her to perch beside me. I guess I owed it to her to tell her an exciting story. It felt similar to when I'd told Peter the tale about Archie, only this time, the fantasy fairy-tale wasn't from my imagination.

'There was a big battle,' I told her, and already, her interest was ignited. 'My friend and I were searching for the lost king. We heard he had been living in the ruins of an old city. It was a long journey, but we eventually found his castle. The structure was crumbling, encased in a shield of twining vines.'

A voice at the door interrupted my story,

'Lilly,' said a tired voice, and I looked to see Peter standing in the doorway, rubbing his eyes as though he'd just woken up. 'Where's Uncle Adrian?'

Lilly bounced up and down on the mattress at the sight of her brother. 'Peter, Peter!' she said. 'Pepper's back!'

Peter's face lit up, the previous fatigue suddenly vanishing.

'Pepper!' he exclaimed with a beaming smile. It took me a while to realise it, but he was looking directly at me. I flicked a confused look at Lilly, and then back at Peter.

'You can see me?'

Peter ran up to me and wrapped me in a firm hug, causing some of the air to squeeze out of my lungs. I grunted against the weight he leaned onto my injured arm. He noticed, and released his hold, though not by much.

Lilly recognised my befuddled expression.

'Since you left,' she explained, 'Peter has been able to see the magical creatures, too! He can see Fifi, and Scarlett, and her friend. And now he can see you, too!'

'Why didn't you tell your uncle this?' I asked her as I helped Peter onto my lap. At seven years old, he was a little large for this position.

'I don't know,' replied Lilly, looking down at her fingers in her lap. 'Uncle Adrian looked angry when I told him about what I could see. I didn't want him to be angry at Peter, too.'

'He wasn't angry,' I assured her. 'I think he was just a little shocked. And confused.'

So, Peter could see the magicks too, now? Adrian had to know about this. I had been led to believe this was an ability people were born with. I had no idea it could be something that developed.

So what changed? The last time I saw him, Peter showed no signs of being able to see the magicks; Lilly even told me as much. I had a vague idea. The story I told him about Archie—perhaps it ignited his imagination. After all, wasn't it the imaginative ones who had the ability?

'Pepper?' Peter asked me, bringing me back to the present. 'What's wrong with your arm?'

I smiled, ready to delve back into story-telling mode. 'Well, Peter, that is a very good question. Why, I was just telling your sister the same story!'

At that point, Peter wriggled off my lap and took a seat next to me on the other side of the bed. I was no sandwiched between the two Calthorpe children as

333

they eagerly awaited their story.

'While I was away,' I began, 'I bumped into Archie.'

'Archie!' said Peter, sitting up straight at the mention of the friendly troll.

'That's right.' I nodded. 'And his phoenix, Belinda. But she preferred to be called Bel.'

'Tell him about the King!' Lilly piped up.

'I'm getting there!' I told her with a chuckle. 'This land is ruled over by an evil king, who is threatening the lives of all the villagers.' I left out the part about him wanting to cross through the portal to take over our world. I didn't want to be responsible for giving them nightmares.

I continued with my story. 'The only way to stop this king was to find his brother; the rightful king of the land. My friend and I were led to believe that he was hiding out in a ruined city, but when we arrived, the place was empty. Wee, all except for one angry ogre. Still living in the years of the battles from years ago, he chased after us. He was going to kill us!'

The children gasped.

'At one point,' I told them, 'he stomped on my arm. That's how it broke. Before long, he had us both pinned to the ground, and was about to gobble us up, when out of the sky came a huge ball of fire!'

'The phoenix!' shouted Peter.

'That's right. Bel swooped down and knocked the ogre out of the way, sacrificing herself for us.'

Both Lilly and Peter stared at me in awe as the story came to its climactic end.

'That's so sad,' Peter said, 'but amazing!'

'I don't understand,' Lilly spoke up. 'Who was the other person? Your friend.'

'That friend was a lovely young man named Therron,' I told her. 'He saved me when I first entered his land. He showed me around, and tried to help me get back home to you. We became great friends.'

My chest suddenly felt empty when I realised I was speaking about Therron in the past tense, as though I didn't expect to see him again.

No, I couldn't let that be. I needed to know where he was, or at least if he was okay. My stomach coiled at the thought Calpacious might have kidnapped him, too.

'Pepper?' spoke Peter, noticing my silence. 'What's wrong?'

'I'll be back in a moment,' I said, and pushed off from the bed, leaving the two bewildered children behind me. I navigated my way back to my room, intending to pick up Therron's book from where I left it the night before. The book would tell me where Therron was, and what was happening to him.

I was certain I'd left the book on the desk, but

when I looked, it wasn't there. I checked on the floor, on the chair, and under the desk, but the book was nowhere to be seen.

Now frantic, I fumbled round the room, searching everywhere I could think of—in drawers, under the duvet, in the kitchen—but I couldn't find it anywhere. Who would take it? Adrian? A member of staff? Or, maybe, another magick?

The more I looked, the more frustrated I got. I was getting hot, and was about to shed my jacket when I heard something from the corridor.

'Lilly?' came the concerned voice of Adrian. 'Where are you?'

Though it was further down the corridor, I heard Lilly exiting her room.

'Is Pepper with you?' he asked. I didn't hear a response, so I assumed Lilly shook her head. 'Could you go and find her, please? I've found something really important she needs to see.'

At that moment, I exited my room and joined them outside Lilly's bedroom.

'You can tell Adrian I'm here,' I said to Lilly, as she had her back to me. She looked over her shoulder, acknowledging my presence, and announced my arrival to Adrian. He placed something in her hand.

'Show this to her,' her said, and she did so. I felt sorry for Lilly, being the one having to communicate our conversation. It couldn't be fun for her.

As soon as Lilly turned round, I recognised the object immediately as Therron's notebook. I grabbed the book off her, and heard Adrian's startled gasp. I suppose, to him, all he could see was a floating notebook.

I opened the front page and flicked through to the most recent entry. When I read what was written there, it was my turn to gasp, and it was all I could do not to drop the book to the floor.

I took off running down the corridor. Lilly called after me, but I ignored her as I dashed for the closet concealing the mirror.

'Pepper, don't!' yelled Adrien. Lilly's shouting must have clued him in that I'd taken off. 'You can't go back there—Calpacious will be expecting it. You'll be putting yourself in danger!'

'And what?' I shouted back, whipping back round to face him. 'Someone is hurting my friend! If I don't go back there now, then he's the one who's in serious danger!'

But I forgot he couldn't hear me. Just as Lilly turned to translate my rant to her uncle, I interrupted.

'You know what?' I said. 'Forget it! I'm going back. And don't you dare send Max after me this time!'

I shoved the book in my jeans pocket and found the

mirror. Its power was definitely weakening, or else it would've hidden itself from me, the way it had before. I couldn't hear if anyone was following me; I didn't care. I placed my hand against the mirror, and closed my eyes as the light got brighter and the familiar pull dragged me back to the land I just escaped from. Back to the tyrant king and his terrible schemes.

Back to Therron.

28

FURTHER COMPLICATIONS

ust like the last time, the trip threw me unconscious. I woke up with a pounding head, but not because I hit it—wherever I'd landed, it was the middle of the day, and the sun was unbearably bright. I buried my face in the crook of my elbow as I curled up from the ground with a groan.

It was too bright to open my eyes, but from the soft, yet grainy, sensation between my fingers, and the sounds of sea birds and rolling waves, I had a pretty good idea of my location.

Eventually, I was able to open my eyes to find

myself lying somewhere along Tantary's beautiful coastline. Only, where?

I reached for the back pocket of my jeans to check Therron's book was still there, only to have a sick feeling form in my throat when I found it empty. My fingers fumbled through the sand around me, and I could only breathe again when they came in contact with the spiral binding. It was still there. It must have fallen out of the pocket during the journey.

I felt a moment of guilt when I recalled the previous events that led me here. I ran off without much of an explanation, or even consideration for what I might be getting myself into. I'd probably sent Adrian into a panic. Maybe I was walking straight into my death. Whatever I'd done, the decision was made, and I had no choice but to follow the path I'd sent myself in.

I pushed myself up from the pale sand and wiped the grit from my clothes. Had I known this was where I would land, I would have chosen some more appropriate clothing—skin-tight jeans and a fleece jacket weren't exactly the most suitable clothes for this kind of weather. I shrugged off my jacket and secured it around my waist, grimacing at my choice of T-shirt. I might have got away with the hoodie, but I would have a hard time explaining to the magicks who the *Avengers* were.

I surveyed my surroundings in an attempt to figure out where I was and where I was going to go from here. Behind me was the solid face of a cliff, rising several metres vertically towards land. There was no way I could climb that. I would have to trek along the beach to find a pathway up to the top. That was, if the tide didn't catch me first.

I looked out towards the sea. The horizon was practically empty, with only a single island visible a few miles out. There were no boats, and no other magicks on the beach with me. The sudden sense of solitude drained any optimism I had left. I threw back my head and rubbed my eyes. It looked like I was going to have to wing it from here.

'Pepper, Pepper!'

What the . . .

I looked around to see who was calling my name... The beach was completely empty, but then I saw a short form run out from behind a nearby rock. The small body charged towards me while giving me a gleeful smile.

'Lilly!' I said, staring at her with wide eyes. 'What on Earth are you doing here?'

She stopped just in front of me and clasped her hands behind her back, rocking forwards and backwards on the balls of her feet. 'I followed you!' she said, looking pleased with herself.

I grabbed her by the shoulders and looked her directly in the eyes. 'You can't be here!' I told her, my breathing erratic.

'It's fine, see?' She stepped back from my grip and span round, revealing the Barbie rucksack strapped to her back. 'I brought food and orange juice and my iPad with me!'

'Lilly.' I tried to get her to look at me, tried to get her to see the gravity of what she had done. 'Does your uncle know you're here?'

The only answer she gave was the biting of her lower lip. I sighed.

'Come on,' I said, taking her hand, 'We need to find a portal and get you back to the manor before Adrian finds out you're missing.'

Lilly did not protest. She simply held onto my hand and followed me as I dragged her along the beach. My confident stride hid the fact that I had absolutely no idea where I was going.

'I'm sorry, Pepper,' Lilly spoke up after a while. 'I didn't mean to make you angry.'

I smiled and squeezed her hand. 'I'm not angry. I'm just . . .' I was scared, but I didn't want her to know. I was having enough trouble keeping a cap on my own fear. I didn't want a trembling five-year-old on my hands, too. '. . . I'm concerned about your uncle not knowing where you are. I really don't think

342

he would be happy with you being here.'

'But why?' she asked, kicking up the glistening sand as we walked. 'You're here! And I know all about the story book people, now. I can help you, and you can look after me! I mean, that's what you're supposed to do—you're my nanny!'

We'd been walking for twenty minutes, and there was still no sign of a way off this beach. I took a seat on a flat rock jutting out from the sand.

'Why are we here?' Lilly asked me as she unzipped her rucksack and rummaged through the goods packed in there. 'I thought all the story book people would live in a town or a hotel or something. Why are we on a beach?'

Lilly fished out a carton of orange juice from her bag. Feeling the dryness of my mouth, I asked if she happened to have another one. She handed me one, and I commenced trying to puncture the top with the pointy plastic straw.

'I'm not entirely sure,' I said in response to her question. 'The portal between these two worlds was created by a wizard many years ago. There are many rules I am not familiar with yet. As far as I know, the portal simply spits you out anywhere. But I suppose that doesn't really explain why *both* of us ended up here.' I took a quenching slurp from the carton.

'So,' she continued, her little eyebrows sinking

down on her forehead, making her chubby face scrunch up in thought. 'I still don't understand. What was in the book my uncle gave you?'

I fished the notebook out from my pocket and laid it on my lap.

'You remember how we told you that every person in this land comes from a book?' She nodded. 'Well this is the book my friend, Therron, comes from.'

'Therron!' Lilly repeated, recognising the name. 'Your friend who helped you fight the ogre!'

'That's the one,' I said. 'I think he might be in danger. In the book, it says he was being chased by something horrible.'

'What?'

'I don't know. The story is told from his perspective—it only tells what Therron sees, and Therron couldn't see who or what was chasing him.'

'Why don't you just write the bad things away?'

'It's not that simple,' I told her with a wan smile. 'I've tried to re-write a story. For some reason, it doesn't seem to work.' I was referring to Calpacious, but she didn't need to know that.

She slumped forwards and rested her cheeks in her hands. 'So, what are you going to do?'

'I'm going to find him,' I told her, though I didn't feel half as confident as I sounded. 'I hoped the portal would lead me straight to him, but now I'm going to have to look for him.'

Lilly was silent for a while as she stared at the tiny, spiral-bound notebook on my thighs.

'What's in the book now?' she asked. 'Has anything else happened?'

I'd been wondering the exact same thing. I supposed, in all honesty, I was too scared to find out what happened since the last time I looked. Did he escape? I hated to consider the alternative.

The ground began to shudder, diverting my attention from the book. Lilly grabbed onto my arm with a whimper. The trembling continued, getting more and more intense. It took me a while to realise it wasn't the ground that was moving—it was the rock we were sitting on. I barely had time to grab Lilly's waist and slide her off the rock with me before it began to rise up out of the sand.

Still keeping a tight arm around the quivering Lilly, I retrieved the notebook from where it dropped to the sand and inched back as the rock continued to grow. It climbed taller and taller, making grinding and splintering sounds as it rose. Lilly let out a shriek as the top of the rock, now feet above us, morphed into a jagged facial structure. I shielded her with my own body.

What had previously been a smooth rock, perfect for sitting on, was now a towering, snarling monster.

The rock monster brought its stony gaze down on us and gave a deafening roar, sending shards of rock debris in our direction. Some of them nicked my skin. I pulled on Lilly's hand to turn and face away from the creature, but another stood directly in our path. I took that moment to take a look around, and realised there was now a total of five hideous rock monsters surrounding us.

'Please!' I called out. With my one good arm supporting Lilly, I had nothing to defend myself with. 'We don't mean you any harm!' But the monsters continued to advance, seaweed-coated mouths upturned in hungry grimaces.

There was nowhere for us to go but backwards, towards the sea. Before long, I felt the tingle of salt water lapping at my ankles. Well, that was another pair of shoes ruined.

'Pepper, look!' Lilly's podgy finger poked out from behind my back. 'They've stopped!'

She was right. We were still edging away from the beasts, but they ceased their advance, stopping just where the waves lapped against the shore.

'They're frightened of the water!' she said, and it certainly seemed that way.

The monsters continued to glare at us, but at least we were no longer at risk of being lunch. I breathed a deep sigh of relief.

'Lilly,' I whispered, trying not to make any sudden movements that might send the creatures into a rage. 'We're going to walk slowly through the water until we can get help, or until they stop following us. Okay? Try not to make any sudden movements.'

Lilly nodded, totally silent.

We began to wade along the shoreline, the rock monsters watching us as we went. After a few steps, they still weren't following us, so I tried to relax a little more.

I decided it was time to check the book. I took it back out from my pocket and began to flip through the pages, until I heard a loud and unexpected yelp and a splash from behind me.

'Lilly!' I screamed, spinning round to find that she was no longer following me. The rock monsters roared at the disturbance, but I paid them no attention as I scanned around for the young girl. 'Lilly, where are you?' I screamed, the sound cutting my throat. My frantic eyes scoured the beach, the water at my feet, and even the surface further out, as sweat started to bead at my temples. She was gone. I'd let my guard down for one second, and she disappeared. What was Adrian going to say? How could I have been so careless?

I scarcely had a moment to gather my thoughts when something cold and slimy grabbed hold of my ankle and plunged me into a pool of darkness.

29

ORDINARY HEROES

To begin with, all I could hear was a sharp ringing in my ears. But, after a while, I started to make out the low humming of male vocals.

When my eyes opened, I saw the humming man standing not too far away from me, wringing out water from what looked like the jacket I'd worn earlier.

It took me a few coughs and splutters before I could get my voice working again.

'Excuse me?' I croaked, gaining the man's attention. With striking features and a windswept hat of cropped hair, I pegged the man to be in his thirties.

I stared at him for probably longer than what was acceptable. He had a difficult face to figure out—a clean-shaven face showing he might be used to a life of sufficiency, but his eyes conveyed a depth of knowing beyond the apparent.

'What happened?' I asked him, groaning as I rolled onto my side. I was dripping wet, and the lingering taste of saltwater tingled my tongue.

'Mermaids,' he answered. 'Vicious creatures, they are.' His upper class accent caught me off guard, adding yet more mystery as to who this character was. 'You're lucky I was around to help.' He reached a hand towards me for me to haul myself up with. 'Looks like you could do without any more broken bones. You can call me Marc, by the way.'

I thanked him as I got to my feet and brushed away some of the dirt that clung to my damp jeans. 'Where's Lilly?' I asked, without thinking he might not know who I was talking about.

'The little red-head?' he asked. 'She's just fine. She woke up a while before you did. The last time I saw her, she was playing over by the stream.'

My eyes followed to where he pointed and, indeed, there she was, swishing her hands in the glittering water of the stream that ran from the forest beyond.

Turning back round, I took note of where we were. Looking out to my left, I saw the calm sea stretching far off into the horizon. Somehow, he managed to get us to the top of the cliff overlooking the beach, with all its rock monsters and mermaids.

'How did you get us up here?'

Marc grinned and tapped the side of his nose. 'Now, where would the fun be if I gave away all my secrets?' he asked, handing me back my soggy jacket. I tied it back around my waist.

'Do you have magic?'

'Not magic, as such,' he said, 'but I'm willing to argue what I have is just as powerful. Now, may I ask what the two of you were doing on that beach?' he said, diverting the attention from himself. 'You should know those sands are ridden with mermaids and petramids.'

'Petramids?' I repeated. 'Is that what those rock creatures are called?'

Marc took a seat on the dry rock of the cliff. 'I had a feeling you were new around here,' he said. His words lacked the shock and fear most magicks would have had. 'The petramids work for the mermaids. They lure people into the water through the force of fear, making it easy for the mermaids to grab their prey by the feet and drag them under. In return, the mermaids give the petramids the bones of their victims—that's what they feed on.'

I shivered at the gruesome imagery Marc had

distilled in my mind. I didn't particularly fancy the idea of those beasts feasting on the remnants of my corpse.

'It was the portal that landed us there,' I explained. The question that had been bouncing around in my head earlier bubbled up to the surface. 'But why?' I asked him. 'I didn't see an open portal on that beach, and yet both of us ended up in the same place, even though we went through at different times. Why is that?'

I could tell I'd asked a weighted question from the way Marc's face drew in as he gazed out to the horizon.

'No one knows precisely how the portals work,' Marc explained. 'The wizard who created it calibrated it to limit the traffic between here and the manor as much as possible. We can only exit this land when a portal appears, which are scheduled to show up once every twenty-four hours. The locations are always the same five places, simply alternated in a fixed order.

'It's coming here from the other side that gets complicated. Our scientists have been trying for years to figure out the pattern, but there just doesn't seem to be one. I feel the truth in it may simply be you don't end up where you want to be; you end up where you need to be.'

'So, you're saying I was supposed to get attacked

by rock monsters and almost eaten by mermaids?'

Marc didn't answer. He just smiled and took a bite of a flat, white biscuit.

'Want one?' he asked, offering me the paper bag that I hadn't noticed he was holding before. They looked unappetising, but I was hungry, so I took one anyway. They were just as bland as I thought they would be.

'Thank you for saving us,' I said to Marc, having wiped the crumbs from my mouth after taking a bite.

'Not a problem,' he answered, finishing his own mouthful. 'Happy to help. Though I should probably tell you some of your possessions got a bit damaged in your struggle with the mermaids.'

'Yeah,' I said, lifting up the still dripping sleeve of my fleece jacket. 'I figured.'

Marc walked over to a pile of something wet and ruined. He picked it up, and a cascade of water dripped from what I now recognised to be Lilly's rucksack, shredded and grimy.

'I tried to recover what I could,' he said, 'but I'm afraid what wasn't torn to pieces by the mermaids was ruined by the water.' He took out Lilly's iPad, its pink case now torn down the middle and the back of it barely hanging on by a thread. 'This seems to be the only thing still intact,' he said, handing me the device. But while the object itself looked unbroken, I knew its

353

little swim had cost it its life. 'There was food and some strange boxes of liquid in there, too, but I'm afraid it's all been destroyed.'

'The book!' The thought sprang into my head. 'I had a little notebook with me,' I said, 'it was in my hands when we went under. Do you know what happened to it?'

'Oh,' said, Marc, 'you mean this one?' He held up Therron's book.

I was quick to retrieve it from him, but I already knew just from looking at it that it was severely damaged. I flicked through the pages, only to find the last few were missing completely, having been torn clean from the rest of the book. His story ended at the point I was kidnapped outside the Old City.

'No!' I cried.

'Hey, hey!' said Marc, holding out his hands in front of him. 'It's fine! Let's see, that belongs to a friend of yours, yes?'

I nodded.

'I know what you're thinking.' He took the book from my weakened hands. 'Look. These are just pages. They're not a real person. Your friend . . .'

'Therron,' I said.

'Therron is perfectly safe, no matter what happens to these pieces of paper here. Okay?'

I didn't ask how he seemed to know what I was

thinking. Instead, I told him, 'Therron was in danger. I came back to save him. But, without the last few pages of his story, I don't know where he is, or if anything else has happened to him!' As my fear and desperation rose, so did the tears behind my eyelids, but Marc did his best to keep me calm.

'Listen,' he said, 'it's going to be okay. I'll help you find him. Come. We should probably go and check on the young mistress, Lilly, down there. Is she your sister?'

'No,' I said, 'I'm her guardian.'

He gave me an odd look, but didn't ask further on the subject. I shoved the ruined notebook back into my pocket, but left the rest of the ruined items where they were—it wasn't as though we needed them anymore—and made our way over towards Lilly, still playing by the stream.

'I never asked,' Marc said as we walked, 'but what's your name?'

'Pepper,' I said, returning his smile. I was beginning to like Marc. It had been a while since I'd met anyone so genuine and happy about life.

'It's a pleasure to meet you, Pepper,' he said with a small nod of his head. 'And, may I ask, for what are you seeking vengeance?'

'Excuse me?' I asked, unsure what he was referring to.

He pointed at the logo on my T-shirt. 'You are an Avenger,' he said, 'yes?'

30

RISING QUESTIONS

*S*called out Lilly's name as we wandered down to the stream where she played.

'Shh,' she urged me, her finger to her lips. 'You'll disturb them!'

'Disturb who?'

Without a word, Lilly pointed at the water flowing at our feet. It wasn't until I took another step closer and lowered myself to her height I saw what she was talking about. Tiny little fish, about the size of fingers, darted around in front of us. And they were not just in the water, either: some of the fish hovered in the air with flapping fins, like little hummingbirds.

'Aren't they beautiful?' spoke Lilly as one of them brushed against her hand. 'This place is amazing,' she said with a whimsical smile. 'Did you see the mermaids? They were so pretty! I've decided I want to stay here for ever and ever.'

I took my feet out from beneath me to sit beside her. I wished I could see things through her eyes, without knowing we almost became mermaid lunch, or that I still had no clue where we were.

'What about Peter?' I asked her. 'And your uncle, and Max? Wouldn't you miss them?'

Her smile turned down. 'I suppose. But I'll be here with you!'

I took in a deep breath and rose up from the bank. I was too mentally exhausted to explain to her the dangers of this land, or maybe I just didn't have the heart to crush her fantasy. Taking her hand, I helped her up, intending to introduce her to Marc, but it seemed I had already been robbed of that pleasure.

'Marc!' she said with a beaming smile. 'Look at what I found!' She pointed at the shimmering flying fish.

'Those are saries,' he told her. 'Friendly creatures. I see you've made friends with them.'

Lilly grinned. 'They're like fairy-fish!' she said, and Marc chuckled.

'Okay,' he said, turning his attention back to me. 'I

suggest we head towards the Tropolis. We can navigate from there, and maybe find a place to stay the night if needs be.'

'No!' I told him. 'We're not resting. The longer we wait, the more danger Therron could be in. We've already wasted enough time as it is—I hoped to be there by now. You told me the portal drops you where you need to be. Well I need to be with Therron. So why am I here and not there?'

My hands shook, and I had to swallow down the burning sensation in the back of my throat which told me tears were imminent. I wasn't sure what made me so irritable—the run-in with hungry mermaids, the lack of food, or the feeling of hopelessness clouding my conscious.

Marc remained silent. He seemed to know exactly what to do to keep me from having another outburst. His calm indifference worked and, after a while, I was able to get my breathing back under control. We were going to find Therron. He was going to be okay.

Marc led the way back to the Tropolis, having already warned us it would be a long journey. Lilly didn't seem to mind too much, taking the whole experience in her stride. She was too mesmerised by the scenes around her to complain. Her enthusiasm kept me entertained as she pointed out all the odd coloured flowers and the occasional magical creature that crossed our path.

'Pepper, look!' she exclaimed at one point. I looked over to see a wild pegasus standing before us. This one tawny in colour with a dappled coat and large, white wings were folded against its flank. The pegasus stood beside a rock on the other side of the grassland we trekked through.

'I've met one of those before,' I told her. 'Therron told me there aren't very many of them left, and they are very special to this land.'

Lilly stared in awe at the magnificent beast as it grazed at the shrubbery beyond.

'How odd,' remarked Marc? 'Some magicks go entire lifetimes without ever seeing one of those, and yet you claim to have seen two in the space of a week. Incredible.'

The pegasus lifted its head and saw us watching it. It wasn't long before the creature galloped off beyond the crest of the hill and was out of sight.

'Aw, we frightened him away!' Lilly said with a sigh, but it wasn't long before something new caught her attention and she went skipping away towards it.

'Thank you so much for helping me,' I said to Marc when it was just the two of us ambling along.

'My pleasure,' he replied. 'I don't get much of a chance to do anything these days. It's nice to do something worthwhile every so often. It's so easy to let life here get you down. Sometimes you just have to keep yourself occupied.'

I knew by now that there was much more to this man's existence than he was letting on. I would have asked, but there was another, more pressing question on my mind.

'How did you know that I saw the other pegasus last week?' I asked. 'You said how strange it was for me to see two pegasuses in the space of a week. How did you know it was only a few days ago?'

I gauged Marc's reaction, but it didn't seem as though I had caught him off-guard.

'I just figured,' he said, 'picking up from things you've said. I like to think I'm pretty good at deducing information about people.'

That, I could vouch for, given how quickly he worked out I was human. Still, his explanation felt lacking.

'Young Lilly over there, for example,' he continued, 'She's the imaginative type. Curious, too. That's healthy for a child her age.'

'Her brother's quite something, too,' I told Marc. 'Perceptive and intelligent. The two of them make quite a pair. I certainly have my hands full looking after them back at the manor!' Not that I'd actually spent all that much time at the manor recently, I thought to myself.

'These children,' Marc said, looking pensive, 'are they any relation to the Calthorpes?'

I nodded. 'Adrian Calthorpe owns the manor— Lilly and Peter are his brother's children.'

Marc's eyebrows drew in as he watched Lilly gazing at a cluster of flowers taller than her up ahead. I wished I knew what he was thinking.

'She's not in any danger, is she?' I asked, referring to Lilly.

'I know this land better than most,' was Marc's reply. 'I'd know if she was getting herself into any trouble, don't worry.'

We slipped into a comfortable silence and walked on that way a while longer. It wasn't until the sun started to disappear behind a blanket of clouds and a light rain began to spit down on us that the long journey really started to affect Lilly.

'I'm tiiiired,' she whined as we neared a dense forest. Tantary certainly owned its fair share of them.

I offered Lilly a piggyback, but Marc mentioned how it was time the three of us all got some rest before we carried on. I was reluctant, but I knew it wouldn't be fair on Lilly to carry on. And so, after entering the shelter of the trees, we found a decent spot to sit in for a while.

'I'm hungry,' was Lilly's next complaint. Marc just smiled, said he would sort it out, and went off in search of some food.

'How much longer?' Lilly asked me when it was just the two of us.

'I don't know,' I told her in honesty, 'but I don't think it will be much longer.'

We must have been walking for over an hour, and I was actually surprised at how well Lilly had coped so far. To tell the truth, I'd started flaking by the time we passed the pegasus.

The two of us perched on the dry ground of the forest against a sturdy tree, the sounds of the rain pattering on the leafy canopy above us. By the time Marc returned with our meal of an unfamiliar forest creature, I could see Lilly was having a hard time staying awake.

Once we finished eating, Lilly rested her head against my shoulder as the twinkling lullaby of the rain lulled her into a deep sleep. I hadn't intended to rest for long, but I just couldn't find the heart to keep her awake. The day's excitement had drained a lot of her energy, and now I, too, was beginning to feel the familiar pull drawing my eyelids to a close.

I wasn't aware I had fallen asleep until a shrill cry made my eyelids fly open. The first thing I was aware of was the empty space beside me where Lilly had been sleeping.

The scream sounded again, and I launched myself

from the ground and dashed towards where the sound came from.

'Lilly!' I yelled. There was another scream. 'Where are you?'

'I'm up here!' said a frantic voice. I peered up to see Lilly hanging several feet above me, suspended from a single branch her top had snagged on. 'Help!' she cried.

'I'm here!' I said, scanning the lower branches to find a way to climb up to reach her. I had been years since my last tree-climbing endeavour, and that was without my arm in a sling. 'Just don't move!'

Keeping my eyes on Lilly at all times, I started to ascend the tree, finding it difficult to find secure purchases for my feet. It looked from here like she had fallen—or been dropped—and a jutting branch had latched on to the fabric of her top. I shouted at her once more not to squirm, for if she did, the material could rip, and that was a long drop for a girl as small as her.

Then I heard it: the sound of tearing fabric. I looked up to see Lilly drop a couple of inches, but she still hung on. This time she didn't scream, though. She just let out a terrified whimper.

'I'm almost there,' I said as I fumbled for another branch to grab onto. I was now just about level with her feet, but from there onwards, the branches became too thin to support my weight. I tried to grab another, but it snapped right off in my hand.

'Lilly,' I told her, 'I can't climb any higher. Can you try and unhook yourself?'

'I can't,' she sobbed, 'I'm scared!'

'Don't worry, you're not going to fall. I'll catch you. Grab on to that branch.'

Blubbering, she reached out a trembling arm to the branch I pointed at, but didn't get very far before another rip was heard, and she dropped even further. Completely disregarding my broken arm, I let go of the tree reached both my arms up towards her waist, catching her body just in time as the material gave in to the will of the tree and she fell towards me. I lurched back, taking the impact of her drop into the branch behind me. Pain throbbed through both my arm and my spine, but I paid them no attention as I clutched the young girl close to me and used my injured arm to get us down from the tree. Two sweaty, shaking arms curled around my neck and into my hair. She said nothing, only panted, as I carried her down to safety.

Once down, she collapsed into my arms, and I supported her trembling body and she sobbed into my hair, my hands stroking her own ginger mop.

I waited for her whimpering to calm a little before I asked her, 'How did you get all the way up there?

Was it an evil magick? Did someone try to hurt you?'

She shook her head against my shoulder.

'It was me,' she said, 'I'm sorry. I thought I saw a fairy, and she flew up into the sky, to the top of the tree. I tried to follow her, but I got stuck and I slipped and I fell.' The tears started up again.

'Shh,' I said as I picked some of the branch debris out of her wild hair. 'It's okay now. I'm just glad you're safe. Are you hurt?'

Lilly pulled away and dropped her gaze, wiping the back of her hand against her wet and swollen cheeks. I turned her around and investigated her back where the branch had caught her. There was a vertical slash in the material of her top leading from the middle all the way to the bottom. I peeled apart the two flaps like curtains and grimaced at the similarly shaped scratch the branch had made in her skin. Luckily, the wound didn't run too deep, but if it wasn't cleansed and dressed soon, it would almost definitely get infected.

'Come on,' I said, 'let's go back to Marc. We'll get to the Tropolis and get you all cleaned up, okay?'

Lilly simply nodded without meeting my gaze, and gripped onto my hand as she followed me back to our temporary camp, but when we returned, something was missing.

Marc was gone.

RACHEL E. WOLLASTON

31

HAPPY REUNIONS

$\mathcal{T}$he small fire was still simmering and his possessions lay on the ground, but there was no sign of Marc, and no indication as to where he could have gone.

'Do you think he's coming back?' Lilly asked as she tightened her grip on my arm. I told her I didn't know.

I beckoned for Lilly to sit with me for a while and wait, hoping maybe he'd just gone to relieve himself, or to find some more food. But, after a whole twenty minutes passed, it really didn't look like he would return. Had he been there when I woke up? I couldn't remember. I don't think I paid any attention. Now I wished I had.

What were we going to do now? The realisation hit me that I was stuck in the middle of an unknown forest with no clue as to which direction I was heading in, with a five-year-old girl who was both injured and exhausted.

It was time to make a decision, but what options did I have? It was either stay here and keep waiting for Marc's return, or wander on blindly in the hopes we might find our way to the Tropolis.

'We have to go,' I told Lilly, but she didn't move. 'Lilly? It's time to go.'

'Look,' she said. I followed the line of her finger to see what caught her attention. A path through the trees was lit by a line of fireflies, casting a warm, yellow glow in the shadow of the setting sun. 'It's a trail!' she said. I was just able to grab a hold of her wrist to stop her from sprinting off ahead.

'Wait!' I said, but I couldn't think of any reason to wait for. Perhaps I needed to take some of Lilly's initiative—to go charging ahead without worrying about what the dangers might be.

'Okay,' I said, 'we'll follow the path, but you must promise to stick beside me at all times, okay?'

Though I could tell she didn't want to, she conceded. Lilly held my hand as we walked through the firefly-lit walkway, gazing in wonder at the sight the whole way. The sky was getting darker now, and the fireflies continue to light our path. A thousand thoughts swirled round in my head. Was this one of Calpacious' traps? Was it a trap Marc had set? Maybe he wasn't as sincere as he made himself out to be. Or were these insects really trying to help us?

We emerged onto a much wider path, one large enough for horses. The track looked familiar, and it wasn't until the fireflies guided us towards a particularly wide tree that I realised where we were. I clutched Lilly's hand tighter and sprinted round to the other side where Therron's house sat.

The front door was shut, but I could see light coming from the inside. I hit the door with my fist until it opened, but it wasn't Therron who opened the wooden door and encompassed me in a relieved hug. It was Tharva.

'Oh! Oh, Pepper!' she said, her voice muffled in the fabric of my jacket I'd donned in the cold of dusk. 'I'm so happy to see you. And you're safe! Oh my. We've been so worried!'

I pushed her short figure away from me and looked her in the eyes, which looked dark and drained from worry.

'Is Therron okay?' I asked her.

'He's all right. But, more to the point, are *you*

okay?'

From behind where she stood in the doorway, I saw a mass of chocolate brown hair over Tharva's shoulder.

'Therron!' I shouted and swerved past Tharva to greet him. I don't know who was the most surprised—me or him—when we flew into an embrace, and stayed there for a few moments. It wasn't until that moment that I understood how much I'd missed him. Coming back to Tantary—hoping to rescue him from whatever was chasing him . . . I thought I was doing it out of loyalty, but it was only now, in his arms, that I realised my reasons might have been more selfish. Therron was more than an acquaintance. I cared what happened to him.

'I'm so glad you're safe,' he spoke into my hair. 'I was so scared something had happened to you.'

'I came back for you. I thought you were in danger.' I had to blink back some of the tears that threatened to spill over. All that journey, all that worry, and here he was, safe.

Therron's hands moved from my waist to my upper arms and lifted my head from his shoulder. 'I'm okay,' he said. 'You're okay. We're both here now.' He was trying to make me feel secure, and it worked. The longer I looked into those moss-green eyes, the safer I felt.

Another voice tore my gaze away.

'And who is this pretty young lass we have here?' asked Tharva, looking at Lilly, who looked guilty to be standing there.

'This is Lilly,' I said, and stepped over towards her. 'She's Mr. Calthorpe's niece.'

'She's from the manor, too?' said Tharva, enthralled. 'Humans were never supposed to enter our land, and now this is the third in only a few days! Why, the portal is barely holding up. I hope you know what you're doing!'

But despite her complaints, Tharva looked to be rather taken with Lilly. When she saw the tree wounds on her back, she asked Therron if he had any salve handy. He did. Tharva proceeded to apply the solution methodically to Lilly's back.

'Hehe, that's cold!' she said, fidgeting on Tharva's knees at the sensation.

Therron turned to me.

'What happened to you?' he asked. 'I'm sure a lot has happened since our last meeting. Where have you been all this time?'

'Before I tell you the whole story,' I said, 'I think first I should tell you both something.' The two of them leaned forwards with fretful expressions. 'Alzabar is dead.'

Tharva's eyes bugged as her eyebrows dropped.

373

'Who told you that?'

'Calpacious.'

'And you trusted him?' She looked incredulous.

'I learnt a lot of things about Calpacious in the time I spent at his castle, but one of them was that he does not joke around.'

'Wait a minute,' Therron interjected, a look of horror on his face. 'Are you saying you were with Calpacious this whole time?'

I decided it was time to sit down. I took a perch on the familiar sofa/bed, and said, 'Lilly, why don't you go and play by the lake for a while? I'm sure Penelope will show you the way.' I'd spotted the little bunny hiding beneath a table in the corner, watching the whole exchange. Tharva had finished applying the salve, and I didn't think the story I had to tell was entirely suitable for her young ears.

'Penelope?' Lilly echoed, and I remembered she didn't know the bunny's Tantary name. I didn't need to explain, though, because the beautiful white creature emerged from beneath the table and brushed her fur against Lilly's legs.

'Fifi!' She grinned. Penelope looked at me and gave a little whisker-wiggle, before hopping out of the door, a gleeful Lilly in tow.

'Tell us exactly what happened,' said Therron, 'beginning from the moment I woke up and you

374

weren't there.'

'I will,' I agreed, 'but only if you tell me what happened to you, and how the two of you got here.' Therron nodded, and so I began my story, starting from the moment I awoke in Calpacious' castle to the peculiar row of fireflies that had led us to Therron's cabin.

'This Marc person said he was taking you to the Tropolis?' Tharva said. 'That doesn't make any sense. The Tropolis is on the other side of Tantary. If you were coming from the South Sea—which it sounds like you were—then that journey should have led you in a north-easterly direction, across the Arndoor River. Why in the world would he send you this way?'

'I have no idea,' I said with a small shrug. 'Like I said, he was gone by the time I woke up, so I was under the impression the whole thing was a set-up, anyway.'

'Unless he brought you this way on purpose,' spoke Therron. 'Is it possible he knew I was here?'

Tharva gave him a rueful smile. 'Oh, Therron,' she said, 'always the optimist.'

'You barely know me,' he said back.

'I've known you long enough. All that talk about how adamant you were Pepper was going to return.'

'And she did.' Therron lifted his chin, and offered

375

her a smile that was almost smug. 'So what makes you so sure I'm wrong this time?'

'Hey,' I said, cutting the two of them off. 'Marc's not really our problem at the moment. I wish I knew why he did what he did, but we really shouldn't be worrying about this right now.'

'You're right,' Tharva said, 'we should be worrying about Max. You said Calpacious was keeping him prisoner?'

'Yes. And using him as blackmail in order to get me to comply.'

'And yet you saw him at the manor. How did he escape?'

'I don't know,' I said in honesty. 'I was going to ask him earlier today but, for one, he couldn't see me thanks to this stupid wristband. And two, apparently he went out this morning to visit his mother. All I want to know is how he got his bracelet off.'

'Does Calpacious know you're back in Tantary?' Therron asked. 'What if he comes after you again?'

That was the very thing I'd silently feared since my return. 'I'm not sure, I said. 'Besides, Therron, you haven't told me what happened to you, yet.'

Therron nodded and took a breath, preparing to recount his story. 'When I first woke up,' he said, 'and you weren't beside me, I panicked. I looked everywhere for you, and feared the worst. I went back to the Old City. I found Archie in the street where we fought the ogre, paying his final respects to Bel. We talked and, eventually, he convinced me to leave the Old City. I had to find you.'

All the while Therron recounted his story, he fidgeted with his fingers. He never looked up from them once.

'I left the city on the back of the griffin and began my search. After a day passed, and I still couldn't find you, I was close to losing all hope. The next day, something strange happened. After a night of sleeping rough in the woods, I woke up to find the griffin missing. And that was when I became aware of another presence in that forest. At first, I thought it was one of the King's guards, but it was fast, and dark—like a shadow. Then there were more things. It felt like a dream, like I was in some warped version of reality. So I tried to run. If it wasn't for Tharva and her psychic abilities which sensed I was in danger, I think. . . I think they might have killed me.'

I considered his words. From the sounds of it, someone had tampered with his story. I doubted anyone got attacked by invisible forces here for no reason. The question was, who would do such a thing? Calpacious?

The three of us sat in silent contemplation for a few moments, before Therron spoke up again.

'Look, I don't think we need to waste any more energy worrying about Calpacious right now. It's nearly night time. I'll start the fire and cook us all a decent supper.'

'On no you don't,' Tharva interrupted, heaving herself up from the stool. 'You two deserve a break after everything that's happened to you. I suggest you both go outside and take a stroll. I'll take care of supper, maybe even young Lilly can give me a hand.'

Therron looked at me, as though waiting for me to agree with her, before he said anything himself. I gave him a nod.

'Okay,' he said. 'Take care of yourself.'

'I'll call you when it's ready,' she said with a grin. 'Now go and get some fresh air.'

Therron walked out the door, but I stayed behind, giving Tharva another hug.

'Thank you so much,' I said.

'It's not a problem, child. I quite enjoy a bit of culinary work from time to time.'

'I mean for everything.' I took a step back so I could match her dark brown gaze. 'For helping Therron, and for being a good friend.'

She beamed and clasped both of my hands. 'It's my pleasure. Now you two go and make the most of the evening.'

I squeezed her hands and smiled before letting go

and heading towards the door.

'By the way . . .'

I stopped and turned back to face the older woman.

'You keep a good hold of Therron. You don't find many like him nowadays. I should know.' I caught her mischievous wink just as I closed the door behind me.

32

STRENGTHENING BONDS

'Y ou know,' said Therron as I followed him through the winding path of trees. 'You never did explain what made you come back.'

'I had to. I only went back to the manor to escape Calpacious—I intended to come back all along.'

In my earlier retelling of my adventures, I omitted the part about reading what happened to him in his book. As far as Therron knew, I'd never even seen his book. It wasn't that I didn't want to tell him, just . . . one thing at a time. That was all either of us could take at the moment.

'But you didn't have to return,' said Therron. 'Calpacious was after you, and you knew Alzabar is dead. When you first came here, you were desperate to find your way back to the manor. Now you've gone through all the hassle of coming back, but for what reason?' He shuffled down a steep slope in the earth and offered out his hand to help me down. 'You can't honestly tell me you came all the way back just for me.'

I held on to his hand to steady my descent. 'Would that be so hard to believe?' I asked him, meeting his gaze. It wasn't held for long, though, as he snatched his eyes down to the floor. He dropped his hand from mine, using it instead to rub the skin of his elbow.

'I guess, maybe. I mean, who am I? Really, Pepper? I'm a character. From a storybook. I'm not even supposed to exist!' His shoulders were hunched, his face turned away from me, but I could see without looking the torment weathering his features.

'No, Therron,' I said, grabbing a hold of his shoulder—an attempt to get him to look in my direction. 'That's not true. If you weren't supposed to exist, then why are you here?'

'That's what I hoped you'd tell me!'

Therron combed his fingers through his hair and let out a deep breath. We'd stopped walking, but his feet refused to remain still.

'Okay, listen,' he said, finally turning to look my way. His green eyes swirled like the inside of a tornado I could not see the end of. 'There's something I never told you. All the magicks here—they all remember their pasts; details of their lives from the story they originated from. I don't have any of that. No past. No story. No life. Don't you understand? How can I be something, when I don't know what I was in the first place?'

I shook my head as I offered him a reassuring smile. 'You've spent so long believing no one could care for you, you don't notice when someone does. And people do. Therron, I care about what happens to you. That's why I came back. I defied everything Adrian said, went against his commands, because I needed to know you were safe.'

I didn't realise my hand had travelled from his shoulder down to his bicep until he took my elbows with both hands. His thumb grazed against the dirtied, white material of my sling, which hadn't done me much good, since I still used that arm anyway to rescue Lilly. I still felt the throbbing that move cost me.

'You have no idea how crazy I went while I was trying to look for you,' he said, gazing at my fractured arm, as though hoping to stare it back together. 'I wish I could put it into words, how I felt, but I doubt it would make much sense.' His brow furrowed and he let out a soft groan as he raised his head back up. 'I'm so sorry you got into this mess. My fault or not, none of this should have ever happened to you.'

'I chose this,' I said. 'Maybe not the broken arm, but it was my choice to help you. I could have let you go off to the Old City on your own, but I went with you. And I would do it again.'

'Thank you. I really mean it. It's taken me a while to realise just how kind people can be. I've seen the worst of a lot of people. It led me to believe there was no good in the world. But now I'm starting to understand maybe it's been me who's been shielding myself from it.' He took a deep breath. 'I'm a coward, Pepper. I'll be the first one to admit that. Not having a past—that scares me. I just don't measure up to everyone else out there. The amount of times I've told myself I should never intervene with the land's problems; that it's not my place . . . I don't know. Maybe you're right. Maybe it's my own self-doubt that I've come to believe. You're the first person who's helped me see past that, and now I'm scared. I'm scared Calpacious will find you. I'm scared that I'm going to let you down. Again.'

I squeezed his arm where I still had a hold of it. 'You never let me down. You spoke about kindness—

there is not a person in this world I have met who is kinder than you. I'm not scared of Calpacious. I broke free of him once—I can do it again.' I was convincing myself as well as him. My mind flashed back to the story in my pocket. Adrian created Therron with unparalleled powers; ones intended to rescue Alzabar with. They were no longer able to fulfil that prophesised role, but it didn't mean they couldn't still be used for good.

'Besides,' I said, breeching the subject with caution. 'I really don't think he knows what he's up against. I mean, you have magic, don't you?'

I lost him then. I let out a dejected sigh as Therron broke free of the hold and resumed raking his fingers through his already unkempt hair. 'I can't use that stuff,' he said. 'You know I can't. I stopped using magic the day I ran away from the Tropolis. It took me months to get it under control, and I barely thought about touching it since.'

'What if I help you?' I suggested. 'I know magic is a commodity difficult to get hold of in Tantary, but I also know it does exist, and it can be controlled.' In my mind, I thought back to Scarlett and Cade, and the way they froze the guards in order for me to escape. I wished I knew what happened to them, and if they were okay. 'I'd bet, with a little help, you'd have your talent under control in no time at all.'

'Talent?' he repeated, 'or curse? No, I won't do it. I've hurt enough people already. I'm not going to put you at risk, too.'

'I'm already at risk,' I reminded him, 'and you are, too. Look, I'm sorry. I didn't mean to push you into doing something you don't want to do. Let's go back to your cabin. I'm sure Tharva could do with some help cooking the dinner.'

I barely started walking away when his hand grabbed my upper arm.

'Wait,' he said, and I span round. He sighed and ruffled his hair once more. 'What is it you want me to do?'

I was so happy to hear him agree, I almost gave him another hug right there and then.

'Practise,' I said.

The smile he gave me was encouraging, though it was a little uncertain.

'Where do you want me to begin?'

I grinned, standing up a little straighter.

'Mend my arm.'

'Your arm?' he repeated. 'No! No way. What if I hurt you even more?'

'You won't.'

'What makes you so sure?'

With my good arm, I lifted one of his hands and placed it on top of the sling. 'Trust,' I said. 'Do you

386

not trust me?'

'I trust you,' he said, staring at the material beneath his fingers. '*I'm* the one I don't trust.'

'Well, *I* trust you.'

With a slow movement, he brought his gaze back to mine, a mixture of emotions muddling in his eyes.

'I want to be able to do this.' His voice was quieter than before. 'More than anything, I do.'

'Then just try.'

Therron took a steadying breath as I untied the sling from around my neck and held my arm out between our bodies. He reached forward and allowed his fingers to hover above the injured bone. He searched my eyes with his one more time for reassurance, and then drew them closed. Concentration crossed over his face as he focussed everything he had into his flexed fingers. He remained that way for all of thirty seconds before his hands dropped back to his sides.

'I can't find it,' he said. 'I've buried the power down for so long. I don't know how to reach it anymore.'

His hand lifted, probably to comb through his hair again, as he tended to do when he was anxious, but I caught his wrist before it could reach his head.

'You're worrying too much,' I told him, 'you have to let go. It's just like taking an exam—the more you stress about it, the harder you make it for yourself.' I could tell from Therron's expression that he had no idea what an exam was, but that was beside the point. Knowing nothing about magic myself, it was pretty much the only thing I could think to relate it to.

'Just relax,' I said, softening my hold on his wrist. 'Let it come naturally.'

Therron nodded, allowing his features to loosen. He closed his eyes once more.

'Open your eyes,' I said with a gentle tone. 'Look at me if it helps.'

He did. Just as I moved to retract my hold on him, he grabbed my hand back. 'No. Don't let go.' But, looking into the emerald pools of his irises, I could tell he was no longer speaking out of fear. He held my gaze with such intensity I almost shrank back, barely noticing the tingle that ran the length of my forearm as his hand brushed over my fingers.

His face was close. Very close, in fact. His free palm reached out and stroked my cheek, and I allowed myself to lean into his touch, my heart singing as his calloused thumb caressed the skin. He glanced down at my lips, as though asking permission. My only response was a slow blink.

Ever so gently, he pressed his lips to mine with a kiss so tender, it wouldn't have harmed the wings of a butterfly. Never before had I experienced a kiss so full of gentility and compassion. I reached up to cup his cheek as I returned it with as much emotion as he gave me.

With as much care as he began, Therron leaned back and looked down at me with dancing eyes which I knew matched my own. His hand now rested against my chin, and I hadn't realised, but my other arm, the one with the injury, had curled its way around the back of his neck. It didn't hurt a bit.

'Therron,' I whispered, grinning for more than one reason. 'You did it.' He cocked his head to the side. 'My arm.'

He unwrapped it from where it lay behind his head and inspected it himself, running the gentle pads of his fingers over the skin. His expression changed from disbelief to wonderment to glee. With a beaming smile, he scooped me up in a heartfelt hug, taking me quite by surprise.

'Thank you so much!' I wasn't sure if he heard the words, since they were muffled by the fabric of his T-shirt.

'Why are you thanking me?' he asked, taking a step back and lowering his hands to mine. 'You're the one who helped me. You believed in me, Pepper. No one has ever done that before. And for that, I owe you everything.'

'You owe me nothing,' I assured him. Then I

thought. 'Just,' I said, watching my fingers weaving through his. 'I don't want to leave you.'

'Then don't.' He tilted my chin upwards with his index finger. But I shook it free.

'It's not that simple. I have a family . . . friends . . . a job. Therron, I want to stay here with you more than anything. This land has become my home. But you must understand I have to go back at some point.' I felt like I was telling myself this more than him.

'Then I'll come with you,' he said. 'I'll go back though the portal with you.'

'I don't know. I think—'

'Please, Pepper,' he said, cutting me off. 'You're the closest thing I have to finding out who I am. There is nothing in this land that can help me. I need you.'

I exhaled and rubbed the side of my face. I couldn't keep this to myself any longer. I had to tell him about the book. About why he'd been written.

Just as I was about to open my mouth to speak, Therron centred my shoulders and planted another, more passionate, kiss on my lips. And just like that, all thoughts I had of telling him the truth vanished from my mind.

'Please,' he said. 'Promise you won't leave me.'

'I won't,' I replied, though I wasn't sure how long I'd be able to keep that promise.

It was getting chilly, and whatever goodies Tharva

was cooking up for us mustn't have been ready yet, as we'd yet to hear from her. So, we decided to wait it out here by the light of the campfire as the sun continued its slow decline.

It seemed Therron's surge of magic hadn't been a one-off. It didn't take long for him to start a small fire in a patch where the foliage was sparser.

I snuggled up close to Therron, and he draped his arm around me. We must have fallen asleep, because the next thing I knew, I was woken up to an angry grip on my shoulder.

33

PAINFUL DISCOVERIES

I yelped at the touch and jumped to my feet, ready to defend myself. I stopped short, though, when I saw it was Therron jostling me awake.

'I'm sorry,' he said, backing up. 'I didn't mean to scare you. You wouldn't wake up.'

I let out my fight or flight instinct in one deep breath as my heart rate slowed back to normal.

'No, it's me,' I said, still a little shaken. 'I can't seem to take my mind off Calpacious. He's still out there. He's still looking for me.'

Therron's arms encircled me in a reassuring hug.

393

'Shh,' he soothed as he stroked the back of my hair, picking out the leaves and pieces of moss that had found their way there. 'It's fine. You're safe.'

'I'm not so sure.'

Therron leaned back and studied the worry in my eyes. 'Why?' he asked. 'What's wrong?'

'I had a dream,' I told him. 'It was about Tharva. I dreamed she worked for Calpacious, and she planned to take us to him. When you woke me up, I thought you were her.'

'But it was just a dream,' Therron said. 'It was nothing to worry about.'

'No.' I pulled away. 'You don't understand. I know why I had that dream!'

Therron waited patiently for me to elaborate.

'Back at the castle,' I explained, 'while the sylphs helped me escape, I overheard something. A conversation between Calpacious and someone else who I couldn't identify. But I'm pretty sure they had a female voice. Calpacious told her I trusted her, and asked her to find out my weakness.'

'Okay,' Therron said, reaching out for me again. 'Don't worry.' Though I could see in his eyes what I said troubled him. 'The main thing is, you heard it, so you know to be wary.'

'Therron, listen to me. There's only one female here who I know and trust.'

Therron's face drained of its colour as he caught my meaning. 'Tharva.'

'What if she really is working for Calpacious?'

'Look. Don't worry. We'll figure something out, okay?' The look in his eyes gave me hope, but it didn't quench the gnawing in my stomach. He ran his thumb over my cheekbone then leaned forwards to steal another sweet kiss.

'Come on,' he said. 'We'd best be heading back. You were only asleep for twenty minutes—I'm sure our supper will be ready by now.'

The thought of Tharva making us supper made my stomach contract, but I knew we had to go back sometime, if only for Lilly. I hoped I was wrong about Tharva. That perhaps I misheard Calpacious, and maybe they weren't talking about me at all.

Upon my urging, Therron snuffed out what was left of the fire with his re-found powers, and we went to leave, when something caught his eye.

'Is that yours?' he asked, pointing to a rather mangled-looking object on the mossy floor. It was Therron's book. He went to pick it up, but I stooped down just in time and snatched it up before he could touch it. My action left him looking at me, perplexed.

'What is that?' he asked as I shoved the ruined notebook into my back pocket.

'It's not important,' I said, and began heading back

towards the cabin. Except, I didn't know which direction the cabin was in.

'Well I think it is.' He grabbed my arm and span me round so I was looking at him again. 'I thought you trusted me, Pepper. What was that? If it's something that's going to get you into trouble, then I need to know.'

I shook myself free. 'This isn't about me!'

Therron looked taken aback by my sudden defensiveness. I took a deep breath to calm myself.

'It's your story,' I told him.

'My story? You mean—'

'Yes, the one from the manor. It is the book that created you.'

This time, Therron ran both his hands through his hair. I chewed on my lower lip as he turned away from me. I wished he would say something.

After a few moments of composing himself, he turned back.

'May I read it?' he asked. His features twitched, but his face remained otherwise stoic. I couldn't tell if he was mad or not.

'I'm . . . not so sure that's a great idea.'

'Why? How bad is it?'

'It's not that.' I dropped my gaze, unable to look him in the eyes. 'Earlier, when Lilly and I had that run-in with the mermaids . . . it got damaged. Half of the story was lost, and what's left is barely legible.'

'You've read it though, haven't you? You know my past.'

I swallowed. 'Are you angry?'

'I don't know,' he replied with a sigh. 'Just, please, Pepper. I want to know the truth. For once in my life, I just want to know who I am.'

I stepped up to him and took his hand. 'Nothing in that book will change you,' I said. 'I know who you are. what's written down isn't important.'

'It's important to me.'

I thought back to earlier, when I almost told him the whole truth. I thought it would make it better, that he would be happier. Now, I wasn't so sure.

'You really want to know?' I asked, and felt my heart drop further when he nodded. 'Even if it hurts?' He said nothing. I took a moment to prepare myself before I revealed to him the thing he both craved and feared.

'Your story came to the manor more recently than those of the other magicks. You already know that.' Still, he remained silent, so I continued. 'But what you probably don't know is that your story was written within the manor. By Mr. Calthorpe.' I had to turn my head away, not wishing to see the conflict my words caused him. 'Adrian Calthorpe already knew Calpacious was up to no good, and having no connection to the magicks, he decided to create a new hero, one with magical powers. This hero was destined to one day rescue the real king, Alzabar, and save both Tantary and my own world.'

Therron still said nothing for a while. It took an effort, but I willed myself to look him in the eyes. His brow was scrunched and a war of emotions toyed with his expression. When he did speak, his words were quiet and pensive.

'Me,' he said. 'That hero is me. Isn't it?' My silence was the only answer I gave. 'How long have you known? Since you came back? Before you met me?'

'Max told me. He told me when he came to Tantary. In Tharva's shop.' I realised then just how long I'd kept this from him.

Therron turned and walked away with brisk steps.

'Wait! Therron!' I called after him, but I struggled to keep up. He'd already taken off, and he knew this forest better than I did. Where I kept stumbling over tree roots and dodging hanging branches, Therron marched straight ahead without any problem.

'Wait!' I shouted. He stopped. Breathless, I caught up to him, but also stopped dead in my tracks when I saw what he was looking at.

His cabin was surrounded by fifteen, no, twenty armed guardsmen dressed in the King's army's uniform, and there was no sign of either Tharva or Lilly.

I prepared to run, but was grabbed at the last minute by a pair of sturdy arms.

'Therron!' I cried out, but he, too, had been captured, his captor dragging him backwards towards his cabin. Therron shouted out one last time before the guard shoved him inside and got to work bolting the door from the outside.

That was the last I saw of him before the guard holding me dragged me, kicking and screaming, into the back of a wooden cart.

I didn't know which fate was the hardest to live with—being re-captured by Calpacious, or Therron hating me.

34

VILE BETRAYERS

I sat in the corner of the crate and folded my arms in front of my chest as we trundled along, pouting. It was dark inside, with only the gaps in the wooden planks letting in the pale moonlight.

We'd been on the road for over an hour now, the first part of which I spent acting hysterical, banging on all sides of the crate, while screaming at the driver who remained mute the whole time.

After my futile efforts, I now sat back against the crate wall, and sulked.

The sounds of the horses' hooves accompanied the

rattling of the wheels as I was jostled about. I scowled even more. Like it wasn't enough they'd found and captured me again, they had to go and box me up like some wild animal.

'Oh, yeah, sure,' I muttered to myself, 'Just go and humiliate me even more. That's right, everyone hide—there's a wild human on the loose. Don't worry, though. We locked her in a cage.' I groaned. 'Didn't even have the decency to knock me unconscious.' I looked up to the wooden roof and shouted through the gaps, 'Hey, can we turn back, please? I think I left my dignity behind.'

I heard a slight chuckle. Well, at least I now knew it was a man driving.

'You know,' I heard him call back, 'you'll be lucky we don't lock you up, the way you keep talking to yourself like that.' It was the first time this whole journey I'd heard a voice other than my own.

'Duh, you already have locked me up.'

'So we have.'

I thought I heard a hint of amusement in the man's voice. Well, at least someone was entertained. Still, I had him speaking now. I decided to make the most out of it.

'This is nice, isn't it?' I said. 'A lovely stroll through the countryside. Though I don't know if you can call it a stroll if you're a captive prisoner. Are we

402

even in the countryside? Perhaps we should install a few windows in the cage.'

'And have you escape?' He chuckled. 'Not a chance.'

'No, I was thinking more of one with bars. Or maybe glass, for a little pizazz. Maybe dress it with a pair of curtains . . . ooh, how about a window box?'

'Are you trying our patience?' asked a new voice.

'I'm just pointing out,' I said, 'that if you want more customers, you might want to put some more thought into making the ride more enjoyable.'

'I don't think, with the types of customers we acquire, we need to worry about things like that,' the second voice continued.

'Suit yourself,' I said with a sigh. 'Though I, for one, would personally benefit from a cushion of some sort. I'm afraid this wood is giving me splinters right where I don't want them!' I made a grunting sound to prove my case. 'Will we be stopping off anywhere along the way?' I asked. 'My legs could do with a bit of a stretch soon. Plus I had a glass of water earlier, and I'm afraid it's gone straight through me.'

'Why didn't we sedate her?' asked the second voice to the man beside him. It sounded like there were only two of them on this journey. So what had happened to the rest of them who were at Therron's house?

'It was you who said we should leave her conscious,' the second voice continued complaining.

The conversation hushed, and I just about made out the first voice asking the other to take the reins. The cart drew to a stop, and I heard him jump down from the front and around the back to where I sat in the crate. I grinned, delighted my plan had worked. Now all I needed was for the guard to open the crate and then I would kick him down and sprint away as fast as I could.

But when the crate door was unlocked, and I saw the guard's face, my jaw fell slack, and all plans of escaping fled from my head. It was Marc.

He gave me an amused smile.

'You do like getting yourself into trouble, don't you?' he said.

I had to refrain myself from reaching out and slapping him in the face.

'What the hell is this?' I asked, my vision flashing red. 'First you save Lilly and me from mermaids, and now you're kidnapping me?'

Marc lifted up his legs and perched on the floor of the cart, beside my crate.

'Now don't go getting wound up, Pepper,' he said, 'it's really not what it looks like.'

'Well, please, explain away!' I said, throwing my arms into the air in exaggeration. 'But from where I'm standing—or, crouching, as the case may be—you've kidnapped me, done goodness knows what to three of my friends, left Lilly and me in the middle of the night, and are dressed in the uniform of the King's army.'

'Okay, I admit it looks pretty bad—'

'Pretty bad?!' I echoed. 'Are you seriously trying to tell me you're not working for Calpacious?'

'No, I am, but—'

'I don't want to hear it,' I said, cutting him off, and slammed the crate door shut in his face, trapping myself back inside.

'Pepper!' He knocked on the wood. 'You need to listen to what I have to say!'

'Says who?'

'Me! Pepper, this could very well save your life!'

'What part of, "I don't want to hear it" do you not understand?'

I heard him sigh, and vaguely made out through the wood the silhouette of him rubbing his eyes.

'I really was trying to help you back then,' he said. 'No, I wasn't taking you in the direction of the Tropolis, but I took you to your friend's house instead. I was called to duty while you were asleep. I wasn't expecting it. I set up that trail of fireflies so you could find your way safely to Therron's hut.'

My plan had been to ignore him, but his words

piqued my interest.

'How?' I asked. 'How did you do that? Is that part of your powers you didn't want to tell me about?'

'This is exactly what I need to let you know,' he answered.

I was left with no choice. I pushed the crate door back open and crawled out before sitting on one of the cart's benches. Marc took the one opposite. He knew I wouldn't escape. Not when he held such valuable explanations.

'You have more influence in this land than you realise,' he told me. 'You just need to learn how to recognise and utilise your powers.'

'What are you talking about? You know I'm human. I don't have any abilities.'

'Now, you know that's a lie,' he said with a pointed look. 'I know Calpacious has told you about the power of your imagination.'

I sighed. Not this again.

'It doesn't work,' I told him. 'Calpacious wanted me to change his character. I tried, and nothing happened.'

'And do you know why?'

'Well, no,' I said. 'What would it matter, anyway?'

'It matters a great deal. How do you feel about Calpacious?'

I grimaced. 'What kind of question is that? I think

he's a slimy, greedy monster.'

'Do you think he could ever change?'

'Of course not!'

'Well, there's your answer.'

'What?' My eyebrows grew closer and closer together as the conversation progressed.

'Nothing will come true if you don't believe it. Imagination is a powerful thing, but belief is just as important. And that is something a lot of people tend to overlook.'

'So,' I said, 'you're saying I need to *believe* Calpacious will escape into my world?'

Marc smiled a little. 'Now, you and I both know that's not going to happen,' he said.

It suddenly came to my attention that the driver of the carriage had been listening in on the whole conversation, and yet hadn't spoken a word. Marc must have caught my anxious gaze.

'Don't worry about him,' he said, 'I've dealt with it.'

His answer just left me even more confused, but I told myself it wasn't at the top of my priorities list at the moment.

'How do you know all of this?' I asked him instead. 'No one else has told me this before, so how come you know?'

Marc got the secretive gleam in his eyes again. 'I

know a great many things,' he said, 'a lot of which you'd never believe if I told you.'

Tired of his cryptic answers, I folded my arms over my chest and reverted back to sulking mode, my eyes staring at the road ahead of us.

Before long, we reached the castle. I should run, I thought to myself, but where would that have got me? Lost in the middle of nowhere, potentially running into some other dangerous creatures I'd never heard of before. Plus, I doubted I could outrun an army of the King's guardsmen. So, I allowed Marc and his companion to grab my arms and tow me towards the castle.

It was the first time I had seen the exterior so close up. It was breath-taking, in a dark and foreboding kind of way. The sound of cascading waterfalls echoed all around, and even though we walked in the middle of the bridge, I saw the knee-trembling height from which we were suspended above the water. Good thing I wasn't afraid of heights.

More guards stood along the bridge, none of them giving us a glance as we passed them. The fact that they stood so still, almost like statues, gave me the creeps.

The door opened for us, and they led me through the main foyer of winding staircases to the double doors at the end. The doors opened to the all-too-familiar throne room, where Calpacious waited with a gloating grin.

The triumphant look on Calpacious' face was sickening. I was so irked with everything by this point, though, that I barely cared.

'It's lovely to see you again, Pepper,' the King said with a haughty smile.

'Yeah, well, I would have brought flowers and a gift basket, but this visit came as quite a surprise,' I remarked.

'Oh, believe me,' he replied, 'this will be much more than just a passing hello. There will be no more help from your little fairy friends, and I have other ways to make you cooperate this time.' His confident smile didn't waver.

'You mean like Max, last time?' I raised an eyebrow. 'Unless you forgot, he escaped, too. I hate to tell you this, but I don't think your security measures are all that great.' I didn't know where this sudden burst of sarcastic confidence came from—it could have been the adrenaline rush—but I certainly hoped it didn't go away any time soon.

'Escaped?' Calpacious repeated, matching my cocky expression. 'Is that what he told you?' He guffawed. 'I let the kid go.'

Well, that was the kick to my stomach. There went all the optimism I had for escaping again.

'Such an ungrateful pain in the neck,' he continued, shaking his head. 'He came to me asking for help, and what did I get? I'm glad I got rid of him when I did.'

I just opened and shut my mouth in shock, not knowing what to say as a thousand new questions swirled in my head. Calpacious gestured for Marc and the other guard to leave, then stood and walked over towards me.

'Follow me,' he said. 'You'll be happy to hear I've assigned you the same room as before.'

Oh, yippee.

'Now, Max came to me because he claimed to have a problem with a certain Story-Boy, I think he called him. I promised him I'd help, just so long as he promised to do everything I told him to.'

'This was all a trick?' I seethed. 'You lied to me! Max was never in any danger. The band on his wrist—none of it was real!' That explained why he escaped so easily, and why he never told me about what happened to him at the castle. And the wounds . . . were they fake? It would certainly have explained why he returned to the manor unscathed.

'Why are you telling me this?' I asked Calpacious.

'So you know this time there is no hoax,' he said. 'This time, you will do EXACTLY as I say. I see you're free of your troublesome sling. Good. That should make it easier for you to write me a story. And as for leverage, well, you only have to follow me to find out.'

I swallowed a lump that had formed in my stomach, my previous confidence having all but dissipated. We entered the main foyer, but instead of going up the stairs as we had previously, Calpacious led me through another door and took me down a flight of eerily familiar stone stairs.

We reached the floor of the dungeon, and it looked every bit as creepy and neglected as I remembered. I now knew Calpacious tended to use his fully-furnished guest rooms for most of his prisoners, so it seemed he only used his dungeon for special occasions. I, apparently, was one of them.

The sconces still weren't functioning, and the dim skylight was the only thing illuminating any rats that might come scurrying my way.

Further down the dungeon corridor, I began to make out the sound of soft breathing, like someone was asleep. Calpacious drew to a stop outside one of cells, and I peered inside to see a small sleeping form on the slate bed.

Lilly.

I moved towards the iron bars, but the King caught me just before I could reach them.

'You should know,' he whispered, his face so

close, his short beard scratched my temple. I leaned away. 'That I really don't want to hurt her. But if that's what it takes to get you to comply, then so be it.'

'You can't do this to her,' I hissed, being careful so as not to wake her—it was easier to believe she was asleep rather than under sedation. 'She's five years old!'

'And that,' Calpacious said with a sneer, 'is exactly why you will do what I want you to do.'

'But why?' I asked. I felt the familiar burning of tears welling up behind my eyes. 'You must have heard by now the portal is weakening anyway. If you waited long enough, you could get through anyway. Why still use me?'

'You think this is still about my powers?' he asked, but I knew he was only patronising me. His flickering gaze searched my face one more time before he whipped around and headed back out of the dungeon. Out of options, I could only follow. He didn't speak again until we got back up to ground level.

'While you were away,' he said, 'I had some time to think. Not only about how to keep you within my walls, but also about what it is, exactly, I want you to do. Why do you think I let you stay away for so long? Do you think I'm weak?' Of course, he didn't expect me to answer. 'That beautiful little wristband of yours, as I'm sure you know by now, turns you into a magick—one of my subjects. And that means I can track you where you are at all times. It's one on the perks of being King.'

'Why are you telling me this?' I asked, wary of where this conversation was heading.

'So you understand,' he said, stopping to turn and face me, 'that you have no power over me. You see me as an evil king. But who I am is a man who is willing to do whatever it takes to get what he needs.'

He continued to lead me up the stairs, taking me to the same room he had me locked in the first time he brought me here. Looking into that gold-laden room flooded me with a conflicting emotion of familiarity and discomfort. The place chilled me to the very core, but something inside me was strangely happy to be somewhere I recognised.

Calpacious pushed me inside and turned to walk away, but just before he did, I called after him, 'Wait! You haven't even told me what you want me to do!'

He looked back at me one more time.

'I want you to write me a monster,' he said, then slammed the door in my face, leaving me on my own once again.

Was that it? Was that all the information he was going to give me?

A monster. What did that even mean? I yelled after

413

him and tried to open the door, but it was locked. After pounding on the door a few more times, I screamed, and slid my back down the door.

For the first time in a long time, I cried. Really cried. I let the tears burn my cheeks, soaking into the cotton fabric of my T-shirt. I didn't even make an effort to wipe them away. In less than a day, I betrayed my boss, lost my best friend, and endangered the little girl I was supposed to look after. And now, locked here in the gold-plated prison, there was nothing I could do to change that.

I wondered what happened to Scarlett and Cade. Calpacious had been so certain they weren't going to rescue me this time. Thoughts of fear pummelled my mind about what he could have possibly done to them. And what about Tharva? Was she the one who led the guards to me?

Calpacious already admitted it was the bracelet that let him find me, but that still didn't answer the question of who he was talking to that day the sylphs rescued me.

And so it was there, against the wooden panel of the door, that I cried myself to sleep.

35

HOPELESS SITUATIONS

woke up late the next morning to a plate of food already in my room, though I hadn't seen anyone. Also, whereas I fell asleep against the door, I now found myself waking up in the comfort of the blood-stained bed. I felt sick, though I wasn't sure if it was from fear or the knowledge that I lay on the blood of Calpacious' previous victims.

Though I was awake, I continued to lie in bed, relishing the comfort I had missed so much over the last couple of days. Eventually, when I was sure I wasn't going to get back to sleep any time soon, I stretched and sat up straight. Being so much calmer

415

than I was the night before, I took in things that previously escaped my notice.

The room was more or less the same as it was the last time I was here—the changing screen on one side; the bejewelled bathtub on the other. There were, however, a few alterations that did not escape my notice. The gold-framed window beside the bed had been fixed with metal bars, hindering any attempts at escape. The writing desk in the corner of the room had also been equipped with more paper and utensils.

But the main difference that really caught my attention was the huge, golden frame hanging opposite the bed. The last time I was here, that frame sported a beautiful mirror which was the centrepiece of the entire room. Today, the mirror had been replaced, and within the frame was a giant glass pane that looked through into the adjoining room.

Of course, I thought, how could I believe Calpacious would allow me the right of privacy? I groaned as I rolled myself out of bed and walked towards the window, hoping to give whoever was spying on me a piece of my mind.

But that wasn't the case. There was no one there watching me. The window looked through to another bedroom, and there, sitting on the floor, was Lilly.

'Lilly!' I shouted, my hands up against the glass. She made no sign that she heard me, simply continued to concentrate on her colouring in. I commenced hitting the glass with my fists, screaming her name again, but there was still no response. In fact, when she did glance up, it didn't even look as though she saw me.

I backed away from the screen. A one-way mirror. So, this was Calpacious' next tactic. There was no denying he wasn't playing around this time. He may not be watching me through that wall, but somehow, he had his eye on me. And if I stepped one foot out of place, then it was Lilly who would suffer the consequences. And I could nothing but stand idly by and watch as it happened.

I screamed and threw a candle holder—the first heavy thing I could find—at the window. Both arms of the candelabra snapped off, but the window didn't so much as crack.

I regretted my temper surge when there was an immediate knock at the door. But it wasn't my door—it was the one in Lilly's room.

Curious, I stepped closer to the glass pane and watched for what was about to happen, my heart in my throat.

The door opened, and an unfamiliar guard walked into her room. Though she was turned away from me, I could tell this guard was female, and Lilly seemed pleased to see her. My guess was they'd already been acquainted.

I could hear everything that went on in that room. At first, I couldn't work out why, as it was apparent Lilly couldn't hear any noise from my side. Then I looked up into the corner of the glass and saw a miniature speaker, transferring everything that happened on that side of the window. Like it wasn't bad enough I had to watch the oblivious Lilly as she suffered from my mistakes. I also had to listen to her tortures.

'Morning, sweetie,' said the guard woman with a cheery voice. 'I've brought you some breakfast.' Behind her came two maids, trundling in a trolley carrying a bowl of Frosties—Lilly's favourite. I remembered that from the manor.

'Can I go and see Pepper yet?' she asked with excitement.

'Pepper's busy at the moment,' the woman explained. 'She's doing a job. If she finishes it, then you might get to see her.'

Lilly's expression dropped at the woman's announcement.

I realised then that this woman hadn't just come in to see Lilly. She knew I was in the next room, and listening to every word she said. What she said was a warning. If I didn't complete my job, Calpacious would make sure I never saw Lilly again. My blood boiled, but I was intrigued to hear what else she had to say, so I kept listening.

'How long is she going to be?' she asked.

'Don't worry. We'll make certain she reaches the deadline.'

Really? The deadline? She wasn't even going to tell me when that would be? Calpacious must have wanted me to keep guessing. But it was perfectly clear that, if I took too long, he would put measures in place to hurry me along. And those measures probably involved Lilly.

'What do you think of my drawing?' Lilly asked, changing the topic. She took the guard's hand and led her over to the colourful sheet of paper on the floor. She picked it up and showed it to her.

'It's supposed to be a fairy,' she said, 'like the ones I saw at my uncle's house.'

The two of them stood closer to me now. I wished the guard woman would turn around to give me a view of her face, but she remained with her back to the window. Or mirror, as it was on their side. I just wanted to get an idea of how old she was. All I could see of her was the black hood of her uniform, covering any glimpse I might have got of her hair.

'I can see,' she said to Lilly.

'I like fairies. They're so pretty, and they make me remember that the world is so beautiful. I didn't colour her in very well though. I went out of the lines a lot.'

'The lines are thin,' the woman said. 'Once you go over, there is no way to change it back. That is the nature of the beast.'

There it was. She was talking to me again, delivering another ambiguous message for me to decipher

The woman said nothing more, and she and the two maids left. Lilly was alone in her room once more. I wanted desperately to go in there, to tell her I was there for her. I wanted to ask her who kidnapped her, and what happened to Tharva.

An ugly thought crossed my mind, and I wondered if, in fact, the woman in the guard's uniform was the delightful shop owner, that maybe it was her who brought Lilly here.

But no, it couldn't be. Could it? Surely, I would have recognised her voice. Or maybe I would have, had it not been transmitted to me via a microphone.

There was a way for me to see Lilly again. A way for me to find out exactly who Tharva was working for. And that was to do what Calpacious wanted me to do.

I glanced over at the desk beside me. It pained me to admit it, but Calpacious had won. He'd found my weakness. There was no way I would allow any harm to come to another because of me, especially a child as young and innocent as Lilly. I swallowed down my pride, and took a seat at the desk. It was time to begin.

A monster, he said. Calpacious was enough of a monster as it was, so why would he need another? What did he want this creature to do? And could he have been any more vague?

The lines are thin.

The guard woman's words still rang through my head. What could she have meant? If the lines were thin, that meant they were easy to cross. Calpacious had thin boundaries, and I knew if I were to cross them, there would be drastic repercussions. But I knew that already. So what else was she referring to?

I tried to knock the thought out of my head and focus on creating this monster, but nothing was coming to me. What would happen if I got it wrong, and created the wrong kind of monster?

'Not my fault,' I grumbled. 'Could've been a little more specific.'

Believe: that was what Marc said.

He said I needed to believe in something in order to make it real. That belief was just as important as the imagination. I still wasn't sure whether or not I trusted Marc, but at least he gave me something to go on. Whatever kind of monster I created, I had to believe in it. And that was going to be the hardest thing of all.

I took a deep breath and lowered my pen to the paper, allowing the words to flow from the pen. I barely paid attention to the words I wrote as my fingers moved the pen elegantly over the page, sweeping up and down, and swirling around the shapes of each letter.

It wasn't until I finished the sentence and looked down that I realised what I wrote.

The nature of the beast.

That was what the guard woman said to Lilly. And then, like a sack of bricks, the meaning hit me.

36

SHOCKING REVELATIONS

For two days, I slaved away at that desk. Barely given enough food to last the day, my stomach was almost constantly making noises.

As much as I could, I kept my eye on Lilly. She didn't receive human contact anymore, except for when they delivered her food. I learnt by now that, for every hour of the daytime I wasn't writing, Lilly lost a meal. Yesterday, I stayed up writing late into the night worrying about the poor girl.

I wished I could simply write myself out of the whole situation, but I knew the rules didn't work that way.

Stupid rules! I wanted to scream, but if I did, I knew they'd take away another one of Lilly's privileges. Thanks to me, she'd already lost the rights to converse with the castle staff, and her complimentary paper and crayons had also been taken from her.

The guard woman's message was clear: 'The lines are thin. Once you go over them, there is no way to change it back. That is the nature of the beast.'

She meant the lines of morality. A beast, a true monster, was one who could cross those lines and give no remorse. Calpacious was like that, but even he had boundaries. What I needed to do was to create a character with no concept of right or wrong. A beast without a soul. That had to be one of the most terrifying things in the world, both this one and the real one.

By the end of the second day, I ran out of things to write. Just reading back through what I wrote made me feel sick to the stomach, and sent shivers down the length of my back. I had no idea I was capable of creating so much raw terror.

The paper I worked on was enchanted. I tried many times to write positive attributes into the monster, but the ink never took to the page. I was forced to create something that would eventually destroy a world I loved. A great sense of self-loathing took over me, and I realised there really was nothing I could do about it.

As I sat there, staring with absent eyes at the notes in front of me, a movement in the floor disturbed me from my dismal train of thought. It felt like the earth had dropped as, in one jerky movement, the whole room plummeted no less than a foot. It took a while for the chandelier and ornaments to stop rattling, but my body still shook long after the impact. On quivering legs, I made my way over to the window. Everything looked normal. But when I turned to the other wall to check on Lilly, she was gone.

'Lilly?' I cried out. I knew it was futile, since she never heard me even when she was in the room. My breathing turned heavy as my heart started to pummel my ribcage. Frantic, I slammed myself into the door and began hitting it with my arms and fists, screaming for someone to let me out, but no one answered.

Tears swelled in my eyes as my hands went limp. My fingers slid down the wooden panel, my left hand catching on the door's handle. There was movement.

I frowned, and then lifted my hand back up to the cold metal. I twisted it. It turned. I pushed the door. It opened.

Without thinking, the first thing I did was charge into Lilly's room. I called out her name again. I checked under the bed and in the wardrobes, but she wasn't there.

No one was there.

I stumbled back out into the corridor, realising I was completely alone. There were no guards, no busy maids—no one. I swallowed my heart, but it did nothing to stop the pounding in my ears. The castle, with its many stairways, was like a maze, but I recalled my way to the bottom. I sprinted the entire way.

Only to come to a dead stop when I reached the main foyer. It was empty, and eerily quiet. What happened? Was I in a dream?

'Hello?' My warbling voice echoed off the walls of the barren halls. I cleared my throat. 'Is there anyone there?'

I wasn't sure, but I thought I heard something. It was so quiet, though, that I couldn't make out what it was. A footstep? A rat? The wind?

I opened my mouth to say something else, but I heard it again. A whisper; my name.

Someone was calling me.

'Who-who is that?'

There was another sound. This one sounded like a strong gust of wind. It was difficult to tell with the surrounding echoes, but it sounded like the voice came from Calpacious' throne room. I inched closer and nudged at one of the double doors. It didn't open.

I figured it must be locked, but pushed a little harder just in case it wasn't. It budged ever so slightly, but slammed itself shut once more. This time, I leaned all my weight against the wooden door and grunted as I forced it open. Straight away, I was blasted in the face by a cold wind. I threw my hand up in front of me to shield my eyes from the gust that tried to blow me backwards.

'Pepper!' I heard it clearer this time. 'Help!'

I looked around, and almost ran back out of the room when I saw that the desperate plea came from none other than King Calpacious himself. In the centre of the room, he stood in the middle of a spinning vortex that was the source of the gusts. He struggled to stay upright at the swirling wind tossed him around.

Startled, I remained towards the back of the room, not daring to get much closer.

'What happened?' I shouted over the raging air currents. 'What's going on?'

'It was her!' Calpacious said as he continued to be thrashed around the room. 'She did this to me! Damn betrayer, she was working for herself all along!' Calpacious' arms flailed as he tried to free himself, but the more he struggled, the stronger a hold the mini tornado kept on him.

'Who? Who did this?'

'Your friend.' Calpacious grunted. 'Oh, get me out of here, girl!'

The breeze whipped at my hair and I struggled to keep it out of my face.

'Who?' I asked again. 'Tharva?'

He groaned out in pain. 'Just get this thing off me!' he ordered.

'How?'

'I don't know . . . use your words. Write me out of it!'

I stared at him, the wild torrents tugging at his dirty blond hair, thrashing it in frenzied formations around his terror-stricken face. He looked truly helpless; a stark contrast to his usual demeanour.

'What would make you think I'd want to help you?' I tried to lock gazes with him, but that was difficult when his body kept spinning in circles. 'After all you've done to me, it would be easy to just leave you here and run away while I can.' To make my point, I turned and moved to put a hand on the door handle.

'Pepper, wait!'

I smiled to myself and turned back around.

'I'm not going to apologise, if that's want you want. Everything I've done has been for the good of my kingdom.'

'Oh really?' I lifted an eyebrow, making him

scowl. 'So killing your brother was what was best?'

'This really isn't the time for this discussion.'

This time I raised both my eyebrows. 'I think this is the perfect time. It's the perfect time for you to tell me why I should bother to help you.' I was testing him, and he knew it.

Calpacious growled. 'Alzabar was never supposed to be king. I was the eldest—I deserved that throne! I only corrected the mistake our parents had made.'

'Your brother might not be able to stop you,' I said, taking a step forwards, 'but there are plenty more people willing to try.' With that, I turned to leave again. This time, I really did intend to leave, but he made me stop once more.

'No, wait!' he said, stopping me again. 'I know what she's doing! If you don't stop her, the whole kingdom is in danger, including you and your friends.'

That made me turn back around.

'Look, I know you hate me, okay, but you have to understand. You know what I had planned, Pepper, but this . . . this is much worse.'

He was still inside the cycle of wind, still being tossed around in circles, but he managed to hold my gaze. His face now told a much different story to the one I was used to reading. Something foreign to his features danced within his grey irises—fear.

I shouldn't have done it. But Therron's face bore into my mind. And so did Scarlett's, Cade's, Marc's, Lilly's, Archie's, and even Bel's. Even Tharva sprang to mind. So I said it.

'Okay. I'll help you. Only because I care about what happens to my friends. But you need to tell me who did this to you. Is it her?' I asked. 'Is it Tharva?'

'No,' Calpacious said, his eyes grave. 'Not Tharva. Prudence Sharpe.'

'Miss Sharpe?!'

I backed away, dumbfounded, until my back collided with the stone wall. No, it couldn't be! For all that I never trusted the woman, I never would have suspected her.

'But what . . . how did she get here?'

'You stupid girl!' Calpacious spat. 'She's a magick. I sent her to the manor to be my lookout, but the traitorous woman had to go and betray me. Now are you going to get me out of this thing or what?'

It seemed I was left with no choice. Remembering what Marc said, I closed my eyes and tried with all my might to believe Calpacious was free. I concentrated so hard I thought my head was going to explode, but eventually, the whistling of the wind in my ears drew to a stop. I opened my eyes and saw Calpacious lying out of breath on the throne room floor, his clothes a mess. It worked! I could scarcely believe it.

He hardly looked like a king at all. Should I have helped him up? Perhaps. But instead, I followed my instincts and stuck to my comfort zone, against the wall. I still didn't trust him.

'I don't understand,' I said, barely giving him a chance to recover. 'How is Miss Sharpe a magick? Everyone at the manor could see her. And if she had dark intentions, she shouldn't have even been able to cross!'

Calpacious pushed himself up, his legs wobbling beneath him.

'Prudence has always been a manipulator of the rules. Perhaps I will never learn how she does it. I just know she needs to be stopped.'

I thought back to the earthquake moments earlier. That must have been her. 'What did she do?' I asked, becoming frantic. 'What did she do to Lilly?'

Calpacious shook his head. 'I don't know. But Prudence is planning on destroying Tantary forever, and everyone in it. She used the portal I intended solely for myself. We made it together—a box, that when activated turns into a super-portal. It can only be used once. She knew I was going to use it, but she tricked me. The wench tricked me! And now she's going to destroy Tantary!'

In his rage, Calpacious kicked at his throne, which

lay on its side from the tornado.

Destroy Tantary? Terror pumped through my veins. 'What do we do to stop her?'

'Someone needs to get to the other side,' he said, 'but it's going to be difficult. The whole point of that portal was that it disabled all the other ones. Wherever she opened it, it will only remain active for the next twenty-four hours, and then no one will ever be able to leave Tantary again. And, if what she has in mind all goes to plan, there won't even be a Tantary left to live in!'

'Well, come on, then!' I said, opening the door to the foyer. 'We need to find that portal before she uses it!'

'Hold on,' Calpacious said, catching up to me. 'There's one more thing.' He paused. 'That monster I told you to create. Did you do it?'

He was right up close to me now, so much so that I had to swallow down a lump of fear in the throat. 'Yes,' I said, hoping to appease him. Then, he did something unexpected. He picked up one of the candelabras standing beside the double doors and threw it across the room, screaming. The stand broke in two, and the candles, blown out from the tornado, scattered over the floor.

'Without a portal to go through, that monster is going to destroy everything in its path! Don't you

432

see? That's how she's going to destroy us! By turning my own weapon against me! Why, if I ever see that witch again . . .'

I didn't let him finish. Instead, I grabbed his arm and towed him out of the castle.

'I don't know where the monster is,' I said as I ran. 'I finished the story, but I have yet to see it. We need to find it and get it to that portal!'

'For heaven's sake, girl!' Calpacious said with a growl, but continued to run alongside me. 'Don't you know anything? If it goes through there, it'll destroy *your* world. I know, because that was what I wanted it to do. The only way to stop it is to kill it.'

At his words, all the blood drained from my face. I did my absolute best to appease Calpacious, by giving him the toughest, strongest monster my mind could conjure. To kill it, it would have to have a weakness. As we ran out of the castle and across the bridge, I nearly stumbled, as I realised it didn't have one.

The land was in a state. All around us, people were screaming, trying to hide. I saw the castle's staff— they must have escaped before I left my room. Perhaps they knew what was going on before I felt the earth move.

I scanned the crowds for Lilly. I had to know she was safe. But there were too many people, all moving too fast for me to look at any faces.

One figure did look familiar, though—a small, white shape hopping through the crowd, coming towards me.

'Penelope!' I stooped down to welcome to little bunny as she jumped up into my arms.

So pleased to see a familiar face, I picked her up and buried my face in her fur. She was covered in dirt and debris, and she clearly came a long way to find me.

She was trying to tell me something. I placed her back down on the ground and crouched to her level. Her nose twitched as she tried to communicate, bouncing up and down on her little feet. I wished I could interpret her movements the way Therron could.

Her fur changed colour in her frustration, cycling through all the hues.

'Please,' I told her, 'you're going to have to slow down. I don't understand.'

She calmed down a bit, but her movements were still frantic. I don't know how or why, but understanding suddenly came to me. I knew precisely what she meant.

Archie and Therron were coming.

37

POWERFUL ENEMIES

*T*ears of relief swelled my cheeks. They were coming. Therron was okay! And what about Max and Adrian? Did they know Prudence was the one behind all of this?

Just then, Penelope's ears twitched, as though she heard something from behind her. She glanced at me once before turning and hopping away. She was fast, but I managed to keep up with her, pushing my way through the bustling crowd, apologising as I bashed into the confused bodies. The village here wasn't nearly the size of the Tropolis, but with everybody out on the streets, the place was crowded.

I had no idea where Calpacious had gone, but I no longer cared. He could do what he pleased for all I was concerned. A victim of Miss Sharpe's evil plan or not, nothing could take away what he did to me.

Every now and then, Penelope would stop and twitch her ears a little before carrying on. She must have sensed something I couldn't. It wasn't until I'd been following her a while that I discovered what.

Penelope came to a stop outside a house in an empty side-street. I heard then what she had—the sound of someone sobbing. Curious, I came to stand beside her, where she faced the front of the building. When I got closer, though, I saw that it wasn't the brick wall she stared at, but a thin partition between two houses. The gap was too small to be an alleyway, but large enough to fit the young girl who sat between the two buildings, sniffing into her skirt.

'Lilly!' I cried out, and the little redhead tilted her damp face up to meet mine. Did Penelope really hear her crying all the way in the village centre?

I crouched down in front of Lilly and gripped both her trembling hands in mine. Her face was red and blotchy, and I realised this was the first time I had ever seen her cry.

'Lilly, what's the matter?'

If she was pleased to see me, she didn't show it. She peered up at me with watery eyes and told me

436

between rasps, 'I'm scared.'

'I know, sweetie,' I said as I pulled her out from her hiding spot, 'I know.' I pulled her close to me, placing her head on my shoulder as I combed my fingers through her un-brushed ringlets. I wanted to ask her how she'd escaped, and to tell her how glad I was to find her, but right then, the only thing she needed was reassurance. Even though I was barely sure myself, that was something I strove to give her.

This wasn't fair. Lilly shouldn't have been here. She should have been at home. And I didn't even mean back at the manor—I meant with her parents. Her parents who were so cruelly taken from her life while she was barely old enough to remember them. She'd told me how she hadn't cried when her parents died. How crying wasn't going to bring them back, and that she needed to save her tears for when they were really needed. She was a tough girl, and yet here she was, sobbing against my shoulder, arms gripped around my waist as though her life depended on it. Being in Tantary, and witnessing its horrors, had caused the shell around her to crack. But if she hadn't been crying, would Penelope have heard and found her?

A protective instinct made me pull Lilly closer to my chest, and a surge of anger at the whole situation made me take her by the hand and drag her all the way back to the village centre—to the safety of the crowds. I had no idea what was going on, but I wasn't about to let Lilly get caught up in all this.

She and Penelope followed me as I led her back through the streets, but just before we entered the commotion, she pulled at my hand. I stopped and turned to see what she wanted.

'I saw her,' she said.

'Saw who?'

'Miss Sharpe. I saw her at the castle. I thought she was being nice at first . . . but then she wasn't. She scared me, so I ran away.' She sucked in her lips as more tears formed in the corners of her eyes. She was referring to the guard woman I saw in the room with her. That was Miss Sharpe?

We were too close to the village centre, so I led her back down the street we came from, away from any listening ears. 'When no one was looking,' she continued when I prompted her, 'I left the castle, and I hid. People came looking for me, but they couldn't find me. And then . . .' She started blubbering and looked down at her muddied shoes. 'The ground moved. And the sky changed colour. It's Miss Sharpe, I know it is!' She brought her nervous gaze back to meet mine. 'And I think this is all my fault because I ran away!'

'No, Lilly, this isn't your fault!' I said, hugging her

438

as she burst into another round of sobs. 'Please, don't think like that!'

I told her this, but silently, I wondered if this was a contributing factor in the sudden turn of events. Prudence had planned this for a long time—at least, according to Calpacious. But perhaps Lilly's escape attempt had been a trigger.

Or a distraction.

The new thought popped into my head, making me wonder whether Lilly's running away had been her own decision, or if it was more manufactured, in that it had been intended all along.

'Lilly?' I spoke up once her rasps died down a little. 'Can you tell me how you managed to get out?'

'I went in the night time,' she said. 'I got lonely, and scared, and when I tried to open the door, it was open.'

'Did no one see you?'

'No. Most people were asleep, and I was very quiet.'

I felt a chill creeping up inside me as she confirmed my fears. Prudence used her situation to her benefit. I'd bet that it was her who left Lilly's door unlocked. Mine, too.

'Pepper!'

I looked behind me to see Calpacious turning into the street. Lilly whimpered in recognition and hid behind me leg.

'Where did you go?' he demanded. 'There are rumours in the village. They say the portal has already been opened. If that is the case, then I'm afraid it is too late.'

My fear spiked once again.

'There must be something someone can do,' I said, but Calpacious looked pessimistic.

'I manufactured that portal,' he said. 'The only way to stop it is to cross through to the human world and destroy it from the outside, and that's only if you can get close enough to it without getting killed.'

So it seemed that, either way you looked at it, we were doomed.

No. I refused to believe that! There was another way to stop this, there had to be!

But still, I had one more question to ask Calpacious.

'What exactly were you planning to do with the portal?' I said. 'If you knew how dangerous it was, then why risk so much just to get to the other side?'

'The portal wasn't complete,' he said with a frown. 'The project was supposed to carry on for another few months. That way, the only land it would destroy would have been the human one, just like I wanted. But Prudence played me like a fool. She never intended for it to get to that state. She had it planned, just like she planned Lilly's escape. She knew I would send all the guards to go and find her.'

So, that was why the castle was so empty? They were all looking for Lilly! Of course, a guard-less castle would have meant Prudence was able to smuggle out the portal without being caught.

'So what about the earthquake?' I asked the King. 'What was all that about?'

'Earthquake?' he echoed. 'What earthquake?'

I shook my head. 'I don't know,' I told him, 'but it felt like the ground dropped. It-it must have happened while you were still trapped inside the tornado.'

Calpacious let out a rather loud cuss words. I winced, hoping Lilly wasn't paying too much attention.

'That was the portal opening,' he explained. 'That means we're too late. She's done it.'

But before I had much time to ruminate on this, Penelope began head-butting my ankle, and she did so with quite some persistence. When I looked at her, she turned her head to face the sky. I did the same, and saw why she was so intent on getting my attention.

Through the clouds appeared the flapping wings of a griffin. Who rode it? Was it Therron?

Lilly spotted it at the same time I did, and the two of us waved our arms in the air as they came to land beside us in the barren side-street.

It wasn't until the bird landed that I noticed. Therron wasn't there.

It was Archie who climbed down from the griffin's back and gave me a hug.

'Great to see you again,' I said.

'I'm glad you're safe. Are you okay?'

I gave a small smile, indicating I did not know how to answer that question. Instead, I asked my own. 'Where's Therron?'

This time it was Archie who didn't know how to respond. 'I don't know,' he said as he checked the griffin's saddle and reins. 'Penelope came to find me when . . .' He trailed off when he caught sight of Calpacious. His gaze flacked back to me in question.

'It's alright,' I told him, 'this isn't his doing. This is the work of Prudence Sharpe—the housekeeper from Calthorpe Manor.'

His eyes widened, but I had no time to explain further. I egged him to continue with his story.

'Um, I sent Penelope ahead to tell you we were coming,' he said, his eyes still casting suspicious glances Calpacious' way. 'I went to rescue Therron, but when I got there, his place was empty. I have no idea where he went.'

I felt bile rise in the back of my throat as I wondered what could have happened to him. A thousand scenarios played out in my mind, few of them ending positively. Conflicting emotions fought in my head, and I remembered the kiss we shared that night. The night he found his book. We had parted on such bad terms. I wished for them to not be the last.

'Excuse me,' Calpacious piped up. I watched as Archie's stance turned defensive. 'But right now, there is a giant, black hole in the middle of my kingdom. Don't you think our time would be better spent discussing that?' He was looking pointedly at Archie, who cleared his throat.

'I saw it,' he said. 'While flying over from Therron's house, I saw something—a swirling black disk in the sky—directly over the Tropolis.'

Archie turned back to the griffin and began to haul himself onto its back.

'Um,' I said, 'what are you doing?'

'I'm a hero.' He shrugged. 'It's kind of my job to deal with these situations. And you're going to have to come, too.'

'What, me?' I took a step backwards. 'No, it's really not my thing. Plus, I can't leave Lilly behind on her own.'

Calpacious looked offended, but he didn't get a chance to speak, as a golden dragon descended from the sky.

'Who says she'll be on her own?' said the rider.

Tharva grinned, seeing my expression. 'Archie told me to follow him,' she explained. 'The King's guards,' she said, shooting Calpacious an accusatory look, 'had me tied to a tree when they kidnapped you. I don't know what would have happened to me if this young man hadn't come and untied me!' She shot a coy smile in Archie's direction. Archie choked out a cough, and I could have been imagining it, but I thought I detected a slight pink hue painting his cheeks.

'Tharva!' Lilly ran up and gave Tharva one of her loving leg-hugs, catching Tharva nearly completely off guard. She stumbled backwards and chuckled at the young girl's affection.

'You go and do what you have to do,' she said with a warm smile as she stroked Lilly's hair. I wondered in that moment how I could have ever considered that she was the one conspiring against me. 'This land needs you, Pepper. More than you realise.'

Hesitant, I turned towards Archie for a second opinion. He nodded, agreeing with what Tharva said. I walked up to Lilly and placed my hand on the small of her back. She turned around, releasing Tharva from her grip.

'Are you going to be okay here?' I asked her. Her little brow was creased, but she nodded. 'I promise I'll come back for you. Okay?'

'Okay.'

I turned back to Tharva.

'Tharva, promise me that, if anything should happen, you and your dragon fly her to safety.'

'I will,' she said. 'There's a standard portal that should open on the other side of the King's forest soon. I'm not sure if it will actually open, but I'll try my best to get her back to the manor.'

I smiled at her kindness, and enveloped her in a large hug.

'Thank you so much,' I said. 'You've been so helpful to me. I'll never forget you.'

Tharva chuckled against my shoulder. She was too short to get her chin over it.

'We're not saying goodbye,' she assured me. 'I'll always be right here for you.' She lent away but held onto my shoulders, keeping me at an arm's length. Pools of water shimmered in her eyes. 'You're a wonderful girl, Pepper. You're the closest thing I've ever had to a daughter. Now, your Therron needs you. We all do. You need to—'

She was cut off by a loud thumping sound that sent tremors through the village and shrieks of distress from the crowd gathered in the streets beyond.

'What was that?' asked Tharva, her eyes wide. Archie looked baffled as he peered around for the source of the noise, and Penelope ran to hide behind

Lilly's legs.

But I knew exactly what it was. It was my monster. It was alive. The shock it had sent through the earth told me it wasn't that close, but it wasn't too far away, either. I knew that monster, and it could move fast.

It wasn't heading towards us, though.

Without waiting a moment longer, I joined Archie on the back of the griffin and we headed straight for the Tropolis; right into the eye of the storm.

38

MAGICAL FRIENDS

*I*t was an eerie sight. Directly over the Tropolis, a huge, black circle hung low in the sky. The closer we got, the darker the sky became. Around the edges of the open portal churned tornado-like clouds, similar to the ones I rescued Calpacious from.

The suction from the portal tore off the roofs from the taller buildings, sending them spiralling up into the abyss. Into the manor.

Where was Therron? I hope so much that he was safe.

Archie landed the griffin a safe distance away, but

447

the sounds of the battering winds and the screams of the fearful residents could still be heard.

'What do we do?' I asked Archie, anticipating that he had already come up with a plan. The griffin was distressed, and he was doing a great job of calming him down. I only wished my nerves were so easily settled.

'We evacuate the city,' he said. 'If what you told me on the way here is true, that the monster is heading for the Tropolis, then we need to get as many people out of harm's way as possible.'

I followed Archie through the entrance in the surrounding trees, into the Tropolis. The city was bustling with terrified people, more than the village we just left, which Calpacious was probably now dealing with.

Archie took control of the situation like a pro. I followed his lead, ushering people out of the village.

'Go to the guard tower,' he told them. 'You should be safe in there until we deal with this situation.'

Magicks of all ages, shapes, and forms joined the rush to evacuate the city. Some were willing to leave, but others needed a little more persuasion.

'Where do you think Prudence is?' I shouted to Archie through the flowing crowds.

'I'm not sure,' he replied. 'I guess she might be on the other side of the portal. I've never met her, but I wouldn't think she'd risk getting hurt in her own schemes.'

'So, to stop her,' I said, 'we have to find a way to get through the portal.'

I looked up. The portal was growing, and was now nearly the side of the whole Tropolis. More debris went flying up into the swirling hole, and I knew there was only one way we were going to get through—by going up.

There was another *thwump*, like the one we heard in the other village. The monster was here.

I anticipated it before it happened. A dark shape blasted through the trees and into the city, sending tree branches splintering into the building. The smaller ones were carried up into the portal.

It was him. The monster Calpacious forced me to create. Just to look at him, to know I was the one who created him, made me feel sick to my stomach.

The remaining villagers screamed and quaked in fear. Those that weren't paralysed in terror sprinted for the exit, but the 3-story high monster was too quick. With a swing of its arm, the villagers went flying across the street. It was unlikely any of them survived.

The monster was a face-less, gender-less, soul-less beast. Taking the form of a shadow, it could crush you to death in a split second, before you even realised what was happening. It slunk around like a billow of smoke, but with the strength of a bulldozer. Where its face was supposed to be were two white, glowing holes marking its eyes.

And I wrote it. I didn't want to, but it was like I had no control over the words that flowed from my pen. Knowing I created something so terrible was far worse than any pain Calpacious could have inflicted on me.

I was so caught up in my grief, I didn't think to duck when the creature's black foot swung towards me. Just before the impact, Archie threw me to the ground and hid me behind what was left of a wall. He was out of breath, but still checked if I was okay.

'You never told me this monster of yours was so . . .' he struggled to find a word. 'Vile.'

I hung my head.

Archie saw my expression and placed an apologetic hand on my shoulder.

'There has to be some way to defeat it,' he continued. 'You know this beast better than anyone. What are its weaknesses?'

I jumped as the sound of another crashing building filled the air.

'That's just the thing,' I told him, 'it doesn't have any!'

And with that, the shadow monster slammed its fist

into the bricks we hid behind, missing us by mere inches. I held my breath, intending to lie still, but Archie grabbed my arm and towed me away, trying to outrun the beast.

'That can't be,' he said as we ran. 'There must be something. A blind spot. A lessened sense. Anything!'

'There isn't anything! The paper I used was enchanted. Every time I tried to write something positive, or considerably weak, the ink didn't take. I'm telling you, there is no way to defeat this monster! He's just going to destroy everything in sight until there is nothing left!'

And to prove my point, the monster jumped over us. Where it was previously on our tails, it now stood directly in front of us, blocking our path. We turned, ready to run in the other direction, but there it was again. It looked at us with its glowing eyes, but I knew there was nothing behind them. No heart, no soul. No hope. There was nothing we could do now.

And Archie knew it, too. We stood stock still as the beast approached, one menacing step at a time. This was it. How ironic that the death of me should be my own creation. In my last conscious thoughts, I closed my eyes, hoping for the process to be quick and painless.

Just then, a sound echoed from a few streets down. I dared to peel open my eyes, and I watched as the

451

monster turned away and headed in the direction of the new sound.

Making as little noise as possible, we crept round the corner to see what caught the monster's attention.

Archie and I both saw him at the same time.

Therron.

He stood on the roof of a building, clanging a metal pole against the chrome surface. He did it on purpose, trying to get the monster's attention.

I opened my mouth to scream to him, but Archie clapped his hand over it before any sound could come out.

'Wait here,' he said quietly, and then, before I could ask what he was doing, he added, 'and stay quiet.' With that, he stood and left, sneaking through the streets towards the exit.

But I couldn't obey him. Not while the monster headed straight for Therron.

'Therron!' I shouted, making the beast turn back to me. 'What are you doing?'

Without taking his eyes off the monster, he thrust out his arms towards it, and out shot two fireballs, hitting it square on the back.

'Practising my magic!' he said with a mischievous grin. I, however, failed to find the humour. The monster, not appreciating the fireballs, now had his attention back to Therron.

'You're going to get yourself killed!'

He didn't answer me, and instead went back to shooting missiles of both fire and water at the monster, which had turned back to me again.

This seemed to be the only way to keep the monster from attacking—by distracting his attention, so he didn't know which of us to attack first. Thinking fast, I grabbed a wooden beam from one of the buildings and a piece of corrugated metal which lay by my feet.

'Over here!' I called, clanging the shard of metal with the beam as I ran down the street. Therron seemed to get the message, and began running over the rooves of the compacted houses, hitting them with the pole as he went.

It was working. The monster didn't know which direction to run in. For a few seconds, it would take off after me, but then with a loud clang from Therron's direction, it would turn and run the other way.

This distracted the monster, but it wasn't going to stop it. I hoped Archie would be back soon, before we tired, and it destroyed us both.

I didn't know where I was going. For the most part, I ran blindly through the streets, giving no thought as to which turnings I took.

Before long, I was lost. What was it with me and

my awful sense of direction?

I stood at the end of a dead-end street, with no way to get out and nowhere to hide. I stopped my clanging and steadied my breathing, listening out for the monster. I heard nothing.

I thought I was safe, but then the sound of creeping footsteps behind me made me still.

My blood pumped through my ears as the being got closer. Soon, I heard its breath. It sent tingles down my neck. Where was Therron? Why couldn't I hear him anymore?

My breathing hitched as a cold hand grabbed my arm and span me round, but it wasn't the monster.

It was Prudence Sharpe.

'Miss Fairfield,' she snarled. 'You've come to see your work in action, I see.'

I tried to take a step away from her, but the grip she had on my arm was too strong.

'This is all your doing,' she said with a smile, looking around at the destruction that lay even in this blocked-off street. 'Every last piece of destruction. It was all you. I've never been a fan of Mr. Calthorpe's decisions, but I think he made a good one by hiring you.'

Fear choked my throat, but I was just able to ask the question that had been gnawing at me.

'Why are you doing this?' I asked her. 'Why are

you destroying Tantary? This is your home!'

'It was!' she said with a snarl, her grip on my arm tightening. Talon-like nails dug into my flesh. 'This place doesn't belong to me now. I've found a much better life, up in the real world. I don't need this dungeon anymore.'

She walked me backwards until my back collided with the crumbling wall at the end of the road.

'If you don't need it,' I said, 'then why destroy it? Why endanger so many innocent people?'

Prudence snarled and pressed her other hand right up against my throat, slamming my head into the wall behind.

'You don't know anything!' I only just heard her through the ringing in my ears. 'The magicks are abominations. They were never meant to exist! You may think you're clever, that you're some kind of hero, but you are nothing but a pawn. And not just for me, either. Think about it— both Calpacious and Mr. Calthorpe used you, too. Fortunately, I was one step ahead of both of them.' She took away the arm holding my wrist in place and reached into her pocket. She pulled out a rolled-up scroll and held it out in front of my face.

'You see, I'm not the one who's going to do the destroying—your monster is. That was my fantastic idea. I actually convinced Calpacious the beast would help him over take your world!' Her chuckle was gritty, like the muscles were dry from under-use.

'How did you get that?' I said, pointing to the scroll containing the monster's story. 'I left that on my desk this morning. No one went back into the castle after I left.'

Prudence grinned. It was a strange look for her, especially after I was used to seeing her so sour back at the manor.

'What you left on your desk wasn't the original story,' she told me. 'I performed a little switcheroo. Quite a nice trick, actually. A friend of yours gave it to me.'

A friend of mine?

Since both my hands were now free, I wrestled with her, trying to force her hand away from my throat. But she was too strong, and in response to me struggle, she pressed even harder. My lungs started to burn.

'That monster responds to me now, and it will destroy this land and everything in it before you can even blink an eye!'

'And what about you?'

She raised an eyebrow at my question. 'Well I'll be going back to the manor, of course. Since Cedrick removed my terrible curse of being bound to this awful land, I'm free to go wherever I like.'

'Cedrick?' The name sounded familiar, but I didn't get the chance to think about it as, from overhead, a dark shape swooped down into the street. Miss Sharpe tried to move away, pressing me even further into the broken wall. Crumbling bricks and shards of metal dug into my skin. I closed my eyes and ducked, but felt only the gust of wind as whatever it was soared back into the sky.

Prudence stepped back, and I watched as she stared at her empty hand, where the scroll had just been. She let out a loud curse word, looking up as Archie came back into view, grinning in triumph as he sat astride his griffin's back. He waved the scroll in his hand in a taunting manner, and then tossed it to his right. My eyes followed its path as it fell and landed in Therron's hands. Still standing on the rooves, he must have crept over here while Prudence had me cornered.

But where was the monster?

Prudence looked disgruntled, but not overly fazed. Gaining the scroll was only a minor victory for us. As a matter of fact, it didn't really do us much good at all—only made an angry Miss Sharpe even more vengeful.

She looked at me with murder in her eyes.

'I've suffered long enough!' she snarled. 'I am not going to have all my hard work ruined by a couple of teenagers and an ugly troll!' Raising her face skywards, she stuck two fingers in her mouth and gave a shrill whistle. Within mere seconds, the monster appeared at the end of the street. It was probably the angle, but he looked larger and more evil than ever.

'Finish them!' yelled Prudence, pointing at the three of us. She took a running leap and jumped up onto a pile of rubble and, a few seconds later, was gone. I heard the griffin's shriek, followed by a cry from Archie. When I looked up, I saw neither of them. I could only assume that the griffin fled in fear.

By now, Therron had climbed down from the tops of the buildings, and stood beside me.

'Pepper,' he said, taking both hands in mine. I could barely hear him over the stomping footsteps of the monster and the churning winds of the portal above. 'About what I said at the cabin.'

'I don't think now is the best time.'

'Well then when would be?' he countered. 'The odds aren't in our favour here, and I didn't think we'll have much time to chat in the afterlife.'

'Therron, please,' I said, squeezing his hands that had found their way into my own. 'Don't talk like that.'

He lowered his head and sighed before continuing. 'I just want to say I'm sorry,' he said. 'For what I said to you that day. It wasn't your fault. I shouldn't have let the shock of finding out about my story make me lash out at you.'

'No, please. I'm the one who's sorry. I was going to tell you, I swear. I just . . . I guess I waited too long.'

I knew he wanted to reply, but there were more pressing matters at hand. The monster stood right before us. It was biding its time, like it would get more fun out of making us wait for our death.

It took a swing, its arm reaching out towards me. I saw its claws coming down, aiming straight for my head. But, just before the impact came, Therron threw the scroll out of his hand and pushed me down to the ground. I heard his cry of pain when the monster's claws tore into his flesh.

39

BRAVE SACRIFICES

*F*ear paralysed my body, and I listened only to the sound of my own frantic breathing. I wasn't even aware everything had gone quiet until I felt the warmth of Therron's body leave mine and I was able to open my eyes again.

The street was empty, the monster nowhere in sight. I looked at Therron, and he turned to face me, a similar look of confusion mirrored in his eyes. The monster was gone. All that was left in its place was the scroll—its story.

Therron and I exchanged equally dumbfounded glances. What just happened?

Therron pushed himself up from the dusty ground and extended out a hand to help me. The silence was disturbing.

'Where do you think he went?' I asked Therron. He didn't answer me. Instead, he stepped over to where the scroll lay on the ground below. Looking tentative, he stooped down and picked it up.

'I threw this,' he said, looking pensive. 'I threw it at the monster's head. I hoped it would distract him.'

I tilted my head, unsure what he meant.

'I think this is the reason he vanished.

'But that doesn't make any sense,' I said, my eyebrows drawing low. 'Why would the monster run away from a piece of paper?'

Therron shook his head, inspecting the paper in question.

'I don't think he ran,' he said. 'I think this is the very reason magicks never see the stories at the manor. He's gone, Pepper. He's been absorbed back into the words that created him.'

I took the scroll off him, peering at it myself. I could see no difference.

'So,' I said, 'are you saying all the monster had to do was touch the words that created him, and that was it? He simply disappeared?'

'I can't see any other explanation.'

Really, I thought? That was all it took? I thought

back to the day Therron discovered his book. He hadn't touched it then, but if he had . . .

I didn't get much time to think, though, as something else caught my eye.

'Therron,' I said, 'you're bleeding.'

Therron looked down at his arm, and saw the layer of blood that caked it; the monster's final legacy.

Therron ran his hand over the wound, closing his eyes. He was trying to heal it.

But it didn't work. I watched as, three times, Therron performed a similar procedure to what he did on my arm, only to come back with the same results: nothing.

Therron frowned.

'What's the matter?' I asked.

'My healing powers,' he said. 'They don't work on myself.'

The gash continued to spew out blood. The wound ran deep. If it wasn't treated soon, he would lose too much blood.

Therron reached down and grabbed the end of his top, moving to rip a shred off, but I stopped him.

'Wait!' I said. 'I . . . I think I might be able to help.'

Therron cocked his head to the side, but when I beckoned him closer, he did as he was told.

I swallowed down my nerves and took a hold of

Therron's arm, only looking him once in the eyes. I couldn't get over how similar this situation felt, only the roles were reversed. For so long, Therron had been in utter denial over his powers. Now I knew what that felt like.

I took a deep breath and I closed my eyes, imagining his skin fully intact and perfectly smooth again. It was hard to concentrate as, even though I couldn't see him, I still felt Therron's gaze boring into me. I heard his sharp inhale, and took that as my cue to open my eyes. When I did, I saw Therron staring at his arm in wonderment. Then he turned to me and grinned, scooping me up in a big hug. I couldn't help it—I smiled too. Despite the portal, that was getting more violent by the second, and the knowledge that Prudence waited somewhere, just around the corner, I actually enjoyed the moment.

Therron kept his hold on me, but lessened his grip. I turned my head away, to see if Prudence was there but, taking my chin between his thumb and forefinger, Therron turned my face back to his.

'I meant what I said,' he told me. 'I really am sorry about everything that happened. I shouldn't have let you get kidnapped. When the guards locked me in my house, they didn't taken into account the fact that I live there. I know that place inside and out—all the loose grouting in the floor, the fact that the chimney warps in the warmer months, and the back exit. The one that leads into the tree behind and under the ground.

'After I escaped, I knew I had to try and find you. I met a man called Marc. Possibly the same one you met. He told me things were under control, and my time would be better spent practising my magic. This morning, he found me again, and told me to come to the Tropolis. I owe a lot to that man—he helped me find you.'

'He made you a hero,' I told him. I nearly laughed at the way he tilted his head in question. 'You've been fighting your powers—your strength—for so long. It took one person for you to realise your potential and embrace your true self.'

'That may be true,' he said. His forest-green eyes absorbed mine. 'But it wasn't Marc who made me see it. It was you.' With that, he leaned in and pressed his soft lips to mine. I melted, wanting the kiss to linger, but a thought occurred to me. I asked before, back at his hut, but a lot had happened since then. I needed to say it again.

'Come with me,' I said. 'Come with me to the manor. Once this is all over, you can come and live with me. In the real world!'

His eyes lit for all of two seconds. 'What makes you so sure we are going to get out of this alive?' he asked.

'I'm not,' I said in honesty. 'But I just need to know that, if we do, I'm not going to lose you again. Please, promise you'll come back with me.'

He smiled, and pecked my mouth once more. 'I promise,' he said.

We turned to leave the street, to find Prudence, when something to our left caught Therron's eye.

A browning, dusty book that looked like it hadn't been opened in decades lay on the street. Therron and I exchanged curious glances, and then he went to pick it up. The pages were damaged and falling apart, and when he opened the front cover, the hinge creaked. He read the first page and I watched as his eyes widened.

'What is it?' I asked.

'It's Prudence's book,' said Therron, flipping the pages over in his hands.

'How did it get here?'

He turned his eyes to me. 'I don't know,' he said, 'but I think it's obvious what we have to do.'

Therron and I ran through the streets. We didn't know where Prudence was, but she was bound to catch up with us soon.

'We need to get to the tower,' Therron said as we ran. 'It's still intact, so maybe, if we get to the top in time, we can jump into the portal.'

I gripped Prudence's book tight in my hand. I heard her following us—just a few streets behind. I had to wait until the opportune moment to throw the book. I couldn't risk missing.

Where was Archie? I hadn't seen him since his griffin flew away in fright. I hoped he was all right. In fact, I wished he would come here right now and take this book out of my hands. We really could have done with his impeccable aim right now.

Finally, after a few wrong turns, we reached the base of the tower. Usually acting as a communal area for the villagers, its steeple towered high up into the sky, pointing right into the centre of the portal. The structure wobbled precariously, and a couple of tiles shot up into the sky. We didn't have long to get up there before the whole steeple was sucked up inside the portal.

But still, we had to wait for Prudence to catch up with us. I got ready, holding the book behind my back, and looked up to the top of the tower. I prayed it didn't go anywhere anytime soon.

It wasn't long before Prudence caught up to us. When she saw we stopped, she slowed down, as though sensing we had something planned.

'Congratulations,' she sneered as she inched closer towards us. 'You defeated the un-defeatable monster. But I'm afraid that what's about to come you won't be able to stop.' She looked up and grinned as a huge rumble shook the ground. More buildings collapsed, and I clung on to Therron as the city continued to rattle.

'You see!' shouted Prudence over the noise. 'It's too late! Cedrick is destroying the portal. You will never be able to get back!'

Cedrick. It was that name again.

'Who is he?' I asked her. 'Who is Cedrick?'

'You've already met him!' said Prudence, still looking pleased with herself. 'Think back. Do you remember going to a certain party back at the manor?'

Adrian's party! The memory hit me. Cedrick was the creep who followed me upstairs—he was the one I hid from in the closet; the reason I was here in the first place! He'd asked me about the mirror. He wanted me to tell him where it was.

And I led him straight to it.

'Cedrick is the one who created this place,' Prudence continued. 'He's the wizard who Marcius Calthorpe went to.'

'But that makes no sense!' Therron countered. 'If Cedrick created this place, then why is he trying to destroy it?'

Prudence now stood directly in front of us. My arm holding the book twitched, but Therron grabbed hold of my wrist. He was right. We needed to hear her explanation first.

'You think this is what he wanted?' she asked us. 'Cedrick has been looking for a way to destroy all the magicks for over a hundred years. A few years ago, he met me, and I agreed to help him. In return, he promised to relieve me of the curse of being a magick, allowing me to be seen by humans and to come and go through the two realms as I please. This portal, the monster—it was all for us. For our life together.'

It all made sense now—why Adrian and Max could see her, and why she worked at the manor. It was so she could spend as much time at the manor as she could without looking suspicious. And it worked.

The ground rumbled again.

'Two more minutes,' she said, 'and then the portal closes for good. You'll both be trapped down here forever! With no access to the real world, I doubt Tantary will last more than a week. You'd better start saying your goodbyes! I can't see you being alive for much longer.'

'Now!' Therron whispered into my ear. I took my cue and launched the book at her, grunting with the force it took. Prudence saw the book coming with only a split second to spare. Dodging to the side, the

469

book just missed her, landing instead several feet behind her. There was no time to try again. We needed to get out of there!

Therron and I scrambled through the door to the tower, knowing that Prudence was right on our tails. We found our way to the stairs and began sprinting up to the top. My legs ached, and I was quite a way behind Therron. He noticed and waited for me, then grabbed my hand and stayed with me as we continued our ascent.

Prudence was fast catching up. The structure groaned in protest at the three sets of feet bolting up its steeple. We were nearly at the top, but so was Prudence. If we went through the portal, so would she.

With Therron's help, I opened the steeple window. No sooner was the latch undone that the pane of glass flew into the sky.

I went to climb out of the window, but Therron grabbed a hold of my shoulders and span me to face him. A dangerous look swirled in his eyes.

'Therron,' I said, frightened. 'What are you doing?'

He looked me in the eyes. 'Just trust me,' he said, and stepped away from me. 'Go! Now!' With that, he raised his hand into the air. There was another rumble, but it didn't come from the outside—it was the tower moving.

Therron stood at the top of the chrome staircase, which began to shudder dangerously. I was about to pull Therron onto the window ledge, to safety, but then I realised: he was doing this.

'Therron!' I called, reached out to him. I screamed as the staircase collapsed beneath him, sending both him and Prudence tumbling downwards, to the very bottom of the tower. I panted. Only the thin wood of the window ledge kept me standing.

I waited, listening for any sounds of life, but all I heard was the moaning on the collapsing tower.

Then, through the darkness, I saw one hand rising up out of the rubble. I heard the echo of Therron's voice: 'Go!'

His voice was weak. He was probably winded. I looked out the window, then back to him. I didn't know what to do.

My vision was blurred as a haze of tears descended in front of them. The steeple wobbled one more time, and that was the last thing I knew before I flew, screaming, up into the sky.

40

FINAL DISCLOSURES

*I*t wasn't like before.

This time, when I entered the portal, I stayed there.

I couldn't move. It was like I was stuck between the two worlds. I was nowhere, and yet everywhere, at the same time.

Everything was white. My feet stood upon a solid surface, yet I could not see where the floor met the walls, or where the walls met the ceiling. It was just white.

'Hello?'

The word was loud to my ears. I almost had to

473

cover them because of the intensity. Soon, the echo subsided, but there was no answer.

I was alone. I span round so many times I made myself dizzy, and yet I saw nothing. Where was I? And how was I supposed to get out of this place?

'Pepper.'

I span around at the sound of my name, and almost jumped out of my skin when I saw someone standing in what had just been an empty space.

'Marc?' I choked out his name. He gave a small nod in greeting. 'Wha—how—where am I?'

'It's nothing to be afraid of,' Marc assured me. 'We're in the portal between the realms. I only stopped you here to speak with you before you go back to the manor.'

I shook my head, stepping away from him.

'I don't understand. How did I get here?'

Marc remained silent, which just infuriated me.

'Who are you?' I asked him. 'I mean, really? You know too much about me, and about my friends. You always seen to be at the right place at the right time. Or the wrong time, depending on how you see it. You rescued Lilly and me from being devoured by mermaids, and yet you helped Calpacious kidnap me.' Marc just looked amused by my accusations. 'You helped Therron be true to himself, and made him see his true potential, and yet you weren't there when we needed your help. So please, just tell me, who are you?'

Marc exhaled and looked around him, as though he expected someone to be eavesdropping on our conversation.

'Okay,' he relented. 'I suppose I owe you that much. I guess a lot of people probably refer to me by my full name: Marcius.'

'Marcius?' I repeated. 'As in Marcius Calthorpe?'

Marc nodded.

Marcius Calthorpe. The original owner of Calthorpe Manor when it was a popular book store, a hundred years ago. The same man who called upon the help of the wizard to send all the magicks to Tantary.

Dumbfounded, it took me a while to find my words. 'If you're Marcius,' I said, 'then what are you doing in Tantary? And why all these years later?'

'I was much like you, Pepper,' he explained, clasping his hands behind his back and taking a more natural stance. 'I had a strong enough imagination, not only to see the magicks, but also to enter their realm. Soon after I had Cedrick create Tantary, I went to visit, to have a look at his work.

'I met Calpacious, back when Alzabar was still king. Calpacious appeared weak and distraught, claiming his brother stole the throne unlawfully.

Being the young and naive man that I was, I believed him. I sided with him, and thought I was doing a good thing when I agreed to help him overthrow his brother. I didn't realise he wanted to kill him. It wasn't until it was all over that I learned Calpacious was banned from the throne because of his instability. But by then, it was too late. I had done a bad deed, and that darkened my soul. From then on, the portal saw me as having bad intentions, and it kept me trapped.

'I've been watching you, Pepper. You, and you friend, Therron. I realised the only way I could protect you both without becoming too involved was to re-forge my alliance with Calpacious and pretend to work for him. That way, I was able to keep an eye on his plans while making sure you two didn't get hurt. But I didn't do a very good job.' He looked down at the stark white floor. 'I've had my eye on the wrong enemy. Once again, by trying to do the right thing, I have let people down. I'm sorry.'

'What you did wasn't wrong,' I said as he looked down at his fingers, entangling between one another. 'You saved us more than once, and I, for one, am more than grateful. You sent us Prudence's book, didn't you?'

'Yes,' he admitted, 'but I should have done more. The book didn't work. There was only a slight chance it would.'

'What happens now?' I asked. 'Prudence is still alive. Therron is trapped down there with her. And what about Lilly and Tharva? I don't even know if they got out in time. I need to go back! I can't just leave them there!'

Marc placed a hand on my shoulder in order to calm me down.

'I understand why you're worried,' he said. 'Therron has magic now. Let him become that hero he was destined to be. Young Lilly made it through the portal safe and sound. Tharva, I'm afraid, wasn't so lucky. The portal is closed for good, but perhaps that is for the best.' He stared into my eyes as I fought back tears.

'I called you here to warn you,' Marc said. 'Prudence is trapped inside Tantary, but Cedrick still roams free. He's at the manor. You have to stop him.'

Marc stepped away from me once, and then continued to walk backwards. The further away he got, the more he faded into the whiteness.

'Wait!' I called after him. 'What am I supposed to do? Where are you going?'

But he didn't answer. He just continued to get further and further away until he'd completely faded.

I felt a cool breeze ruffling at my hair, followed by a familiar tugging sensation. I tried to run. I wasn't ready. I didn't want to go back. Tantary still needed me! Therron needed me!

But the portal had a will of its own. Before long, it sent me hurtling through the air at top speed.

41

LASTING LEGACIES

I was thrust through the portal with such a force that I went careening into the wall opposite. As I landed, I heard the grunt of someone I'd crashed into along with the raining of mirror shards. I tried to get up from my crumpled position on the floor, the broken shards of the portal mirror digging in to me as I moved.

'What the hell are you doing?' asked an irate voice, making my head hurt more than the impact had. 'Do you go looking for trouble, girl? Get out of my way!'

I recognised the voice of the creepy Cedrick guy. I opened my eyes to see the mirror lying half broken beside me. Max stood against the wall, holding Cedrick back by keeping his arms firmly behind his back. Cedrick struggled, but Max seemed to have a pretty strong hold on him. On the other side of me stood Adrian, hugging a trembling Lilly.

I called her name and extended my arms out to embrace her, thrilled to see she made it back through the portal. Adrian, however, wouldn't let her leave his grip for fear of Cedrick. And possibly the blood which I felt slithering down my forehead.

'Let me go!' yelled Cedrick, thrashing against Max's hold. 'What I'm doing is for the good of everyone. That portal was never supposed to exist!'

'Don't listen to him,' I told Max, then turned to the screaming man. 'I know who you are,' I said. 'Everyone, meet the man who created Tantary in the first place—the wizard hired by Marcius Calthorpe.'

Cedrick looked momentary stupefied, but he soon snapped out of it. He began to laugh. 'You think that makes any difference?' he asked. 'So what if I created it? Surely that makes me all the more entitled to shut it down.'

'Miss Sharpe works for you,' I continued. I wasn't looking at Max or Adrian, but I could almost sense their shock increasing, the more information I divulged. 'She created that portal especially for you. She created it so you could close the connection between the realms for good.'

The facts I told had no impact on the situation, but I had a plan. With my fingers behind my back, I gestured for Adrian to pick up the mirror behind me. The portal was still open. Although it was weak, I felt the air tugging me back towards it.

'Well, that portal is nearly closed now,' I continued, 'and do you see Prudence anywhere? No. That's because she's not coming back. She's trapped down there forever.'

'Pah!' Cedrick scoffed. 'As though I care about what happens to her! She gave me what I needed. She's of no use to me now.'

I smiled a little. 'That's not the part that concerns you,' I told him. 'Your problem is that we're sending you to the same fate.'

Only a momentary look of confusion crossed over Cedrick's face before Adrian, now behind him, brought the mirror down over the man's head. There was a bright flash, and within seconds, Cedrick disappeared into the portal.

The mirror began to shake, startling Adrian. He dropped it in shock, and I leaned away, expecting what was left of it to shatter on the floor below.

But it didn't. Instead, the mirror simply bounced in mid-air and hovered in the middle of the hallway. The bright halo surrounding it never faded, and I watched in amazement as the jagged splinters of glass on the floor below rose and, one by one, reattached themselves to the broken artefact. I stepped back and gripped onto Lilly's hand, hoping to shield her from the flying shards. Maybe it was guilt. Perhaps I felt bad about not doing enough to protect her back in Tantary. Here she was, a five-year-old girl, probably scarred for life having been through things no child her age should have. When she followed me into Tantary, she thought she was in for the adventure of a lifetime. If only I had stopped her. If only I had found a way to get her back home earlier. Protecting the children from fictional kings and vengeful housekeepers probably wasn't in my job description, but I felt like I failed her. Like I'd failed Adrian.

All these thoughts flew through my head as the mirror restored itself. Just seeing the magical, glowing item reminded me of how this house used to belong to a normal, everyday family. And then I came along. And look what I'd done to it.

Max, who'd held Cedrick away from the mirror, stood and watched in wonderment as the mirror span, spiralling higher and higher into the air. Then, all of a sudden, it ceased its glowing, and fell down to the carpeted floor, landing with a thud as it rolled a few times on its edges, and then came to a stop.

Adrian was the first one to step towards the

restored mirror.

'What was that?' he asked, breathless.

'I was hoping you knew,' was Max's answer.

I did what Adrian was too frightened to do. I bent down and scooped up the mirror from where it had landed on the floor.

'It's closed,' I said. Tears once again bobbed to the surface.

Lilly, now free of Adrian's grasp, came to inspect it herself. 'But,' she said, 'that can't be right! What about Therron and Tharva?'

Max put a hand on each of our shoulders.

'Maybe this is for the best,' he said. 'Those characters were never supposed to exist, so maybe this was supposed to happen.'

I knew that, but that didn't stop the streams of warm tears which finally broke free of their dam and drizzled down my cheeks.

Adrian took the mirror from me as I sank silently to the ground.

'I'm sorry,' he said. 'I really am. I had no idea this was going to happen.'

No one said anything for a while. I don't think anyone knew what to say. I just sat in the middle of the hallway, gasping as tears absorbed into my clothes. I failed. I failed everyone, both at the manor and in Tantary. And now I was the one who would suffer for it.

After a few moments, Lilly crouched down on the ground next to me, where she wrapped me in one of her loving hugs. I bundled her up onto my lap and rocked her, slowly, back and forth, her arms around my neck.

'It's okay,' Lilly said into my ear as we hugged. 'Maybe it will work later.'

I squeezed her a little tighter. 'Maybe,' I said. But, I knew it wouldn't.

Max and Adrian didn't seem to know what to do. When tears started to speck Lilly's cheeks, too, Adrian made his way over to us. He reached a hand out for Lilly. Just before she took it, she said to me, 'I'm going to miss them.'

I smiled back at her through wet lashes. 'Not half as much as I am, sweetie.'

That night, there was a soft knock at my bedroom door. The tears had barely stopped flowing since that afternoon. Taking in a deep breath, I wiped the residual dampness from my cheeks and answered. Max entered the room, offering me a smile that did not meet his eyes. He looked like he wanted to give me a hug, but apparently decided against it.

'How are you doing?' he asked, taking in my flushed cheeks and swollen eyes. He went to take a seat on the chest at the end of my bed; his usual perch.

I shrugged. 'It doesn't hurt any less. It wouldn't be so bad if . . .' I sighed. 'I just wish I knew what happened to him. I want to think he managed to get away from Prudence and Cedrick, but I-I just don't know.' My words came out strangled as my tear ducts threatened to spill over again. 'What do you think happened to Tantary?' I asked. 'Do you think it survived?'

'I only wish I knew. All we know is that the portal closed. For good, it seems. I'm not quite sure how that would have impacted the land.'

I couldn't keep it in any longer. Water clouded my sight once more and I cried soundlessly.

'Hey,' he said, standing up. This time, he did give me a hug. 'Don't worry. Therron was blessed to have had a life. As an entity who wasn't even supposed to have that much, he was very lucky. Even more so that he met you. Therron is where he belongs now—in the words of a storybook. It may not be fair, but it is the way it's supposed to be.'

I shook my head against his shoulder.

'No,' I said, 'it's not like that. His book is destroyed. I ruined it!'

'It doesn't look that way from here.'

I turned and wiped the tears from my eyes to see what he was looking at. Right there, on the dressing table, sat a spiral-bound notebook, untouched and untarnished. The pristine, green cover shone in the light from the window, reflecting onto the wall behind. Almost in a trance, I made my way over to the book, and picked it up. My heart raced in my ears, though I knew what lay inside even before I peeled open the front cover.

Therron's story.

This time, when the tears came, they tasted of rueful joy. His story was restored. Maybe that meant he was okay. My fingers ran the length of the unopened pages.

'Go on, then,' urged Max, knowing what I was thinking. 'Go to the end of the story. Find out how it ends.'

My fingers itched to do just that, but I hesitated.

'What if it's bad?' I asked.

'It won't be,' he said.

'You don't know that.'

'And you won't know until you open it.'

I nodded. And, with a shaky breath, I flipped the book to its final pages. Tears flowed freely down my face as a limp smile tugged at the corners of my lips.

Epilogue

*T*he months went by, and the sorrow became easier to live with. Though the memories of all that happened still hurt, I could live with myself, safe in the knowledge that things were as they were meant to be. That, at least, Max had been right about.

Though Adrian suggested that, under the circumstances, it might be an idea for me to go home, I continued to stay at the manor. I loved the children very much, and wished to carry out the rest of my year here. Or perhaps that was just what I told myself.

We rarely spoke of Tantary, or of the events that plagued us all for so long. Things carried on as normal. Had you known no better, it would have been easy to believe none of it ever happened.

Not a day went by when I didn't think about them, though. Beautiful memories of Therron, Tharva, Archie, and everyone else painted my every waking thought. I cherished them, like blooming spring flowers you knew wouldn't last forever.

Perhaps the true reason why I didn't want to leave the manor was that, just by being here, I felt close to them. Close to him. And that was a feeling I wasn't ready to give up. Not yet, anyway.

Therron's story wrote itself, right up to the end. His sacrifice gave him strength in his magic—the strength to overcome the evils that were Prudence and Cedrick. Even Calpacious received his just desserts. It was a struggle, but eventually, his act of bravery was recognised, and the whole of Tantary praised him. Within time, he was appointed as their new ruler.

Therron ruled with a kind and gentle heart—the kind the magicks had not seen since the days of Alzabar. His powers were no longer feared, but respected, as he used them for the good of everyone around him. And I couldn't have been prouder.

One thing about the story had changed, though. He never met me.

In the last few months, I had read and re-read the whole of Therron's story. My name was not mentioned once. It was like I was never there. The story told of Therron coming into his powers on his own. Perhaps I would be the only person in existence to ever know otherwise.

But it was for the best. He was never supposed to have met me, so it was probably a good thing he had no memory of our time together.

That was what I told myself, at least.

One cold, February night, I lay in my bed at the manor. The thoughts of all that had passed flitted through my mind, hindering my ability to sleep. It became like this occasionally—an irksome side effect that came with all the adventures I faced.

As I lay tossing and turning, unable to drift into a pleasant slumber, I heard a sound. A whisper.

My name.

The voice was quiet, like it came from the back of my mind. Blaming tiredness, I pushed the thought away and dove deeper into my covers.

'Pepper.'

I was aware of a soft light illuminating the room. Slowly, I opened my eyes. And there he stood, watching me from across the room.

My movements were slow as I slid out of the bedclothes and walked forward, half expecting the vision before me to dissolve into nothingness. But it didn't.

Therron walked towards me, a smile on his face. He looked the same, though somehow different, as though wisdom had aged him.

'Therron?' I whispered, my nightdress swishing as I walked. 'Is that really you?'

Therron said nothing, just grinned, and I walked straight into his arms. He caught me, and held me close. I did not count the time for which we remained in that embrace, for time had no matter. We simply stood, and hugged, as Therron's fingers brushed down the length of my hair.

'You came back,' I whispered, barely finding my breath.

'Of course I did,' he said back. He nuzzled his head into the crook of my neck.

'But how—'

'It doesn't matter. But I don't have much time left. I shouldn't be here, but I just had to come and see you one more time.' His tender hands ran down my arms, catching my fingers at the bottom. 'You gave this to me, Pepper,' he said, 'you gave me my strength. I owe you everything I have.'

I opened my mouth to protest, but he swiftly closed it, pressing his thumb down onto my lips.

'I have to go now,' he said, stepping away. 'I'm only sorry I could not have stayed longer.'

'Therron, wait!' I reached out my arm. He caught my wrist.

'Pepper.' The way he said my name was soft, like the word itself was fragile. 'I'm sorry. Someday, I will see you again. I promise.'

'Wait!' I lunged forwards. My fingers grazed the top of his chest as his body shimmered. All too soon, he was gone.

I stood there for a while, staring at the blank space where he once stood. I could no longer fight the tears that sprang to the surface.

There came a knock at the door, and a groggy-eyed Max entered the room.

'What's the matter?' he asked. 'Are you okay?'

I blinked a few times, releasing some of the teardrops that clung to my lashes.

'Nothing,' I said. I looked once again to the spot where Therron had disappeared, and I smiled.

'It was just a dream.'

KINGDOM

About the Author

Rachel E. Wollaston is a self-taught author from Gloucester, UK. Born in 1997, story writing has been a passion of hers ever since the day she could put pen to paper. It has been her dream to publish a book that would inspire others, just like the books she read inspired her.

Besides writing, the young author also enjoys a range of other artistic hobbies, such as dancing, painting, and crafting. She currently lives at home with her loving mother and sister and ever-growing family of cats.

Find out more about Rachel by visiting her online at **www.rachelewollaston.com**, or on Facebook as **Rachel E. Wollaston.**

495

A Note from the Author

Thank you so much for reading my debut novel, Kingdom. If you enjoyed it, please stay in touch by visiting me online, where you can sign up to my newsletter to receive exciting updates and other big announcements!

You can find me online at:
www.rachelewollaston.com

Or on Facebook at:
https://www.facebook.com/rachelewollaston9127549/?ref=aymt_homepage_panel

Made in the USA
Charleston, SC
21 July 2016